HELL-O-WEEN

THE SCARES NEVER END

It's Halloween night.

Two buds decide to play a trick on the class brain.

They take him to a local landmark, a cavern rumored to be bottomless. Their plan is to go down far enough to get him lost, then leave him there.

They bring along their girlfriends and some others, thinking it will be fun.

They're wrong.

Something lives in the cavern. Something from out of its depths.

Now that something is after them. Unless they can reach the surface, this Halloween will be their last.

Books by David Robbins

Endworld Universe

ENDWORLD
WILDERNESS
WHITE APACHE BLOOD FEUD
A GIRL, THE END OF THE WORLD AND EVERYTHING

Series

ANGEL U
DAVY CROCKETT

Horror

PRANK NIGHT SPOOK NIGHT
HELL-O-WEEN THE WERELING
THE WRATH SPECTRE

Novels

HIT RADIO BLOOD CULT

Westerns

GUNS ON THE PRAIRIE THUNDER VALLEY
RIDE TO VALOR TOWN TAMERS
BADLANDERS DIABLO
THE RETURN OF THE VIRGINIAN

Movie Novelizations

MEN OF HONOR PROOF OF LIFE
TWISTED

Nonfiction

HEAVYE TRAFFIC
(A history of the DEA)

HELL-O-WEEN

by

David Robbins

Published by Mad Hornet Pub.
Printed in the United States of America
ISBN: 978-1-950096-06-0

Dedicated to Judy, Joshua
and Shane

FROM THE LEADVILLE CHRONICLE
1892

GOLD FEVER CLAIMS MORE LIVES

PAGOSA SPRINGS---August 5

More prospectors have been lost in the mountains. From Pagosa Springs comes word of four men who ventured into the notorious Caverna del Diablo in search of Spanish gold two weeks ago.

No one heard anything from them until this past Monday when a single member of the quartet was found wandering in the forest northwest of town by a party of elk hunters.

The prospector, identified as F. J. Hildreth, was in a hysterical state and raved on about finding the gateway to Hell.

Sheriff Travers reports that a search will be launched in a few days but he is not optimistic about the chances of finding the missing prospectors. By his reckoning, nine men have lost their lives in the Caverna del Diablo in the past decade, and he told this reporter that, 'For two bits I'd fill the cave entrance with dynamite and seal it. It's too blamed dangerous. Anyone who goes down in there must be hankering to die."

Chapter 1

"Yo, dweeb! Are you ready to go monster hunting?"

Seventeen year-old Cory Fleming knew those words were addressed to him even though the speaker was behind him. He also knew who it was and knew why the word 'dweeb' had been stressed to give the insult extra emphasis. He pushed his glasses higher on the bridge of his nose, a nervous habit he had formed years ago, before he reluctantly spun around and said, "Don't call me that, Wes. I don't like it."

Wesley Eagen, seated behind the steering wheel of the brand-new jeep he had just angled over to the curb, blinked in surprise, then laughed. "Whoa! The worm turns."

The three other high school seniors in the jeep all smirked at Cory, who withered inside under their looks of ill-concealed contempt. Across from Wesley sat Leslie Vanderhorst, daughter of the richest man in Pagosa Springs. Behind Wes was a fellow star member of the football team, Jay Thorpe, and next to Jay sat Stacy Curvin, the vivacious blonde who was a shoo-in to be Homecoming Queen that year. "Hello", Cory said, then added the thought uppermost on his mind. "Where's Ann?"

"Where do you think?" Wesley retorted, and jerked his thumb over his shoulder. "She's riding with Scott."

Cory shifted as a second jeep braked behind the first. He saw Scott Miklin driving and frowned ever so slightly.

This is stupid, stupid, stupid! he told himself. He had no business going out to the cave with guys and girls who wouldn't give him the time of day in school except to knock on him when the mood struck them. Then his gaze fell on the brunette beside Scott, and he forgot all of his worries as her rosy mouth curled in a genuinely friendly smile.

"Hi, Cory. Glad you could make it," Ann Weatherby said.

"Wouldn't miss it for the world," Cory lied. The only reason he had accepted Scott's invitation was because of Ann. If she wasn't going he would have told Scott to get screwed---tactfully, of course.

"Hello, Cory," chimed in the bleached blonde seated behind Scott. Terri Sheehan was Ann's best friend. Where Ann went, Terri went. What Ann did, Terri did. They had been inseparable since childhood.

"Terri," Cory said, stepping over to their jeep, a brown model almost as new as Wesley's red one. He simply nodded at Scott.

"How's it hanging, brother?" Scott Miklin asked in his New England accent. Born and raised in Massachusetts, he had moved with his family to Colorado a year and a half ago. In that time he had become one of the most popular guys at Pagosa Springs Senior High. At least once a month he held parties at his house that were the talk of the school. "You all set?"

"Yeah," Cory replied. "But are you sure I shouldn't bring some food and a flashlight?"

Scott nodded at a green backpack resting on the console between his seat and Ann's. "We have everything we'll need. Hop in and we'll get this show on the road." .

Although Cory would much rather have sat next to

Ann, he climbed in the back with Terri Sheehan and buckled his seat belt.

"Good idea," Scott said, grinning. "We wouldn't want you to fall out. Some of the back country roads are rough." He faced front and honked his horn. "Lead the way, Wes!"

Wesley Eagen gave the thumbs-up sign, checked the traffic flow on U.S. Highway 160 and accelerated.

"Here we go, ladies and germs," Scott said, stomping on the gas pedal and pulling out so quickly that his passengers were slammed against the backrests of their seats.

"Scott, please," Ann said in reproach.

"Oh, sorry," Milkin responded, his blue eyes twinkling, giving her a grin that revealed all of his perfect white teeth. He reached out to stroke her neck. "Didn't mean to rattle your bones, babe. I'll be careful from here on out."

Cory averted his gaze, unable to bear the sight of Scott touching her. He absently stared up at the Pizza House situated on a low hill to the north of the highway, regretting the fact he hadn't gone there after school instead of agreeing to meet Scott's crowd for this insane trip to the cave. For someone who got all A's, sometimes he displayed the intelligence of a lobotomized baboon.

"So tell me, Cory, " Scott said, "ever been to this Cavern-del-whatever before?"

"It's called La Caverna del Diablo," Cory said. "But most call it Caverna del Diablo for short. Got its name from the Spanish conquistadors who came to this region searching for gold. And yes, I was there once with my dad. We only went in partway."

"Why only part of the way?" Scott asked. "Afraid the monster would nail you?" He chuckled at his little joke, and winked at Ann.

Cory ignored the barb. "No one has ever gone all the

way. It's one of the biggest caverns in the entire country, maybe the whole world. Several groups of professional spelunkers have gone down in, but even they weren't able to find the bottom."

"What the hell are spelunkers?"

"People who explore caves," Cory explained. "They have a national organization, and there are several grottos here in Colorado."

"What the hell are grottos?"

"Local spelunker clubs. My uncle belongs to one up in Fort Collins. They spend their weekends traveling to caves all over the state. He invited me along on a trip to the Groaning Cave once and I had a great time. We went in over a thousand feet."

"Sounds like fun," Scott said with all the enthusiasm he might apply to being consumed by a great white shark.

"Gosh, you sure know a lot, Cory," Terri interjected, brushing her short bangs aside. "I'm glad you came along. I've never been in a cave before, and frankly I'm not too keen on the idea."

"There's nothing to be afraid of," Cory assured her.

Terri's brown eyes narrowed. "But what about all this monster business? They say it killed someone a long time ago."

Scott cackled. "Oh, really! Don't tell me you believe that bullshit, Terri? Only a moron would think there really is a monster down in there."

"Of course I don't," Terri said defensively. "I was just wondering about the legend, that's all."

"Well, I'm sure digithead can tell you," Scott replied. "He knows everything. That's why everyone calls him a walking encyclopedia."

Cory scowled and looked away so Scott wouldn't notice

in the rearview mirror. The wind stirred his brown hair and felt cool on his face, relieving some of his burning anger. He was such a twink! He should have known better than to expect to be treated differently after so many years of being viewed as Pagosa Springs's prime dork. And all because he would rather read a good book than go see a stupid slasher movie or work on a science experiment instead of cruising for foxes or guzzling six-packs until he dropped. Oh, he had his share of close friends, mainly brains like him. But the jocks and the in-crowd had always looked down their collective noses at him and undoubtedly always would.

"Cory?" Terri said. "About the monster?"

"Oh. Sorry. There are Native American legends about a creature of some kind. And a few prospectors and others from the early days claimed to have encountered something."

"See?" Scott said. "Digithead knows everything."

Cory sat in morose silence, idly observing the magnificent scenery as the jeeps passed beyond the town limits of Pagosa Springs and traveled southwest on 160 until they came to a dirt road.

Wesley and Scott turned onto it, and for the next few miles the only buildings they saw were ranch houses and barns. Soon a sign appeared informing them that they were about to enter the San Juan National Forest, and a minute later they were hemmed in on both sides by virgin wilderness. A green sea of towering somber pines surrounded them.

Far to the north reared the mysterious San Juan Mountains, one of the least explored regions in the entire United States. Jagged peaks over two and a half miles high were capped with sparkling snow, resembling ghostly spires as they shimmered in the late afternoon sun.

Cory looked to the east and spied the pale full moon already above the horizon. Good, he thought. The trick or treaters would have the benefit of bright moonlight when they made their rounds. His younger brother, Bert, who was only six, would be going out with their mother. He recalled how Bert had begged him to go along and how he had refused. "Halloween is for kids," he said, pretending not to notice the hurt in Bert's innocent eyes. Guilt assailed him, and he sank back in his seat.

Here he was, the big, mature high school senior on his way to the infamous Caverna del Diablo to spend Halloween with other seniors who felt it was beneath their dignity to go out trick or treating at their age. Instead, they were going to spend the evening in a supposedly monster-haunted cave. Now that he viewed the matter objectively he realized they were being as juvenile as his little brother, maybe more so. At least his brother had the good sense not to enter a cave where a number of people had disappeared.

“Say, Cory," Ann Weatherby unexpectedly said, twisting in her seat. "What have you been up to lately?"

"Oh, the usual," he responded, deliberately avoiding her gaze.

"You haven't been over in a long time," Ann said.

Cory shrugged. "Been busy. You know how it is."

"I miss our talks.”

Scott Miklin glanced over his right shoulder. "That's right, dude. Ann tells me the two of you have been next-door neighbors since you were munchkins. Grew up together and all that."

"We're good friends," Cory said, although deep down he longed to be much more. Ann Weatherby had always held a special place in his heart, especially after that time when they were ten and had hidden in her father's shed so they could play doctor undisturbed. Playing doctor had always been a favorite game of theirs. But after that day they had never played it again, nor had Ann spoken to him for two years.

"And in all that time you never ever hit on her?" Scott inquired ever so politely.

"Scott!" Ann said.

"Sorry, babe," Scott responded, smiling sweetly. "But your good friend must have rocks for brains. If you were my neighbor I would have latched onto you ages ago."

Cory felt his cheeks tingle and hoped he wasn't blushing. Memories of that day in the shed overwhelmed him, and he squirmed uncomfortably. Dear God! What had he been thinking? And at his age, too! Who would ever expect a ten year-old to do such a thing?

"You promised that you wouldn't give Cory a hard time," Ann criticized Scott.

"And I'm keeping my word," Scott retorted indignantly. He glanced at Cory once more. "Hey, dude, do you think I'm picking on you?"

"Not at all," Cory said, secretly wishing he could bash Scott's head in with a baseball bat.

"See." Scott gloated at Ann. "I promised you we'd all be on our best behavior and we will be. You'll see. Your good friend will feel right at home."

Why did Scott keep referring to him that way? Cory wondered. Ann gave him a reassuring smile, and he smiled back, then made bold to ask, "Whose idea was this?"

"What do you mean?" she rejoined.

"Who came up with the idea to ask me to come along?" Cory clarified, dreading her answer.

“I did," Ann confessed. "You don't get out much, and I

figured you would like to have some fun. Scott agreed and invited you. Is there something wrong?"

"No," Cory said, his stomach doing flip-flops. So there it was. But why should she be concerned about his well-being after all this time? It was true that she had become friendly again two years after the shed incident and he had spent many a lazy afternoon shooting the breeze with her about everything under the sun, but they weren't as close as they were before the shed. And since, thanks to her outstanding looks and outgoing nature, she had easily fitted into the most exclusive clique in school, they rarely mingled socially. Now all of a sudden she wanted him to come along on an outing deep into the mountains? It made no sense.

The dirt road forked and the two jeeps swung to the left. Immediately the road narrowed and became rockier. Countless ruts marred the surface, the result of heavy erosion caused by frequent thunderstorms during the spring and summer months. Wesley and Scott had to steer carefully to avoid becoming hung up or damaging the undercarriages on their jeeps. From that point onward only four-wheel-drive vehicles could negotiate the twisting roadway. At that time of year and so late in the day it was unlikely they would encounter other four-wheelers.

To the west loomed magnificent Horse Mountain. South of it, invisible from where they were, was Chimney Rock. In the summer the area would be crawling with campers and hikers, but this late in the season only hunters penetrated any distance into the national forest, and they seldom if ever ventured into the area near the cave.

Old-timers like Cory's grandfather swore there was little game in the general vicinity of the Cavema del Diablo although the mountains around it teemed with mule deer and bears.

"Hey, Cory," Scott said, "you didn't tell your folks what we're doing, did you?"

"No," Cory replied. "I kept it a secret like you wanted." He wished now he had told his mom and dad. If something went wrong and they wound up stranded, it would be nice to know a rescue party would be sent to find them. But Scott had insisted on keeping their jaunt to themselves, and he'd had a valid reason. The cave was in a remote area, and although it wasn't hard to find and contained no hazards for those who stayed in the upper levels, there was always an element of risk involved. It was unlikely any of their parents would have permitted them to go.

"Excellent," Scott said, then asked suspiciously, "What did you tell them?"

"That I was going to be at Zack McCoy's until late, working on our joint entry in the science fair. They know we've been developing a project to demonstrate how industrial and automobile pollution deranges the global ecosystem and---."

"Yeah, yeah," Scott interrupted. "Just so they won't come looking for you." He snickered. "We don't need our parents messing up all our plans. This is shaping up to be one def Halloween. Besides, we're old enough to decide what we want to do without them looking over our shoulders every damn minute of every day."

Terri shifted and opened her mouth to say something but apparently changed her mind and glumly stared down at her lap. The short black skirt she wore was riding high on her pudgy thighs and she smoothed it down.

Cory looked at Ann. "What did you tell your folks?"

"That I was spending the night at Terri's. Terri told her parents that she was spending the night with me. With luck they won't suspect a thing."

The road started to climb and the air became cooler. Dense walls of vegetation partially obstructed their views to the right and the left. After five minutes the road slanted to the northwest, skirting Horse Mountain and bearing into the very heart of the foreboding San Juan Mountains. They came over a rise, descended a hill and crossed a shallow creek between a pair of deep pools.

"Look at those," Ann commented. "I bet my dad would like to fish here. He's always looking for new spots."

"He'd be wasting his time," Cory informed her. "This is Devil Creek. Hardly any fish in it. Something to do with enhanced acidity in the water. I once read an article on the imbalance in a regional science journal. They say this is the only stream in the state that has the problem."

Scott took his eyes off the road long enough to caustically ask, "Is there anything you don't know?"

Again Cory lapsed into silence. Despite himself, he was intimidated by Scott's attitude. All those years of being the brunt of countless jokes about his IQ had taken their emotional toll. Rather than make an issue of an insult and perhaps spark a fight, he had learned to keep his mouth shut and weather the slings and barbs of his callous classmates. He'd been in more than his share of scraps when he was younger, and he'd learned the hard way that earning a bloody nose or a black eye in the defense of his dignity wasn't worth it.

The bumpy road wound ever deeper into the San Juan's. They continued to climb steadily, and the temperature continued to gradually drop. Through valleys and over mountains they went, at times carefully navigating a ribbon of roadway that seemed glued to the sheer side of a cliff while above them perched massive boulders capable of crushing their vehicles to bits should a rock slide start.

"Geez," Terri breathed at one point as they crested a ridge thousands of feet above a verdant valley. "This gives me the creeps. What if we go over the side?"

"Then they'll be scraping us up with putty knives," Scott said, and laughed.

"I don't think that's funny," Terri said anxiously. "I'm not very fond of heights."

"Don't worry. We won't go over the edge," Ann assured her, and shot Scott a hard glance.

Cory saw Miklin look at her, grin and blow her a kiss. Peeved, he gazed past them out the windshield and was alarmed to behold a sharp curve abruptly appear. With a start he realized the jeep was making straight for the brink "Look out!" he cried, leaning forward, and listened in dismay to the screeching of the tires as Scott slammed on the brakes and the wheels locked. The jeep went into a skid, raising a cloud of dust as it slid closer and closer to the rim.

Terri screamed.

Ann gripped the dashboard with both hands.

Stark fear rippled down Cory's spine. He saw the edge sweep toward them and mentally ticked off the distance. Ten feet. Eight feet. Six feet. He threw an arm out to clutch Ann's shoulder and hold her steady so she wouldn't crash through the windshield when they went over. Then the jeep slowed dramatically, gravel spewing out from under its skewing tires, and came to a lurching halt within inches of eternity. For a minute no one uttered a word as dirt and small stones cascaded over the brink and rained down on a section of woodland over a thousand feet below.

"Damn you!" Terri Sheehan finally exclaimed, glaring at Scott. "You nearly got us all killed!"

"Oh, bull. I had everything under control," Scott retorted

angrily.

Cory exhaled in relief. Ann turned to regard him with a strange expression, and he became aware that his hand still rested on her shoulder. "Oh, sorry," he mumbled, jerking it back. "I thought you might go through the windshield."

"Thank you," Ann said softly.

"Hell!" Scott growled in irritation. "Let's catch up with the others before they become worried about us." He spun the steering wheel and got them back in the middle of the road.

Leaning back, Cory closed his eyes and waited for his racing pulse to return to normal. His heart thumped heavily. Another second or two and they would all have been goners. The mishap reminded him that their jaunt into the remote mountains wasn't to be taken lightly. Up to a dozen or more people lost their lives from a variety of causes each and every year in Colorado's vast wilderness. They might become lost while out hunting or hiking and succumb to hypothermia. They might be skiing out of bounds and be caught in an avalanche. Or, like Scott, they might fail to pay attention to the serpentine mountain highways and roads and pay for their neglect with their mangled bodies.

The close call had a positive effect on Scott. He now devoted his entire attention to driving and maintained a prudent speed for the next six miles.

Gradually the sun sank toward the horizon. In the valleys the dark shadows lengthened. The heights were still aglow for awhile, but eventually the crags and peaks were likewise shrouded in twilight.

Wes and Scott flicked on their jeep headlights.

A thin ring of rosy sunlight crowned the mountains to the west when the two vehicles rumbled up a steep incline and came out in a great natural bowl hemmed in on three sides by enormous cliffs that gave the illusion of touching the few gray clouds drifting like eerie wraiths across the murky sky. At the base of the cliff to the north was an immense black opening.

"Hot damn!" Scott whooped. "We're here!"

Cory stared at the inky entrance to the Caverna del Diablo and felt his mouth go inexplicably dry.

Chapter 2

Wesley Eagen slid out of his father's new jeep, stretched and breathed deep. The rarified air was like a cold spash of water to his lungs, invigorating him. All that bouncing had jarred his kidneys mercilessly, and he couldn't wait to relieve himself. He turned as Scott parked next to his vehicle, killed the engine and hopped out. "About damn time we got here," he said. "It better be worth it."

"It will, Wes," Scott said, grinning. "Trust me, bro."

Everyone else was piling out.

The sight of Cory Fleming caused Wes to turn away so the dork wouldn't see the anger that hardened his features. He had to will himself to calm down, to not let his hatred show. After all the trouble Scott and him had gone to in making this an outing Fleming would regret for the rest of his life, he didn't want to ruin everything by giving it away. He composed himself just as a hand touched his left arm.

"You okay, lover?"

Wes turned and nearly bumped into Leslie Vanderhorst. She was standing so close to him that her full breasts brushed against his chest. Not that he minded. He inhaled the tantalizing fragrance of her perfume, gazed into her lake-blue eyes, and impulsively grabbed her to plant a kiss on her full red lips. Of all the babes he had ever dated, she was the best, the creme de la creme, as his French teacher might say.

"What was that for?" she asked, giggling.

"Can't a guy kiss his girl without the third degree?" Wes

said and playfully gave her thigh a light pinch.

"You looked upset a second ago," Leslie said.

"Me? When do I ever let anything get to me?"

"Hardly ever," Leslie admitted, idly brushing at her hip-length red hair. Her lavender blouse, which fit her as tightly as her skin, threatened to burst with the movement.

It was all Wes could do not to grab hold of her globes and squeeze until she squealed. Next to Stacy Curvin, Leslie had the best body in the whole student body at Pagosa Springs High School. And he wasn't the only guy who thought so. Before he came along she had dated every jock in the school, never sticking with one for very long. Then, two months ago, he had gone out with her for the first time and screwed her senseless in the back seat of his father's Caddy. Ever since, she had been exclusively his.

Scott Miklin cleared his throat. "Let's pass out the backpacks, people. Everyone will need a flashlight. And anyone who has to take a leak should do so before we get down in the cave." He caught Wes's eye and nodded at a cluster of bushes ten yards from the jeeps.

"I need to empty the old bladder," Wesley said and trailed Scott to the bushes. Once they were out of sight of the others, he unzipped his fly and began saturating the soil at his feet. "What's up?"

Scott had turned sideways. He grunted as he sprayed a rock and said over his shoulder, "So far, so good. Cory doesn't suspect a thing."

“I can hardly wait to roast that son of a bitch," Wes said.

"Just don't give everything away before we're down far enough. We want him where it won't be easy for him to get out of the cave once the fun begins."

Wes chuckled in keen anticipation. "I can't believe the dweeb was stupid enough to fall for this. How could he think that we really wanted him along?"

"It's Ann," Scott said gruffly.

"You still figure Cory has the hots for her?"

"I know the bastard does. I was keeping my eye on him in the rearview mirror all the way up here. You should have seen the way he looked at her, like a lousy puppy in love."

"Think she likes him?"

"I don't know," Scott said. "I've only been out with her twice." He stopped peeing and shook his pecker, spattering a few lingering drops on the ground. "I really don't give a damn one way or the other. She was the bait to get him here."

Wesley slipped his manhood back into his pants. "I appreciate all the trouble you've gone to for me. Hope I can pay you back one day."

"Once you told me that you wanted to nail his ass, it was the least I could do," Scott said, zipping up and pivoting. "We're best buddies, aren't we?"

"You know it," Wes agreed, and sniffed. "Say, did you bring some stuff along?"

Scott grinned. "Does a bear crap in the woods?."

"Excellent," Wes said and led the way back to the jeeps. Leslie, Ann, and Terri were chatting away next to his. Everyone else, including that prick Cory, was straying in from different directions, having heeded the call of nature. In a pile in front of Scott's jeep were the four backpacks. Nearby were four flashlights.

Jay Thorpe, who topped out at six-foot-two and weighed two hundred and fifty pounds, whooped and jabbed a finger at the cave entrance. "What a bodacious way to spend Halloween! It will be just like back in caveman times." He thumped his huge chest like a gorilla and did a pathetic imitation of a Tarzan yell, then beamed at his cleverness. Stacy Curvin, his girlfriend, was the only one who bothered to laugh.

Wesley had always considered Jay as being about ninety bricks shy of a hundred brick load, but he wasn't about to say so when Jay could, and would, break every bone in his body without working up a sweat. Another reason Wes never made fun of the hulking mass of muscle was that Jay qualified as the football team's best guard, and since as quarterback Wes relied on Jay to protect him from onrushing opponents who wanted to separate his head from his body, Wes always made it a point to never, ever antagonize Pagosa Springs's answer to King Kong.

Scott stepped over to their gear. "Each of the guys will take a backpack and a flashlight."

"What about us?" Ann asked.

"Your hands will be free to do with them as you please," Scott replied and leered suggestively. "And I trust you ladies know what to do with them."

"Don't be crude," Ann chided.

Stacy Curvin, every inch a blonde bombshell, her thin pink top and short pink shorts leaving nothing to the imagination, looked at Ann and frowned. "Who died and appointed you the Virgin Mary?"

"Why, Stacy," Ann replied coolly, "I'm surprised you've even heard of her."

Wes winced. The last thing they needed was for the girls to get into it right now. A serious argument or a cat fight would jeopardize the whole deal. The girls might want to be taken home, spoiling his well-laid plans. He saw Stacy ball her fist and take a step toward Ann, who tensed for the worst.

"Ladies! Ladies!" Scott cried, moving quickly between them with his arms extended to keep them from each other's throat. "What's with all this hostility? We're all friends, aren't we? And didn't we drive all this way to spend a bitchin' Halloween in the cave?" He glanced at each of them. "It would be a shame to spoil everything because the two of you can't control your tempers." He paused and lowered his voice, pretending he didn't want anyone else to hear but them. "What is it? The time of the month?"

Jay roared, and as if on cue Stacy laughed heartily.

Wes noticed that Ann didn't so much as crack a grin. Now there was a cold mama! he told himself, which was a pity. Ann Weatherby was almost as choice a fox as Stacy or Leslie but where those two knew how to treat a guy to a great time, Ann had a reputation for being as frigid as an iceberg. She'd neck heavy and let a guy play finger tag with her box, but she refused to go all the way. Must have been her upbringing, he reasoned. Her parents warped her for life.

"If you want a flashlight," Scott was telling Ann, "you can have mine." He leaned down and picked up one. "But as you can see these are big mothers. Four of them will light up the cave as if it were daylight in there." He motioned for her to take the one he held. "I just figured you'd want your hands free in case we have to do any climbing."

"Oh," Ann said. "You keep it then. I'll be fine."

Wesley grinned. He had to hand it to Scott. The guy had a golden tongue. If Scott ever became a car salesman he'd sell more cars in one month than most salesmen did in a year.

"What do you have in those backpacks?" Cory asked.

"Munchies galore, rope in case we need it, spare batteries and plenty of candles and matches," Scott answered. "Why? Don't you think I'm smart enough to pack everything we'd need?"

“I never said that,' Cory replied, walking over and taking one of the red packs. "I was just curious." He hefted it, testing its weight. "Did you bring a compass?"

"What the hell do we need a compass for? We go down, we come up. It's as simple as that."

Cory slipped an arm into one of the straps on his backpack. "There are reportedly hundreds of passageways in the Caverna del Diablo, and many of them twist and turn every which way. It's like a maze down there. The cave hasn't even been fully mapped yet. Only about a third of the tunnels, if that, have been properly measured and documented by the speleological society."

"The what?"

"Those spelunkers I told you about."

Scott gestured angrily at the cave with his flashlight. "We don't need a damn compass and we sure don't need a stinking map. We're high school seniors. I think we're bright enough to find our way out." He nodded at the packs. "And for your information, in one of those I put a rock hammer and chisel. We can mark the tunnels we take if we have to and find our way back up easily."

"Sounds good to me," Wes spoke up, annoyed that Cory saw fit to question Scott's judgement. By common consent Scott was the leader of their little foray into the depths of the cave, as he was on most of their outings whether it be to the big mall in Durango or a hike into the national forest.

”I guess that will have to do,” Cory said, his voice lacking conviction.

Jay Thorpe jabbed a thick finger at him. "If you don't like it, Fleming, you don't have to come in with us. Stay out here with the jeeps and twiddle your thumbs."

Panic seized Wesley. He was afraid Jay would antagonize

Cory and the dweeb would change his mind and decide to stay up above. If that happened, all their scheming would have been wasted. In order to pacify the geek, as much as he disliked doing so, he came to the bastard's defense. "Lighten up, you guys. Cory is a brain, remember? It's only natural for him to consider every angle. We should be grateful he's so concerned about our safety."

Scott caught on instantly. "Yeah, Wes is right. Sorry, Cory. Nothing personal."

"No harm done, fellas," Cory said, putting his other arm through the opposite strap.

"What I don't like," Leslie Vanderhorst said to Wes, "is not being able to take our cell phones. Why did you say we should leave them home?"

Wes didn't tell her that he didn't want their victim to be able to call for help. "You explain for her Cory, would you? You're our science guy."

"There's not much science to it," Cory said. "We're too far out, Les, is all. Cell phones are useless in the cavern. You can't call, text, nothing."

"Well, that sucks," Leslie said. "I wanted to take selfies."

Wes claimed one of the backpacks and a flashlight for himself. He adjusted the straps to give the pack a snug fit, then tested the push-button switch on the flashlight. A wide beam of incredibly bright light stabbed the darkness, illuminating the cavern entrance and the rock wall surrounding it. "You weren't kidding about these things, Scott. I could reach the moon with this baby," he said, tilting the beam toward the impassive lunar face dominating the heavens.

Scott and Jay donned their backpacks, and everyone moved toward the enormous dark mouth that seemed to be gaping wide to admit them.

"Hey, listen!" Terri Sheehan exclaimed.

They all halted, and Wes turned toward her, straining his ears to catch the faintest sounds. But there were none "I don't hear a thing," he said.

"That's just it. There should be animal and insect noises, yet it's as quiet as a tomb. It's not natural," Terri said.

"The cliffs probably block off most sounds," Wes said. Next to Cory Fleming, he despised Terri the most. It wasn't her personality, since he never hung around with her and didn't know her well enough to know what she was like. He despised her because she was a leech, a bimbo who glued herself to a more attractive and popular friend, in this case Ann Weatherby, and got a free ride as a result. Because everyone knew the two were like sisters, whenever anyone wanted to invite Ann to a party or to go somewhere they had to invite Terri along too. Terri didn't earn her social status. She was Ann's shadow, nothing more.

"Oh, I never thought of that," she responded.

"We can't all be an Einstein," Wes said, resisting an urge to give Fleming a meaningful look so everyone would know who he meant. Instead, he hiked up a path to the cave and played his flashlight beam over the imposing cliffs on either side. The others joined him.

"Hey, what are those?" Stacy asked, pointing at a spot just above the opening.

Cory, Scott and Jay trained their lights on the smooth rock wall.

"Whoa!" Wes said, amused by the sight their combined illumination revealed.

Ages ago a series of symbols had been painted on the stone surface. The passage of time and the onslaught of the elements had eroded them to where they were barely legible. Not so, though, with the bizarre figure painted in bright red underneath the symbols. Almost the size of a full-grown man, the creature depicted had a repulsive face, a bulky torso, and legs like the rear legs of an elk. Hairless and slightly stooped, it also sported fingers that were more like talons and twin knobs a few inches long jutting upward from the top of its forehead.

Leslie giggled. "That thing looks like the Devil."

"Some religious nut must have painted it," Stacy said.

"Not exactly," Cory stated. "Experts say the symbols were painted by the Spanish centuries ago."

"What do they mean?" Leslie asked.

"No one knows for certain," Cory said.

To Wes the symbols made no sense whatsoever. There were four of them arranged in a row, as if they formed a sentence. On the far left was what appeared to be an odd sort of hat or helmet with a creased crown that came to a point at the front. Next to it were two curved lines aligned vertically so that their curves touched, while down the center of each ran a straight line. The third symbol was a crude cross, the vertical post thicker and pointed at the top. And finally the fourth consisted of a rectangle bisected by short vertical lines. It was all Greek to him.

"What about that monster?" Terri inquired. "Did the Spanish paint that, too?"

"The experts don't think so, but they have no idea who did," Cory said. "Oddly, the paint never fades. They guess it has something to do with the rare pigments used."

Terri moved closer and stared at the crimson form. "It does look like the Devil, doesn't it?"

"Don't be stupid," Wes snapped. "It's some goblin or other. Those old-timers were superstitious bozos."

"I wouldn't dismiss Terri's statement out of hand," Cory said. "This *is* the Caverna del Diablo."

"Yeah? So?" Wes said, peeved yet again by Fleming's know-everything attitude.

"The Caverna del Diablo is Spanish for the Cavern of the Devil."

Wes glanced at the red creature again. Maybe there was a similarity between it and the pictures of Satan he remembered from Sunday School. But so the hell what? He'd stopped going to church when he turned sixteen because by then he'd learned the truth. All those boring sermons and all that constant quoting from the Bible had just been so much mumbo-jumbo the church used to keep their dumb sheep in line. He knew better now. He wasn't anyone's fool. "Big frigging deal," he said. "The Devil is nothing but a fairy tale. Only an idiot would think it's real."

"I'm not an idiot," Ann Weatherby said, "and I happen to believe there is such a thing as the Devil."

"Yeah, me too," Terri said.

Scott stepped forward. "Does it matter one way or the other? Whether the Devil does or doesn't exist, I doubt he lives in this cave. So why don't we quit bickering and get on with it? We're wasting valuable time."

"You've got that straight, dude," Jay declared while moving into the opening. Stacy walked by his side with her hand in his. "Let's cut the bullshit and explore this sucker."

"Now you're talking," Wes said.

"I'll take the lead," Scott offered and stepped a few yards in advance of the group. "Keep close to one another, and if you should stray off and get lost give a yell and the rest of us will come running." He looked at Cory. "Is that adequate or should we tie the rope around our waists?"

Wes could almost see Cory squirm inside. The dork didn't like the sarcasm in Scott's tone but he wasn't man enough to do anything about it.

"The rope shouldn't be necessary," Cory said.

"Then let's go," Scott said cheerfully, starting forward.

Beyond the entrance was a spacious chamber with a high vaulted ceiling. In the dust at their feet were scores of footprints left by previous souls brave enough to venture into the unknown.

Wes was behind Jay and Stacy. He admired the way her tight ass wiggled when she walked, then quickly glanced away when Leslie came up beside him.

"Wasn't that painting a little spooky?" she asked almost in a whisper, as if afraid to raise her voice in the cavern.

"Only for kids," Wesley responded, letting his eyes rove over her assets. Why had he risked life and limb ogling Jay's girl when he had one who was every bit as gorgeous? Leslie's full breasts were enough to make any guy drool. And if all went right, he'd be holding them in his hot hands before the night was out. The thought made his manhood twitch, and he grinned.

"Are you laughing at me? Do you think I'm a kid?"

"No, of course not," Wes said and lied to avoid arousing her touchy temper. "I was thinking of all the fun we're going to have with the--" Suddenly he stopped, aware he was about to blurt out the secret behind inviting Cory along. Only Scott and he knew the real reason they'd asked the son of a bitch to come. The others might not appreciate the humor of it, not even Jay. Thorpe was a monster on the playing field but he had a soft heart at times. Once Jay had caught a guy tying firecrackers to a cat's tail and beaten the poor slob within an inch of his life. Another time an idiot had thrown a balloon filled with water at Jay's younger sister at the swimming pool. It had taken three lifeguards to pull Jay off the sap to stop Jay from drowning him.

"With the what?" Leslie probed. "What were you about

to say?"

Wesley's mind raced. "With the bunch of beautiful babes we have with us tonight," he said and leaned toward her so only she would hear. "Myself, I can't wait to get you alone for a while. We haven't necked in over a week, and I'm going through withdrawal. I've started to act weird." He contorted his face in a goofy expression to demonstrate his point.

"Oh, you!" Leslie said, laughing. "You've always been weird if you ask me." She took his hand. "That's part of your charm."

They crossed the chamber and came to a narrow tunnel, the four flashlights bathing the immediate area around them in light bright enough to read by.

Scott paused at the tunnel and swept it with his beam, then beckoned for them to follow and entered the passage.

Wes glanced over his shoulder and saw Cory and Ann walking together. Bringing up the rear, and looking as if she would rather be anywhere than in the cave, was Terri. He snickered and kept going into the tunnel. The walls were as smooth as polished glass, the passage barely the width of his shoulders. Halfway through he had to turn sideways for a few feet. It was then, with his back to one wall and his nose almost touching the other, that an intense sensation of claustrophobia hit him. For a fleeting instant he felt completely hemmed in and helpless. He stopped and fought back an urge to flee.

"Why'd you stop, lover?" Leslie asked.

"No reason," Wes answered and took another step. The sensation subsided as quickly as it had struck, and within seconds he stepped from the tunnel into another large chamber, only this one was totally different from the first.

The ceiling was twenty feet high and dotted with small

stalactites, slender formations much like icicles in shape. Spaced at random along the floor were outlandish rock formations, some half as high as the ceiling, others so tiny they could be stepped over.

"Wow, " Leslie said as they advanced. "This is rad."

"It gets better below," Cory commented. "Some of the chambers and rooms are spectacular."

"Rooms?" Wes said, eager for any chance to make a fool of the chump who had cost him the championship and a new Corvette. "Rooms are what you find in a house. In case you hadn't noticed, Fleming, we're in a cave."

"Precisely," Cory said. "And spelunkers, the people who explore caves, refer to parts of a cave that are bigger than passages but smaller than chambers as rooms. Anyone who knows anything about caves knows that."

Wes wanted to slug Fleming then and there. How dare the geek try to show him up for a moron in front of his girl and all the others! He turned and glared, ready to wade in if Fleming so much as grinned. But, as usual, Scott intervened.

"Cory, enough already about the damn spelunkers. And Wes, let's stick close together, shall we?"

Frustrated, Wes resumed wending his way through the chamber. He hardly noticed the marvelous formations. In his mind's eye he was reliving that day in May when he competed in the school's annual archery competition. Archery had always been a special love of his, ever since childhood when he was first introduced to the story of Robin Hood. Nowadays his compound bow hung on a polished mahogany rack above his bed.

Every Sunday for years he had tried to get in a half hour of practice, a habit that helped develop the keen eye and steady nerves he found so useful in playing baseball, football and basketball. He was an outstanding all-around athlete and enjoyed high prospects for being awarded a scholarship. But archery remained his first love, and he had always taken special satisfaction in winning the archery championship.

Until last May.

Who would have thought it? Beaten by Cory Fleming, who had never entered an archery competition in his life. By Cory Fleming, who had never joined an archery team before. By Cory Fleming, the dork of dorks.

His ears burned at the memory of the ribbing his friends had given him. They had delighted in rubbing his nose in his loss. 'Hey, Wes, we heard Fleming gave you the shaft!' 'Wes, next time you should remember to string your bow.' 'Maybe you should take on Fleming at checkers!'

Had he lost to anyone other than Cory, no one would have given a damn. Instead, his defeat had become a running joke that seemed to go on forever. The jibes had tapered off a couple of weeks after the match, but seldom did a month gone by that someone didn't remind him of his loss. And although he laughed along with his friends, deep down he'd simmered.

The ribbing, bad as it had been, wasn't the worst aspect of losing.

For almost a whole school year he had looked forward to the new Corvette his dad had promised him. As usual, there had been strings attached.

Since grade school his parents had enticed him to get better grades and to perform better at sports by offering to reward his performance with his heart's desire. In grade school they had given him money and toys. Later it had been money and clothes. In high school there had been a vacation in Bermuda, an unchaperoned weekend of skiing at Vail, and the usual money.

So it had been only natural for his father to set conditions if he wanted to earn the car. All Wes had to do was be picked as first-string quarterback on the football team, have a winning season pitching for the baseball team, and win the archery competition.

When his father made the proposal, Wes had laughed. The car was as good as his! he told himself. The football coach had made him first-string quarterback the season before and was bound to do so again. He was one of the top two pitchers on the baseball team, his fastball the talk of the league. And he had won the archery trophy during his sophomore year and was certain to repeat.

Or so he thought.

Then Cory Fleming came along and beat him by ten points.

Ten stinking points.

He had tried explaining to his father that Cory's win was a fluke, a once in a lifetime occurrence, and that technically he had deserved the top trophy because he was a far better bowman. But his dad refused to break their agreement, and since he had failed to live up to the conditions, he wasn't awarded the new Corvette.

Cory Fleming had cost him the car of his dreams. Right then and there he had vowed to---"

Wes!" Leslie suddenly exclaimed, grabbing his arm hard, her fingernails digging into him.

"What?" Wes responded, distracted by his thoughts. "What's the matter?"

"Don't you hear it?" Leslie whispered.

Wes looked around in confusion and realized everyone else had stopped.

It was then the he heard the eerie sound wafting up from

the Stygian depths of the cave, a quavering moan like that of an anguished soul in torment.

Chapter 3

Cory Fleming stopped dead in his tracks on hearing the moan. He saw Wesley halt and gape, and he would have laughed if not for being preoccupied with the sound. What in the world was it? Something touched his hand and he jumped, then was embarrassed when he glanced down and discovered Ann's hand had bumped his.

"Sorry," she said.

The moan howled through the cavern for over a minute, rising and falling like the wail of a coyote. As abruptly as it had started, it ceased

"What the hell was that?" Jay blurted.

"The wind," Scott said. "There are a lot of hidden cracks in caves this size up near the surface where the wind can get in." He shifted so he could see Cory. "Isn't that right, Fleming?"

"Yep," Cory responded, although bothered by a feeling that in this instance the wind had not been responsible. Which was utterly ridiculous. No animals lived in the Caverna del Diablo. He dispelled the feeling with a shake of his head and moved out when Leslie and Wes did.

They crossed the chamber, went through a long, wide passage, then stopped in a circular area. Ahead the passage forked.

"Now which way?" Scott wondered aloud, shining his flashlight down both branches. "Fleming, you were in here before. Which way did you take?"

"We took the right fork," Cory said. "It takes you down

to what's called the Rainbow Room, where the ceiling is all different colors. It's the most popular spot in the whole cave, and families go down there a lot to have picnics."

"Way cool!" Stacy said. "Let's go."

Scott turned. "This is Halloween, remember? The whole purpose for coming out here was to have some fun, to put a little excitement into our lives." He indicated the right fork. "Where's the fun in taking the branch everyone else takes? And who cares about a dumb Rainbow Room? We're not here for a picnic. We're here to do some monster hunting and scare ourselves shitless. Isn't that what Halloween is all about?"

"Right on," Wes said. "I vote we take the left branch." He imitated the voice of a certain actor on television. "Let's boldly go where no one has gone before."

"Whatever you guys decide is fine," Cory said, although secretly he would have been happier going to the Rainbow Room. He knew the route, and the passages were so arranged that it was impossible for anyone to become lost. The left fork was a whole different story. It was reputed to be a maze down there.

"Girls?" Scott said.

Stacy grinned and rubbed against Jay. “I go where my hunk goes."

"The left branch is okay with me," Leslie said.

Ann pursed her lips and gazed uncertainly at the forks. “I know this is Halloween and all, but shouldn't we play it safe? No one knows we're here and if something happens we could be in trouble."

"Spare me the gloom and doom," Scott responded. "We're all big kids now, honey. The left branch will be more of a challenge." He reached out to tap Jay’s backpack. "You have nothing to worry about. We came prepared for every contingency."

Ann shrugged. "I suppose it's okay."

"And you, Terri?" Scott asked.

"I don't much care one way or the other. I just want to get out of here as soon as possible."

Wesley laughed. "Scared already? Hell, we've hardly gone more than a couple of hundred yards."

"This place is spooky," Terri said, gazing apprehensively at the shadows ringing the ceiling.

"That's the whole point," Scott declared happily, "Just think! We're the only ones in here. We have the whole cave to ourselves, thousands of feet of tunnels where we can party to our heart's content. And I've brought all we need to do just that."

Cory didn't like the sound of that. If the others drank heavily it would invite an accident. "What exactly did you bring?"

"Wait and see," Scott replied, and wheeled around to stride into the left tunnel.

With grave misgivings, Cory held back at the fork to allow Ann and Terri to go in front of him, then shined his light on the tunnel floor ahead so they could see any obstacles. He wondered why Ann was hanging back near him instead of walking up front with Scott. He stared at her long hair, at the curve of her back, and finally at her hips as they swayed provocatively with every step. Lord, she was beautiful! And he was a fool to think he had a chance with her. She had made that plain years ago.

So why did he keep on hoping?

The passage narrowed, then curved to the left for fifty yards. A cool breeze blew on their faces until they arrived at a chamber filled with rimstone dams. From there they carefully negotiated a steep incline until it bottomed out in a pit littered with tiny fragments of rock mixed with dirt.

A cloud of dust enveloped them and set them all to coughing as they crossed the pit to another tunnel.

Cory covered his mouth with his left hand until they were out of the dust. The new tunnel had a high ceiling creased in the center by a thin cleft. He detected a faint whisper of chill air and licked his forefinger to determine the direction it came from. But when he raised his arm the air seemed to strike his finger from all sides at once, making it impossible to tell.

Next they entered a room where the ceiling was covered with calcium helictites, worm-like protrusions of varying sizes. The floor slanted downward ever so gradually, and after passing under an arch that glittered when struck by their flashlight beams, they encountered another fork.

Scott stopped and examined both. "Okay, gang, which way now?"

It didn't matter to Cory. They hadn't listened to his advice the last time, so he didn't bother to voice an opinion until everyone else had voted to take the left branch and Scott looked directly at him.

"And you, brain? What do you say?"

"You're the leader, Scott. Whichever one you pick is fine with me," Cory answered.

"We're trying to keep this democratic, Fleming. Isn't that the way our old civics teacher says things should be run? So out with it. Vote like everyone else."

Cory became uncomfortably aware that some of the others were gazing impatiently at him. "The left fork is okay," he quickly said.

"Figured it would be," Scott said, and chuckled. He aimed his flashlight straight ahead and headed out.

Twenty minutes of traversing various tunnels brought

them to the narrowest passage so far. They had to turn sideways again to squeeze through.

Cory was the last to enter. He removed his backpack and dangled it at his side, then eased in. Ordinarily confined spaces never bothered him but in this instance he abruptly experienced an unreasoning flood of fear that erupted from the core of his being and pervaded his every pore. He paused, his breath catching in his throat, then fought off the fear and moved on. It was silly to be afraid, he told himself. The walls weren't about to close in and crush him. The cave had existed for centuries, and it was highly unlikely any part of it would collapse while they were inside. The walls and ceiling were solid rock, as sturdy and as safe as a concrete bunker.

Partway along, the passage angled sharply to the left. He saw Terri go around the corner, leaving him momentarily cut off from the others. With hurried steps he went to catch up when a second bout of fear overcame him. Shuddering uncontrollably, he leaned his forehead on the wall and took deep breaths. What was going on? Logically, there was no reason to feel as he did. Yet here he was acting like a six year old terrified of the dark instead of a high school senior. That thought comforted him. He was almost a man, damn it, not a child any longer. He had to get his act together.

Cory moved to the corner, slid past it and froze in bewilderment. His bright beam of light illuminated the passage for almost a hundred feet---and no one was there! The others shouldn't be more than a dozen yards in front of him. Stunned, he hastened forward but stopped in midstride when a blast of cool air hit him and Ann's voice called out.

"Cory? We're in here. Are you coming?"

He turned, surprised to see a gap in the wall. Stepping into it, he found a broad passage slanting to the right. Twenty feet off waited Ann and Terri, their figures silhouetted by the glow of the flashlights ahead.

"What the hell is the holdup back there?" Scott bellowed.

Cory hastened to the girls. "Sorry. I was studying an interesting quartz vein," he said, filled with guilt by the lie. But he wasn't about to make a fool of himself and confess the truth. Avoiding their eyes, he gazed toward the head of the line and yelled, "We're okay. Keep going."

"Don't fall behind like that," Terri said. "We'd hate to lose you." She lowered her voice. "You're the only guy in this bunch I trust."

"Terri!" Ann said.

"Well, I'm right, and you know it," Terri said defensively. I know you like Scott and all but I don't think he's so great. You've heard the rumors that have been going around school about him."

"What rumors?" Cory asked.

"Never mind," Ann said angrily, facing Terri. "I credited you with better sense than to talk about someone behind their back. Rumors don't mean a thing, as you should well know."

Cory could have sworn that Terri blushed. He hadn't heard any rumors about Miklin, but then his circle of friends was small and limited to those normally excluded from the gab sessions in the hallways and at the lunch tables.

Wesley's shout interrupted their conversation. "Are you three with us or what? Get the lead out of your butts."

Ann spun and hastened away.

"What's this all about?" Cory inquired as he trailed after Terri.

"Why ask me? I never know anything."

Cory detected the hurt in her tone and felt sorry for her. Terri had few friends besides Ann. Like him, she was shunned by the majority of her peers. They shared the mutual bond of being social outcasts. He decided to shoot the breeze with her later and get to know her a little better. Outcasts should stick together, he reasoned, because they needed friends as much as anyone else. Perhaps even more. Being a social pariah was a terrible stigma.

The tunnel tilted downward by gradual degrees, twisting and turning every forty to fifty feet. The it broadened out, the walls shrouded in flickering shadows. Twice they passed narrow passages, offshoots of the one they followed, and each time Scott stuck to the main tunnel.

Cory was bothered by the fact that Scott wasn't bothering to mark their route in some way. The deeper they progressed, the greater the risk of becoming lost. Speaking up, though, might invite criticism, and he was determined not to come across as a wimp again.

The cool breeze intensified, as if they were directly under a fissure that reached to the surface far above. Faint rustlings seemed to emanate from the stalactites overhead.

Pondering whether to secretly make marks of his own, Cory had his eyes on the ground when he heard an indistinct squeal high up. He swept his flashlight beam vertical but saw no movement. Had it been his imagination or did bats dwell this far down? Or were there mice in the cave? There had been no evidence of animal droppings so he was inclined to doubt wildlife lived there. It must have been a freak of the wind.

Excited yells broke out ahead.

Cory lowered the beam and discovered that the tunnel led to a chamber. He was the last to enter, and he gaped in delighted amazement at the staggering dimensions

Mile High Stadium in Denver, home to the Denver Broncos, would not begin to fill it. Moonmilk, composed of crystals of hydromagnesite and water, covered the walls in a dazzling.white coat that resembled a layer of plaster of Paris. Caramel-colored formations adorned the upper rim. Gypsum encrustations layered large sections of the roof.

"Oh, this is so beautiful!" Leslie Vanderhorst exclaimed.

"Out of sight!" Stacy agreed, spinning in a circle as she surveyed the natural wonder.

"How about if we stop and rest here?" Scott proposed. "We can break out the munchies and tell scary stories to put us in the Halloween spirit."

Cory listened as everyone agreed. He roved his beam over the wall behind them, then blinked in disbelief "Hey!" he declared. "Look!"

Everyone turned.

There were three tunnels, not just one, arranged in a row along the base of the cavern wall at regular intervals of ten feet or so. The openings were virtually identical, high and smooth and lacking any distinguishing marks.

"How do we know which tunnel is the one we used?" Terri asked.

"It'Il be the one with all the footprints;" Scott replied, gesturing at the floor. "Look. No one else has been down in this part of the cave for ages."

Cory glanced down and realized Miklin was right. Other than their own tracks, the dust underfoot was undisturbed. What if no one else had ever been in this particular chamber? That gap in the wall he had nearly missed back a ways was virtually invisible unless someone happened to turn or glance over at just the right moment. It was possible that even professional explorers were unaware of its existence. "We shouldn't wander off too far," he cautioned, forgetting himself in his worry for their safety.

Wesley snickered. "Afraid the boogeyman will get you, Fleming? And here I thought you Einstein types don't believe in monsters!"

"We don't," Cory said.

"Not even Bigfoot?" Terri asked.

Scott turned. "How about if we save the monster talk until we make ourselves nice and comfortable? Then we can scare ourselves silly."

"Screw the monsters," Jay said. "I want something to eat. I'm starved."

"You're always starved, honeybuns," Stacy told him, and then placed a finger on her chin and pretended to be deep in thought. "You know, it might be radical to the fifth dimension to get horizontal with a monster like Bigfoot. Just imagine the size of him!"

"How gross," Leslie said and laughed.

"How crude," Ann amended.

"What's the matter?" Stacy shot back "Couldn't you handle a magnum that size? Why, I bet you've never even had your plumbing snaked."

Jay and Wesley roared.

"That's enough!" Scott said. "We're all supposed to be friends on this outing of ours. So no more cuts, all right?" He gave Stacy a hard look until Jay did the same to him. Then he pivoted and pointed at a large flat boulder twenty yards away. "Let's kick back and relax over there."

Cory moved toward it, glad Scott had come to Ann's rescue. Another instant and he would have made a remark that would have brought Jay down on his head like a ton of bricks. Jay defended Stacy's honor vigorously, and any insult, however slight, was sure to bring immediate retaliation. Everyone in high school knew it was certain suicide to mess with Stacy.

He stripped off his backpack and placed it on the boulder. The rest of the guys were doing the same. Stacy and Leslie had gone around the boulder to sit on the other side, away from Ann and Terri. The rift promised trouble ahead. Stacy wasn't the type to take being called 'crude' lightly.

Scott and Wesley began opening their backpacks and pulling out packages of food. There were pretzels, potato chips, cheese crackers, sausages and more.

“You’ve got enough here to feed an army,” Leslie joked.

"We knew Jay was coming," Scott said and gave Jay a beaming smile to emphasize the comment had been a joke and not a dig. He reached into a second backpack and extracted a six-pack of beer, then another and another.

"About damn time!" Jay Thorpe declared, grabbing one of the cans and popping the tab with a flick of his thick wrist. In great gulps, he downed the contents in seconds, tossed the can aside, and let out with a belch that stirred the dust on the boulder.

Stacy, Wes and Scott all laughed.

Butterflies formed in Cory’s stomach. He suppressed a frown and gazed at the three tunnels, afraid his feelings would be reflected in his eyes. Of all the stupid stunts! No one with half a mind would get drunk in the depths of an enormous cavern when all their wits might be needed to find their way back out. Again a beer can popped, and he glanced around to find Wes trying to duplicate Jay's feat. Both of them were as dumb as bricks.

Scott opened a beer for himself and jerked a thumb at the collection of eats. "Help yourselves, people."

Any appetite Cory had developed on the trek into the cave had evaporated in the heat of his annoyance. He stood, picked up his flashlight and trained it on the ceiling to admire the gypsum.

"What's the matter, Fleming?" Wes asked. "Aren't you hungry?"

"Not at the moment."

"Get it while it lasts. We wouldn't want you stumbling around in the dark hungry."

Puzzled by the remark, Cory turned.

Wes and Scott were smirking at him as if they were ravenous cats and he was a helpless canary. Their expressions shifted and became models of polite friendliness.

Now what the hell was that all about?

Chapter 4

Jay Thorpe polished off his sixth beer, tossed the can as far as he could, and listened to it clatter among a cluster of weird rock formations. He had to take a leak, and after ogling Stacy for the past 20 minutes he was in the mood to relieve another basic need. He grabbed Stacy's arm and said, "Let's go for a walk."

About to take a bite from a pretzel, Stacy cocked an eye and grinned. "What do you have in mind/"

"Let's go and you'll find out," Jay said. Vivid memories of the night before, when they had made it in a thicket, fueled his lust and sparked a twitching in his loins. He pulled her along as he headed for the opposite end of the chamber from the three tunnels. They needed privacy. She was always ready and willing, and although she didn't care where they got it on, she drew the line at letting anyone watch.

"Stay close, Jay," Scott called. "You didn't take a flashlight. We don't want you getting lost."

"Yeah, yeah," Jay responded, then said softly to Stacy, "Sometimes that guy is worse than my mother. Him and Wes, both. They treat me like I don't have any smarts at all."

"Wes has always been a snotnose," Stacy reminded him. "He sucks up to you because without you, his ass would have been grass many times over. You're the one who keeps the other teams off his butt."

"True," Jay said, amazed at her insight. He'd never even

considered that Wesley's friendship was based on his football ability, but now that she mentioned it the idea made a lot of sense. Wesley was a rich snot, while he came from a blue-collar family. Wesley's dad was a real estate bigwig. His dad worked as a maintenance man. It always struck him as a bit odd that Wes hung around with him so much. Stacy must be right. She usually was, which only made him love her the more. He didn't mind that she was more intelligent. In his opinion, her smarts and his brawn made a perfect combination. Little did she know that he planned to pop the question at the school prom in the Spring. "What about Scott?" he asked.

"That's simple. He likes anyone Wes likes. Hell, he wouldn't do anything to get his best customer mad. His kind sucks up to anyone who has the green for their goodies."

“I know," Jay said. He'd already figured that much out for himself, not that it really mattered to him one way or the other. He hung out with Wes because Wes always had money to blow and there was no end of partying, food and beer. So if Wes wanted Scott to tag along, it was okay by him.

"How far are we going?" Stacy asked, glancing at the shadowy formations among which they were wending.

"Don't tell me you're scared," Jay teased. He pressed on until they were at the limit of the glow cast by the flashlights. Looking back, he saw the others flapping their gums. Nearby reared yet another strange formation, this one the size of a van. He hauled Stacy behind it. "How about here?”

She studied their surroundings and smiled. "Sort of kinky, but I like it, honeybuns. I've never made it in a cave before."

"Hold that thought," Jay said, moving off to take his leak. He liked beer, but the damn stuff went through him like water through a sieve.

"Don't take too long."

The hint of tension in her voice amused Jay. He was sure she was nervous about being so far down in the cave, but he wasn't going to make an issue of it. If he got her angry he risked having her tell him to go take a flying leap. It would take hours to calm her down, and by then they would be back on the surface. She might be too pooped to pop.

He took care of his business quickly, zipped up his jeans and strolled back.

Stacy was leaning on the formation, her arms crossed under her breasts, her right leg bent seductively. "Looking for a good time, sailor?"

"Ain't I always," Jay replied, halting in front of her, his chest brushing against hers. She puckered and blew him a silent kiss, then giggled. Her hip-length blonde hair seemed to shine even in the gloom, drawing his thick fingers as a flame would draw moths. He stroked it, enjoying its silken texture, entwining his fingers.

"Is that all you want to play with?" she taunted.

"Not hardly," Jay responded, and suddenly swooped his hands to her breasts. She stiffened and gasped as he squeezed, feeling her nipples bud and harden under his palm. The sheer pink blouse she had on did little to conceal her charms, and he now yanked it up so he could reach underneath and cup both of her gorgeous mounds in his huge hands.

"I like it when you play rough," Stacy said huskily.

"Then you're in for a treat, babe," Jay assured her, wedging his thigh between her legs and molding his massive form to hers so he could plant a kiss. She opened her mouth to receive his tongue and gripped his broad shoulders. Beneath his belt his manhood surged to attention, rising to its full enormous height. It wasn't for nothing that many of his teammates had nicknamed him "the Bull." No one else at Pagosa Springs High could boast a boner his size.

Stacy moaned as he continued to massage her breasts, and ground her legs into him.

The tantalizing perfume she wore was enough to send Jay into seventh heaven. Combined with the exquisite feel of her body, it stoked his desire. He lowered his right hand to the junction of her legs and slid his forefinger between them. The heat she radiated could have melted a tank. He rubbed against her pink shorts, and she squirmed deliciously.

“Ohhh, honeybuns," she breathed when he broke for air.

Jay clamped his lips on her right tit and sucked. She cooed and wiggled so he sucked harder while continuing to rub her furnace. Her warm breath fanned his ear and her fingers gripped his hair. He wanted her in the worst way but had no intention of rushing things. Quickies never appealed to him. When he got his rocks off, he liked to savor every second.

He transferred his mouth to her other breast and gave it the same treatment. The bottom of her shorts were now moist, and he deftly slipped his finger under her lacy undies and into her hot hole. For a moment she held herself still, then she began grinding into his hand as if she were riding a bucking horse.

"Uhhh," Stacy said, her eyes closed, her head tossed back. "What you do to me!"

Jay traced a path with his tongue down to her tight

tummy, then licked her right side all the way up to her arm. She drew his face to hers, and they locked lips once more. He chose that moment to begin working his forefinger as if it were a plunger, letting the friction build and build. His hand becamc drenched with her juices as she thrashed madly.

"Do me, honeybuns. Please do me."

"Not yet, babe," Jay responded. He was about to pick her up and lay her on the floor when he remembered the thick layer of dust. She would be annoyed if he got her clothes dirty. Fair enough. He'd be the perfect gentleman and make it while standing.

He tugged her shorts over her hips and down her legs, having to bend until he could remove them. Rather than drop them in the dust, he wadded them into a ball and tucked them under his belt. Then he unzipped, adjusted his jeans so he could expose his pole and immediately felt her hands close on it.

"My big boy," Stacy said, leering. "My big, lovable honeybuns."

"Ready for the main event?"

"I was born ready."

Back at the flat boulder Cory grabbed a handful of potato chips and took a bite out of the biggest. The salty tangy flavor made his mouth water but did little to revive his appetite. For the past ten minutes he had suffered through Wes, Scott and Leslie bragging about a party held at Eagen's house several weeks ago. They rated it as the best party all year since a third of the participants had become so drunk they passed out, others had stripped down to their birthdays suits and taken a plunge in the pool, and the tight end had been caught in the shower with not one, not two, but three of the cheerleaders. Who ever said life was dull?

"Let's get to the nitty-gritty," Scott was now saying. "We came down here because it's Halloween and we might get to see the monster. You heard Fleming earlier, didn't you? How people have claimed there's something down here since the gold-hunting days?"

"It began before that," Cory said.

"What?" Scott said, not too pleased at being interrupted.

"There were the Native Americans, remember? And then the Spaniards. Those symbols we saw were made by them. Supposedly, they came into the cave in search of gold and were driven out by a demon."

"A demon!" Scott laughed. "Hell, they were probably chased out by a bear and told the demon story to cover their asses."

Cory continued. "The Utes who lived in this region also claimed that a horrible creature terrorized their tribe. It was supposed to live in the cavern, which was why they would never set up their lodges anywhere near it. Some of their bravest warriors ventured in to challenge the thing, and that was the last anyone saw of them."

"They probably got lost and couldn't find their way out," Wesley said. "And everyone knows Indians were afraid of their own shadows."

"Tell that to Custer," Cory retorted, and went on quickly, ignoring Wesley's glare. "Then along came the trappers and mountain men. They were the ones who named Devil Creek after something that kept raiding their camps at night and killing their horses. And some of them."

"It could have been a grizzly or a mountain lion," Scott said.

"They didn't think so."

Terri was hanging on every word. She leaned forward and asked, "Is that it? There are no recent reports, right?" She sounded vastly relieved.

"A few," Cory said. "Back in the twenties a couple was found torn to shreds in a side passage."

"A bear," Scott said. "I'd bet anything."

"And in the sixties three people were discovered with their throats slit," Cory detailed. "All the blood had been drained from their bodies and their clothes were nowhere around."

"Tell the rest of it," Scott said gruffly, and gave Ann a reassuring smile. "I heard about that one. The police decided the three were murdered and arrested a suspect."

"So no one has died in the cave since then?" Ann inquired.

"Nope," Scott said. He stood, stretched, and began gathering up their munchies. "And now that Fleming has so kindly put us in the right mood, we can have some real fun."

"What do you have in mind?" Ann asked.

"Oh, a little exploring, a little monster hunting, and a little peekaboo," Scott said as he stuffed the packages into a backpack.

"I'd rather not," Terri said.

Wes frowned. "Hey, if you want to go back to the surface, be our guest. We're not about to spoil Halloween because you might wet your panties."

Ann angrily came up off the boulder and jabbed a finger at him. "Don't talk to her like that."

"He didn't mean anything by it," Scott said, and encompassed them all in a friendly look. "What say we stop getting on each other's nerves and get down to some serious partying?"

Cory noted that Scott hadn't bothered to stick their trash in the packs. Empty beer cans were lying scattered about, as were the plastic holders the cans had come in, and wrappers and whatnot. "Did you bring any garbage bags?"

"What in the world for?" Scott said. He surveyed the boulder. "Oh, you mean this mess. Leave it for one of those ecology buffs to clean up. A few wrappers and cans won't hurt anything." He lifted a backpack and slid his arms under the straps.

Wesley was doing the same.

Cory glanced at Ann, who was being unusually quiet. What was going through her mind? Was she as sorry she had tagged along as he was? Who knew? Maybe she liked being with a jerk like Miklin.

Scott turned and cupped his hands to his mouth. "Yo, Jay! Are you going to take all night?"

From the far end of the chamber came, "Up yours."

"Are they doing what I think they're doing?" Terri said.

Leslie, sipping at a beer, nodded. "What else? That Thorpe is an animal. Stacy says he likes to do it twice a day, three times on Sunday." She shook her head in amazement. "I don't know how she handles all that screwing. I mean, there's such a thing as too much, even with sex."

"How would Terri know?" Wes said, and cackled.

"That does it," Ann snapped. She stood and took Terri's hand. "Come on. We're going back to the jeeps. I've put up with all the insults I'm going to take."

"Ann, wait," Scott said, moving around the boulder to cut her off. "What's with you tonight? You're ready to fly off the handle every time Wes opens his mouth."

"I want to go home."

"Right this minute? What about the long drive here? What about this being Halloween? Don't you want to have a few cheap thrills?"

"No."

"You'd spoil the night for the rest of us? I didn't think you were so selfish."

Cory saw Ann bow her head and knew the argument had worked. He felt his dislike of Scott growing by the minute. The guy said whatever it took to have his own way. And after that strange look Miklin and Eagen had given him earlier, he didn't trust either of them as far as he could throw the giant boulder.

"All right," Ann said softly. "We'll stay a while longer."

"That's my girl," Scott, and pecked her on the cheek.

From out of the shadows strolled Jay and Stacy, arm in arm. Jay grinned like a little boy who had just successfully raided the cookie jar. Stacy wore a contented expression. They came up and Jay gazed around in surprise. "Hey, where's the rest of the brews? I'm thirsty enough to drain a well."

"Later, big guy," Scott said. "We want to get this show on the road. Put on your pack and grab your flashlight. You can take the lead."

"Where to?" Jay responded as he obeyed.

"Pick a tunnel. Any one will do."

Cory, reluctant to join in the so-called fun, took his time shrugging into his pack. The others had all moved out, Jay and Stacy in the lead, Ann, Terri and Leslie right behind them, when he finally moved away from the boulder. Five yards in front of him were Scott and Wes, whispering and chuckling. What now? he mused.

On the other side were three more tunnels. Jay shone his light over them as he approached. Without hesitation he entered the one on the far left. "Watch your head in here," he shouted, ducking low and disappearing.

The girls dutifully filed in.

Scott was almost to the opening when he stopped. So did Wes. They faced Cory and waited for him to catch up.

"We wouldn't want to lose you," Wes said, grinning from ear to ear.

"I'm not about to get lost," Cory said. If anything, he was the least likely of all of them.

Scott suddenly glanced over Cory's shoulder as if he had spotted something back in the chamber. "What the hell is that?" he exclaimed.

Cory spun and went to sweep his flashlight from right to left when he was struck in the small of his back. The blow knocked him to his knees. Before he could hope to react the flashlight was roughly torn from his hand and a shove sent him sprawling onto his stomach.

He heard Scott and Wes laughing as he struggled to his knees. They were already gone, vanished down the tunnel. He could see the glow of their flashlights becoming rapidly dimmer as they sped off.

Darkness abruptly enveloped him like a glove.

Furious, Cory rose and darted forward, but in his haste he tripped over his own feet and toppled, throwing his arms out in a vain effort to recover his balance.

Too late he realized he was going to smash into the rock wall, and an instant later he did.

Excruciating pain flared in his forehead and wet drops splattered onto his cheeks. Dizziness flooded through him. He smacked onto the ground, tasted dirt in his mouth, and tried to rise.

The dizziness intensified, becoming a tidal wave that drowned him in acute vertigo.

Cory struggled again to stand. Gritting his teeth, he was almost up when his head wound took its toll.

Everything faded to black.

Chapter 5

Ann Weatherby was unhappy. Nothing was going as she had planned, and to make matters worse she was winding ever deeper into the Caverna del Diablo, which was the very last thing she wanted to do. The gloomy confines of the cave gave her the creeps. She longed to be back on the surface but hesitated to raise the issue again since the others would make fun of her.

This was what she got for letting Scott talk her out of going back earlier.

The five minutes since leaving the big chamber had been spent in following twisting passages into the very bowels of the mountain. Although the tunnels were wide and the going easy, she felt as if she were in the depths of a monumental tomb and kept imagining what would happen if the ceiling should unexpectedly collapse.

When Scott initially invited her, she envisioned a pleasant evening of strolling about in passages closer to the cave entrance. Had she known that Scott intended to penetrate into unexplored subterranean regions, she never would have agreed to go.

Speaking of the devil, where was he?

Ann looked over her shoulder for the third time in the past minute but there was still saw no sign of Scott, Wes or Cory, which struck her as strange. Jay and Stacy were only a few feet ahead, Jay's flashlight their only source of illumination. Behind her came Terri and Leslie, neither appearing very pleased by the turn of events. But for once

Leslie didn't seem to mind being in Terri's company.

"How much farther are we going to go?" Stacy asked her boyfriend.

Jay looped a brawny arm around her trim waist and smirked. "As far as you want, babe."

Every time Ann saw them acting so lovey-dovey, she felt uncomfortable. Why, she couldn't say. She had nothing against either of them. Jay was a typical jock, Stacy his babe. She wasn't close to either although she had talked to Stacy on occasion. "Jay," she now said.

Neither of them heard.

"Jay!" Ann repeated, louder this time, and halted.

The hulking bruiser stopped and glanced at her. "What is it, Weatherby?"

"Where are the others?"

"Huh?"

Ann pointed back the way they had come. "There's no sign of Scott, Wes and Cory. Where could they be?"

"I don't know," Jay said in surprise, aiming his beam past her. "I thought they were with us the whole time. Why didn't you say something sooner?"

"I kept expecting them to catch up."

"Let's go find them," Leslie proposed. "I want to be with Wes."

It figures, Ann thought, but made no comment. Wesley and Leslie were flip sides of the same coin, spoiled rich kids who had been born with silver spoons in their mouths. She knew Leslie well. Back in junior high they had been close friends until Leslie developed an interest in boys.

"Let me lead," Jay said, stepping around them, Stacy as usual glued to the end of his arm. The flashlight probed into the darkness, revealing a few stalactites on the ceiling and their distinct footprints in the dust. He began retracing their route.

Ann let Terri and Leslie go before her. She brought up the rear, thinking of Cory and hoping he was okay. By all rights she shouldn't care one way or the other, but she did. Even after what he had done, even after keeping her distance from him for years, she still liked him, liked him a lot. All those times they had played together as kids, all the fun they had. It seemed as if it was only yesterday.

What was that?

Ann halted and twisted, certain a faint noise had disturbed the heavy silence behind her. A scratching noise, like a fingernail scraping along a rock. Could it be the guys? Were they playing some sort of trick? It was Halloween, after all. The scratching wasn't repeated, and she decided she had been mistaken.

"Something wrong?" Terri asked, slowing down.

"No," Ann said, and quickened her pace to rejoin her companions. "I'm just hearing things."

"Oh?" Terri peered into the black blanket of emptiness and shuddered as if from a cold wind. "Don't joke about something like that. Not even a little."

"Sorry," Ann responded. She saw Jay, Stacy and Leslie negotiate a bend. Instantly the light dimmed, "Whoops. We'd better move it or they'll leave us behind."

Terri took one look and gasped. She sped toward the bend as if her life depended on it. Amused by her friend's terror, Ann smiled and ran around the corner. She had to dig in her toes to stop in order to avoid colliding with Terri and the other girls. A few feet away stood Jay, his flashlight trained on the cave floor.

"What the hell!" he blurted, as he crouched to touch the ground. "This is impossible."

Ann joined the rest in moving forward. She stared over

Jay's broad shoulder, realized why he was so upset, and recoiled in shock. Common sense told she must be wrong. They had gone less than ten yards since turning around and the tunnel hadn't forked. This was the passage they had followed since leaving the huge chamber. She was sure of it.

"I don't understand," Leslie said. "What's the big deal?"

"The floor," Jay said, his voice strained. "Look at the floor!"

Leslie did. "I am. So?"

"So where the hell are our footprints?"

Comprehension made Leslie cover her mouth with her hand and mumble, "Oh, my God!"

Jay took a few steps, his beam roving ahead of them to reveal that for as far as the light extended, the floor was the same---coated with a layer of undisturbed, smooth dust. "I just don't get it," he said.

"This is the right tunnel," Stacy said, touching the left-hand wall. "I know it is."

Terri fidgeted nervously. "Let's just keep going, okay? The sooner we get the hell out of here, the better I'll feel."

"Yeah," Leslie said. "And we have to find Wes and the other guys. Don't forget them."

"Come on," Jay said, beckoning. "And stay close. I don't want to lose anyone else."

Once again Ann was the last in line. She hugged Terri's heels, her mind awhirl as she tried to make sense of the unfolding events. Maybe those blockheads Scott and Wes had planned the whole thing. Maybe they had somehow erased all the footprints. If so, how could they have done it? With a broom, by sweeping dust over the tracks? Possibly, she reasoned, but no one had brought a broom into the cavern. Then another idea blossomed. What if

Scott and Wes had visited the cave earlier in the week and stashed the broom and additional items for later use? They were notorious practical jokers, and she wouldn't put anything past them. Convinced she must be tight, she mentioned her deduction to the others.

"You know," Leslie responded, "Wes has been hinting that he planned something special for tonight. And I know Scott was in on it but they wouldn't breathe a word to me."

"They've been whispering together a lot lately," Stacy said, "and a stunt like this would be right up their alley."

"I have news for those two," Jay announced. "I don't like having tricks played on me. Wherever they are, when I get my hands on them, they're going to be a pair of very sorry troopers."

"Where the hell are we?" Wesley snapped, flashing his light at the varied columns and formations adorning the chamber in which they found themselves after hiking for over ten minutes.

"More importantly," Scott countered, "where the hell are Jay and the girls? We should have caught up with them by now."

"Beats me," Wes said, his annoyance mounting. He couldn't see how they had lost Godzilla and the foxes. One moment they had shoved that geek Fleming to the ground and left him in the dark without a flashlight, and the next they had raced along the passage after Jay and the rest. They should have rejoined the others within a minute or two at the most. Yet here they were, all alone. The thought disturbed him.

"Hey, I have an idea," Scott said, turning his beam on the floor. He searched every square inch of the cavern, then looked at Wes. "The only tracks are ours."

"How can that be?" Wes said. "We didn't pass any forks."

"I know."

Confounded, Wes scoured the ground in all directions, then stepped closer to Scott and locked eyes. "There must have been a fork we didn't see. Either that, or those airheads are playing a joke on us."

"Well retrace our steps until we find their tracks, then follow them," Scott said and started off. "I should have thought of this sooner."

"We can't all be Cory Fleming," Wes said, and laughed. Confident they would soon be reunited with the others, he whistled as he walked and ran the two flashlights he held over the walls and ceiling.

Scott noticed the twin beams shooting overhead. He glanced over his shoulder, his mouth curling downward. "Put Fleming's flashlight in your pack. There's no sense in letting his batteries go dead."

"You said that you brought spares," Wes said.

"Two," Scott revealed. "But to be safe, let's save the light for when we really need it."\

Wes flicked off the extra flashlight and began to remove his backpack. The tone of voice Scott had used rankled him but he held his tongue. Sometimes, he, reflected, his good buddy Scott was a bit too bossy for his taste.

But it wasn't worth fighting over, not when doing so might turn Scott against him, forcing him to go elsewhere fo his candy---which reminded him. "Hey, any chance of getting some stuff?"

"Later, Wes. This is more important."

"I could really use some."

"You're always ready to blast," Scott said. He chuckled. "Your damn nose is like a bottomless pit. I've never seen anyone go through snow like you do."

"I have the money."

"It's not the green, dude," Scott said impatiently, and stopped. Hands on his hips, he rotated and stared at Wesley as he might a misbehaving child. "Don't you get it yet? We're lost."

"Like hell we are!" Wes said, finding the notion laughable. "We just took a wrong turn somewhere, that's all. We'll find our way out easy."

"We won't if you get high. And what about Leslie?"

"What about her?"

"You wanted to screw her tonight, right? Isn't that what you've been telling me all week? How you couldn't wait to get her alone down here and get your rocks off?"

"Yeah. So?" Wes rejoined, not certain he liked having it rubbed in his face. The sexual aspect of his relationship with his girlfriend was personal. He might brag about her every so often, but no one else had the right to talk about her as if she were a common slut.

"So we have to get her home by midnight," Scott was saying. "Every minute we waste is less time you can spend with her. If you want me to sell you the coke right this second, fine. But don't blame me if you don't have time for Leslie later."

"I can wait for the snow," Wes said, struggling to keep his resentment from showing.

"Good," Scott said. He resumed their backtracking, his flashlight clearly revealing the prints they had made on the way into the tunnel.

Wes sullenly tramped along behind. This was the first time Scott had ever refused to sell him coke, even temporarily, and he took the refusal as a personal insult. After all the money he had spent on the stuff, after all the bread Scott had made off of him, he felt it was his right to be granted coke on demand. Maybe he should find another source. It would serve Scott right.

He unzipped the top of the backpack and stuffed the extra flashlight inside, then zipped it back up. Slipping into the straps, he settled the pack on his back again. His anger gradually subsided. Thinking about ditching Scott for another dealer was all well and good except for one small detail---Scott was the only dealer he knew.

Pagosa Springs was hardly the drug capital of the Western Hemisphere. Until Scott came along, those who wanted coke had to go all the way to Durango. Wes had never gone in for the stuff himself, not until Scott taught him the ropes. Scott had taught a lot of them the ropes. With his slick Eastern ways, his Massachusetts cool as it were, Scott had become the center of his very own clique shortly after arriving in Colorado. And soon Scott had offered those he could trust delights they couldn't buy at the corner drugstore.

Wes had been honored to be considered one of Scott's best friends. He'd grown to admire the glib Easterner who had an answer for everything and whose motto could be summed up as, "Party until you drop!" For Wes, who had become a bit bored by life and the same old dull daily routine, Scott was a godsend. Wes found his horizons broadened like never before, found a new thrill in simply being alive.

So maybe staying pissed off at Scott wasn't such a great idea.

He trudged along, contenting himself by daydreaming about what he intended to do with Leslie later and reminiscing about their past marathon bouts in the sack, when suddenly Scott called out sharply.

"Hey, look at this!"

Wes glanced up to find that Scott had stopped at a point where the passage turned to the right and was closely examining the wall on the left. "What did you find?" he asked, stepping forward.

Scott merely nodded at the spot he had examined.

It was a passage, narrow at the bend but wider farther in, as their flashlights plainly revealed. The tunnel from the huge chamber had indeed forked, but so abruptly that anyone in a hurry might miss it. In their eagerness to outdistance Fleming so he would be left stranded, and laughing their heads off as they had been doing, they had gone right by it.

"Damn," Scott muttered, turning his beam on the ground. Plainly revealed were the tracks of their companions, all pointing deeper into the cavern. "So this is where we lost them." He turned his flashlight to the right. Not twenty feet away was the entrance to the huge chamber.

"They must be on their way back by now," Wes said. "Maybe we should wait for them on that big boulder where we ate the food."

"And what if they don't come back? What if they find another way to the surface? Let's pick up the pace and we'll overtake them in no time," Scott suggested, moving out before Wes could comment.

"Say, what do you think happened to Fleming?"

"Since he didn't take the same tunnel we did, he's probably rejoined Jay and the girls by now."

The idea bothered Wes. He didn't like the notion of that geek being with Leslie when he wasn't around. Who knew what the bastard might say to make him look small in her eyes? "Go a little faster," he prompted.

They hurried, discovering the passage twisted and

turned like none they had encountered so far. One minute it bore to the right, the next to the left. They had the footprints to guide them and made excellent progress.

Wes was gleefully envisioning how he would break Fleming into tiny pieces if Cory had badmouthed him to Leslie, when he saw Scott stop on the proverbial dime, then glance at him in confusion.

"What do you make of this?"

The tracks they had been following ended---not at a fork or a side passage or the entrance to a room or chamber, but right there in the middle of the tunnel. Ahead lay a gray mantle of undisturbed dust.

"I don't know what to make of it," Wes admitted.

"They couldn't just vanish into thin air," Scott said, scouring the passage.

Wes turned to the left and right, his eyes narrowing when he spied something lying at the base of the wall, bundled material of some sort. He stepped nearer to pick it up, coughing as the material unfolded in his grasp and spewed dust all over him. It appeared to be a large square piece from an old blue blanket, about the size of a dish towel and coated with dirt, its edges frayed. "Hey," he said.

Scott turned, then snatched the blanket and studied it under his light. "That son of a bitch," he snapped.

"Who?" Wes responded, confused.

"Who else? Cory Fleming."

"Huh?"

"Sometimes, good buddy, you can be as dense as a brick," Scott said and sank to a knee. He began rubbing the dirty blanket over the last set of trucks. In seconds he totally obliterated them and restored the floor to its normal dusty condition.

A light bulb went off in Wes's mind and he balled his

left fist. "The dork found that thing and used it to erase the rest of the prints!"

Scott nodded. "Fleming must have seen we took a wrong turn and he's trying to pay us back for the trick we played." Scowling, he threw the piece of blanket down in disgust. "The prick probably found this somewhere along the way."

"Yeah," Wes said, then was bothered by a doubt. "But how did he find it without a flashlight? How did he see we took that turn without a light?"

"Hmm," Scott said, rising. "You know, I wouldn't put it past that digithead to have brought his own flashlight, one of those about the size of a pencil."

"So he could hide it in his pocket and we'd be none the wiser?" Wes declared, admiring the geek's resourcefulness despite himself. "When I get my hands on that creep he's going to be sorry he messed with us."

"First we have to catch him," Scott said, pivoting. "I say we jog from here on out. Since they're walking we should spot their lights in less than five minutes."

"Go for it, brother," Wes urged, and broke into a dog trot. As the first-string quarterback he was in superb physical shape. Daily, he ran anywhere from three to five miles. On alternate days he pumped weights for an hour. He also rigorously stuck to a regimen of calisthenics that heightened his stamina and agility.

The tunnel continued to wend along like a gigantic snake, with numerous switchbacks and curves, the width occasionally narrowing drastically, then broadening again. Every so often, a sluggish breeze fanned the air.

Wes, gazing over his friend's shoulder, spied yet another bend. He took it, jogging hard, and had to step nimbly to one side in order to keep from ramming into Scott's back when Scott halted without warning. "Why'd you---?" he began, then spotted the reason and gaped in astonishment.

"This can't be," Scott said.

"No way," Wes agreed.

Ten feet in front of them, completely blocking the passage, was an immense rock slab.

Wes advanced, running his flashlight over the edges to see if there were any gaps large enough for someone to squeeze through.

The slab fit as snugly as a door.

Scott was searching the walls on both sides. "This is a dead end," he said, sounding shocked. "There are no other tunnels."

"We must have missed a fork," Wes said. "They sure didn't come this way."

"No, they couldn't have," Scott concurred.

At that moment, from the other side of the massive slab, faint but nevertheless distinct, came a chilling sound that caused goosebumps to break out all over both of them---the piercing scream of a terrified woman.

Chapter 6

A tidal wave of pain pounded at Cory Fleming's head, the first sensation he became aware of as he struggled back to consciousness. His eyes opened, and it was like gazing at the sky on a black as pitch night when clouds obscured the moon and the stars. An inky void enveloped him.

He might as well be adrift in deepest, darkest space or at the very bottom of the sea where no light could penetrate. For a moment he blinked in confusion, disoriented, wondering where he was and how he got there.

His memory returned with a vivid rush and he sat up. Immediately, he regretted his rash action. The pain flared, becoming infinitely worse, the pounding in his head like the beating of a drum.

An involuntary gasp escaped his lips. He reached up and touched his forehead, flinching when his fingers contacted a gash over two inches long and a quarter of an inch wide. Dried blood caked his lower brow, part of his nose, and had formed into thin streaks down across his cheeks and chin.

How long had he been unconscious?

He tried to read his watch but failed, although slowly but surely his eyes were adjusting to the murky conditions and he could distinguish various large shapes on the floor of the cavern. Rock formations, he deduced. He was grateful his glasses were still intact. Without them he would be completely helpless, unable to see his hand in front of his face.

Wincing from the effort, he slowly stood and took stock. His flashlight was gone. He still had a backpack but hadn't examined it yet and had no idea what might be inside. For all he knew the pack might be crammed with a bunch of rags or whatever else Scott and Wes had tossed in to make him think he was carrying food.

Scott and Wes.

Thinking of them made his blood boil. They'd set him up, set him up but good. The whole thing must have been planned from the beginning as some sort of juvenile Halloween prank. Thanks to them he was stranded in the depths of the Caverna del Diablo. It would take hours to find his way to the surface.

Who was he kidding?

It might take days.

He aligned his glasses on his nose and turned. Across the chamber were the gaping maws of the three tunnels, one of which had brought them there.

But which?

The gravity of his situation hit him then. Without a light, he couldn't retrace his route by following their footprints in the dust.

Panic clutched at his soul. What if he never found his way out? What if he wandered along endlessly until he succumbed to hunger and thirst? What if the others intended to leave him there, to ride back to Pagosa Springs and never tell anyone where he was?

He pressed a hand to his injured brow, willing himself to calm down. Surely Ann wouldn't allow the rest to just ride off and abandon him. She would convince them to mount a search. At the very least she would tell his parents when she got back to town. Unless---.

A staggering thought caused him to close his eyes and groan. Could it be possible Ann was in league with Scott and Wes? Did that explain why she had invited him along in the first place? Was she the bait Scott and Wes had used to lure him into their little trap? If so, their plan had worked perfectly, all because deep down he still cared for her, indeed, he had carried a torch for her since childhood.

Ann had probably sensed how he felt and mentioned it to Scott.

Cory felt like the world's prize idiot. When word of the ruse got around school, which it was certain to do since Wes and Scott would be unable to resist the temptation to brag, he'd become the laughingstock of Pagosa Springs. His stupidity in falling for their trick would serve to confirm his reputation as a dork, and he could expect a whole new round of jokes about his manliness to spread by word of mouth among his peers.

His panic was replaced by anger at the deception, and the angrier he became, the less panic he felt.

He moved toward the tunnels. He had an important decision to make, one that might make the difference between survival and the unappealing alternative.

Which of the three would take him back to the surface?

Cory knelt and lightly ran his fingers over the ground near the tunnel on the right, then the middle tunnel, and last the tunnel on the left.

The task proved hopeless. He thought his hand brushed a few shallow marks here and there but he wasn't certain. There was simply no way to ascertain which tunnel their tracks came from in the dark.

He would have to rely on logic instead. Standing, he moved from opening to opening, trying to determine if there was a difference in the air current that might give him a clue. He got the impression that the air coming out of the right tunnel was cooler, which might mean it was more directly linked to the outer world where at that moment the Rockies were enveloped by the chill of night.

Cory hesitated, afraid of making a mistake. He took several steps into the tunnel, then backed out and went a few feet into the middle one. Once more he backed out and looked at the third.

Maybe, rather than head for the surface, it would be smarter to try and overtake the others. They had food and flashlights. So what if they laughed their heads off? So what if they made fun of him?

No, he didn't want that.

Back to the surface it was.

He entered the right-hand tunnel, staying in the center where there was less likelihood of bumping into something. The walls were black slates, the ceiling invisible. Thanks to the layer of fine dust on the ground, the cave floor was a pale ribbon that stretched into seeming emptiness.

Cory thought about opening his pack to check the contents but opted to hold off until he stopped to rest. If he was lucky, if he didn't become lost, if he didn't slip and break a leg or worse, he might reach the surface in an hour--an hour and a half, tops. If not, he would hike until he dropped.

The silence became oppressive. Except for the shuffling of his feet, the cavern was like a tomb.

He listened intently, hoping against hope to hear distant voices. The tunnel mocked him with its eerie stillness. It was hard to imagine that on the surface teemed a lush world vibrant with life, with ceaseless motion and bright colors and continual sounds.

The Caverna del Diablo was like another world, a nether realm of eternal quiet undisturbed by the activity above. Small wonder that the early Spaniards and the Indians had regarded it with awe and fear.

He walked and walked, looking for spots he must have passed on the way down.

Nothing was familiar.

How far he went he had no idea. He was on the verge of turning around in the belief he had picked the wrong passage when he came to a room he vaguely thought was one the group had passed through earlier. In the dark positive identification was impossible. He had to rely on his best judgement, and his judgement told him to press on.

Cory became thirsty but ignored the sensation. He couldn't ignore the pain in his head, though, which to his relief had dwindled to a dull ache. Periodic twinges made him grimace. Otherwise, he felt fine.

Over and over he told himself that soon he would be back on the surface. Soon he would either be on his way to Pagosa Springs with the chumps who had played this dirty trick on him, or else, if the jeeps were gone, he would get a roaring fire going and wait until daylight to begin the long hike back.

He rounded a curve, then halted in astonishment. Before him unfolded a wondrous room where the ceiling glowed, starkly revealing scores of arresting stalactites and stalagmites. He'd heard of such a rare phenomenon but had never witnessed it. Advancing to a blunt stalagmite the size of a stool, he sat down to admire the golden glow and take a short break so he could examine his backpack.

Suddenly he realized something that caused fleeting anxiety. At no time on the downward trek had they gone through a room remotely resembling this one, which meant he had taken the wrong tunnel. One of the other tunnels must have been the one that linked the huge chamber to the outer world.

Now he either turned around and retraced his steps or else he kept his fingers crossed and continued in the direction he was going.

Cory unzipped the backpack and rummaged inside. He found the rope Scott had mentioned, coiled neatly and filling most of the pack, plus a pair of spare batteries. That was it. There was no food, no water, not even beer, which at that point he would have drank if only to calm his nerves.

An oversight occurred to him as he closed the pack. At no time had he thought to ask Scott if they had brought water. Knowing Miklin as he did, he doubted it. Scott had probably only included beer because to Scott beer was the only refreshment that mattered.

He tried not to dwell on the fact that the human body could go far longer without food than it could without water. Being three-fourths water itself, it required water to function. If a person went without for more than a few days, severe dehydration set in, causing symptoms such as nausea, poor mental reasoning and sluggish muscle response.

Shouldering the pack, Cory started to stand when he saw something move on the far side of the room. For a moment he thought his imagination was getting the better of him, yet when he cocked his head he saw a shape flick from one stalagmite to another. His mouth instantly went dry, his pulse raced. It must be an animal, he deduced.

As he slowly stood, the shape glided into the open. He saw it was almost as tall as he was and as thin as a broomstick. No animal had a shape like that.

Fighting down a surge of raw fear, Cory gulped and licked his lips. He took a tentative step.

The thing, whatever it was, moved a corresponding distance back.

His scalped tingled as he took another stride. The creature retreated as before. Was it afraid of him? He became emboldened by the possibility. Perhaps it was an animal after all, and since most wild animals fled on contact with humans, he forced his lips apart and called out, "Scat! Get out of here! I don't want you around!"

The thing stayed where it was.

Cory's newfound resolve evaporated. He moved his head back and forth trying to get a better view of the creature. Incredibly, the thing seemed to jump to the left when he moved his head to the left and to the right when he moved his head to the right. How could it perform such a feat? he marveled.

The obvious conclusion struck him. No creature known to man was capable of doing so.

He began backing up. To his horror, the inky shape stalked toward him. With every step he took, it came closer. Frantic, he glanced around, seeking something he could use as a weapon. He was shocked to suddenly see similar creatures materialize no matter which direction he looked. His horror became rampant terror, and he whirled to flee.

There, blocking the tunnel, was yet another thin figure.

"What are you?" Cory screeched, and saw the figure bounce up and down with the movement of his glasses on his nose. How could that be?

He reached up to adjust his glasses and felt a smooth substance on the temple piece, a coating that covered the metal.

Understanding burst like a nova in his mind, and he tossed back his head and laughed.

His glasses!

His stupid glasses!

He removed them and touched both lenses. On the right one he found a thin line of dried blood from the wound in his head. There was the explanation. It had literally been right in front of his eyes the whole time.

In the dark of the tunnel the line of blood had been invisible, blending into the surrounding darkness. But here, in this dimly lit room, the line had seemed to have a life of its own. He had deceived himself into thinking the thin shape was much farther away than it actually was.

Cory laughed again, feeling his nervous tension drain away. He raised a finger to his mouth and licked it, then applied the moisture to the lens, rubbing vigorously. Several times he repeated the procedure, finally using the bottom of his shirt to wipe both lenses clean. Satisfied, he perched the glasses on his nose and resumed walking.

The thin shapes were gone.

At the opposite end of the room was another passageway, narrow and black. He stopped, uncertain, until a puff of cool air reminded him there must be a means of attaining the surface somewhere ahead.

Onward he went.

The walls brushed his shoulders every few strides. Somehow he got the feeling the cave floor underfoot had not been trod on in ages although he had no real proof. Overhead, the ceiling sank lower and lower, giving him the impression he was walking through solid rock. A sense of hopelessness closed in on him and he battled it with humor: *Here I am! Cory Fleming, the human mole! The envy of mice and shrews everywhere*! He laughed, but the laugh sounded flat and hollow.

Not far along he noticed a change in the tunnel that made him frown. The ground was tilting downward! He became certain that every step he took took him that much farther from the surface but he pressed on because a breeze was fanning his face.

A warm breeze, not a cold one.

The tunnel went on and on.

Cory noticed the walls became farther apart. The ceiling was again lost in shadow. An opening of some sort, a great Stygian hole, presented itself as the floor became level.

Boldly stepping through, he halted and gazed about for the exit he believed lay close at hand.

The full magnitude of the astounding vista numbed his brain, rendering him speechless, his senses staggered, his mind incapable of functioning.

A chamber of tremendous magnitude stretched ahead as if to the far horizon, more like a world unto itself than a section of a cavern. The ceiling, as in the room earlier, radiated unearthly light. So did the floor, which was not a floor at all but resembled the Grand Canyon in its breadth and scope, with countless ravines and small canyons forming an alien landscape. Gargantuan spires reared higher than any skyscraper ever built, mingled among stone arches and outlandish forms that added to the spectral atmosphere.

"I must be dreaming!" Cory blurted. He felt dazed and weak at the knees

Putting a hand out, he leaned on the side of the opening. Why was it he had never heard of this spectacular chamber before? How could it go undiscovered over the decades? The truth slammed into him with the brutal force of a sledge hammer.

No one else had ever been in this part of the Caverna del Diablo!

He moved forward, his gaze roving over the exceptional scenery. Without warning his right foot bumped an object in his path and he absently looked down, expecting to see a rock or a mound of earth.

A skull grinned up at him.

Cory staggered backward as if drunk until his back collided with the wall. Stupefied, he gaped at a wide area dotted with skeletons. Scores of bones mingled with other things. Beyond the appalling collection was a drop-off to the bottom of this lost world, hundreds of feet below.

Cory realized he was holding his breath. Slowly, he relaxed.

His mind kicked into gear, and he started to logically assess the situation. There were fourteen skulls he could see, perhaps more were buried. All of the bones had been picked clean of flesh and were as white as ivory.

Taking an anxious breath, Cory ventured closer. He saw a bronze helmet lying a few feet to his left. Shocked, he recognized it as the kind worn by Spanish conquistadors, those intrepid explorers who had penetrated deep into North America centuries ago in search of the fabled Seven Cities of Cibolla where reputedly Indians lived in opulent splendor. Near the helmet was a sword. A yard away, jutting upward from the mass of bones and relics, was a tarnished breastplate.

Cory took another step.

Farther in, lying on top of the bones, was an ancient stone tomahawk of the type used by the Indians who had first inhabited the Rookies. Next to it was what appeared to be a wooden club.

He halted, his toes almost touching a skull, and tried to make sense of the strange assortment.

There must an explanation! he told himself. As one who had always taken pride in his scientific ability and his logical reasoning, he was convinced that every problem, every puzzle, could be solved through the use of keen intellect. This instance would be no different.

Quite obviously, the skeletons were from men who had entered the Caverna del Diablo and never made it back to the surface. He knew both the Spaniards and the Utes were known to have visited the cave. These bones, then, were all that remained of the brave conquistadors and warriors who had contributed to the legend of the infamous cave by vanishing within its depths. But why were they all piled here at the very edge of the staggering precipice that overlooked the mysterious realm below? Surely not every single man had made it this far only to die on the spot? Someone must have brought their bodies here. Who? And why?

He examined the skull. Not being an expert, he couldn't determine its age, but he did notice something peculiar. Scratch marks covered it from crown to chin, some a quarter of an inch deep, as if gouged with a knife. A leg bone nearby was even stranger. Not only were there scratch marks, but there also appeared to be teeth marks ringing a section where the bone had been cracked. Evidently animals had gotten to it.

Mystified, he stood. There must be wildlife down here. Something had gnawed on the bones and scratched the skulls? Giant mice? He chuckled at his joke and scanned the area again, seeking clues he might have missed.

His gaze strayed out over the chamber. He admired a towering spire, saw an arch twice the height of his house-

--and then tingled from head to toe when he detected movement.

Cory's eyes narrowed. He must be imagining things, he told himself. But no. There it was again. Something was moving down there. Perhaps a quarter of a mile away, at the base of a canyon wall, in deep shadow.

The distance prevented him from noting details. He could only tell that it was big and walked on two legs, and that fact alone caused his heart to beat madly. If the thing was on two legs, it must be human. The only large animals in Colorado that did so were bears, but infrequently. Could there be people living below?

All kinds of crazy thoughts raced through his head. What if there was a lost tribe of Indians living in the cave? A tribe that entered ages ago and decided to stay? Or what if it was a prospector? The Rockies were home to a lot of colorful hermits who lived way off by themselves in the remotest regions and scratched out a meager existence by panning for precious metals. Maybe one of them was exploring the nether region or had taken to living there.

If so, how had the man gotten down? No rope would be long enough. Dozens would have to be used. Unless they sprouted wings and flew like a bird, it seemed impossible.

Cory cupped his hands to his mouth to call out in the belief that if it was a prospector, the man might help him reach the surface. He froze, though, when a feeling of imminent danger came over him.

Annoyed by his foolishness, he was all set to yell when the thing in the canyon stepped into the open.

Cory took one look, gasped, and fled back along the tunnel as fast as his legs would carry him.

Chapter 7

"Did you girls hear something?" Jay Thorpe asked. He was certain he had detected a scraping noise from somewhere up ahead. He aimed his flashlight down the passageway but saw nothing out of the ordinary.

"Not me, babe," Stacy said, giving his brawny hand a playful squeeze.

"I didn't," Leslie said.

Jay glanced at Ann and Terri.

Both shook their heads.

"I guess it was nothing," he told them, and resumed hiking toward the chamber where he expected to find Scott, Wes and Cory, eating and laughing merrily at the great trick they had played. Well, they'd be laughing out of their ears after he got through with them.

"How much farther, honeybuns?" Stacy asked.

"I don't know," Jay admitted, then added to reassure her, "Not far, I bet."

"I hope you're right," Stacy said. "This whole deal has turned into a major drag. I'm not having any fun and I'm royally pissed."

"You're not half as pissed as I am," Leslie snapped. "Wes should know better than to pull a stunt like this with me! I'll rip the sucker's eyes out." She grinned wickedly. "Better yet, I won't let him lay so much as a finger on me for the next month or so. I'll have him climbing the walls and begging for a little nookie."

"I wonder---' Ann said, then stopped.

"You wonder what?" Leslie prompted.

"I can see Scott and Wes playing a dumb joke like this, but never Cory. I wonder if he's really in on it."

"He's not with us so he must be with Wes and Scott," Leslie said.

"I suppose," Ann said, not sounding convinced.

Jay suddenly heard the scratching sound again, louder this time, leaving no doubt in his mind.

"Hey, I heard that!" Stacy exclaimed.

"Me, too," Leslie confirmed. "What the hell was it?"

"Probably Scott and Wes and more of their damn games," Terri said bitterly. "If I could, I'd punch their lights out. I'm sorry I ever agreed to come."

Leslie glanced at her. "No one twisted your arm, girlie. You came because Ann came. The two of you are Siamese twins."

"We are not," Terri responded. "And don't call me girlie."

With a sigh Jay stopped and turned. "Give me a break, ladies," he said, attempting to keep his irritation under control. "Here I am trying to find a way out of this mess and all you do is---" He abruptly broke off, listening to a peculiar dull thud from farther along the tunnel, like the sound produced when a kicker punted a football, only much louder.

The girls were all frozen, Terri with her mouth hanging open.

"Must be those sons of bitches," Stacy said after a bit, sliding closer to Jay.

"I'll kill Wes!" Leslie declared. "I really will."

"You'll have to wait your turn," Ann said.

"Come on," Jay growled, and inadvertently almost yanked Stacy off her feet when he stormed along the passageway, pulling her in his wake. He'd had enough of their practical jokes. In a couple of minutes they would be back at the big chamber. Then those clowns were going to pay the piper.

As was often the case when Jay became angry, he thought of nothing but the cause of his anger and how he would vent his temper. He paid scant attention to the tunnel.

Suddenly his beam struck a solid object directly in their path, and he gaped in consternation.

Damned if that didn't look like a wall, he told himself. But that couldn't be. He went on, his flashlight trained on the spot, and was within twenty feet of it before he admitted the awful truth. Stunned, he stopped.

"What the hell is going on?" Stacy said. "This is a dead end."

"It can't be," Ann said. "We didn't pass any turnoffs. This is the tunnel we were following."

"You're crazy," Leslie said. She walked up and gave the rock wall a solid thump with her fist. "What did this do? Pop out of nowhere?"

The only possible answer gave Jay a case of the willies. He touched the smooth surface, racking his brain for another explanation. He would be the first to admit that he was never much of a heavy thinker. Now he taxed his mental powers to their limit in an effort to come up with a solution. There was only one he could think of. It shocked him so, he had to try twice before he could speak. "Someone must have put this here."

"Are you stoned?" Stacy said, snickering.

"Never straighter," Jay said. "Somebody deliberately blocked off the tunnel with this thing. Remember those noises we heard?"

Leslie uttered a brittle laugh. "Is this a joke? If it is, I don't like it."

"It's no joke." Jay swept his beam over the slab. As he was turning, a cool breeze washed over him from the left. He looked, and was amazed to see the opening to another passage.

One of the girls gasped.

Stacy pressed herself into his side, her nails biting into his biceps. "What the hell?"

"That wasn't there before," Terri said in the tone of a little girl scared to death of the dark. "I'm positive."

"So am I," Jay said.

"Maybe Scott and Wes set this up," Leslie suggested.

"Get real," Ann said. "That slab must weigh tons. How did they move it? Why put it there? And where did this new passage come from? We didn't see it before."

"I don't have all the answers," Leslie said. "But you can't tell me that someone else just happened to come along and put the damn thing here. Either Scott and Wes were responsible or we took a wrong turn somewhere."

"The main question," Terri interjected, "is what do we do now?"

Jay was pondering the same problem. Should they turn around? Or should they take this new passage and keep their fingers crossed that it led them to the big chamber or up to the surface? He presented the choice to the girls.

"We take this new one," Leslie answered first.

"No!" Terri blurted.

Leslie glanced sharply at her. "What the hell is the matter with you? I'm getting sick of the way you're acting. If you're scared, why don't you bury your head in the ground like an ostrich and wait until we send someone down to bring you out?"

Ann put a hand on Terri's shoulder and glared at Leslie.

"Leave her alone."

"Sheehan's little protector," Leslie said sarcastically. She was on the verge of adding another insult when an iron hand clamped on her forearm and applied so much pressure that she let out an, "Ouch!"

"Enough is enough," Jay said, releasing his hold. "In case it hasn't hit you yet, Les, we're in trouble. Something really weird is going down. Like my coach is always telling us guys on the football team, we have to pull together to get out of this mess. So quit picking fights."

Leslie was about to tear into him verbally, but when she gazed into his eyes, she checked herself and simply nodded. "All right," she mumbled. "Just get us the hell out of this stinking place."

"I'll do my best," Jay said, and turned to Ann. "What do you think? Go back or go on?"

"Go on'" Ann said, nodding at the new passage. "The other way will take us farther away from the chamber where we last saw Cory, Wes and Scott. This one might take us to them."

"Please, no," Terri pleaded.

"Why not?" Jay said.

"I can't explain it," Terri said. "I just have this odd sort of feeling that if we go down this new tunnel something terrible will happen."

Undecided, Jay hesitated. Even though he was certain someone had somehow rolled the slab into place, he had no idea what their motive might be. Like Ann, he doubted Wes and Scott had done it. But if not them, who? He guessed it would have taken five or six extremely strong men, maybe more. Out of the blue a possibility occurred to him, and he grinned at his own cleverness. "Maybe we're all worked up over nothing," he said.

"How so, honeybuns?" Stacy asked.

"It just hit me. What if Wes let others in on the tricks he wanted to play? What if he asked them for help?"

"Like who?"

"Like a bunch of the guys from the team. They could have followed us up here from town but hung far enough back that none of us saw them."

"Of course!" Leslie cried. "Those jerks snuck in after us and trailed us all the way down." She laughed and pointed at the rock slab. "And a bunch of those morons would have no trouble moving that thing. They eat raw hormones for snacks."

"I'll bet you're right," Stacy concurred, her hands on her hips. "Those guys would do anything for Wes, and they'd jump at the chance to pull one over on us."

"I'll clobber 'em," Jay said, peeved because he hadn't been included in the practical joke. How dare those bozos play a prank on him!

"I don't know," Ann said. "I'd like to believe you but it seems to me that Wes and his buddies are going to a lot trouble at our expense. I mean, if it is them, this is the most elaborate prank I've ever heard of."

"Never underestimate my Wes," Leslie stated proudly. "He has a devious mind. So, for that matter, does Scott. Between the two of those devils, I wouldn't put anything past them."

Stacy leaned on Jay's shoulder and rose on her toes to peck him on the cheek. "Pretty sharp, handsome, figuring that out. Those idiots who claim that all you have between your ears are muscles don't know what the hell they're talking about."

Jay instantly bristled. "Who said that?"

"It doesn't matter."

"It does to me," Jay said. "No one insults me and gets away with it."

"I know, honeybuns," Stacy said. "But can you rein in that temper of yours until we're safe and sound back on the surface? Right now I want to get my ass out of here."

"If that's what you want," Jay said. Whirling, he stalked into the new passage, eager to find Wes and wring the S.O.B's neck. He heard Terri utter a low, "No, please!", but ignored her.

The tunnel wound to the right into a small room that smelled musty, then slanted to the left and gradually dipped lower. Total darkness obscured the ceiling. The walls were as smooth as glass and reflected the light brilliantly

Engrossed in trying to figure out who had been cutting on him behind his back, Jay simmered. It ticked him off no end that anyone would talk him down in front of Stacy. He knew himself well enough to know that he was teetering on the brink of one of his infrequent rages. Although he tried to control his temper, at times he went off the deep end. And there was never any way to predict what would set him off. He disliked becoming so mad but was powerless to prevent it.

One incident in particular stood out in his mind. He had been twelve at the time, playing baseball with his younger cousin when an older neighborhood kid came by and swiped their bat. The neighbor had teased them, pretending to hold out the bat for them to take and then snatching it away before they could grab it. Once, when his cousin tried, the bat smacked his cousin's knuckles and his cousin cried out in pain. That was all it took. Jay barreled into the neighbor like a battering ram, knocking the older kid over and straddling him, then clamping his fingers around the kid's neck and squeezing for all he was worth. The kid had wheezed and sputtered and tried to break free, his face turning beet red. If not for Jay's cousin suddenly stepping forward and pleading for Jay to let go, the kid might have been history.

Jay never thought of himself as a violent person, though. Oh, he loved playing football and bashing heads with other guys on the field, but that was different from the wild rages that brought out the worst in him. Football was a sport. His temper was strictly personal.

After five minutes the tunnel floor leveled off then climbed. Stalactites adorned the roof. Out of the gloom a fork materialized.

"Oh, great," Stacy said.

"Which way now?" Leslie asked.

"This way," Jay said, indicating the right branch. He'd learned his lesson back at the slab. If he put the decision to a vote the girls would debate the choice forever. So to keep them on the go he decided to pick the passages from then on.

Past the junction the tunnel widened considerably while the ceiling dipped low until there was barely three feet between the top of Jay's head and the rock surface. He was sweeping the flashlight back and forth when he spied something lying directly in their path.

"Hey, look," he said, moving forward to examine it.

Partially covered by dust was an old wooden bow.

"That must have belonged to an Indian," Stacy said. "Remember Fleming told us about a tribe that used to live in these parts? The Utes, I think they were called."

"It was the Utes," Ann confirmed. "And they still do."

"Maybe we should take it with us," Leslie said. "It might be worth something."

Jay straightened. "If you want to lug it around, be my guest. Me, I just want to find the way out." Adjusting the shoulder straps on his backpack to make it more comfortable, he moved on. His stomach rumbled but he ignored it. That was another of his problems. He was always hungry. No matter how much he ate at a single sitting, he'd be hungry again in an hour or two. His mom liked to joke that he had a bottomless pit for a gut. Thinking of her made him smile. He was sorry he had lied to her in order to come to the cavern with Wes and Scott. He'd told her he was spending the night at another friend's. Should she call, the friend was going to cover for him by claiming he was asleep.

Another object appeared. This time it was part of a leather sheath, the colored beads and much of the fringe still intact.

"Think this belonged to the same Indian?" Leslie wondered.

"Who knows?" Stacy said. "Who cares? Keep going, Jay. We must be close to the chamber by now."

He was of the same opinion. When a turn loomed before them he bore to the right, then halted in annoyance. Instead of a passage, he found the ceiling lowered to within several feet of the floor, leaving a crawl space barely large enough for a person to negotiate.

"Oh shit!" Stacy said.

Jay knelt and extended his right arm. The beam showed him the crawl space ran for as far as he could see, probably farther. "I'll go first," he announced

"Count me out," Leslie said.

"Why?"

“I'm not about to get down on my hands and knees and make like a marmot. I'll get my clothes all dirty."

Stacy laughed. "Would you rather spend the rest of your life in this armpit of a cave? If we don't get out of this maze, I can guarantee that your clothes will be the least of your worries."

Leslie mumbled a few words, but by then Jay was inside the crawl space and moving at a rapid clip. The closed confines didn't bother him half as much as what Stacy had said. The damn cave *was* a stinking maze, and the farther they went the worse it got. He hoped they'd find a way out soon.

If they became lost, he'd be embarrassed to the max when a rescue party showed up to lead their butts to the surface. Then a disturbing fact occurred to him. No one knew they were there except for Wes, Scott and Cory. If something should happen to those three, the rest of them would be stranded in the Caverna del Diablo.

He shut the thought from his mind as he continued to crawl. If there was one lesson he had learned from his years in sports, it was that mental attitude made all the difference between winning and losing, success and failure, persevering and giving up. As the coach of the football team was so fond of repeating, "Think positive and kick butt!" In this instance, if he let himself give in to a bunch of negative thoughts about how helpless they would be if they became stranded, then he wouldn't function at his best.

The end of the crawl space abruptly appeared. He could tell there was a chamber or a room ahead and said over his shoulder, "We're almost to the end."

"Good," Stacy said.'"My knees are killing me."

Jay reached an opening and extended his flashlight. About the size of the school gym, there was a room filled with stalagmites and stalactites plus strange formations.

Easing out, he straightened, then turned to give Stacy an assist.

"Damn. This isn't the chamber we want," Stacy said as he uncoiled.

"We'll reach it soon, babe," Jay said. "We must be close by now."

Leslie emerged and brushed dirt from her clothes while scanning their surroundings. "I'm growing sick and tired of this wandering around. Wes will be lucky if I don't dump his ass."

Jay politely gave Ann a hand, then turned to study the other side for a way out. Across from them was a narrow tunnel. "Let's keep going," he prompted and took several steps before a cry from Ann stopped him dead in his tracks.

"Where's Terri?"

Jay spun and saw Ann peering into the crawl space, a hand pressed to her throat. "What do you mean?" he demanded, stepping to her side. "She should have been right behind you." Bending, he aimed the beam down the crawl space and felt his pulse quicken upon discovering it was empty. "Terri? Where the hell are you?"

She didn't answer.

Dust sifted in the crawl space. Otherwise, nothing moved.

"Oh, God!" Ann exclaimed.

"Calm down," Jay said. "She must be in there. Maybe she hit her head or something. I'll go check." He crawled in and started back.

"What about us?" Stacy called.

"Stay put. I won't be a minute," Jay promised, moving as fast as he could, his flashlight revealing the trail they had made.

"Give a yell if you can hear me, Terri!" Jay shouted.

With no result.

Where the hell could she be? Jay wondered. He figured she had been afraid to enter the crawl space and was still back at the beginning, shivering in her undies.

Jay hurried, not at all pleased at being separated from Stacy. He spied the opening ahead and grinned, but the very next moment his grin was erased by a horrifying sound from somewhere far off---the hair-raising sound of a woman screaming at the top of her lungs.

Chapter 8

Terri Sheehan had never been so scared in her life.

One second she had been standing behind Ann, waiting her turn to enter the crawl space, and the next a huge hand had clamped on her mouth from behind and an arm as hard as solid steel had looped around her stomach and lifted her bodily from the cave floor. Shocked to her core, she had dumbly gawked at the backs of her friends as she was silently spirited away from them at frightening speed. Belatedly, she stirred to terrified life, kicking and thrashing and trying to wrench her mouth free so she could scream. Whoever held her never broke stride, and a second later they rounded a comer and her friends were no longer in sight.

No! Terri wailed in her mind. *This can't be happening*! Tears formed in the comers of her eyes. She pounded the arm encircling her waist but it had no effect. In a flash of inspiration she gouged her nails into her abductor's flesh---or tried to. Her nails barely scraped the skin.

Suddenly the hand over her mouth shifted to cover her nose as well and clamped down, cutting off her air. Panic washed over her as she realized her kidnapper was trying to suffocate her. She struggled with all her strength, kicking and scratching madly. In the end all her efforts did was hasten the inevitable. A veil of nothingness enveloped her, and she mercifully faded into oblivion.

Terri became vaguely conscious of a swaying motion

that became more pronounced as she slowly revived. She was aware of an arm about her waist and that she dangled like a limp rag at the side of whoever had kidnapped her. Grateful to be alive, she held herself still and took stock. The hand had been removed from her mouth so she could scream if she wished, but something told her that if she did no one would hear and she would arouse the wrath of her captor.

They were moving along an inky tunnel at a bewildering speed. She was amazed. How could anyone carry her so effortlessly? Not even Jay could do it. Thinking of him and his great rippling muscles almost prompted her to scream anyway. If anyone could save her, he was the one.

She could hear her kidnapper breathing. Every now and then he would grunt. An unusual odor tingled her nose, similar to the scent of a new leather coat only ten times stronger. Her left hand brushed against her abductors leg and she was startled to feel bare skin. Was he naked? Was it a pervert who lurked in the Caverna del Diablo and preyed on girls? Grisly images of what he might do to her made her close her eyes and tremble.

Her captor abruptly halted.

Terri, petrified, held her breath. Had he felt the movement and suspected she had revived? A hand touched her hair and she nearly recoiled in dread. Long fingers stroked the strands, then a fingernail lightly scraped her neck. It was replaced a second later by warm breath. She trembled again. She couldn't help it.

Her kidnapper uttered a sound remarkably like the rattling of a rattlesnake's tail, then resumed their speedy travel.

How had he done that? Terri wondered. A possible answer formed unbidden into her brain, but it was so outrageously fantastic that she immediately chided herself for letting her imagination get out of hand. But how *did* the man do it? She had never heard anyone imitate a rattler so perfectly.

Emotionally agonizing minutes dragged by as they wound ever deeper into Caverna del Diablo. Initially she hoped her abductor would soon stop, until she realized that once he did, he might turn his undivided attention to her.

Terri thought of the others and told herself Jay would be on their trail by now. Ann or someone else must have noticed she was missing and her kidnapper's tracks would be easy for Jay to follow. If she could just hang in there and keep her kidnapper from doing her harm, before long she would be rescued.

She focused on that hope to the exclusion of all else.

Her abductor came to an incline, and for the next ten minutes or more they descended. The air became warm, almost stuffy. She dared a peek and saw smooth walls on either side and loose gravel underfoot.

Small rocks clattered down the slope, forming a cloud of white dust that tickled her nose and made her want to sneeze. Fortunately her captor was moving rapidly. She doubted he would notice if she moved her arm, which she now did so she could pinch her nose and keep from giving herself away.

As long as he believed she was unconscious, he might leave her alone. Such was her second hope.

When, at long last, they reached level ground, she was grateful for the respite. Her stomach and shoulders ached and she felt slightly dizzy from having her head upside down for so long. She noticed a new scent, like that of burnt food. She also felt a strong wind on her skin. To her surprise, it was positively hot, in sharp contrast to the breeze in the tunnels.

Her kidnapper was flowing over the cave floor at the fastest clip so far. If she didn't know better she would swear he was going 50 or 60 miles an hour. She saw dirt and rocks and boulders and belatedly realized there was light somewhere above. Dim light, to be sure, but at least she could see again.

No sooner did she smile at being able to see than they moved into an area of deep shadow. She had the impression there was a high wall on their right. From up ahead arose a faint gurgling noise that grew in volume. The air acquired a dank quality.

Just then a cramp lanced her stomach, and she was debating whether to try and shift in her captor's arm to make herself more comfortable when without warning she was dumped unceremoniously on the hard ground.

Terri lay still on her side, her eyelids pressed tight, her body tense, waiting for her captor's next move. Shuffling footsteps moved away. She waited until she could no longer hear them, then cracked her eyes open and studied her surroundings.

Complete astonishment gripped her.

Not ten feet off was an immense pool of what appeared to be yellowish-brown water. At the very center the water bubbled and foamed, the source of the gurgling she had heard. On all sides but one towered sheer cliffs. Massive boulders dotted her vicinity. Overhead, so far up the stalactites seemed like toothpicks, was a ceiling that glowed with an eerie light.

She twisted, searching for her abductor, but saw no one. Her throat and mouth were dry, and with the idea of quenching her thirst she crawled to the pool and dipped her left forefinger into the water. Too late she felt the heat.

Pain seared her like a razor-sharp knife and she jerked her hand back. The water was hot enough to boil the flesh from her body! Her poor finger was blistered from the nail to the knuckle. She instinctively raised the finger to her lips to suck on it and relieve some of the anguish when it occurred to her that the water might be poisonous. Instead, she wiped the finger on her pants and held it in her right hand.

Ripples of torment brought home the point of how stupid she had been. She knew nothing about caves but she should know better than to assume any water she found was drinkable. Satisfying her thirst would have to wait. The temperature in that pool must be hot enough to cook a lobster.

Since Pagosa Springs was famous for its hot springs, she figured the pool must be connected to the same underground system that lured thousands of tourists every year.

Terri rose to her knees and looked around. To her right the cliffs branched out to form a narrow canyon. At the far end was a flat plain. If she could get out and find the incline, she might be able to work her way back to her friends.

The thought goaded her into running toward the plain. Her legs were wobbly at first, until her circulation was fully restored. Then she sprinted, puffing and huffing, her blouse working its way out of her black skirt. Her heart drummed wildly. Other than the pounding of her shoes the canyon was quiet.

Her footfalls seemed to echo off the cliffs, adding to her fear because her captor was certain to hear them.

She covered half the distance and began to slow down.

A sharp pang under her ribs made every stride a grueling effort. This was what she got for being so badly out of shape. If she had bothered to go jogging every afternoon with her mom as her mom wanted, she'd be able to run a lot farther.

Terri faltered, gasping for air. She glanced back. A tremor shook her on spying a huge figure standing near the pool. Her abductor was back and had seen her! She faced the end of the canyon and pumped her legs in a frenzy of desperation, groaning low in her throat at the prospect of being thwarted.

Please give me strength! she prayed. *Don't let him catch me again*!

She covered twenty yards. Thirty. Forty. She was almost to the plain, her legs protesting every step. Each breath was labored anguish. Her head drooped, her knees threatened to buckle, and she was on the verge of collapse when she glanced up, skidded to a halt, and screamed.

Her captor was in front of her. For the first time she saw him clearly, and the sight shriveled her soul.

It was seven feet tall and possessed a physique that radiated raw power. Its arms bulged with muscle, and its chest was three times the size of a professional wrestler's. Most distinctive of all was its hideous face, a horrid mix of reptilian and human features dominated by slanted eyes that blazed with an inner red light.

It was completely naked, its skin like that of a snake. But no snake alive had skin the like this, a striking red tint the same color as human blood.

"Oh, God!" Terri exclaimed, aghast. She remembered the figure that had been painted above the entrance to the cavern and recognized this creature as the thing depicted. Some of the details were different, but this was it, a living, breathing, gruesome nightmare that regarded her coldly.

She took a step back and saw something move behind the thing, a flicker caused by the waving of a sinuous forked tail.

Shaking uncontrollably, she retreated farther. "Please don't hurl me!" she pleaded.

The creature made no reply but the fire in its eyes grew brighter.

"Please!" Terri repeated, and whirled to flee. She took a single step and fingers that might have been forged from metal closed on her upper arms and she was lifted bodily from the ground and hurled through the air. The cave floor seemed to rush up to meet her.

She smashed onto her right side, the breath whooshing out of her lungs, and lay there dazed.

Terror pervaded her being. She tried to collect her thoughts and put a hand on the ground to rise. From behind her came a whisper of sound and she was seized again, this time in one mighty arm. She recoiled in anticipation of being thrown but the creature merely carried her toward the pool.

Lord, help me! Terri inwardly wailed. How could this be happening? *Why* was it happening? Such creatures couldn't possibly exist. They were supposed to be legends, things of myth believed in by superstitious, primitive people in the same vein as dragons and fairies.

What did it want? Why had it abducted her? A number of ghastly possibilities occurred to her, and she had to dispel the gruesome thoughts to retain her self-control, not to mention her very sanity.

She would have screamed if not for a firm conviction the creature would become violent.

When it let go she was unprepared. Still, she managed

to land on her hands and knees and kept her head averted. By the gurgling she knew they were close to the boiling water. What was so special about the spot that the creature came back to it? She heard the soft pad of its feet as it moved to the pool, followed by splashing.

Risking a look, she discovered the creature was washing its crimson hands. But how could it bear to touch the scalding water? Flabbergasted, she saw the creature put its palms on the ground and bend down to take long, loud sips.

What in heaven's name *was* it?

Terri recalled Leslie making a comment to the effect that the painting above the entrance had looked like the Devil. Indeed, this thing did. But it couldn't possibly be the real Satan she had heard the minister refer to in his sermons.

The creature stood and turned.

As desperately as Terri wanted to run, she was unable to set her body into motion. Her limbs were mush. Her brain was a vacuum empty of all save pure fear as the thing came toward her. She gazed up into its red orbs and wished she would die then and there.

No such luck.

Terri whined when the creature sat down beside her, picked her up, and deposited her in its lap. She shook in terror as it began stroking her hair with one hand while rubbing her back with the other. Bile rose in her throat, and she dreaded being sick. The next moment that became the least of her worries because the thing suddenly put a massive hand on her breast.

Terri lost it. Throwing back her head, she screeched like a banshee and clawed at the thing, trying to tear the hand from her body. Unfazed, the creature gave her breast a squeeze, and she nearly fainted. The cavern spun. Dimly, she was aware of its hands roving over her at will. One hand dipped under her skirt. She feebly tried to stop it but the creature was too immensely strong.

It groped her, exploring between her legs and tugging at her panties. A long nail lightly traced a line from her underwear to her knee.

Terri stared numbly at the pool. She wished she would pass out. Barring that, she wished she could enclose her mind in an impenetrable mental vault and not emerge until the creature was done playing with her. But she couldn't ignore the hand that had crept under her blouse and was massaging her breasts any more than she could the other hand stroking her legs.

She knew what it was up to. There was no denying the obvious. The obscene abomination was taking its deliberate time, compounding her humiliation.

A hand fell on the back of her neck and her head was roughly twisted upward until her face was inches from the creature's. She tried to pull away but was held fast in an unbreakable vise.

The thing smiled.

Terri saw tapered teeth and smelled fetid breath. She almost gagged. Eyes wide, she beheld its tongue slither out of its mouth, a thin, forked tongue, a smaller version of the creature's forked tail. Nausea welled within her as the tip touched her lips. She pressed her mouth tightly shut and was again frustrated. Its tongue slid into her mouth, filling her with a sulphuric taste, entwining with her own, causing her to shudder in disgust.

Mercifully, her senses succumbed to the loathsome violation and she fainted. How long she was in limbo she had no idea, but when next her eyes opened, she blinked in joyous astonishment at finding the creature had gone.

Her joy was short-lived, though, disappearing a second later when she realized she was naked.

She sat up, her hand brushing a garment lying at her side. She grabbed it, thinking it was her blouse, but found in her hand a single sleeve. Scattered in profusion all around her were bits and pieces of the rest of her clothes. Without thinking she leaped to her feet and fled, fixing on the end of the canyon as her salvation. If she could only locate a way out before the thing came back!

Suddenly the creature was right there, running at her side as if mimicking her or taunting her.

Sobbing, Terri angled to the right. It kept pace for ten yards, then caught her up in both hands and halted. She was elevated until her navel was level with its mouth. Anger flooded through her when the creature's tongue darted out and licked her bellybutton.

"Leave me alone!" she shouted, squirming uselessly. "Damn you all to hell!

The creature's mouth twisted in what could only be construed as a grin.

Terri continued to squirm. She gasped when the thing began licking her all over as if she were an oversized lollipop, its tongue running up over her belly, then along her right side to her arm. She trembled uncontrollably and her teeth chattered.

The monstrosity raised its head, then flicked its tongue at her ear. Taking a seat, the creature again let its hands roam over her body, exploring every nook and cranny.

Terri twisted helplessly in its grasp. She felt sick and longed to faint again to spare hers from whatever vile act was to follow. Those leathery hands caressed her shoulders, her neck, her arms. "Please," she mumbled. The thing shifted its attention to her breasts and squeezed until her head swam with pain.

"Spare me!" she wailed, her consciousness slipping.

The last sensations she felt before an inky void claimed her was that of having her breasts ripped from her body and the creature's teeth sinking into her throat.

Chapter 9

No sooner did the scream die away than Jay scrambled out of the crawl space. He aimed his flashlight down the tunnel but it showed nothing but the dusty walls and the ceiling.

He took several strides, certain Terri was the one who had screamed and intending to go to her aid.

Suddenly he stopped short. His beam revealed a series of footprints on top of those the five of them had made earlier, enormous tracks at least eighteen inches long and twelve inches wide. Even more remarkable, each footprint exhibited only three large toes.

"What the hell!" Jay exclaimed, crouching to place his hand in the center of one of the tracks. The impression dwarfed his hand. Awed, he straightened and tried to envision the size of the thing that made the footprints.

It must be huge, even bigger than he was. And it must have Terri.

Jay glanced at the crawl space, uncertain of what do. Maybe, he reflected, the scream and the tracks were more pranks, courtesy of Scott and Wes. He looked at the footprints again. They could have been faked. But what about the scream? That had seemed terribly realistic.

Something deep inside told him that his buddies hadn't been responsible. And although his mind balked at the notion, he accepted the evidence at hand and concluded Terri had been taken by whatever made the tracks.

Jay began chewing on his lower lip, a habit he had when

thinking heavily. Normally he avoided serious reflection. Give him a brew and his babe and let him play sports whenever he wanted and he was a supremely content trooper.

It explained why his performance on the playing field was so outstanding while his classroom performance was mediocre at best.

Should he go after Terri? The tracks would be easy to follow. But going after Terri meant leaving Stacy, Leslie and Ann. If he took them with him they might find their lives endangered by the thing that took Terri, and under no circumstances whatsoever would he put Stacy in a situation where she was at risk. He loved her more than he did life itself.

Jay listened but there were no more screams. Reluctantly, he returned to the crawl space and headed back to the other girls.

Guilt racked him. He tried not to think of what might be happening to Terri.

He debated telling the others what he had found. If he mentioned the tracks he might wind up with three terrified females on his hands. Maybe it would be best to fib. He could always come clean later, and for all he knew he was wrong and Scott and Wes *were* up to their usual tricks.

If he told the girls there was some sort of monster in the cavern and later it turned out his friends had pulled a fast one, he'd look like the prize chump of Pagosa Springs Senior High School. The kids at school would never let him hear the end of it.

Having made up his mind, Jay put a smile on his face as he emerged and found three anxious faces fixed on his. "Miss me?" he quipped.

“What the hell happened back there?" Leslie snapped.

"We thought we heard a scream."

"Where's Terri? Is she all right?" Ann asked.

Stacy promptly added, "Is everything cool, honeybuns?"

Jay forced a laugh. "Whoa there, ladies. One at a time." He stepped past them so he could sweep the room with his beam. Nothing out of the ordinary was visible. Plastering a smile on his lips , he rotated. "Now then, none of you have anything to worry about. Terri is gone but I saw other footprints with hers leading back along the tunnel and I figure Scott and Wes are with her now."

"What about the scream?" Ann pressed him.

"Did you hear it clearly?" Jay said, knowing full well the crawl space would have distorted and muffled the sound.

"Not really," Leslie said.

"Well, I did. And I can tell you that it was as phony as a three-dollar bill. Right after the scream I heard someone laughing, and we all know what that means."

Leslie had the look of a hungry hawk about to swoop down on its prey. "Wes and Scott are playing more of their damn jokes! I can't wait to get my hands on that sucker!"

"I find it hard to believe," Ann said. "Neither Scott nor Wes cares much for Terri and she knows it. Why would she go along with one of their juvenile pranks?"

"How should I know?" Jay responded with a shrug. "You can ask her when we find them." He started toward the tunnel across the way, certain Ann didn't believe him and not about to let her give him the third degree. Hiking briskly, his nerves on edge, he crossed the room and halted to verify all three girls were right behind him before stepping into the next passageway.

Fifteen minutes of traveling a twisting course brought them to a chamber containing more stalagmites than anywhere they had seen so far. The high ceiling was vaulted like a cathedral and sparkled when the flashlight beam struck it.

Jay wended his way among the forest of stalagmites, feeling more and more uneasy the farther he went. He tried to convince himself there was nothing to worry about. If a flesh and blood beast had made those strange tracks, it was undoubtedly a long ways off. He and the girls had nothing to fear.

He was convincing himself of that fact when he rounded a squat stalagmite and halted on seeing a fissure bisecting the chamber floor. "Damn," he said, stepping cautiously to the brink. Eight feet separated the two sides. He could get a running start and jump the gap but what about the girls?

"Oh, wonderful," Leslie groused. "How are we supposed to get to the other side?"

"We don't," Ann said. "I vote we turn around and go back."

"No," Jay said.

"Let's put it to a vote," Ann said. "What do the others say?"

"None of us have wings so we can forget continuing this way," Leslie said.

"We have to," Jay said more gruffly than he intended. If they retraced their route, they stood a good chance of running into the thing that took Terri. He had to keep the three girls moving in the direction they were going. But how? Leslie had a point. Without wings there was no way they could get across. He swung his beam to the right and the left, seeking a point where the fissure wasn't as wide. Instead, he spotted a stone bridge.

"Look there," he said, moving closer, It appeared to be five feet wide, a foot thick, and arched in the middle.

"You've got to be kidding!" Leslie said.

Stacy came up alongside Jay. "Do you really expect us to step out on that? What if it can't hold our weight."

"It looks sturdy," Jay said, although secretly he had his doubts. "To be on the safe side I'll go first." Halting, he gingerly placed a foot on the pitted surface to test if the bridge would support him.

"Do you have a death wish?" Leslie asked.

"Not funny," Stacy said.

Jay paid no attention to their bickering. He eased his other foot out and stood stock still, barely breathing. The bridge gave no indication of imminent collapse so he took another step, his legs tensed to leap for the rim should he be proven wrong.

"Be careful, lover," Stacy urged.

Jay bobbed his chin and eased out farther, his arms at his sides. His flashlight played over the bottom, revealing dirt and jagged boulders thirty feet below. If the bridge were to buckle and he couldn't reach either rim, the fall might kill him. He licked his lips, then dared another step that bumped a pebble which plummeted over the side, clattering when it hit the boulders.

Stacy had her hands pressed to her throat. "Oh God, sweetie! Watch yourself!""

What did she expect? Jay wondered. That he'd suddenly start break dancing? He grinned at his wit and moved onto the arched portion, treading carefully for fear of slipping.

"I can't stand to watch," Stacy said, covering her eyes. "Let me know if he makes it."

"I'll make it," Jay shot back, ruffled by her lack of confidence. He crossed the arch quickly, then took a breath and bolted the remaining distance. Once he stood on firm ground he beamed and motioned at the girls while training his flashlight on the bridge so they could see clearly. "All right. Who's next?"

"Do we have to?" Leslie asked.

"You sure as hell do," Jay said. "Come on. We don't have all night."

"I'll go," Ann offered.

"No. Let me," Stacy said. Without waiting for a reply, she rushed onto the bridge, her shapely legs pumping. Rather than step onto the arch, she vaulted over it, and when her feet came down the bridge shuddered, cascading dust into the fissure.

"Stacy!" Leslie cried.

Jay, his heart pounding, his mouth dry, held his right arm out. The instant her hand touched his, he seized hold and hauled her off the span so fast, she nearly tripped. "Don't ever pull a stunt like that again," he said, inwardly quaking at the mere thought of losing her.

"Chill out, handsome," Stacy said. "You damn near pulled my arm out of its socket."

"Here I come," Leslie called out.

Facing around, Jay opened his mouth to tell Leslie to take it easy when she suddenly imitated Stacy's example, fear lining her face as she made a mad dash.

"No!" Jay blurted, too late.

Leslie jumped over the arch. Her right foot smacked down and all of them heard the loud crack that ensued. She took two more strides, the span splitting and crumbling under her, and executed a frantic leap.

Jay caught hold of her arm and pulled her to safety, then stood, aghast, as the section near his sneakers gave way, breaking completely off and tumbling into the fissure.

Leslie exhaled in relief. "That could have been me!" she exclaimed.

"What about Ann?" Stacy said.

Jay aimed his flashlight across the fissure.

Ann was staring down at the smashed bits of bridge. The rest of the span was intact but she would have to jump the final three feet to reach the side they were on. "Wonderful," she said.

"Think you can do it?" Jay said.

Ann moved a few inches out onto the bridge and gave it a close scrutiny. "I'm afraid the whole thing will break off if I try."

"You only live once, girlie," Leslie said. "Go for the gusto. I made it. You can, too."

Annoyed, Jay turned on her. "If you'd taken your time this wouldn't have happened. Now she's stranded over there, and there isn't a damn thing we can do to help her."

"I did the same as Stacy," Leslie angrily replied. "Why are you getting on my case and not hers?"

Rather than answer, Jay played his light over the chamber, seeking a means of getting Ann across. All he saw were stalagmites and dust.

Close by was a stalagmite that had tipped over and broken ages ago. He walked over and picked up a large chunk that must weigh ten pounds or better.

"What are you doing?" Stacy said.

"Testing the bridge to see if it's safe for Ann to use," Jay said. Hefting the piece of stalagmite, he aimed at the center of the span and heaved. The chunk hit with a loud thud. More dust and fragments rained into the fissure but the bridge held. "What do you think?" he called to Ann.

"I can try," she said, not sounding at all pleased at the prospect. "Tell me, though. Scott mentioned bringing rope on this expedition of ours. Do you have it in your backpack?"

"Let me see." Jay quickly stripped off the pack and

checked. Inside was food, a six-pack of beer, a box of wooden matches, a rock hammer and a chisel. "No rope," he announced.

"At least we won't starve," Leslie said.

Until that very moment Jay had never quite realized how inconsiderate Leslie could be. He'd always rated her as too stuck-up for her own good, but as he looked at her, he saw her in a whole new light. She was all smiles because they had eats. Ann's predicament meant nothing to her. Indignant, he said curtly, "You'll get something to eat when I say you can and not before."

"Who died and made you leader?"

"I'm the only guy here in case you haven't noticed."

Leslie reacted as if he had slapped her on the cheek. "What the hell does that mean? Just because you're male you get to boss us around? In case you haven't noticed, that macho crap doesn't cut it anymore. If I get hungry I'll eat whether you like it or not.

"Go ahead and try," Jay invited her.

The growl in his voice made Leslie take a step back. She glanced at Stacy. "What is this bogus? Do you put up with this crap? I can tell you right now that I won't. When Wes is out of line I let him know it, and you should do the same with this gorilla of yours."

"I don't need your advice on how to run my life," Stacy said. "And if you ever call Jay a gorilla again I'll rip your face off."

"You two are perfect for each other, you know that?" Leslie said, then fell silent, her faced flushed as she folded her arms across her chest.

Jay zipped up the backpack and fixed the flashlight on Ann. Her conspicuous anxiety made him wish he could fly. "I'm not about to leave you here alone, but I'll be damned if I know how to get you safely to our side. Do you have any ideas?"

"I wish I did."

"How about if I try the bridge from this end? I can jump out to it, and if it supports my weight we know it will support yours."

Both Ann and Stacy said "No!" in unison.

"I don't want you killed, lover," Stacy said. "You weigh more than two of us combined. Go out on that bridge and you're history."

"We can't just leave her there," Jay said.

Ann shifted to stare back the way they had come. "I have an idea."

"I'm all ears," Jay said.

"Maybe if I hurry I can catch up with Terri, Scott and Wes. You heard her laughing, didn't you? It shouldn't take me long."

Vivid images of the enormous three-toed tracks branded themselves on Jay's mind. "You'd be stumbling around in the dark. It would be easy to become lost and there's no telling where you'd wind up."

"I can't think of anything else to try."

"There must be a better way," Jay insisted. "Let me look around this chamber and see what I can find." He hurried off, sweeping the flashlight back and forth, hoping against hope for a miracle. If Ann went back she might run into the thing that grabbed Terri. He never should have lied to them. Now he either had to admit the truth or pull a rabbit out of the hat and get her across the gap. A sweep of the rest of the chamber, though, turned up zip. There was nothing he could use. Dejected, he walked toward the fissure and girded himself for the tongue-lashings they would give him once they learned about his deception.

Suddenly Jay stopped and aimed his flashlight at the mouth of a tunnel to his rear, positive he had heard a faint noise---a scraping sound, like before. The tunnel slanted to the left just inside the opening, and he was unable to see what lay beyond. Although tempted to take a look, he didn't want to leave the girls alone for too long, not with whatever made those tracks on the loose.

"What the hell is keeping you?" Leslie shouted.

Jay hastened to their side. Neither Stacy nor Leslie had budged from the spot where they had stood when he left. "I came up empty-handed," he said and turned the light on Ann. "How are you holding up?"

"Fine," she answered softly.

Peering into the gap, Jay had an idea. "Hey! What if we inspect the fissure from one end to the other? Maybe it narrows at some point and you can jump across."

"It's worth trying," Ann sid. "And please try to keep some of the light on my side so I don't fall in."

Jay stayed close to the edge, his fingers crossed. He wanted to inform them of the huge footprints but the words seemed to catch in his throat. "I wish to hell we'd never gotten separated from the others," he mentioned to keep the conversation going as he struggled to muster the courage to tell what he knew.

“I wish to hell I'd never come," Ann said. "This outing has turned into a fiasco, and Scott and Wes are to blame."

Leslie came to her boyfriend's defense. "Don't blame Wes. It's not his fault we're lost. If our fearless leader had half a brain we'd be up on the surface by now, on our way home."

"Lay off Jay," Stacy said.

"I'm sick and tired of you threatening me," Leslie said.

So much for getting a conversation going, Jay mused.

He noticed a point twenty yards off where the fissure narrowed to about six feet, which still wasn't enough.

His thoughts strayed to Scott, Wes and Cory, and he speculated on where they might be. If, as he believed, they weren't involved in Terri's disappearance, and if those tracks had been made by the thing that was, maybe the same creature had taken them.

"If only this were narrower," Ann said, stepping to the rim at the point he had noticed. She frowned and leaned forward.

"Don't get too close to the edge," Jay advised. "That's a long drop."

"Tell me something I don't know," Ann said, taking a step back and stamping her foot in frustration.

To Jay's dismay the ground under her abruptly gave way. As if in slow motion he saw the earth collapse and saw Ann throw her arms out and desperately try to leap to a firmer footing, but the dirt and stones poured into the fissure so swiftly she was unable to stop herself from being carried over the brink, and in a twinkling she plummeted into the fissure.

Chapter 10

"What the hell was that?" Wes blurted as the scream faded, his palm slick on his flashlight handle, his mouth bone dry.

"One of the girls," Scott said.

"Leslie!" Wes cried, and furiously threw himself at the smooth slab blocking their route. He slammed his shoulder against it and shoved with all his might.

It didn't budge.

"We've got to reach her!" Wes shouted. "Help me!"

Scott stayed where he was. "First of all, we don't know who it was. And second of all, how?" He gestured at the slab. "It must weigh more than our whole team combined."

"There has to be a way!" Wes grunted, gouging his heels into the cave floor to gain more leverage.

"You're wasting your time, bro," Scott said. "We have to go back and take another tunnel."

"Like hell!" Wes snarled, continuing to push. His face was red, his veins bulging. The slab didn't move a fraction. He pushed and pushed until his shoulder ached so bad, he couldn't push any more. Stepping back, panting, he gave the slab a fierce kick.

"Are you done making a fool of yourself?" Scott said.

"Go to hell."

"Simmer down and listen to reason."

Wes whirled on his friend. "How can you be so calm when one of them is in trouble? Les might be lying somewhere with a broken leg or whatever, and you stand there like we're getting set to order at Pizza House."

"Unless you brought dynamite, we're not going any further," Scott said. "As I tried to tell you, we need to backtrack and find another way."

"Then let's find it," Wes said, taking the lead this time. Part of his irritation had nothing to do with his failure to budge the slab.

He was mad at himself for being one of the geniuses who planned this trip to the Caverna del Diablo. Ever since they ditched Cory Fleming, nothing had gone right. And he had a terrible feeling that things were going to get worse before they got better. Come to think of it, why should he blame himself when the whole mess was all that geek's fault? Fleming was a jinx as well as a dork. Everyone knew that. Look it what happened during the archery contest! Fleming had jinxed his chances to win and lost him the Corvette of his dreams.

"Slow down, will you?" Scott said. "You'll wear both of us out before we find anyone."

Wes realized he had been practically running, his long legs taking strides Scott couldn't match. He slowed, his blood still on fire, filled with regret that Fleming wasn't there right that minute so he could pound the bastard to a pulp.

"Are you still in the mood for some blow?" Scott asked.

The question caused Wes to break stride. He stopped and turned, s familiar hunger creeping over him. "Now?" he said, thinking of Leslie. Reaching her quickly was imperative.

'Why not?" Scott said. "Coke always helps me unwind, and with all that's happening I'm pretty wound up. So are you."

"Got that right," Wes said, his hunger warring with his

conscience. He knew what would happen if he indulged. Snorting cocaine always made him so spaced out he felt like he could fly. Back when he started, his ability to concentrate and think coherently had not been as drastically affected as it was now. The longer he used it, the more of an airhead he became during his highs. And lately he had noticed another disturbing trend. He was using more and more of the stuff in order to reach a plateau that lesser amounts used to produce. If he kept going at his current rate, pretty soon he'd need to win the Colorado Lottery to support his habit.

"Is your answer yes or no?" Scott said.

Wes remembered that horrible scream, licked his lips, and answered with full knowledge of the consequences. "A million times yes."

How far Cory Fleming ran he had no way of knowing. He raced recklessly along tunnel after tunnel, heedless of the risk of being injured if he should trip in the dark or crash into a wall or boulder. His only concern was putting as much distance between the creature he had seen in the vast chamber and himself.

Red!

The thing had been red!

As the old cliche went, if he hadn't seen whatever it was with his own eyes, he would never believe such a creature existed. What could it have been? Why had the mere sight of it sparked such intense fear? Was it an animal or something else?

The same questions repeated themselves over and over, and by the time he finally stopped in a small room to take a breather, he still had no answers.

The painted image of the being at the entrance to the

Caverna del Diablo popped into his mind. Both the creature in the depths and the painting were red. Coincidence? Or had he actually glimpsed a descendant of the legendary monster? His scientific nature rebelled at such a crazy idea, but there was no denying the testimony of his own eyes.

Oh, God, what was he going to do?

Cory leaned against a wall and tried to stabilize his erratic breathing. His lungs hurt like mad, his stomach was queasy, and his legs were sore from exercising muscles he seldom used.

He speculated on whether he had imagined the whole incident. Maybe a trick of the lighting had made him think he saw a living creature where none existed.

No, Cory told himself, he had seen it, all right, and he must stop trying to convince himself otherwise. A scientist should never be afraid to face new facts, no matter how inconsistent they might appear at first glance, and the fact of the matter was that an unknown creature lurked in the bowels of the Caverna del Diablo, a beast no doubt related to the thing encountered by the Spanish conquistadors and the Ute warriors.

It couldn't possibly be the'same one, not after so many centuries.

He remembered the collection of bones, and shuddered. They took on a whole new meaning. The creature must have placed them there. It must be carnivorous, roaming the immense cavern in search of prey and feasting on whatever or whoever was foolhardy enough to enter its subterranean domain.

The Spaniards and the Utes had been right in warning everyone to stay away.

An alarming conclusion increased his apprehension.

There must be more than one! In order to perpetuate the species, a viable core colony or pack must exist. Either that, or the creature enjoyed an incredibly long lifespan, which he was inclined to doubt.

But why weren't the things spotted more often? he wondered. Did they only venture into the upper levels every now and then? If so, what did they subsist on in the depths? Were they like bears, capable of hibernating for lengthy stretches? Of were they so totally alien to any known species that their capabilities were beyond human ken?

Of one aspect he felt fairly positive. The thing wasn't the Devil. Not the Biblical entity believed responsible for all the evil and wickedness in the world. Not the high being of light who had rebelled against God.

Then what else might it be?

As with most boys, he had gone through a phase during his childhood where he had been fascinated by monsters of every shape and size. Vampires, werewolves, aliens from outer space, you name it, they were part of his childhood fare. Movies, monster magazines, comics and books, he had indulged in it all. The phase lasted about a year, and in that time he had been exposed to pictures and descriptions of hundreds of savage beasties and grotesque beings.

The red creature he had seen resembled one kind more than any other. A nefarious breed said to plague humankind from the dawn of recorded history. Creatures reputed to be in thrall to the Devil and to comprise his infernal army in Hell. It was a breed chronicled in the records of every ancient nation, a breed that reportedly hated humanity and wanted to wipe human beings from the face of the planet.

Demons.

In particular, Cory recalled a reproduction of a painting in a book on supernatural beings such as sprites, gremlins, centaurs, gargoyles and others. The painting, done by a medieval master during the Middle Ages, showed the realm of Hades, complete with a gigantic winged Devil and a horde of demons, red-skinned creatures sporting small horns and barbed tails.

But that was preposterous.

Wasn't it?

Cory straightened and moved across the room, his logic reasserting itself. How could any person in their right mind believe in the existence of literal demons? Such creatures were the product of superstition. He was supposed to be an aspiring scientist and scientists didn't accept the existence of anything without concrete proof. So what if he had seen a strange biped deep down in the cavern? So what if it had been red? It could very well have been someone wearing red clothing.

Cory wiped his perspiring brow with the back of his hand and tried not to think about how hungry and thirsty he was. It had been stupid to run so far without good cause. Now he had depleted his body's energy and would need food and water, neither of which he had.

Damn him for being so dumb.

Cory hiked on, completely lost, resisting the raw despair that tried to overwhelm him.

Winning a battle required the right mental attitude, and he knew he was in a battle for his life. It was the Caverna del Diablo against him. If he didn't succumb to fear, if he applied his deductive powers and conserved his strength, he might survive. *Might*? No, he *would* survive, and then he wold pay Wes and Scott back for what they had done to him. He didn't know exactly how, but he would come up with a way.

Suddenly, from somewhere in the dark far behind him, arose a faint sound uncannily similar to the rattling of a rattlesnake.

Surprised, Cory stopped and looked back. What could it have been? So far as he knew, rattlers didn't penetrate this deep into the cave. It must have been something else. Then he heard it again, nearer. Whatever was making the sounds was coming in his direction.

He swallowed hard and ran, annoyed at letting irrational fright dictate his actions. Yet he had to admit that he was scared, an extremely unscientific attitude, to say the least. Instinct was in control, and his every instinct, his intuition, told him that he must avoid the source of those strange sounds at all costs.

So he fled again, winding along the bowels of the earth until he reached a fork where three tunnels branched off. His eyes by then were fairly well adjusted to the lack of light, and he could see the openings even if he couldn't distinguish details.

Which one should he take? On impulse he took the passage on his right and almost immediately the cave floor angled upward, which was encouraging.

Cory settled into a rhythm, sweating profusely, tempted to discard the backpack so he could go faster but knowing he might need some of the contents later.

Another fork appeared and he again took the right one. The floor continued to gradually rise.

Every step was bringing him closer to the surface and safety.

Then rattling broke the stillness. But this time, instead of being closer, it was distant as to be barely audible.

Good, Cory thought and smiled. He shouldn't have to

worry about whatever was back there catching him. Slowing to a walk, he slid out of the backpack and held it by the strap. His shirt was plastered to his body, his feet ached. He had gotten more exercise since entering the cavern than he had in the past year.

Chuckling, he walked around a corner into another of those chambers where the ceiling glowed. He halted, braced his butt against a stalagmite, and scanned for an exit. There were two, a narrow tunnel off to the left and a wide tunnel directly ahead.

He was in no hurry. A little rest would rejuvenate him for the next stage of his ascent. Squatting, he thought about Ann. Was she safe? Since she was with the others and they had flashlights and food, she must be. All of them were probably in the jeeps, heading homeward.

But why should he care what she was doing? She must have been in on the prank Scott and Wes played. After eight years she was still trying to get back at him for a childish mistake in judgement.

His mind flashed back to that day in the shed. The two of them had kissed and hugged until they were both warm and tingly, and then she had suggested they play doctor, her favorite. Their version called for her to point out a spot on her body and claim it hurt, then he would kiss it better. That day they became more carried away than usual, and Ann had pulled up her shirt so that he could kiss her skin. Swept up in the passion of the moment, he had begun kissing every square inch of her body while his hands roved up and down. Since he had known virtually nothing of the female anatomy, he didn't realize there were certain parts of a girl's body that were taboo for a boy to touch. So he had been surprised when Ann suddenly stepped back, her face registering total shock.

He was even more surprised when she hauled off and smacked him so hard, his ears rang. She had pulled her shirt down, smacked him again, and raced out of the shed with tears streaming down her red cheeks. Not until a year a half later, when his dad got around to explaining about the birds and the bees, had he understood why Ann reacted the way she did. By then it was too late to apologize, and since she had not been speaking to him at the time, doing so was moot.

So much for his first true love.

Ever since, he had carried a torch for her. Stupid as it sounded, he never developed a deep affection for any other girl. He'd dated occasionally. A few of the girls he liked. But none captured his heart the way Ann did.

How happy he was when she finally broke her silence and talked to him! From that day on, he was utmostly careful about how he acted around her so as to never antagonize her again. His fear made him seem shy in her presence but that wasn't it at all.

And now this.

He should be mad at her but he wasn't. He should despise her for being a party to the prank but he didn't. In his heart of hearts he still cared for her. Was he being foolish? Hopelessly romantic? Probably, but he didn't care.

Cory walked toward the wide tunnel. Fatigue and anxiety gnawed at him. More than anything else he craved to curl up in a soft bed and sleep for twelve hours. Near the tunnel he paused to glance over his shoulder, and it was then he heard the rattling noise again.

Only this time it came from right outside the chamber.

In four bounds Cory was behind a thick stalagmite. He held the backpack close to his side, his nerves jangling. Peeking out, he saw something shuffle into view, coming out of the tunnel that had brought him here.

It stood apparently surveying the chamber, and when satisfied the chamber was empty, moved into the open.

Cory's breath caught in his throat. Before his astounded gaze stalked the embodiment of the creature in the painting at the cave entrance. It was the same as those in the medieval painting of Hades.

A demon. An honest-to-God real, live demon.

The creature halted and gazed at the ceiling. Its lips moved, and from its throat issued the familiar sound of a rattlesnake.

Stupefied, Cory watched as the creature moved in a circle as if admiring a particular section of the ceiling. He had no idea what it was doing. All he could think of was that this shouldn't be happening, that it was impossible, that demons didn't exist and never had.

With quick steps the thing moved to the wide tunnel and cocked its head, evidently listening. Its huge hands, capped by long nails, were clenching and unclenching as if in anger.

What was it upset about? Cory wondered. He had to exhale and did so slowly so as not to make any noise. The demon took another step, and he began to relax in the belief it was leaving and he was safe when suddenly the creature whirled and stared into the chamber, stared directly at the stalagmite shielding him.

It must know he was there!

Chapter 11

Ann Weatherby's heart was in her mouth as she plummeted over the brink of the fissure. Frantically she tried to regain her balance but gravity was stronger. She twisted as she fell, heard someone scream, and clawed at the side of the fissure to try and halt her descent. Pain lanced her hands as the tips of some of her fingernails were snapped off. She threw back her head to scream herself when her feet hit the bottom. Agony speared up her spine, the impact stunning her so that she sagged and her forehead hit the wall.

"Ann! Ann! Are you all right?"

Jay's words seemed to reverberate in her skull. She was aware of being alive but felt sure both of her legs and possibly her back must be broken. Through a haze of anguish she managed to lift her head and peer upward where the bright circle of light from the flashlight pinpointed the position of her friends. She squinted, much of her pain surprisingly subsiding, and looked down at herself.

All she could see was her thighs a few inches above the knees and then the floor of the fissure. The sight panicked her and she wildly struggled, only to behold the ground around her thighs shift and more of her legs appear. Slowly the significance sank into her dazed mind. She had fallen into a layer of loose dirt that must be over two feet deep, if not more. Her legs were intact! And they weren't broken! The dirt had cushioned her, saving her from serious injury.

"Ann, how badly are you hurt?" Jay called down.

She craned her neck, smiling in relief. "I don't think I'm hurt badly at all," she responded. Except for her hands, he felt okay. She tried moving her legs. It was like trying to walk through water, only more difficult.

"Are you sure?"

Ann nodded while gingerly trying to lift first her right leg, then her left. She couldn't lift them alll the way out but there wasn't any pain.

"But you fell so far," Leslie yelled.

"Really?" Ann said curtly.

"Can you climb out?" Stacy said.

Her relief at being spared from harm dissolved. She studied both walls and saw nowhere she could gain a handhold. The fall had trapped her in the fissure.

"Can you?" Stacy prompted.

"I don't see how."

"Damn it!" Jay snapped. "I wish we had the rope. I wonder who does?"

"What does it matter?" Leslie said. "We don't even know where any of the others are. Now what are we going to do? I, for one, don't intend to wait around here forever."

"Boy, are you a real cheesehead," Jay said.

"What are you cutting on me for?"

"Because you have the consideration of a rock. Ann is in serious shit, you idiot, and all you can think of is yourself. I wish you were the one who fell in, not her," Jay said.

"Just wait, Thorpe. I'm going to tell Wes all about how you've treated me. He won't like it one bit."

"So tell him. See if I care."

"He'll talk to the coach and have you kicked off the team."

"Don't make me laugh. If the coach was to give one of us the boot, it wouldn't be me. I'm not a coke head."

"Are you threatening to tell the coach on Wes?"

"I don't have to. The way he's been playing lately, the coach will figure it out for himself. Now keep your mouth shut and let me think."

"With what?"

Ann stopped listening and and struggled to get a leg free. She raised it out of the dirt as high as her ankle, then had to give up. She couldn't get her leg all the way out. Walking would be impossible. If she was to get around she must do so another way. Bend, she lay on top of the dirt and discovered it would support her weight. By wriggling her legs, she felt them loosen to where she could ease them out and lie flat on the dirt. She began to crawl.

Dust got into her nose and she sneezed.

"Clever move," Jay shouted.

But what good had it done her? Ann mused. She snaked to a boulder low enough for her to grip the top with both hands. If she had hit it instead of landing in the dirt, the fall would have killed her. Tightening her grip, she pulled herself up until she could take a seat.

Jay was sweeping the flashlight along the fissure in both directions. "There has to be somewhere you can climb out," he stated. "I'll look for you."

Ann watched him move along the rim and prayed he would find a way. The high walls reared like a stone prison, imbuing her with dread at the idea of being stuck down there while the others went for help. Even if the three of them reached the surface, it would take hours to drive to Pagosa Springs and organize a rescue party. And there was no guarantee the rescuers would find her since it was unlikely Jay, Stacy or Leslie would be able to find their way back to the fissure.

"Don't worry, Ann," Stacy said. "You'll be fine. On Monday you'll be back in school and have forgotten that any of this ever happened."

"I'll never forget this nightmare," Ann said, conscious of the darkness closing in on her as Jay moved farther away.

"I hear that," Stacy said.

Jay had gone about twenty yards, his beam illuminating the fissure. He abruptly halted and trained it on a spot at the base of the opposite wall. "Hey, Ann, come and take at look at this. Is that a tunnel?"

Hopefully, Ann slid off the boulder onto her stomach and crawled as rapidly as she was able. Dust caked her clothes and hands. The tips of her fingers, where her nails had broken, hurt terribly. Sh refrained from examining them. Ever since she was little she had been squeamish about personal injuries.

She came to the area bathed by the beam.

Apparently Stacy and Leslie had kept abreast of her because Stacy yelled from directly above.

"What is that?"

At the bottom of the wall was a black area the shape of a half-moon. Four feet high and twice that in length, it might just be a hole.

Ann snaked closer. Suddenly she saw her hands clearly. Three of her fingernails on her right hand and two on her left had broken off, and several of her fingers were gashed. A strip of skin dangled from her right forefinger. She felt nauseous, fought off the sensation, and moved to the opening.

"Are you okay?" Jay asked.

"Fine," Ann lied, peering in. She dimly made out what appeared to be a room or chamber. "Move the flashlight around to get a better angle," she yelled up, and was gratified when the beam revealed a short slope of loose earth angling down into a room. Straight across from her was the vague outline of a tunnel.

"What's in there?" Jay asked.

Ann described what she saw. "I have no idea where that tunnel will take me," she concluded, "but it's a way out of the fissure. I don't have any choice except to follow it even though I don't much like the idea of wandering around in the dark."

"If only we had another flashlight," Jay said.

"You could give her ours," Leslie said sarcastically.

"Or I can throw you down there so she'll have some company," Jay retorted.

"You wouldn't dare."

"Keep flapping your gums, bitch, and you'll learn the hard way."

"Who are you calling a bitch?"

As if Ann didn't have enough weighing heavily on her mind, what with her injuries and the dire straits she was in, the constant bickering of her companions was like rubbing salt on her raw emotions. She wanted to shout at them to shut the hell up.

She also wanted to kick herself for coming to the Caverna del Diablo in the first place. Scott wasn't her type. She didn't feel especially close to him. He was simply a handsome guy who had asked her out a few times and she had agreed to go, more out of a desire to alleviate the boredom of staying home and watching the idiot box than any interest in him as a boyfriend.

"Ann, I don't think you should go in there," Jay said. "There's no telling what could happen. Stay where you are until we get back with help."

She twisted onto her side to stare up at them. In the peripheral glow of the flashlight their faces appeared like pale ghosts detached from corporal forms. "And how long will that be, Jay?"

Jay shrugged. "There's no telling."

"Even if you make it out and get help, how can you be certain you can locate this fissure again?"

Jay gazed around the chamber, and frowned. "To be honest, Ann, I don't know if I can."

"You can use the hammer and chisel to mark the passages we take, can't you?" Stacy asked.

"That's right!" Jay exclaimed, and hastily removed his backpack. He extracted the rock hammer and chisel and held them aloft. "See, Ann? It'll be easy for us to find you. I'll carve notches in every damn tunnel between here and the surface."

A flicker of hope flared in Ann's soul. A rescue team could easily follow a marked trail and have her out quickly. All she must endure was the long wait between the time Jay and the others left until the rescue team arrived. Which meant long hours spent alone in Stygian gloom in the depths of the earth. The very thought terrified her.

"What do you say?" Jay asked. "Will you sit tight until we get help? I promise well hustle our asses off."

"I'II stay right here," Ann said reluctantly.

"We'll make the stay easier on you," Jay said, reaching into the backpack again. He pulled out bags of potato chips and pretzels and extended his right arm out over the fissure. "You can munch on these while you wait."

"Hold on there, buster," Leslie said. "What if we need the food ourselves?"

"We still have some," Jay said, and let go of the bags. They fell straight and landed with twin plops, swirling small clouds of dust into the air.

Ann crawled over. "Thank you, Jay," she shouted. "This will help a lot."

"Okay, then," Jay said. He was clearly reluctant to leave her. "We'll be on our way." He trained the flashlight on her, his face twisted in worry. "I hate this. Is there anything else we can do that you can think of?"

There was, Ann realized. "I could use that box of matches."

"You've got them," Jay told her, and rummaged in the pack again.

"Now just a damn minute," Leslie objected. "I don't mind going hungry on her account but I draw the line at giving her the matches. What if we need them later to see with? Or to start a fire or something?"

"There's nothing in this cave we could use to start a fire," Jay said. "And we have the flashlight. We don't need the matches." He lifted the box out.

"Don't give her all of them!" Leslie said.

Jay glared at Leslie, then deliberately held his arm over the fissure and pitched the box toward Ann. It tumbled end over end and smacked down within inches of her left arm. "Now you won't be in the dark all the time," he said.

"Thank you, Jay," Ann shouted. "I won't forget this. You're a good guy."

"Yeah, he sure is," Stacy said, smiling at him.

Ann clutched the matches as if they were the source of life itself. If she used them sparingly they might last until help arrived, and in the process give her some peace of mind.

"Keep your chin up, kiddo," Jay said with a grin. He zipped the pack closed, shrugged into the straps, and waved. "By morning you'll be sound asleep in your own bed."

"I hope so."

Jay moved off. Stacy waved, then she and Leslie followed him. Almost immediately darkness reclaimed the fissure.

Ann listened but was unable to hear their footsteps or their voices. After a minute she knew they were gone and she was alone. *Alone*. The word conjured up frightening memories of her childhood when more than once she had become scared to death while lying in her room at night. Her fertile mind had fabricated all sorts of monsters and demons lurking in every shadowy comer or peering at her from out of the closet. Time and again she had asked her parents for a night light and they always refused, saying night lights were for 'babies'.

Her father, in particular, was always stressing self-reliance. "The only way to conquer your fears is to face them head-on," he constantly asserted.

Easy for him to say, Ann reflected. He'd never been stuck in her situation.

Her hands were hurting but she suppressed the pain. They would get worse before the night was done, and she regretted not having water to clean them. If they should become infected the agony would be unbearable.

Sliding against the wall, she sat up and rested her back on the smooth stone. She placed the two bags and the box of matches between her legs, then gingerly opened the bag she believed contained the pretzels. Being careful not to bump her fingers, she reached inside and pulled a pretzel out.

The cavern was disturbingly silent.

Ann took a bite, savoring the salty taste, and chewed hungrily. Her thoughts drifted to Cory. Was he with Scott and Wes? Had he actually participated in their asinine prank? She didn't believe that for a minute. Cory was too level-headed, too serious in his thinking, too mature to ever pull the kind of stunts Scott and Wes delighted in.

She had her doubts about the prank, itself. Yes, it would have been easy for those two idiots to erase tracks. But how had they moved that massive slab that blocked the tunnel? They would have needed a lot of help. Although the idea that other members of the football team had shadowed them to the cavern and were helping Scott and Wes was plausible, somehow she doubted that was the case.

She'd had doubts, too, about the wisdom of asking Cory to come along. Scott and Wes had been strangely insistent. She only gave in because she knew that Cory rarely went anywhere. He spent all his time on his computer or with his nose buried in books. In all the years she'd known him, he'd never had a steady girlfriend.

As his closest friend she felt obligated to do something to break him out of his cocoon. Humans were social beings. Living in isolation was detrimental to a person's mental and emotional health. The exalted thought made her grin.

But poor Cory. A lot of the others at school considered him a loser. Not that she ever did. But many had branded him a misfit and refused to have anything to do with him. How he tolerated their attitude she would never know. He must have a shell like a turtle.

Ann pursed her lips. Why was he so much on her mind lately? Seldom did a day go by where she didn't think about him. She had even taken to calling him more frequently than usual and sitting next to the living room window so she would spot him leaving his house and could go out and talk to him. He was easy to talk to. And he never tried to hit on her, like a lot of the guys did. He treated her with respect.

Terri had started to tease her about hanging around with him so much, hinting there must be a deeper reason, which was patently ridiculous. Terri was her BFF and as sweet as could be, but she knew nothing about girl-boy relationships. If a boy so much as talked to Terri nicely, she almost swooned at their feet.

That made Ann think of the scream. Jay had thought it was part of the prank. Ann disagreed. Never in a million years would Terri help Scott and Wes scare them.

Suddenly something clattered among the boulders off to the right.

Ann sat up, puzzled. It sounded like a pebble fell from above. She glanced up, scanning the top of the fissure. Although the dark veil prevented her from seeing much, she distinctly made out a huge figure poised on the rim.

As she laid eyes on it, the figure moved.

Chapter 12

"Where the hell are we?

"Who the hell knows?"

Wes Eagen snickered and swung his flashlight in a circle, surveying the chamber in which they found themselves. "This sure ain't the one where we stopped earlier."

Scott nodded. "I'd say we're lost, old buddy."

They both laughed.

"Oh, well," Wes said. "Shit happens." He resumed hiking, not in the least bothered by their situation. Confidence flowed through his veins, supreme confidence in his ability to tackle any problem, to surmount any difficulty. He was Wesley Aaron Eagen, star quarterback, the guy all the girls wanted and every other guy envied. He was the best at everything he did, which was why he always came out on top, why he was a natural-born winner. He'd find his way out of the stupid cave before too long. It was inevitable.

"You know, I've been thinking," Scott said.

"About what?"

"This cave would be a great place to stash some of my goodies. No one would ever find the stuff. It's a lot safer than keeping it in my room or down in the basement where one of my folks might stumble across it."

"You're crazy. You'd ride all the way out here every time someone wanted to make a buy?"

"Get real. I'd keep plenty handy for my everyday needs. But let's say I wanted to stash a couple of kilos of Mary Jane. Can you think of a better spot?"

Wes could think of a dozen but he kept his mouth shut. Scott sometimes became as goofy as all get-out when high, saying the dumbest things and coming up with the looniest notions. If Scott wanted to store drugs in this rotten cave, that was his business. But Wes suspected that once Scott came down to earth he would change his mind.

Wes approached a passage and searched the cave floor for footprints. There had been no sign of the others, not so much as a single track, for the better part of an hour. It would serve those idiots right if they were never found, even Leslie. She should have stuck by his side instead of traipsing off with Jay and the rest of the bimbos.

Wes turned a corner. Ahead, the tunnel forked. He halted to get Scott's opinion. "Which way this time?"

"Left."

"Any reason?"

"I'm left-handed."

"Makes sense to me," Wes said, and went on. His stomach rumbled, calling to mind his hunger. "Hey, do we have any beer left?"

"You want a beer after all that coke you snorted? Don't you know better than to mix your poisons?"

"Do we or don't we?"

"You bet your ass we do."

"Hand one over."

They stopped and Scott opened his backpack, producing a six-pack with a flourish. "Here we go, bro. I guess I'll have one, too. If we're going to spend the rest of our life in this armpit of a cave, we might as well do it totally blitzed."

"We'll be out in an hour," Wes predicted. "Leave it to me. I've lived in Colorado since day one and I know how to survive in these mountains. Hell, I was even a cub scout for a while. I'll get us out."

"Is it okay if I don't hold my breath?" Scott said, and cackled.

"You wait and see," Wes said, miffed by his friend's lack of confidence. He opened his can, took a long swig, and let out a belch.

"Pig," Scott said, and did the same.

Holding the beer in his left hand and the flashlight in his right, Wes advanced. "You know what really gets my goat?"

"Paper clips."

“What?” Wes looked at him. “Why in hell would they get my goat?”

“I don’t know,” Scott said, and inanely grinned. “It was the first thing that popped into my head.”

“Brother,” Wes said. “No, what’s gets my goat is that we’ve been down in this frigging cave all this time and we haven't seen any sign of the so-called monster. What's this world coming to when you can't trust a crazy legend to be true?"

Scott chortled. "It's the drugs, man. Haven't you heard? There's too much dope in this country and it's ruining everything. The schools, the inner cities, even us rural types. Everyone is getting swacked on either coke, grass, crack, the big H, you name it. I know. I listen to the news. I read it on-line. Anything having to do with drugs, I’m there. Drugs are my life."

"Why?"

"What?"

"I've never asked why you’re so into them that you seel them, and I've always been meaning to. It's not exactly the safest line of work. If the coke doesn't get you, the cops will. You must have a reason for doing it."

"That I do, bucko," Scott said, nodding. He polished off

half of his beer in large gulps, then wiped his sleeve across his dripping mouth. "And I'll tell you a secret I've never told anyone. I do it because I hate my old man."

"Your dad? What did he ever do to you?"

"Everything, dude. The man is the ultimate wuss. I mean, he's so liberal he thinks the Democratic party is right wing."

"I don't get it," Wes admitted. He never paid much attention to politics. His political science and history classes bored him to tears. Who cares who wrote the Declaration of Independence or who shot Abraham Lincoln? It all happened centuries ago to people long dead. None of that jazz was relevant any more.

"Okay. Let me explain," Scott said, and took a sip of brew. "My old man, as you know, is a newspaper editor. Journalism is his life. It's all he talks about and thinks about. Every day at mealtime I've had to listen to him ramble on about how he has all the answers to all of society's problems. If we had the right President, we'd have this country running like clockwork in no time. If he could educate young people the way he wanted, our schools would turn out perfect citizens." Scott swore."I'm sick to death of hearing his same tired garbage day after day. Follow me so far?"

"Not exactly," Wes said.

"What is it you don't understand?"

"What's a liberal?"

"You're kidding?"

"I'm not Cory Fleming. Yeah, I've heard the word before. But I never pay any attention. Politics is people who don't have anything better to do with their lives."

"Wow," Scott said.

"What?"

"Back to my dad," Scott said. "The important point is that my old man is the biggest hypocrite who ever lived. He claims his kind have all the answers to everything. Mom left him because he's such a jerk. They used to argue all the time, and I'd listen at their door. She used to tell him that he knew how to talk a good life but he sure as hell didn't know how to live one."

Wes said nothing. He still didn't see where all this was leading and was embarrassed to admit it.

"Do you know my old man never once came to any of the ballgames I played in when I was a kid? Do you know he never once took me fishing or hunting?"

"Why not?"

"Because he thinks sports are stupid, hunting is for Neanderthals, and fishing is for guys who never grew up. He was always dragging me off to art shows and museums and crap like that."

Now it was Wes who said, "Wow. How could anyone not like sports?"

"Something else about him I hate," Scott went on passionately. "He likes to manipulate people. All those editorials and stories he writes are slanted so he can get his view across. He considers what he calls 'average people' to be jerks and dimwits."

Wes had listened to enough. "How the hell does all this tie in with you selling drugs?"

"I'm getting to that."

"I hope so."

"My dad likes to think of himself as a rebel. He smokes a little pot now and then. He steals pens and tablets from work. He runs red lights."

"Who doesn't?" Wes responded. "Will you get to the damn point before the suspense kills me?"

"Don't you see?" Scott said. "My old man acts like he's perfect and most everyone else is either a mental defective or just plain dumb. Yet he's just as screwed up. Probably more than most."

Wes wanted to hit him. "So what?"

"So all my life I've had to put up with him preaching at me from his soap box and have him looking down his nose at me because I liked to do the same things other boys did."

"So? So? So?" Wes said in exasperation. He'd forgotten how long-winded Scott could be when he was high.

"Once, a few years back, he sat me down at the kitchen table and told me how disappointed he was that I didn't have any intention of following in his footsteps. He said he had high hopes for me when I was young but I'd never come around to his way of thinking. And then he grinned and said the thing that I remember the most." Scott paused. "He said that he supposed he should be grateful that at least I wasn't a criminal and hadn't wound up in prison."

"So you went right out and became a dealer?"

"Not overnight, but eventually, yeah. I like drugs, and it was a way to rub his nose in it. Understand now?"

"Yeah," Wes lied. He didn't have the slightest idea what Scott meant. How did dealing dope get back at Scott's old man for being a lousy father? Jesus, give him his dad any day. Now there was a man who understood what made a guy tick---sports, girls and gobs of money. What else did life have to offer?

"After I got into the dealing I grew to love it," Scott went on. "I mean, all the foxes and the money and being so damn popular. All of a sudden I had more friends than I knew what to do with. There's nothing like it."

"Your dad doesn't suspect?"

"Hell, no. The man is an idiot. Any lie I feed him, he

believes."

Wes's flashlight revealed another bend. He was almost to it when from their rear arose a sound so bizarre he stopped short in astonishment. At first he entertained the ridiculous idea someone was shaking a baby rattle. For thirty seconds the rattling filled the tunnel, then abruptly ceased.

Scott had spun and was sweeping his beam down the passageway. "What the hell was that?"

"I don't know."

"Aren't you the one who knows these mountains? Was it some kind of animal?"

"To me it sounded like a rattlesnake," Wes said. "But I didn't know there are snakes down this far."

"Let's go see," Scott said and began to retrace their steps.

"I think we should keep going."

"What's the matter? Are you scared?" Scott teased. He polished off his beer, then tossed the can aside. It banged against the wall and made considerable noise when it hit the tunnel floor.

From beyond a corner up ahead came a series of tremendously loud thumps, as if someone was pounding the wall.

Scott halted. "Damn, that sure as hell isn't a snake."

Wes was at a loss to explain it and felt vaguely uneasy until an obvious possibility occurred to him. "Hey," he whispered so the person doing the pounding wouldn't hear. "Maybe it's the dork."

"Fleming?"

"Did any other dorks tag along?"

A wicked grin creased Scott's mouth. "He's trying to scare us, if that it? He wants to play games, does he? Well, let's give the prick what he wants." Scott quickly removed his backpack.

The thumping was repeated.

Scott snickered.

"What are you planning to do?" Wes asked.

"He must be right around that corner," Scott said. "You stay here and talk real loud so he thinks we're still here." He chuckled. "I'm going to sneak up on the son of a bitch."

"What will you do when you catch him?"

"What do you think?" Scott deposited the pack at Wes's feet. Then he handed over his flashlight. "I don't want him to see me coming until it's too late."

"Watch yourself"

"With Fleming? Was that a joke? What can a wimp like him do to me?" Scott smirked.

"He might be pissed off because we ditched him and be out for revenge."

"What's he going to do? Smack my hand and tell me, what a bad boy I've been?" With a wink Scott turned and tiptoed toward the bend.

Wes broke into a fit of laughter, but at a hard look from Scott he caught himself and cleared his throat. "The others must be around here somewhere," he stated loud enough for Cory Fleming to hear him. "All we have to do is keep looking and they'll turn up." He snickered as Scott neared the bend, and again caught himself. "Say, who do you think will win the game this weekend between the Broncos and Seattle? I put my money on Denver. The Seahawks always have a hard time of it at Mile High Stadium. Must be the altitude."

Scott paused at the comer to look back and grin and give him a thumb's up.

Wes gave a little wave and resumed chatting to the air. "Yeah, Denver will beat Seattle by eighteen points or I don't know anything about football. I also laid some bread down on the Philadelphia Eagles."

The thumping stopped.

Scott darted from view.

"Nail the sucker!" Wes yelled, running forward be in on the kill. "Give it to him good!" He was ten feet from the bend when he heard a strangled cry and knew Scott had caught Fleming, There was the sound of a solid blow, a thud, and then another cry, a piercing wail that brought goosebumps to Wes's skin and made him stop dead in his tracks. Was that Fleming? Scott must be killing him! He took another step, wanting to give his friend a hand, when the wail transformed into an articulate cry that definitely didn't come from Cory Fleming's throat.

It was Scott, shrieking at the top of his lungs.

"Weeessssssss! Help meeeee!"

Startled, Wes felt the short hairs at the nape of his neck prickle. He thought that Scott must be playing a joke on him. The next instant, however, there was a distinct snap, reminding him of the sound made when someone broke a dry branch in half, and Scott vented a bloodcurdling scream.

Wes wanted to go to his friend's aid but couldn't. He was rooted to the spot, petrified, afraid to help Scott and afraid to flee.

There was another chilling snap.

Then it got worse.

Scott began blubbering incoherently. He alternately whined and bawled and screeched. Mixed in with his pathetic cries were crunching sounds and low grunts, as if something was eating him alive.

Wes took a faltering step closer. His body had broken out in a cold sweat. This must be a prank, he told himself.

Scott was having some fun at his expense. Any moment now Scott would pop in sight laughing his fool head off.

Any moment now.

But the crunching and blubbering went on and on. He tried to call out but couldn't seem to find his voice.

A quavering shriek reverberated in the tunnel.

Suddenly fainthearted, Wes backed away. He heard a new sound totally unlike any he had ever known, and Scott's cries became muffled as if someone had a hand pressed over his mouth.

What was happening back there?

Firming his resolve, Wes reversed direction and moved toward the bend, a flashlight in each hand. He couldn't just run off and desert his best friend. He had to find out what was going on.

At that juncture the blubbering stopped.

A second later an oval object sailed out and fell to the cave floor not three yards from Wes's feet.

The twin beams brilliantly revealed every grisly feature. The blood-spattered hair. The jagged flesh ringing the neck. The protruding, partially severed tongue.

It was Scott Miklin's head.

Chapter 13

Cory Fleming became as rigid and motionless as the stalagmite he was hiding behind as the demon gazed in his direction. He froze, scared to even blink because the thing might detect the movement.

The demon stared intently, its eyes shimmering with flames of fire. Then, unexpectedly, the thing pivoted and loped out the wide tunnel so rapidly that Cory couldn't believe it was gone.

Was it hunting him?

Dazed, he stayed where he was, debating his next move.

The thing must know he was in the cavern. It had spotted him earlier, when he first caught sight of it, and now it was after him. What would it do if it caught him? He thought again of that pile of bones.

He looked down and his gaze fell on his own tracks. In its haste the demon hadn't bothered to glance at the floor. Thank God! His life, for the time being, had been spared.

Cory donned his backpack. Should he go on or go back? Going back would take him near the enormous underground world chamber where the demons, or whatever they were, apparently dwelled.

And since the creature had gone off up the wide tunnel, that left him to take the other one. As soon as he left the room with the glowing roof, darkness again descended.

Cory ran, the backpack slapping against his shoulder blade. He was constantly on the lookout for dark patches against the backdrop of the lighter dusty floor, patches that might be obstacles such as small boulders or stalagmites.

The ground angled upward, but he knew enough not to count on the tunnel taking him to the surface. The Caverna del Diablo was so vast, with hundreds if not thousands of tunnels twisting every which way and rising and falling more frequently than a roller coaster, that it was impossible to determine whether he was nearing the cavern entrance or merely going deeper into the vast maze.

Cory ran until he was too tired to run any more. Then he walked, sweat dribbling down his back and sides. He tried to see the face of his watch. Even though he held the timepiece right in front of his eyes he couldn't tell the time. He made a mental note to ask his folks for a digital for Christmas, one that not only glowed in the dark but could perform fifty-six separate functions and do everything except microwave food.

By his estimation he had been traveling for forty minutes when, after a sharp turn and a dip, he entered a spacious room. Halting, he scanned the walls but didn't see another way out.

The far wall seemed different somehow so he moved forward to investigate. On drawing within a few feet of it, he realized it wasn't a wall at all but rather a high mound of earth. Above it, there looked to be a hole in the shape of a crescent moon.

He was debating whether to investigate it when a timid voice addressed him.

"Who's there?"

Cory's heart beat like a triphammer. He knew that voice as well as he did his own. No, better! Incredulous, he stared up at the top of the mound, at that opening. "Ann? That's you, isn't it?"

"Oh, God! Cory!"

Cory started up the slope but she was quicker, diving feet first through the opening and sliding swiftly down the mound. Grinning happily, he held out his arms to help her up but she needed no assistance.

Ann leaped to her feet when still a yard off and literally threw herself at him, almost bowling him over, causing him to teeter backwards until his feet were on level ground. She uttered a low sob and embraced him, her lips close to his cheek, her warm breath fanning his ear.

"It's you! It's really and truly you!"

Cory didn't know what to say. An odd lump constricted his throat. He inhaled the pleasant scent of her hair and felt her breasts flush with his chest. Suddenly the room became five to ten degrees warmer.

“I thought you were the thing I saw earlier," Ann said.

Instantly, Cory's elation dissipated. “What thing?” he said, still holding her close and wishing he could go on holding her like that forever.

“About half an hour or so, I guess. I saw something at the top of the fissure. It jumped across and kept going.”

“Fissure?”

“It's on the other side of that hole I came out of,” Ann explained.

Cory wondered if it had been the same creature he saw, or another. He tried to calculate the time frame but was distracted by the feel of her, the warmth of her, the sheer joy of being with her. "Where are the others? I haven't seen anyone since Scott and Wes played their stupid trick on me.”

Ann stepped back. "What trick?"

Briefly, Cory told her about being pushed and his flashlight taken, and his wanderings since. He mentioned the vast chamber but refrained from telling her about the creatures he had seen. There was no sense in scaring her more than she already was, although he knew he must inform her soon. "I had no idea you were nearby when I came into this room," he said and grinned. "Had I known you were here I would have been here sooner."

"I've never been so glad to see anyone in my life."

Those words were ambrosia to Cory's soul. He went to take her hands when she flinched and drew them away.

"I hurt myself," she said.

"How?"

Ann related everything that had happened to her since last they saw one another, including Terri's disappearance and her fall into the fissure. "I was sitting up there nibbling on a pretzel when I heard something and looked through the opening. I couldn't tell who it was but I knew it wasn't the big thing that jumped across the fissure."

"You have food?" Cory asked excitedly.

"Some pretzels and some potato chips. Oh, and a box of matches. I left them up there," Ann said, turning and pointing at the half-moon opening.

"Wait here. I'll get them," Cory offered. He went up the slope stooped over, scrambling energetically, his stomach rumbling in anticipation. Finding the bags and box proved easy, and he hastily returned to Ann.

"Don't ever leave me again," she said.

"What?" Cory responded, knowing she couldn't possibly mean what he thought she meant.

"This place gives me the creeps. I can't stand being alone. Promise me you won't go off and leave me until after we're back on the surface."

"You have my word," Cory said, striving to hide his disappointment.

"Is something wrong?"

"No," Cory equivocated. He was set to tear into one of the bags when he recalled her hands. "Take a seat so I can see how bad off you are."

"I'll be okay."

"Take a seat," Cory insisted, and knelt next to her when she sat down. Placing the bags of chips and pretzels beside her, he opened the matchbox and removed a wooden match. The box was only half-full. "How many have you used?"

"None. After seeing that thing I didn't want to draw attention to myself by using them."

"Smart move," Cory said. He struck the match on the side of the box and held the match up. The sight of her fingers made him cringe inwardly. They were covered with dried blood and a piece of skin hung from her right forefinger. "They must hurt like crazy."

"Only when I breathe."

Cory smiled and moved the flame closer to the dangling piece of skin attached to her finger by a thin strip. "I can pull that off for you."

"Must you?"

"It will pick up a lot of dust and will sting like crazy if you brush your hand against something."

"You're right, of course." Ann took a breath. "Go ahead."

"Close your eyes," Cory directed. Once she complied, he gripped the skin tightly and gave a sharp yank. Other than a flickering frown she gave no indication of feeling pain. "All done," he said, casting the piece over his shoulder. The flame chose that moment to go out.

"Thanks," Ann said.

"We have to get you to a doctor. You say there's no way out of that fissure?"

"Not unless you can leap tall buildings at a single

bound."

"Then we'll go back down the tunnel I used to come in and look for a passage out," Cory said with as much confidence as he could muster. He unslung the backpack, placed both the chip and pretzel bags inside after removing three pretzels, and eased it over his arms. The box of matches he tucked into his front pocket so they would be handy in an emergency. "Are you ready?"

"Home, James, and don't spare the gas."

Cory admired her spunk. After all she had been through she could still make jokes. He took her by the right wrist and led her into the tunnel. She could hardly object under the circumstances.

"What do you figure that thing was I saw?" Ann said.

Cory hesitated. Here it was---the moment of truth. Should he lie or fill her in? "I know what it is." Confident she would handle the revelation intelligently and calmly, he left nothing out. Her arm grew tense when he described the creatures but she maintained her composure.

"This is a nightmare," Ann said when he was done. "A nightmare brought to life."

"If we're lucky we'll be able to avoid them," Cory said. "The cavern is tremendous. Those things can't be everywhere at once."

"We don't know that. What if they are demons, like you believe? They might be able to accomplish feats we can only dream of." Ann paused. "Demons? Did I really say that? This whole business is insane."

"People have been reporting strange creatures in caves since time began," Cory said. "Not just from the U.S. either, but from all over the globe. Huge lizards, albino amphibians, bats the size of condors, and things that resemble men but aren't men."

"Let's change the subject."

"Don't worry. I'll do my best to get you to safety. I won't let anything happen to you if I can prevent it."

"I know I can count on you," Ann said.

Cory saw the white of her teeth against the canvas of inky murk. Despite the danger they were in, he was ecstatic. He had her all to himself and could, if he dared get up the courage to tell her his true feelings. For the moment he was content to walk along, feeling her skin on his hand and occasionally having her brush against him

"I'll never go out with Scott Miklin again," Ann declared out of the blue. "The trick he and Wes played on you was despicable. Is your head still hurting?"

"Not that much."

"Cory, I had no idea Scott and Wes were planning to do that to you. Please believe me."

The sincerity in her tone was self-evident. "I do," Cory said.

"It's partly my fault, though," Ann sadly said. "I was the one who invited you. I'm sorry I put you through all this."

"Inviting me was a kind thing to do," Cory said. "You can't blame yourself for how those two behaved." He gave her wrist a light squeeze. "I'm glad you did. You're the nicest, prettiest girl I know, and I like spending time with you."

"Why, thank you, kind sir," Ann said lightheartedly. "If you could see me in the dark, you'd laugh at how I'm blushing."

"I mean it," Cory said, then wondered if he had made too big an issue of it because she fell silent.

At length they reached the chamber where he had seen the creature. He took her straight across and was almost to the far side when she stopped and gasped, her eyes on the floor.

"I had no idea!"

There in the dust were the thing's gargantuan footprints, each bearing the impression of only three toes.

Cory had been aware of them before but in his haste to quit the chamber he hadn't taken the time to examine them. He remedied his oversight, sinking to one knee to gauge the dimensions of the prints and learn what little else he could from them. Each was a foot and a half in length and about twelve inches in width. The tracks alone were enough to confirm that no creature known to science had made them. Unlike human tracks, where the heel of the foot produced a heavier impression than the ball and the toes, these prints indicated the creature's weight was evenly distributed along the entire sole. Its toes were circular, and at the tip of each was a line in the dirt that might have been made by claws.

"Let's get ot of here," Ann urged. "Please."

Cory didn't need prompting. As they hurried along the tunnel he thought about Terri's disappearance and its implications. There was a chance Wes and Scott were to blame but he personally believed the creature was the culprit. What would it have done with her? Killed her on the spot? Or take her back to that vast realm and finish her off there?

He contemplated going to Terri's rescue but thought better of the idea. For one thing, she might already be dead and he would be wasting the effort. For another, he wasn't sure he could find that immense realm again. But the clincher was Ann. Going there would expose Ann to the same fate as Terri's, which he wouldn't do under any circumstances.

When the tunnel forked he took the left branch, one he

hadn't used. Immediately the ground sloped upward. At the top the tunnel widened and leveled.

The walls were faintly phosphorescent, enabling them to see a few feet in any direction.

"Too bad the entire cave isn't like this," Ann said, breaking their lon g silence.

"It would make life easier," Cory agreed.

"What causes the glowing?"

"If I had to make a guess I'd say the luminosity is produced by the slow oxidation of phosphorus in the walls."

Ann grinned. "I love it when you talk like that. No wonder everybody thinks you're another Albert Einstein."

"Sorry," Cory said, embarrassed by the comparison. Too many times he'd heard the same statement in an insulting vein. At school he consciously kept his speech simplistic so the other kids wouldn't rib him.

"No need to apologize," Ann told him. "It's a refreshing change from guys who only talk about themselves or sports or cars, as if that's all that matters in the whole universe." She sighed. "Girls have to put up with a lot of crap from guys, Cory. You must know that females mature earlier than males. About the time girls are starting to have serious thoughts about a career or motherhood boys are just entering their second childhood, doing quaint things like having belching contests or drag racing or trying to see how far they can go with every girl they meet."

"Not all guys are like that," Cory said, trying to come up with something else to talk about. The subject of sex made him uncomfortable, especially since he had never gone all the way. If the raunchy talk in the locker room during gym class was reliable, he must be the only guy in Pagosa Springs High who had yet to make the big score

"You're a rare exception, and I never appreciated how much that means until now."

"Oh?" Cory said, his hopes again flaring at the hint of affection in her words.

"Yeah. If Wes or Scott had found me, I'd be forced to listen to Wes's endless talk about football and Scott go on and on about the parties he's thrown."

"You know those two," Cory said, disappointed once again.

"Which reminds me," Ann said. "Have you heard any rumors going around school about Scott? Terri brought it up earlier but I snapped at her and shouldn't have."

"What kind of rumors?"

"There's been talk that he's heavy into drugs and might even be a pusher."

"I've never heard a word, but then I'm not the most popular guy in school. No one bothers to confide in me."

"I figured the stories were just wild talk. He's never offered to sell me any drugs."

"Maybe he's selective about who he picks to be his customers," Cory said. "Or maybe he's afraid you'd go to the police if you learned the truth."

"I would at that," Ann said. "Anyone who'd ruin the lives of others just to get rich quick should be locked up and have the key thrown away."

Cory felt the same way. A cousin of his in Portland had become a drug addict several years ago. Her family had gone through sheer hell before she was finally able to kick the habit and get her life in order. She still attended support sessions weekly and went to therapy so she wouldn't give in to temptation and go back to using.

The tunnel narrowed. Soon it bore left and they were were plunged into darkness.

A strong, cool breeze hit their faces, coming from above.

Cory glanced up and was startled to behold a patch of stars way up high. The ceiling had to be hundreds of feet overhead. In the middle was an opening to the surface. If only they could reach it! He halted, mesmerized by the elusive promise of escape. But the opening was so high up, it might as well be on the moon.

Cory took another step and his right foot bumped a small stone. He heard it strike something, then clatter downward, the noise growing fainter and fainter until he couldn't hear it any more.

"Don't move," Cory cautioned. He took the matches from his pocket. On striking one, he saw a stalagmite a few feet away. Beyond yawned the mouth of a great pit. If they had kept going they would have fallen in.

"We have to turn around," Ann said.

"Let's see first," Cory said and edged to the rim. By lowering his arm as far as he could, he determined the sides were smooth. Judging by the curvature of the wall, he estimated the circumference as thirty feet or more. He couldn't see the other side or the bottom.

"You're not thinking of going down in there?" Ann said.

"For all we know there might be a tunnel to the surface down below" Cory said. "We can't afford not to check."

"How are you going to get down? You don't know how deep it is. You certainly can't jump."

"Take these and keep one lit," Cory instructed as he gave her the match box. Unzipping the backpack, he removed the rope. Then, stepping to the stalagmite, he fashioned a loop.

"What if the rope doesn't hold?" Ann said.

"It's a new rope and it's thick enough to bear my weight."

"But what if you reach the end and still don't touch

bottom? Or what if you slip and fall? How will I get you out?"

Cory gave her arm a reassuring squeeze. "Stop worrying. I'll be fine. If I don't reach the bottom I'll climb back up. As simple as that."

"And if you slip?" Ann persisted.

"If we're to get out of this mess we may have to take a few chances. Since we don't have a flashlight the only way to find out if there is a tunnel is to go have a look."

"I wish you wouldn't."

Cory began tying knots at regular intervals of a foot or so. When he was done, he secured the loop over the stalagmite, and pitched the rope over the rim. Averting his eyes from Ann's, he turned, straddled the rope, and gripped it in both hands. "Wish me, luck."

"Oh, God," Ann said. "Be careful. I don't want anything to happen to you."

His ears burning, Cory eased down slowly. His shoulders and upper arms bore the strain. His feet flat against the side, he took his sweet time.

"Are you okay?"

Cory grunted and continued lower, his shoulders protesting. Except for gym class he rarely exercised, an oversight he intended to remedy provided he lived long enough.

The rope was thirty long but seemed twice that. His arms were trembling when he reached the twenty-eighth knot. He was almost at the end. Gripping harder, he carefully lowered his legs to see what happened.

His feet made made contact with solid ground.

Cory gingerly felt around with his toes until he was certain it was safe, then he let go and relaxed.

"Cory?" Ann anxiously called down.

"I made it," Cory replied. "Hang on a second."

Pivoting, Cory moved along the base of the pit. Soon his probing fingers found an entrance to another passageway. Retracing his steps until the rope bumped against his cheek, he seized hold and craned his neck to see Ann. "There's a tunnel down here," he shouted. "Your turn to climb down."

"Here I come."

Ann shook her left hand and the match went out, enfolding the rim in pitch black.

"Take your time. Rest when you have to," Cory advised, trying not to think of the horrible consequences should she slip in the early stage of her descent. "I'll hold the rope steady for you."

He thought he heard rustling, then dust rained on his shoulders. "Have you started yet?"

"Just did," Ann yelled. "Had to put on the backpack first."

Invisible pins pricked Cory's skin as he waited in breathless eagerness for her to reach the bottom. He would have brought the pack himself, but he'd wanted her to have the munchies in case something happened to him.

The rope shook in his hands, and he braced his feet. Already he was planning the next phase of their search. If the tunnel should prove to be a dead end they would return to the pit and climb out. By then they would be in need of rest. After a few chips and pretzels they would press on, refreshed.

At no time must he give in to the growing sense of desperation eating at his insides. They would find a way out. They had to---or perish.

Suddenly Ann's foot brushed against his hair.

Moving aside so she could reach the pit floor, he reached up, found her waist, and guided her to his side.

"Glad you could drop in," Cory joked, letting his hands linger on her hips.

"The next time I'll use a parachute," Ann responded.

Cory laughed and impulsively pursed his lips to kiss her. In the nick of time he caught himself and jerked his hands away as if they were on fire.

"Something the matter?"

"No. What could be wrong?"

"I don't bite, you know."

Was that an invitation? Did she know he had almost kissed her? Cory's head swam with thoughts better left alone until they were safe and sound. They were standing nose to nose, her warm breath caressing his face, and he swore he could feel the heat of her body through his clothes.

"We'd better get moving," he said huskily.

"Yes."

Neither of them moved.

Cory could distinguish the whites of her eyes but was unable to read her expression. "Let me have the matches," he said.

"I stuck them in my pocket." Ann drew the box out and holding it close to his chest.

As Cory took them his fingers enfolded hers, and it was as if an electrical charge zapped his body. He tingled all over and broke out in a sweat. His manhood leaped to attention, too, bulging against his pants.

"Cory---," Ann started to speak.

Suddenly the rope swung against Cory's left cheek. "What are you doing with the rope?" he asked.

"Me? I'm not touching it."

As the rope swung away, Cory grabbed at it but missed. Bewildered, he opened the matchbox and swiftly lit a match. As the tiny flame crackled to life he saw the end of the rope retreating into the darkness above as someone---or *something*---pulled it up.

"No!" Cory cried, and leaped. His fingers raked the air and down he came, striking the wall with his shoulder.

An instant later the rope vanished.

Chapter 14

Jay Thorpe's muscles rippled as he swung the rock hammer again and again, the tip of the chisel biting into the rock wall with every blow. This was the fourth arrow he had made and he was becoming adept at completing them fast, which still didn't satisfy the snippy bitch standing behind him

"Must we stop at every damn fork to do this?" Leslie said, impatiently tapping her right foot as she waited for him to get done.

"We do if we want to find Ann again."

"At this rate we won't get out of this stinking cave until Christmas."

Stacy stepped closer and placed a hand on Jay's back. "Quit your griping, Les. Jay is doing the best he can. I swear you're going to drive us both nuts if you don't stop your damn complaining."

"You'd be upset too if we were with my hunk instead of yours and you had no idea where Jay was," Leslie shot back. "Can I help it if I miss Wes?"

"You wanted to kill him for his little prank, remember?"

"I'll kill him, all right. Then I'll screw his brains out and have him begging for more," Leslie said.

"You're *such* a slut," Stacy said.

"Takes one to know one."

The arrow completed, Jay stood and admired his handiwork. When the rescue party entered the Caverna del Diablo they would have no difficulty in locating Ann.

He felt profoundly guilty over having left her and fervently wished it hadn't been necessary. By leaving a trail of arrows any moron could follow and guaranteeing her rescue, he partially soothed his guilt.

"Are you two at it again?" he said while putting the hammer and the chisel into his backpack.

"Let's just get on with this, shall we?" Leslie said.

Jay sighed. The two of them had been arguing since they left the fissure, and he had taken about all he was going to. It was hard to believe they were best friends. Or used to be before coming to the damn cavern.

He entered a new tunnel, the flashlight in his right hand. Was the beam a bit weaker than it had been earlier? As a test he held the flashlight at waist height and roughly gauged how much of the passage the beam illuminated. Yep, the battery was wearing down, which was to be expected since he had the flashlight on all the time. He debated on whether to turn it off to conserve the battery but decided against it.

Walking in the dark was bound to upset the girls even more than they already were. Then, too, he felt confident they would soon be back at the jeeps. There was no cause for worry. So he kept the light on and hiked boldly along the narrow passage.

"Wait up," Stacy said, taking his left hand. "I don't want to walk with Grumpy."

"Aren't you being hard on her?"

"She's the one who can't stop shooting her mouth off," Stacy said. "As if things aren't bad enough, we have to listen to her bitch. I never realized how much of a crybaby she is."

Leslie abruptly grabbed Stacy's shoulder and spun her around. "Enough is enough! I heard that! And I'm tired of your petty insults."

"What do you aim to do about it?" Stacy said, clenching her fists.

Jay moved between them. "Girls, please! Settle this once we're out of the cave."

"We'll settle it now," Stacy said, stepping past Jay and giving Leslie a hard push.

Leslie returned the favor, and a moment later the two of them were going at it like alley cats, punching and clawing and tearing at each other's hair.

"Damn it," Jay grumbled as he snatched at Stacy's arm. But she pulled free.

Now what was he supposed to do? Jay asked himself. Put a stop to the fight or let them get it out of their systems? Rather than step in and possibly have Stacy be mad at him, he stood next to the wall and watched them go at it. Neither appeared to be doing serious damage although they were flailing away like madwomen.

Stacy raked Leslie's cheek with her nails and Leslie retaliated by yanking on Stacy's hair. Clenching, they kicked and screeched, raising a fine swirl of dust.

Jay began to find the fight amusing and not a little arousing. Stacy had torn the front of Leslie's blouse, exposing the upper half of Leslie's right breast. And Stacy's own honeydews were heaving from her strenuous exertion. Grinning, he licked his lips and waited for the outcome.

The fight was decided when Stacy hooked a leg behind Leslie's ankle and shoved, sending Leslie crashing to the floor."

Had enough, bitch?" Stacy sid, her features livid.

Leslie put her hands on the ground and was all set to get up when she glanced down and saw her ripped blouse. "Look at what you did!" she wailed. "This cost thirty-four dollars! My mother will have a fit."

"Serves you right," Stacy said. "Lay a hand on me again and I'll rip all your clothes off."

Jay's eyes lit up at the image of Leslie naked and ripe for the plucking. She was as much of a fox as Stacy and there had been occasions when he imagined what it would be like to get horizontal with her. He'd never followed through on his lustful urges, though, because he knew Stacy would dump him if she ever found out. After she castrated him, of course.

Leslie suddenly burst into tears, her hands over her eyes, her shoulders shaking uncontrollably.

"What a baby!" Stacy said.

Moved to pity, Jay came forward and rested a hand on Leslie's arm. "Come on," he tried to soothe her "It's not as bad as all that. Get up and we can keep going."

Leslie cried louder.

"Leave her be," Stacy said. "She got what she deserved."

Jay was turning when Leslie swept up off the floor and embraced him, burying her face in his shirt and sobbing pitiably. Shocked, he delicately tried to pry her loose but her arms were corded bands. "Get a grip, Les", he said, and cast a sheepish glance at Stacy, who was positively furious. Leslie's breasts poked against him, jiggling with every heave of her shoulders, bringing his organ to a full erection. He became hot all over and nervously licked his lips.

"Let go of her," Stacy said.

"Me?" Jay responded. "She's the one doing the holding here." Again he tried to pry Leslie off, although not nearly as hard as he tried before.

Stacy, in a huff, turned and folded her arms, her spine as stiff as a two-by-four.

Smirking, Jay took advantage of the situation to place his hands on Leslie's back and begin rubbing up and down. "There, there," he said. "Shape up, will you?"

Leslie's sobs became fewer and less severe. She shifted her head to one side and sniffled loudly.

Keeping a watchful eye on Stacy, Jay allowed his hand to drift around Leslie's back to her right breast, brushing it lightly with his palm. To his amazement, she ground her hips into him. He thought he would explode in his jeans. "Feeling better now?" he asked, struggling to keep his tone even.

"Yes," Leslie said, looking up, her eyes wide as if in surprise. Her cheeks were moist, her nose red. "I'm sorry. I don't know what got into me."

"It's the strain," Jay said, glancing at Stacy. He started to pull away when Leslie did an incredible thing; she gripped his hand and pressed it to her exposed breast. For a second her hard nipple mashed into his palm, and then she released him, her mouth curling in an enigmatic smile.

"I'll be okay," Leslie said, adjusting her blouse to cover as much of her breast as she could. "Thank you."

Stacy finally turned. "Are you done being the Good Samaritan?" she demanded of Jay

"Hey, don't blame me. You two started this."

"I'm to blame," Leslie said contritely, looking at Stacy. "Will you ever forgive me for being such a jerk? I promise it won't happen again."

"No problem," Stacy said, taken aback by the admission. "Like honeybuns said, it's the strain getting to us. All this lousy wandering around is enough to make anyone bitchy."

Jay slipped past her to take the lead and to prevent her from noticing the bulge in his pants. The flashlight flickered, then steadied. He wondered who had the backpack containing the extra batteries and figured it must be Scott or Wes. They would be sure to keep the spares handy.

As he hiked he thought about Terri. There had been no sign of any unusual tracks, and not so much as a glimpse of the creature that might have made those he saw. Was he wrong? Had Terri's scream been faked? Was it all part of some game Wes and Scott were playing?

Thinking of Wes brought Leslie to mind. Why had she deliberately turned him on? What was she trying to prove? She was supposed to be Wes's babe, yet she acted as if she had the hots for him. Should he follow through and see if she was serious?

Jay grinned. Sure, the thought of poking her got him excited but he was risking romantic suicide if he did it. And how could he even entertain the notion of losing Stacy when she meant so much to him? He glanced over his shoulder at the two of them, now walking quietly side-by-side, and drank in the beauty of their lovely bodies. Both of them smiled.

Fifteen minutes later Jay entered a room where the ceiling glowed dimly. There were two exits, a narrow tunnel on the right and another passage across the way. He clicked off the flashlight and leaned against a stalagmite. "How about a short break?"

Leslie nodded and brushed her bangs out of her eyes.

"I need to weewee," Stacy announced. "Which tunnel aren't we taking?"

Jay pointed at the passage on the opposite side of the room. "We'll leave that way."

"Fine, Stacy said. "Give me a minute." She hurried into the narrow tunnel without looking back.

Here was the perfect chance for Jay to learn whether

Leslie wanted him or not. But he hesitated to make the first move, fearful of being seen by Stacy. He gazed at Leslie, who smirked and reached up to cup her breast.

"Did you like it?" she whispered. "If you did, there's more where that came from."

He was in front of her in two strides, his big hands covering her globes and squeezing as his lips locked on hers and his tongue darted into her mouth. He felt her hand slide between their bodies and stroke his pole. Burning with desire, he lowered his left hand to the junction of her smooth thighs and rubbed his forefinger against her crack. She squirmed and cooed, her tongue deliciously sweet as she kissed him. It took all of his self-control not to rip her blouse and pants off right then and there. As it was he had to force himself to push her back. Then he quickly stepped a few feet away and tried to recover his composure before his woman returned.

Not five seconds elapsed before Stacy did, grinning and asking, "Anyone else have to use the facilities?"

"I'm fine," Jay said, shrugging out of the backpack. "What do you say to some food and some brew?"

"I'm thirsty enough to drink a river," Leslie answered, her hips swaying slightly as she gave him a meaningful stare.

Jay swiftly opened the pack, hoping Stacy hadn't noticed. He pulled out the six-pack and gave each of them a can, then popped another and gulped the tangy beer greedily, trying to quench the fire in his loins. Damn, that girl could kiss! And there was no doubt she was warm for his form. All he had to do was think of a way to be alone with her. Suddenly a hand fell on his wrist and he inadvertently jumped, spilling beer on himself as he hastily lowered the can.

Beside him Stacy broke into laughter. "Jesus, lighten up, honeybuns. You're wound up as tight as can be."

"Sorry. I didn't know who it was," Jay blurted, and immediately regretted his rashness.

"Who else would it be?" Stacy asked suspiciously.

"No one," Jay said, taking another swallow so she couldn't see his eyes. That was too close for comfort. He had to be careful from now on and not say or do anything that would give Stacy the slightest cause to suspect he was hot for Leslie. If he played his cards right he could have his cake and eat it too, as the old saying went.

Stacy grabbed a box of cheese crackers from the backpack and took out a handful. "Anyone else want some?"

"I do," Leslie said, sashaying up. She made a point of smiling at Jay the whole time.

What the hell was she trying to do? Jay wondered in a panic. If Leslie kept it up, Stacy would figure out what was going on. Fortunately Leslie turned away and stared at the ceiling.

"Any idea what makes it glow like that?"

"Beats me," Stacy said. "It's pretty, though."

"I bet Einstein would know," Jay said. "He's the only guy I know of who gets straight A's in every stinking class. Can you believe it? Every stinking class. I wish I had his smarts."

"You'll do fine with the brains you have if you don't overreach your limits," Stacy said.

Jay nodded although he had no idea what she meant. He took the cracker box from her and jammed a half dozen into his mouth at once.

"Maybe we should go easy on the food for now," Stacy said. "We might need it later on."

Leslie turned. "I have no idea how close we are to

surface. Do either of you?"

All Jay could do was shake his head while chomping on the crackers. He carefully avoided looking at Leslie and let his gaze wander around the room. By chance he glanced down at the cave floor and beheld a sight that turned him into a block of ice, his mouth hanging open in the act of chewing. His pulse rate speeded up. It couldn't be! But there, etched in the dust, was one of the monstrous footprints complete with the three odd toes.

"What are you ... ?" Stacy began, and looked at the ground. A sharp intake of breath signified she saw the track.

Jay spotted others, some partially smudged by their own prints. He closed his mouth and gulped, then began a systematic sweep of the floor. He found other tracks. Human tracks. They told him that someone else had recently been through this very room, perhaps one of their friends. The size shape indicated it had been Scott, West or Corey. Not Terri. Whoever, the tracks were as clear as those of the creature.

"Son of a bitch!" Leslie exclaimed after studying the line of impressions. "What made those huge tracks? A bear?

"No bear has three toes," Stacy said.

"How would you know?" Leslie said.

"I watch the Discovery Channel."

"Stacy is right," Jay confirmed to forestall another argument. "These tracks weren't made by a bear. And they're the same kind as the ones I saw earlier."

Both girls swung toward him.

"Whoa, there," Leslie said. "What tracks did you see? You never told us about them."

"Yeah," Stacy said. "Spill the beans, lover."

Cursing his stupidity, Jay recounted how he found

similar tracks when he went after Terri. "I didn't say anything at the time because I didn't want to worry you."

"Who's worried?" Leslie said. "I don't care what you guys think. It has to be a bear. There are no other animals in Colorado that leave tracks this size."

"Then why are there only three toes?" Stacy said.

"Maybe some of its toes didn't show up clearly," Leslie answered. "Who knows?" She beamed at Jay. "And even if it is a bear, we don't have anything to worry about with your boyfriend here. He can handle anything that comes along."

"Really?" Stacy said, her voice dripping acid.

"Bear or not," Jay said hastily, "I don't want to run into the thing. We don't have any weapons."

"So?" Leslie said. "Nine times out of ten bears run from people they encounter. My dad told me that.

"What if this is the tenth time?" Stacy said.

"We should be more concerned about whoever is ahead of us," Jay said. "I think we should try and catch up." He ascertained that whoever it was had entered the same narrow tunnel where Stacy heeded nature's call.

"Forget it. I'm not going in there," Leslie said. "It'll probably take us back in the direction we came from. And what if we run into the bear? No, let's keep going like we are so we can get out of this damn cave that much sooner."

Stacy touched one of the sneaker prints with her toe. "What if this was Wes?"

"I doubt it," Leslie said. "He's with Scott and that dork, Fleming. I don't think he'd be traipsing around by his lonesome" She muttered something, then said, "Hell, for all we know, there might even be someone else in the cavern."

Jay didn't believe that for a second but he held his

tongue. More arguing would waste precious time. His main concern was getting the girls to safety, and with that in mind he hurriedly removed the hammer and chisel and marked the tunnel they were about to take as quickly as he could.

"What's the big rush?" Leslie asked with a snicker. "Afraid the bogeyman will get us?"

Ignoring her, Jay replaced the tools and resumed their trek, switching on the flashlight once they were in the murky passageway.

Damn, he was hungry. The crackers had barely whetted his appetite. He longed for a nice, thick, juicy steak with all the trimmings, his favorite meal in all the world. He imagined a simmering platter, the steak heaped high with succulent mushrooms, beside it a baked potato smothered in butter. His mouth watered, and he felt an ache in the pit of his stomach. Another hour or so and he'd be tempted to rip open the backpack and devour every last bit of food they had left.

The tunnel, as was typical, pursued a sinuous course.

Jay occasionally trained his beam on the tracks in the dust.

Long minutes of steady hiking brought them to a fork. He halted, scanned the ground, and saw the strange tracks going into the right-hand passage. "We'll go up this one," he announced, taking the other branch before anyone could object.

They covered a hundred yards in silence.

"Is it me or is the flashlight getting weaker?" Stacy asked as they crossed a wide room where the roof was covered with thin stalactites.

"It is a bit" Jay conceded.

"We'd better find the entrance before it goes out

completely."

"Don't I know it," Jay said, bothered by the idea of being lost in the dark with the thing that made those three-toed tracks. Consequently he picked up speed, moving as rapidly as the girls could comfortably manage, his long legs effortlessly eating up the distance.

The tunnel floor elevated upward by gradual degrees, inspiring him to hope they were finally on the right track. His hopes were dashed, however, when before too long the tunnel widened and they found themselves on the rim of a precipice over a hundred feet in height.

He pointed the flashlight at the bottom, then stiffened on hearing a bizarre noise to their rear, a noise similar to one he'd heard a year or so ago when he had been out hiking with his dad and had nearly stepped on a snake sunning itself on a flat rock.

It was like the buzzing of a rattlesnake's tail.

Chapter 15

Scott is dead! *Scott is dead*!

Those words echoed over and over in Wesley Eagen's head as he raced pell-mell down a tunnel, oblivious to his surroundings, aware only of the raw fear dominating his being. His legs churned, his arms pumped, and the twin flashlights moved up and down with the rhythm of his movements, casting eerie shadows on the walls.

He had been running for over five minutes. His chest ached abominably. Still he forged on, panic-stricken that he would share the same terrible fate as his best friend.

What had done it?

What had killed Scott?

He couldn't conceive of any animal capable of ripping a man's head from his shoulders except a bear, and there were no bears in the Caverna del Diablo, so far as anyone knew. Were mountain lions capable of such an atrocious feat? He recalled reading about a jogger slain by a cougar only a month before, but in that instance the big cat had leaped on the unfortunate man from behind and snapped the jogger's neck with a single swipe of its powerful paw. The man hadn't been decapitated.

Wes came to a curve and halted to catch his breath, leaning on the wall for support. Beads of perspiration trickled down his brow. His shirt was clammy and stuck to his sides. Shifting, he aimed both flashlights back down the tunnel but saw nothing in pursuit. Evidently the animal had been too busy consuming Scott to bother giving chase.

Wesley slumped, his mind awhirl, everything catching up with him at once. What with the coke and the beer and now the grisly death of Scott, he could scarcely form a coherent train of thought. Get a hold on yourself! he mentally thundered. The lark to the cave had become a matter of literal life and death, and he needed to get himself under control.

He must devote all his energies to escaping from the cavern. Finding the others was out of the question. They would have to fend for themselves. Even Les. He frowned, thinking of her torn to pieces and being feasted on by some unknown beast, and then he shrugged. She was practically a grown woman and could take care of herself.

He had to look out for number one.

In a certain respect he was lucky. The thing had jumped Scott first, so now he knew they were in danger and wouldn't blunder into another attack. He also had three flashlights. His own, Scott's, and Fleming's in his backpack. So he need not worry about being in the dark when one failed. Too bad he didn't have the spare batteries too. Who did? he wondered, and suddenly cursed aloud.

He'd forgotten all about Scott's backpack. In his haste to flee he had left it lying back there on the tunnel floor. Maybe the batteries were in it. He debated whether to go back and rated the idea as insane. The beast was back there.

A few batteries weren't worth his life.

Wes hastened along the passage. He switched off the flashlight in his left hand but held it ready for instant use. Bright lights often scared off or confused animals, which was why it was illegal to hunt game at night using spotlights. All a hunter had to do was shine a light on a buck or doe and the dumb animal would stand there and stare at the glare, hypnotized in a sense, giving the hunter plenty of time to aim and put a bullet in its brain. He knew the technique well because he had hunted illegally a number of times.

There was no harm in the practice that he could see. Colorado had an abundance of mule deer. A buck or doe less wouldn't make any difference come rutting season.

Wes had a thought that made him chuckle. Scott's coke was in the backpack he'd left behind. What would happen if the animal got into the pack and inhaled some of the blow? He imagined a wasted bear or cougar bumbling around the cave, bumping into walls and staggering all over the place.

The passage wound haphazardly. No forks appeared.

He was beginning to think he had made a mistake and would wind up at a dead end when he emerged into an enormous chamber much like the one in which they had eaten in earlier. He headed for the far side, seeking an exit, and was halfway across before it dawned on him that there was only the one way in and out.

Perturbed, he pivoted and began to retrace his steps. But he had only taken a couple when from out in the tunnel there issued the nerve-jangling rattle he had heard just prior to Scott's death.

The animal was following him!

Instantly Wes turned off the flashlight and dived behind a rock formation. He huddled against it, shivering as if from intense cold.

The rattling grew louder.

Suddenly the creature was in the chamber. Footfalls heralded its arrival, as did heavy, raspy breathing.

Wes quaked in fear. His heart was doing a tango in his chest. He tried willing it to stop, without success. He wondered if the beast could sniff him out even if he stayed still.

The footsteps ceased. But Wes didn't know if that meant the creature was standing and listening or whether it was creeping toward him.

His every nerve was on fire.

The seconds were like hours, each unending unto itself, stretching his self-discipline to its limits.

Was that a footstep?

A tremendous urge to relieve his bladder flooded through him. Wes almost wet his jeans. He touched his forehead to the stone, fervently wishing this was a dream and he would wake up safe in his bed. He would phone Scott and tell him to forget about going to the Caverna del Diablo, and he would never, ever, go near the stinking place as long as he lived.

A hand fell on his shoulder.

Wes cried out and leaped erect, spinning as he did to see the outline of an enormous creature that towered over him like a mammoth grizzly. His reaction was automatic. He extended both arms and switched on both flashlights.

Caught full in the glare was the living embodiment of the being painted at the entrance to the cave, a monster with reddish skin and a long forked tail that waved in the air like a cobra. Its eyes blazed with fire. Amazingly, great, ponderous breasts bulged high on its chest, breasts every inch as naked as the rest of the creature's body.

All this Wes observed the moment his twin beams struck the thing.

It recoiled, hissing like hundreds of vipers, and back-pedaled while covering its eyes with its hands.

In a flash of insight Wes comprehended the reason. The thing couldn't endure bright light! He fixed both beams on its face and cackled crazily when it whirled and raced behind a large boulder.

Wes got out of there. He backed away, keeping both flashlight beams on the creature's hiding place so it couldn't give chase. His confidence grew with every step. Whatever the hell that thing was, he could keep it at bay until he reached the surface provided he did so before his flashlights went dead.

At the tunnel he paused. The creature still hadn't shown itself.

Grinning, Wes spun and sped off, repeatedly glancing back to see if it came after him. It didn't. His fear drained from him like water from a sink, leaving him rejuvenated and brimming with newfound courage. If he kept his head he would survive. He would win just as he always did. Well, almost always. Not that he could fault himself for his loss to Cory Fleming. That had been a one in a million fluke.

Wes suddenly realized the dork might run into the same creature, and laughed. If that happened, Fleming was as good as dead.

The big brain didn't have a flashlight.

"Catch it!" Ann shouted.

"Too late," Cory said, frowning up into the enshrouding blackness. The rope was gone. He should have held onto it and pulled it off the stalagmite the moment she touched the ground.

"Who would do such a thing?" Ann said.

"Not who. *What.*" Cory corrected her. "If it was Wes or Scott they'd be laughing their fool heads off and insulting us for being such idiots."

“You think one of those things is responsible?”

“I'd bet my life on it."

They both fell silent and heard scraping, followed by a

loud hiss.

"Dear God!" Ann gasped. "What if it comes down after us? How will we fight it?"

"We won't even try. We'll run," Cory said. He noticed the match was about burn to within a fraction of his fingers. "Quick. Light another match before this one goes out. It can probably see better than us in the dark and we don't want to be taken by surprise."

Ann grabbed the box and fumbled awkwardly because of her injured fingers before she got one lit.

"Now back into the tunnel," Cory directed. "Take it slow and cup your hand around the match."

He waited until she was in motion, then followed, prepared to defend her with his life if the creature should jump down to attack them. Having seen the thing close up he had no illusions about its capabilities. Such a massive brute, layered thick with muscle, would possess remarkable strength and agility. He would be no match for it in a physical confrontation. Somehow, he must rely on his intellect to prevail, which was easier said than done.

"What now?" Ann asked, stopping a few yards into the passage. "The match is almost out."

"We run," Cory said.

Grabbing her left wrist, he fled into the depths. They ran side-by-side, their shoulders brushing, pacing themselves so they could cover more distance.

"Will it come after us?" Ann wondered at one point.

"Probably."

"What will we do?"

"I'm open to ideas," Cory said.

None were forthcoming. They were both in the same boat. Lacking knowledge of the creature's weaknesses, if any, they had no insights into how to defeat the thing, if that was at all possible.

Cory had to give it credit for pulling the rope up. Clearly, it was smarter than he'd given it credit for being. How smart, though? Did it, say, have an intelligence comparable to a dog's? A chimpanzee's? Or a human's? The difference might mean everything to their chances of survival.

Another chilling possibility hit him. What if the creature was *more* intelligent than they were? If it was a demon, as he'd surmised, then it might be able to outthink them as easily as they could outthink a small child. Demons were notoriously devious and cruel. If the creature did indeed fit that profile, then the thing might be toying with them. Perhaps it knew they were hopelessly lost and was letting them tire themselves out before moving in for the kill. He mustn't make the mistake of underestimating it.

"My hands are bleeding again," Ann mentioned.

"When we can stop I'll see what I can do," Cory said.

Bit by bit the tunnel walls closed in on them, giving Cory the impression they were speeding through solid earth. He noted with dismay the the floor was tilting down, which made it unlikely they were nearing the entrance.

"We're going deeper," Ann said, a tremor in her voice.

"I know. Chin up. We'll make it out yet."

"Thank you, Cory."

"For what?" he asked in surprise.

"For being you."

Now what was that supposed to mean? Cory wondered, and felt her other hand close on his wrist and squeeze. Was there deeper significance to her comment? He didn't know what to think. One minute she intimated she truly cared for him. The next, she treated him as she would any close friend. Was she sending mixed signals, or was he simply making an emotional mountain out of her clear-cut actions and words? Perhaps he saw hidden meanings where there were none because he wanted to see them. He wanted her to like him. Hell, he wanted her to love him. Maybe wishful thinking had tainted his perspective.

They passed through a series of rooms. After four in a row Cory drew to a halt just inside the next passage.

"We'll rest for a bit."

"Do you think it's safe to stop?" Ann asked, staring back.

"Maybe not. But we won't do ourselves any good if we're too exhausted to put up much of a fight."

Cory was shocked when she unexpectedly leaned on him and rested her cheek on his chest.

"This might seem cruel to say but I'm glad you're here," Ann said softly. "Without your help Id be lying back in that fissure, easy prey for the creature."

"I haven't done much," Cory said.

"You 're too modest," Ann said, and kissed him on the chin.

Cory felt warm all over. There she was, doing it again! Was the kiss just a friendly act, or was she expressing deeper feelings? How was a guy to know how to react to a girl when females were so confusing? Maybe he should ask his dad. After twenty-one years of marriage his father must understand women thoroughly.

"Why don't you hand over the backpack?" he suggested.

"I don't mind wearing it," Ann said. "Without the rope it's not very heavy."

"Humor me," Cory said, not wanting to burden her. If the demon closed in, she would need all the speed she could muster.

"Such a gentleman. All right, my knight errant." Ann stood back and wriggled out of the straps. "It's all yours."

He grabbed the backpack and was about to slip it over

his right arm when he spied an unusual object less than a yard away on the floor of the room.

Either his eyes were deceiving him in the near total darkness or the object had the aspect of metal rather than rock. It was also of much lighter color than any of the nearby formations.

"Give me the matches," Cory said,.

Striking one, he lowered it toward the object. He'd found another Spanish-style helmet.

"What is that?" Ann asked.

"If my guess is right, this once belonged to a conquistador," Cory replied. He lifted the helmet in his left hand. The crown had been dented, as if from a powerful blow, and the bottom bore scratch marks. "I saw others like this one at the same spot where I saw the bones I told you about."

"What's that under it?"

Cory looked and was discovered a piece of wood the thickness of his wrist, and maybe six inches long. One end had been charred, convincing him the piece was all that remained of a torch the conquistador had brought into the cavern. Ordinarily the passage of so much time would have reduced the wood to dust, but lying deep in the cave where it had been sheltered from the elements, and being further protected by the helmet, had enabled the piece to remain intact. Gingerly, he touched it, afraid it would crumple at the slightest pressure. The wood was dry but he could hold the end that wasn't charred in his hand without the wood breaking apart.

"Should we try to light it?" Ann said.

"Not yet," Cory said. "We may need it later." He gave the piece to her. "Would you put it in the backpack for now?"

"Gladly, sir," Ann said, stepping behind him.

He heard the zipper being worked, and she said, "Ouch."

"Are you okay?"

"I made the mistake of brushing a finger against the pack and scraped one of the cuts."

"Sorry. I should have done it."

"Don't be ridiculous. I'm not helpless."

Cory waited for her to finish. The match went out so he lit another, then turned. "Let me have a look at your hands again."

"I'm fine," Ann said. "They don't hurt nearly half as much."

"Let me see," Cory insisted, taking her left hand in his.

All of her fingers were caked with a fine layer of dust. Dried blood covered those that had been torn open. Only a middle finger showed signs of swelling.

As yet there was no infection, but the risk was very real if she didn't wash her hands soon and apply antiseptic to kill any germs. Her right hand was in much the same shape.

"Will I live?" Ann joked.

"You'd better," Cory said. "I've gotten used to your company." He gazed fondly into her eyes, girding himself to tell her how he truly felt, when the second match hissed out and they were again embraced by darkness.

"Maybe we should haul butt," Ann said. That thing might be after us."

"Let's go," Cory said. His foot bumped the helmet and he paused. If the demon did catch them he would need a weapon. So far all he had seen were rock, which would probably have as much effect as throwing stones at a tank. Or he could use the helmet to bash it senseless. It was heavy and the top came to a point. He wedged the box of matches into his pocket, then bent and grabbed the ancient headpiece.

"You're bringing that with us?"

Cory explained while taking her wrist and resuming their flight. "Keep your eyes peeled for anything else we can use. I'm not letting that thing get us without a fight."

"My hero," Ann said, but there was no sarcasm in her voice. "And to think I wouldn't give you the time of day for such a long time. You've always treated me with kindness and respect, Cory, which is more than I can say about some guys I've known."

"Ann, there's something I'd like to say," Cory said, glad he wasn't facing her or he might not have the nerve. "I should have said it long ago. It's about--."'

"It's about what happened in the shed," Ann said, cutting him off. "You know, I've been thinking about that a lot lately. I was so young. We both were. And young girls are taught by their mothers to never, ever let a boy touch them where you touched me."

"But I didn't---," Cory began, and again she interrupted.

"You didn't mean to do it," Ann said. "I know that now. Back then I thought you were being indecent, even sinful. I thought you had done the worst thing a boy could do to a girl, and I felt deeply hurt and betrayed because I liked you and trusted you." She paused. "Now I see the incident in a whole new light. Neither of us knew anything about sex. You were as ignorant as I was of the human body. We were two dumb kids playing doctor, and your touching me was an accident."

"Exactly," Cory said, flooded with relief. They had finally gotten the mess out in the open. And, wonder of wonders, she saw his side at last! He felt positively giddy.

"I'm sorry it took me so long to realize you weren't the worst lecher in the Western Hemisphere."

Cory laughed. "Better late than never."

"So we can be close friends again?"

"Whatever you want," Cory replied, although he would rather have confessed he wanted to be much more to her than a bosom buddy.

"Good. No matter what happens next, at least we've cleared the air. We can start over again."

"I'm glad---!' Cory started to say, and was cut off once again. But this time Ann wasn't responsible.

This time he stopped because of a sound coming from somewhere behind them, a thumping sound as if someone was beating on the cave wall. He heard Ann's intake of breath and felt his own skin crawl.

"It's the creature!"

Chapter 16

"What the hell is that?" Leslie Vanderhorst said, spinning so fast she nearly tripped over her own feet and caused dust to sprinkle over the edge of the precipice.

Jay also spun. He trained the flashlight along the tunnel but saw nothing. Right away he thought of the strange tracks and wondered if the thing that made them was also making the rattling noise

"Should we go see?" Stacy said.

"I'd rather not," Jay said.

"Why?" Leslie said. She had recovered her composure and took a step. "It might be Wes or Scott playing one of their tricks."

"I don't think it is," Jay said.

"If you're scared I'll go by myself," Leslie stated and nonchalantly began to walk off.

"No!" Jay exclaimed, grabbing her arm, his gut instinct telling him there was more to the situation than their dipstick friends indulging in a childish prank. "We should stick together until we're out of this damn cave. If we become separated we might never find each other."

"Don't have a cow," Leslie said. "I'm only going down the tunnel a short way. I'll be fine."

"We'll go together," Jay said, stepping in front of her before he let go because he suspected she might try to run on ahead. He advanced cautiously, his flashlight fixed on a bend in the passage. Where previously the beam would have lit up the whole stretch of tunnel, now the bend was barely discernible.

"Those tracks have turned you into a worrywart," Leslie remarked.

Jay glanced at Stacy, who hadn't uttered a word and seemed oddly distracted, then at the bend. What he wouldn't give to have his dad's .357 Magnum or shotgun right at that moment! He hefted the flashlight, pondering whether to use it as a club if his instincts were proven right.

The rattling stopped.

"It's got to be those two clowns," Leslie said. "This is just their style."

Jay didn't bother to comment. He stayed close to the wall until he was only a few feet from the bend, then he boldly dashed forward and swept the flashlight around the corner.

The next section of passage was empty but this time there was proof his hunch had been on target, for mixed in the dust among the tracks they had left were more of the three-toed variety.

"There's no one here," he said, and tried to draw back away before the girls could see.

"Look!" Stacy said, pointing. "That animal has been following us."

"Well, what do you know?" Leslie said, stepping over to study the impressions. She thoughtfully stroked her chin, then grinned. "The two of you were right. I now seriously doubt these were made by a bear."

"You do?" Stacy said.

"Yep. I'm convinced Wes and Scott are to blame."

"For crying out loud," Jay said.

"Hear me out," Leslie said. "You've both seen those phony Bigfoot feet sold in stores, haven't you? The kind you can put on to run around in the woods and leave a bunch of tracks so folks will think a real Bigfoot did it?"

"I've seen them," Jay said.

"Well, the way I see it, Wes and Scott got hold of a pair and modified them to look like the tracks we have here. All they'd have to do is cut off a couple of toes and presto, instant alien monster feet."

Despite himself, Jay had to concede the idea made more sense than there being an unknown animal roaming the tunnels of the Caverna del Diablo. And the stunt was typical of ones Wes and Scott had previously pulled. He felt mildly foolish for not having come up with the explanation himself.

"Could be," Stacy said, but the way she did implied she wasn't completely convinced.

"You should have let me run on ahead," Leslie told Jay. "By now I'd be giving my Wes a piece of my mind."

"If it is them why didn't they stick around?" Stacy asked. "They've carried this game far enough."

"Those two space cadets never know when to quit," Leslie said. "They'll keep this up until we catch them in the act or they become bored."

"How did they make the rattling sounds?" Stacy queried.

"Maybe they bought a rattlesnake tail or killed a rattler to get it," Leslie speculated. "I wouldn't put anything past those two."

For the first time since Terri had vanished, Jay relaxed a little. Leslie had a logical answer for everything. Although he was still annoyed that Wes and Scott hadn't taken him into their confidence, he grudgingly admired them for their clever scheme. It was no wonder those two guys were the life of every party.

"Let's try to catch those clowns," Leslie proposed. Turning, she raced down the tunnel, beckoning for them to follow.

"Wait!" Jay shouted,. knowing full well she wouldn't. Sighing, he glanced at Stacy and together they jogged after her.

Leslie was running flat out.

"Be careful!" Jay called. "You might hurt yourself."

Already Leslie was near the limit of the flashlight's illumination and about to turn another bend.

"What an airhead," Stacy said.

Jay saw Leslie reach the corner.

She suddenly skidded to a stop and gaped at something beyond. Staggering back, she pressed her hands to her face and cringed in fear.

"What's this bogus?" Stacy said. "Is she playing games with us now?"

"Les?" Jay said. He reached the bend several strides ahead of Stacy. Glancing down the passage, bringing the flashlight to bear, he was mystified to see only the walls and ceiling until his gaze dropped to the ground within inches of his toes.

Pure horror seized him at the sight of a severed human hand lying palm up. The fingers were formed into claws, the flesh grimy and discolored with strips of skin dangling from the bottom.

"Son of a bitch!" Jay blurted, and felt Stacy's hand close on his arm.

"Is it real?"

"Looks that way," Jay said, stooping and lowering the flashlight.

The long fingernails were painted red, the fingers pudgy and pale. On the ring finger was a thin golden ring with a red stone in the setting

"Oh, God!" Stacy whispered. "It's one of Terri's hands!

I recognize the ring she was wearing."

"Are you sure?" Jay said absently, so shocked he could barely think.

"Of course I'm sure!" Stacy gasped. "That's her birthstone, a ruby. Her mother gave that ring to her for her last birthday."

Leslie picked that moment to burst into tears. "No, no, no!" she said over and over again.

"Hell!" Jay exclaimed. He backed away, pulling Stacy with him, the two of then gazing apprehensively along the tunnel.

"Whatever did that will come back," Stacy predicted.

"We don't want to be here when it does," Jay said. Facing Les, he put a hand on her shoulder. "Listen, we have to get the out of here. Shape up and move your butt."

Stuttering and blubbering, Leslie seemed to be trying to melt into the wall to escape the horrid sight.

"Come on!" Jay said, shaking her roughly, with no result. He lifted his hand, on the verge of slapping her to bring her around, when she dabbed at her eyes, coughed and croaked a question.

"Where can we go that will be safe?"

"Anywhere," Jay said. "Just so we stay on the move and don't give whatever killed Terri a chance to get us."

Grasping her wrist, Jay hauled her after him as he retraced their steps to the precipice. Stacy stayed glued to his other side. Once on the rim he swept the light over the sheer rock face again, seeking a means to the bottom. They didn't dare go back the other way. The thing might be waiting for them.

"There!" Stacy cried, pointing to their right. "What's that?"

He swiveled and spied a narrow ledge or shelf that ran

diagonally from the top to the bottom. It couldn't be more than eleven or twelve inches wide. A misstep from that height would cost them their life. "We'll use that only as a last resort," he said, and moved along the rim to find an alternate route. A complete sweep turned up none.

"Listen," Stacy said.

Far off arose a faint rattling.

"It's coming for us!" Leslie whined, beginning to tremble.

"Then we won't be here when it arrives," Jay said, stepping to the spot where the ledge jutted from the cliff. "Who wants to go first?"

"Down there?" Leslie responded, recoiling in terror. "You must be nuts. None of us will make it."

"We all will," Jay sid, snatching her arm. She fought him, trying to pull free, but he held fast.

"Maybe you should take the lead, honeybuns," Stacy proposed. "We'll put her between us so we can stop her if she starts to fall."

The suggestion was sound but Jay hesitated. He preferred to have Stacy close to him where he could grab her if she should slip. With Leslie between them he might not be able to come to her rescue in time.

"Well?" Stacy prompted as the rattling became louder.

"All right," Jay reluctantly said, and eased onto the ledge. When Leslie pulled back he glared at her. "Do that once more and I'll throw you over the side. You need to get a grip, Les, until we're at the bottom. Mess up now and we all could die. Understand?"

Her lips trembling, her eyes rimmed with ears, Leslie nodded and gulped. "I'll do my best."

Jay released her. Keeping his back to the cliff, the flashlight in his right hand and aimed back up the ledge, he used short steps to descend until his head was below the rim. Then he stopped and waited for Leslie. She balked until prodded by Stacy, but once she started she came down quickly and and nearly knocked him off his perch when she clutched at his shirt. "Take it easy, girl," he chided. "Unless you're fixing to scrape me up with a spatula after I hit the ground."

"Sorry."

Jay waited tensely while Stacy edged down. He admired the way she held her head up and refused to stare out over the abyss. Looking down from high elevations sometimes made a person dizzy. He kept his own gaze on the girls as he continued to descend, his heels scraping the wall with each sideways step.

The rattling, he realized, had stopped.

An ordeal of grueling proportions ensued. They moved at a snail's pace, their shoe§ shuffling slowly, their backbones as straight as broomsticks, no one venturing to utter a word or so much as sneeze.

After a while it seemed to Jay as if he were suspended in a great void. On all sides, and above and below, lay a mantle of impenetrable darkness broken only by the slowly dying beam of his flashlight. They were in an alien world where sunshine was unheard of and gloom prevailed. His sole contacts with reality were his shoulder blades and his heels; if not for them touching the stone, he would have sworn he was a balloon drifting slowly to the ground, detached from all earthly ties.

"How much farther?" Leslie asked.

"I don't know and I'm not looking to find out," Jay said. "Just keep going." He tilted his head to verify Stacy was still with them before snaking lower. "How are you holding up, babe?"

"Just peachy."

He lost track of time.

Instead of uselessly trying to guess how far they had gone, he concentrated on every movement, making them precise.

He half-expected Leslie to give them trouble but she didn't once complain. Maybe the thought of what was after them had had a sobering effect.

When at long, long last, Jay sensed they were almost to the bottom, he glanced down and saw the floor less than a yard below. Grinning, he jumped and pivoted to survey the rim.

If the thing was up there it was hiding.

"I never want to do something like that again," Stacy said as she stepped off the ledge. "My heart was in my mouth from beginning to end."

"How are you?" Jay asked Leslie.

"Better," she replied, biting her lower lip. "I'm sorry about the way I behaved when I saw the hand. It just blew me away, you know? You guys were right on the mark. There is some kind of animal in this rotten cave, and it wants to kill us."

"It won't if I can help it," Jay pledged. He turned the flashlight on the chamber, discovering the usual stalagmites, stalactites and assorted outlandish formations. Twenty yards off was a tunnel. "Keep your fingers crossed that we find a way to the surface."

The passage was wide and smooth, barren of tracks.

"The thing hasn't ever been here," Stacy said. "Maybe it's afraid to come down the cliff."

“I wouldn't count on that," Jay said. The creature must know the cavern like the back of its hand. It must be familiar with every passage, every tunnel, every room, chamber and dead end. It must know every shortcut, too, which meant it could get ahead of them and lie in wait at a convenient spot.

He must be on his guard every second from now on.

His immediate concern was the flashlight. If he was to judge by the strength of the beam, they would be lucky if there was an hour of battery power left. Hopelessly lost as they were, locating the entrance in sixty minutes would take a miracle.

He walked rapidly, aware the girls were pressed to keep up but anxious to put as much yardage behind them as they could. If he was wrong about the animal knowing shortcuts, by the time it climbed down the precipice they would be long gone.

They traversed a spacious room and another length of tunnel, then reached a second room where the walls cast a pale radiance.

"We'll rest for a couple of minutes," Jay said.

"I could use another beer," Leslie said.

"Sorry, not yet. I know you, remember? Two beers can make you ditzy as a loon, and you'd best stay straight until we're in the clear."

"If we ever are."

Jay walked over to Stacy, draped his brawny arm across her shoulders, and kissed her on the neck. "Sorry I dragged you along and got you into this damn mess. I should have told Scott and Wes to take a flying leap and stayed home to cuddle with you in front of the tube."

"Don't blame yourself, lover. We both figured spending Halloween at the Caverna del Diablo would be a blast. We were looking forward to going monster hunting," Stacy added bitterly.

"The monster!" Leslie cried, clapping her hands. "That's it! That's what killed Terri and what is after us! The famous monster, the red thing painted up top by those Spaniards or whoever. Not some stupid animal! It all makes sense now." The whites of her eyes resembled saucers. "Don't you see? It's Halloween, when all the spooks and goblins and demons are supposed to come out and roam the earth. It's the night of witches and werewolves and ghosts, the night of the walking dead." She cowered against a stalagmite. "We're goners! We're all goners!"

"You're losing it again," Jay warned. He slid his arm off Stacy and stepped in front of Les. "Listen to me. That monster jive is a bunch of crap."

"Are you blind? What else could have killed Terri?" Leslie replied, then suddenly placed a hand on her forehead. "Oh, no! What if it got Wes and Scott? Or Ann?"

"Or Cory," Stacy said.

Jay glanced at her. "Don't tell me you believe this garbage? There are no such things as monsters."

"You saw the tracks. You saw the hand. And you know there are no wild animals down this deep. As much as I hate to admit it, yeah, honeybuns, I think Les is right."

"You've both flipped."

"I'm worried," Stacy said.

Jay chewed on his lower lip, trying to sort everything out. Why was he resisting the idea so much? He could tell Stacy was sincerely scared, which impressed him more than the tracks and the severed hand combined. During the year and a half they had been dating, he'd never known her to show any fear whatsoever. Not even when they were drag racing, hurtling down a road at over 100 miles an hour. Not when they went cliff climbing, as they did a few times each summer. Not even when her old man had caught them necking heavy in her bedroom one night. She was always cool and collected--- until now.

Okay. He would assume the girls were right, that the legendary monster of the Caverna del Diablo was real and somehow alive and stalking them. What should he do? Running aimlessly was pointless. They had to find a way out, but in the meantime they must be able to protect themselves in case the monster attacked. He stripped off the backpack, removed the rock hammer and grinned. "If that thing shows up I'll bash it's head in." Putting on the pack, he rose. "Let's go."

Jay exited the room, Stacy right behind him, Leslie sticking close to her. The narrow passage twisted this way and that. His flashlight became noticeably weaker, and he feared the battery would die much sooner than he had anticipated.

They reached a section of tunnel where the ceiling had partially collapsed, littering the floor with chunks of stone, small rocks and dirt. Their feet crunched underfoot, and they had to step carefully to avoid tripping. Ahead, past the debris, the passage narrowed even more to about the width of an average doorway.

Jay had the flashlight trained on the ground in front of him and was almost to the end of the clutter when he shifted to check on the girls.

It was then, out of the comer of his eye, that he saw a shape materialize in front of him.

Chapter 17

Cory Fleming and Ann Weatherby ran for their lives, They ran in mutual silence, enveloped in blackness, as the thumping grew fainter and fainter. Through two rooms they went and finally up an incline composed of loose earth that made traction difficult. At the top they stopped and looked back.

"I don't see anything," Ann whispered.

"Neither do I but it doesn't mean a thing," Cory replied, taking her wrist in his left hand. The heavy helmet in his right gave him little reassurance. Against a demon the size of the one he had seen, using it would be like swatting a buffalo with a handkerchief.

The tunnel was level for fifty yards then another incline led them upward. Out of nowhere a strong cool breeze whipped their hair.

"That feels good," Ann said softly.

"There must be a cleft in the ceiling," Cory said.

The inky darkness overhead made finding it impossible. He was encouraged by the fact the passage was leading them progressively higher, and he entertained the slim hope that they would come out somewhere near the entrance. He surveyed the tunnel ahead, aware of a subtle difference he couldn't pinpoint. Something didn't seem right, though.

"Do you---?" Cory went to ask, when the ground unexpectedly gave way under his feet and he fell, aware that Ann had fallen, too. Terror seized him at the thought of plunging into a virtually bottomless chasm or a deep fissure and having every bone in their bodies smashed to bits when they hit bottom.

"No!" Ann cried.

They abruptly contacted solid ground, a slope that threw them off-balance. Unable to check their momentum, they tumbled and rolled until they came to a stop side-by-side.

Cory was on his back, the piece of wood in the backpack gouging into his spine. He sat up, taking stock, and reached out to touch Ann. "Are you okay, gorgeous?"

"I think so," she said uncertainly, sitting up. "What the hell happened?"

"I'm not sure." Cory realized he was still holding the conquistador helmet. Releasing it, he extracted the box of matches from his pocket and hastily lit one, then raised his arm on high to increase the radius of the glow.

They had inadvertently stumbled into a bowl-shaped pit. Twenty feet in diameter and less than ten feet deep, the sides slanted up at an angle that would allow for an easy climb out.

"We were lucky," Ann said.

Nodding, Cory rose to his knees and looked behind him. His skin crawled on seeing a skull lying nearby. Other bones were scattered about. One, a thigh bone, was underneath him. It, not the piece of wood, had been gouging his spine. He quickly stood up.

Ann turned and gasped.

Tattered strips of clothing were mixed among the bones. A pair of boots lay a couple of yards away. To their right, partially buried by loose earth, was a wide leather strap of some sort. A hat, or what was left of it after the ravages of time had taken their toll, lay near the bag.

Cory lit a second match. He squatted to briefly examine

the skull and bones and found no evidence of scratch marks or teeth marks. Whoever this man had been, he apparently died of natural causes.

Cory moved to the leather strap and brushed off enough loose dirt to grip it and heave. To his amazement, out came a pair of saddlebags, still intact.

"This poor soul must have died a long time ago," Ann commented.

"Yeah," Cory said, depositing the saddlebags so he could unfasten a buckle securing one of the flaps. He unfastened the other buckle, then upended the twin pouches and let the contents cascade out.

The assortment was incredible. A pipe, a pack of tobacco, a bundle wrapped in buckskin, a large key, a pair of crumpled socks, five short steel bits, a flask containing a yellow liquid, a spare shirt, a six-inch knife in a leather sheath, and, wonder of wonders, a compass! He threw the saddlebags down and snatched up the compass. The needle quivered as he moved his arm, the colored tip swinging in endless circles, first clockwise, then counterclockwise. "It's broken," he remarked. "Or else the ferrous mineral content in the cave is so high that the needle can't get a fix on the North Magnetic Pole."

"Would it help us get out of here even if it did work?"

"It might," Cory said. "The cave entrance is supposed to be at the south end of the cavern. if we knew which direction was due south we could concentrate on the tunnels in that direction. One would eventually take us to the surface."

"What's this?" Ann asked, picking up the buckskin bundle. She unwrapped it in her lap, exposing a score of thin brown strips that gave off a sharp odor. "Yuck. What is this stuff?"

"Jerky," Cory said, putting down the compass to take a piece. The match flared out, forcing him to light another before he could hold the meat up to his nose and sniff. “Venison, if I don't miss my guess. From a mule deer, I bet. Crudely cut. I'd say our friend here packed in his own food supply."

"Is it edible?"

"There's only one way to find out," Cory said. He nibbled on an end. The meat tasted salty and slightly bitter but not rancid. "I think it is if you're not too squeamish. I've heard tell jerky will last forever under the right conditions."

Ann picked up a strip. "What if it makes us sick?"

"Don't eat one if you don't want to. We still have pretzels and chips left. We can save the jerky until we run out of them."

"Good idea, handsome."

Cory handed the jerky over for her to wrap, then glanced at her face. Had she just called him handsome? Him? Cory Fleming? The El Geeko Supremo of their high school? Was she repaying his compliment in referring to her as gorgeous? Or had she meant it? The last notion made him grin. No female in their right mind would seriously regard him as good-looking. He was the bookish type, the type other guys always threw sand on at the beach or shoved aside in the school hallway, the type who never, ever got the girl of his dreams. Yet there she was, a foot away, staring at him as if perplexed.

"What's that funny look?”

"I’ll tell you another time," Cory hedged. Picking up the knife, he unfastened his belt and strapped the leather sheath around his waist. The blade wasn't razor-sharp but it would suffice. At least he had a serviceable weapon.

Ann lifted the flask. "What do you think this stuff is?"

"Obviously our late friend took a nip now and then," Cory sai. Gripping the bottle, he unscrewed the top. A pungent odor wafted to his nostrils. He took a breath, then pressed the flask to his lips and sipped. Immediately, a burning sensation seared his mouth and travelled down his throat, causing him to double over and cough violently. His stomach was set on fire. For a few seconds he thought he might be sick but the sensation quickly subsided.

"Are you all right?" Ann asked, her hand on his shoulder.

"Fine," Cory rasped. "But you'd better do the driving when we head home." Chuckling, he capped the flask. "This stuff must be one hundred proof. Well take it with us."

"Are you planning to get drunk?"

"It might come in handy in other respects," Cory said but didn't elaborate. He removed the backpack and began stuffing in everything they had found, even the crumpled socks.

"You're taking all that junk?" Ann asked, sounding surprised.

"Everything. Look around and see if there's anything else." Cory was going to zip up the pack when he changed his mind and withdrew two of the steel bits. Each was six inches long and tapered to a point. He wedged them under his belt, one on either side of the buckle.

Ann was watching him "What are they?"

"Tools used by miners and prospectors. They're sharp enough to do some real damage at close quarters.

"This guy must have been a prospector then."

"Most likely," Cory said. Again his match went out and he struck another. "He probably came into the cavern to look for gold or silver."

"Think he dug this pit?"

"Maybe, but I suspect a section of the tunnel just buckled."

Cory bent to scour the bottom. The flame sputtered so he held his hand still. In the middle of the bones a metallic surface glittered. Curious, he leaned down and discovered a metal spike jutting from the earth. He used his left hand to scrape sufficient dirt aside to see the spike better. It was curved, thicker at the base than the top. The shape brought a certain implement to mind, and he suddenly began furiously scooping the dirt away, eager to learn if his deduction was correct. Shortly he had most of the head and part of the handle uncovered. Rising, he gripped the head in his left hand and pulled with all of his strength. Gradually the tool came free and he held it aloft, beaming like a kid who had just been given a new toy. "Look!" he exclaimed.

"What is it?"

"A pick. And it's in one piece!" Cory exulted. Now he had a real weapon. Between the pick and the knife he might be able to keep the demon at bay, if not even slay it. He noticed reddish rust on the tapered end and held the head closer to the match. "I wonder. . ." he mused aloud.

"About what?"

"I have an idea how this prospector died," Cory said, and wagged the pick. "I think he fell in here just like we did, and landed on his pick. The point punctured his chest, maybe perforating his heart or his lung."

Ann was ten feet off, stooped low. "Hey. Over here. I found something, too."

"What?" Cory asked, just as the match went out. He was growing tired of constantly striking new ones but did so one more time.

Ann was walking toward him, grinning. Clutched in her

hand was an antique lantern.

"Son of a gun!" Cory said in delight.

"Think it still works?"

"It all depends if there's any fuel left."

Cory set down the pick and grasped the lantern by its handle. He placed it between them, knelt, and raised the globe. "This is an old carbide lantern," he disclosed. "It used coal oil for fuel, which is just another name for kerosene."

The wick was dry but firm to the touch. Would it burn? Cory opened the tank and sniffed. The distinctive acrid aroma of kerosene was still strong. By poking a finger in the hole he learned the tank was half-full with a gummy substance that showed up as black on his fingertip when he pulled his finger out.

"No go?" Ann said.

"No," Cory said, then had an idea. "Get me that flask out of the pack, would you?" While he waited he tried to stir the substance with his finger.

"Here," Ann said, producing the whiskey.

"This may not work so don't get your hopes up," Cory told her, passing her the box of matches. She lit one.

Cory tilted the lantern, poured some of the alcohol into the tank, then closed the tank and swung the lantern back and forth to slosh the whiskey around. After a minute he added more alcohol, then gently shook the lantern until his arms were tired. Again he inserted a finger.

The whiskey was doing as he planned, mixing with what was left of the kerosene and liquefying the gummy substance. He kept adding small amounts and shaking the lantern until the fuel tank was two-thirds full. Then he coated his forefinger with the mixture and applied a layer to the wick.

Ann observed his every move intently. "I never would

have thought of this," she said. "You're a genius."

"It could be a waste of our time," Cory said, putting the lantern down. He wiped his fingers on his pants, then took the matchbox and anxiously lit a match. His fingers were shaking as he applied the flame to the wick and waited with bated breath. The wick sputtered and gave off black smoke but stubbornly refused to catch. He held the match there until the flame went out, then lit another.

"Please let it work," Ann prayed.

This time the wick crackled loudly and spewed off more black smoke, yet it still wouldn't light.

"Once more into the breach," Cory quipped, striking a third match. He crossed the fingers of his left hand, then pressed the burning tip hard against the wick. A puff of black smoke shrouded his face, making him cough and lower his chin to avoid inhaling more. He heard a squeal from Ann and looked up to see the wick glowing feebly.

"Catch, damn you!" Cory snapped, holding the match in place, not caring if it burned down to his fingers. The wick flared and stabilized and the smoke changed to a gray hue. Overjoyed, he tossed the match over his shoulder and lowered the glass globe.

A warm golden glow bathed the pair of them.

"You did it!" Ann exclaimed. Sliding around the lantern, she threw her arms around his neck.

Cory felt her breasts mash into his chest. They were nose to nose, her breath on his cheeks, when suddenly she pressed her lips on his and gave him the kind of kiss he had only read about in books and magazines, a passionate kiss where her supple tongue entwined with his while her fingers ran through his hair and her body flamed hotter than the lantern. Shocked, he nonetheless responded ardently, his manhood rising to the occasion. From within her came a low moan. When, at length, she broke the kiss and leaned back, there were tears in the comers of her eyes. He gaped, bewildered. "Did I do something wrong?"

"No," Ann said, looking away. She wiped the back of her hand across her eyes. "I'm the one who did. I shouldn't have done that."

"Why not?" Cory asked, grinning to show her no harm had been done. "I didn't mind."

"It wasn't fair to you."

"Me?"

"Here you are trying so hard to get us out of this nightmare alive and I go and take advantage of you."

Had he heard correctly? Maybe there was something wrong with his ears. First she called him handsome---and now this. Cory tried to put himself in her shoes and figure out what she meant but he was at a total loss. "I don't understand," he conceded.

"You think of yourself as my friend," Ann said. "Even if I now know I care for you as more than a friend, I have no right to throw myself at you at a time like this. You have enough on your mind without being bothered by me."

"Bothered? Are you wacko, woman, or what? I love you. I think I've always loved you."

Ann stared, astonished. Her mouth worked but no sounds came out until she said hoarsely, "You're joking, right?"

"Do I look like I'm joking?" Cory countered and was nearly bowled over when she threw herself against him and clasped him so tightly it hurt. Her face rested on his left shoulder and she trembled as if crying. Baffled, he rubbed her back and stroked her hair, wondering how she had stroked his with her fingers in such bad condition. Which brought to mind the whiskey. "How are your hands?" he asked.

"What?"

"Your hands. Your fingers. I have another idea."

Ann cleared her throat, sniffed a few times, and moved back. Tear tracks marked her cheeks. Her eyes glistened. "Sorry. You must think I'm an idiot."

"Quit apologizing. And don't call this a nightmare. It just turned into my dream come true."

"Why didn't you ever say anything?" Ann asked, then shook her head, adding, "No. There's no need to answer. I can imagine why."

Cory gazed at her with all the love in his heart, the pent-up feelings he had suppressed for seven years nearly overwhelming him. He almost broke into tears himself. But now was hardly the time or place. As much as he wanted to hold her, to comfort her, he must keep the danger they were in uppermost in mind. He put a palm on her moist cheek.

"We'll have plenty of time to talk after we're safe. Right now I want to disinfect your fingers, but I warn you it will smart."

"How?" she asked.

"The whiskey," Cory answered, retrieving the flask. He held the open bottle over her right hand. "Hold out all your fingers." She obeyed, and he slowly trickled the alcohol over her ravaged nails and torn skin.

Ann arched her back but made no outcry.

When he was done he closed the flask and slid it into the backpack. "There. That stuff is strong enough to kill any and all germs. You won't become infected now."

"Thank you," Ann said softly.

"We'd best boogie," Cory advised, slipping on the backpack. He lifted the pick, then the lantern.

"I should carry something."

"With your hands in the shape they are?" Cory said. He started up the far side of the bowl, marveling at the wondrous turn of events. For the first time in his life the future held the promise of romance. He had someone he could take on dates, someone he could share the lunch hour with at school, someone to buy special gifts for, someone he could smother with the affection smoldering within him.

Cory grinned. All Ann had done was kiss him and he was ready to walk her down the aisle. Talk about getting carried away! He must take their relationship one step at a time. Once they were out of the cavern he would ask her for a date, and if all went well he would ask for another and another, and when he was ultimately satisfied she cared for him as much as he did for her, only then would he make a fool of himself and do something ridiculous like buy her an incredibly expensive gift or ask her to wear his class ring.

He stepped onto the rim and turned to help her up. She was smiling at him, but her smile changed to horror as her gaze went over his shoulder. Her mouth opened to scream.

Cory heard the patter of onrushing feet and whirled. He glimpsed a muscular red arm. A blow struck his forehead. Stars exploded before his eyes like fireworks on the fourth of July. Dimly, he was aware of his feet leaving the ground and of sailing like an ungainly bird until he crashed down with a gut-wrenching shock that made the tunnel spin wildly.

Ann screamed.

Cory tried to get up, to go to her aid, when his mind switched off as abruptly as a light bulb.

Chapter 18

"Boo!" Wesley Eagen shouted and extended his arms toward Jay Thorpe, switching on both flashlights as he did. The fleeting fright on Jay's face was too comical for words. Wes burst into hearty laughter and jabbed a hand at his teammate. "You should see your face!"

Jay's fright vanished instantly, to be replaced by anger. He waved the rock hammer menacingly and took a stride closer to Wes. "You stupid son of a bitch! Don't you have any brains? A joke like that could get you killed."

"Oh, yeah?" Wes said while trying to bring his mirth under control.

"Yeah," Jay snapped. "For a second there I thought you were the monster and I was all set to bash your head in with this." He wagged the hammer and glowered.

"Calm down, big guy," Wes said, chuckling. "You don't have to worry about gruesome. That thing is a wimp."

"What the hell are you talking about?"

"I've seen the it," Wes said. "And I learned it can't stand bright light. All I have to do is point my flashlight at it and it runs off like a big coward."

Out of nowhere Leslie threw herself past Jay and flung her arms around Wesley. "Lover! Lover! You don't know how good it is to see you again!" She squeezed him close, her cheek against his neck, her entire body trembling from the intensity of her jubilation.

"Missed me, did you?" Wes said, conscious of her breasts rubbing his chest and her hips flush with his.

"You know it," Leslie declared, kissing his cheeks, his brow, his nose, his chin. She pulled back and giggled in girlish delight.

"What the hell happened to you?" Wes said, noting the hole in her blouse and streaks of dirt on her clothing and skin.

"Stacy and I had a little disagreement."

Wes saw Stacy step up on Jay's right.

"What's the big idea of beating on my girl?"

Stacy ignored the question. "You say you've seen the monster? What does it look like?"

"Just like that thing painted above the cave entrance," Wes said, "only a lot bigger and uglier." He paused. "It killed Scott."

The others registered shock and sorrow.

"He's not the only one," Jay said. "Terri is dead, too. We found one of her hands lying in a tunnel."

“Her damn hand?”

Jay nodded.

“I saw Scott's head,” Wes said. “Have you seen any sign of Fleming?"

"We figured he was with you guys."

"We became separated," Wes said, and let it go at that. There was no sense in admitting the truth since Jay and Stacy might hold it against him, especially Jay, who was a softy at heart. He tilted his head to peer past them. "Hey, where's Ann? Don't tell me the monster nailed her ass too?"

"She was alive the last we saw her," Jay said, and detailed what happened at the fissure, finishing with, "I didn't like leaving her but there was no choice. At least I've marked every passage we've taken since then so the rescue team can find her again."

"Now all we have to do is find a way out of this hellhole,"

Wes said, looping an arm around Leslie's slim waist. He could see part of her breast through her torn blouse and the sight of it rising and falling as she breathed set his organ to pulsing. Maybe he could salvage something from this farce after all.

"How did you find us?" Stacy said.

"I didn't," Wes said. "It's more like we found each other. I've been wandering around these rotten tunnels it seems like forever. A couple of minutes ago I thought I heard someone coming so I slid into a crack in the wall and turned off my flashlights. I figured it the creature came at me again I'd zap it in the eyes. Then I recognized your voices and decided to spring a surprise on you." He looked at Jay. "No hard feelings?"

"No," Jay said. "But don't do it again. I meant what I said. If anything comes at me, I'II swing first and ask questions later."

"You have my word," Wes said solemnly. He glanced at Jay's flashlight. "Looks as if your battery is almost dead."

"It is. I was worried we'd be clumping around in the dark before too long."

"Here. Take one of these," Wes said, offering the flashlight in his left hand. "It was Scott's and he won't be needing it."

"Thanks, buddy," Jay said gratefully.

"It's no big deal," Wes said. "I . ..," he began, and caught himself, about to say he had Fleming's flashlight in his backpack. Instead, he said, "...... wouldn't want anything to happen to any of you. God only knows how concerned I've been. I could barely think straight."

Leslie put a hand on his arm and gave a tender squeeze. "I knew you'd come to my rescue."

"You know it," Wes said with a grin. He pecked her neck

and rubbed the small of her back, his manhood starting to rise. Somehow he had to get her alone so he could indulge himself.

Jay turned off the weak flashlight and handed it to Stacy. "Okay. What now? Go back the way you came? There's nothing back our way."

"Sure," Wes said. "You and Stacy can take the lead. Leslie and I will be right behind you."

"Fair enough," Jay said, moving forward. Stacy trailed along, a finger looped in his leather belt.

"Now then," Wes said as he turned to Les, "why don't you tell me again how much you missed me?"

"I truly did," Leslie said, sighing and resting her head on his shoulder. "I wanted you with me in the worst way."

"Do tell," Wes said. He waited until they reached a bend, then stopped and faced her.

"What are you up to?" Leslie asked, staring at the comer around which Jay and Stacy had disappeared.

"Oh, about six inches," Wes joked, and took her hand in his to rub her knuckles along the length of his organ. Her cheeks flushed pink and she licked her red lips.

"You're not serious?"

"Try me."

"Here and now? What if Jay comes back to see what's keeping us?"

"We'll see his flashlight beam and I'll tell him to get lost for a while." Wes switched off his own light. Gripped her bottom, he ground her body into his so she would feel how hard he was. It never failed to stoke her passion.

"But . . ." Leslie protested---or tried to.

Wes covered her mouth with his. She hesitated briefly, then responded as she always did, with unrestrained desire, her hands roaming over his back as their tongues danced a sensuous tango. His free hand strayed to the hole in her blouse, his fingers slipping in to fondle her hardening nipple. She squirmed and cooed..

"I want you, babe," Wes said huskily when he broke for air. He leaned to the right and let the flashlight drop a couple of feet to the cave floor, then applied both hands to her twin mounds, massaging them through the sheer material.

"What about the monster?" Leslie asked softly.

"I told you. The thing is scared of bright light. If it shows up I'll turn the flashlight on it." Wes began kissing and lathering her neck. A tiny voice in the back of his mind told him he was taking an enormous risk but he didn't care. He was high and as horny as hell and wanted to screw Les silly.

Monster or no monster, that was exactly what he was going to do.

Wes tugged on her blouse to free it from her pants and swiftly unbuttoned it to expose her glorious breasts. As big as ripe cantaloupes, they swayed as she moved. He cupped them, reveling in their softness and the pliant way they molded to his fingers. Some nights he could play with them for hours. Not tonight. Tonight his manhood positively throbbed.

"Oh, honey," Leslie breathed in his ear,

"The best is yet to come," Wes said. He began lowering her pants to get at her panty hose. Why she always wore the hosiery he didn't know, but she always did. Whether she was wearing a dress, shorts or pants, she had on panty hose underneath. Maybe it was something her mother made her do.

He glanced at the bend, which was barely visible, and saw the glow of Jay's flashlight growing dimmer. The dummy hadn't even realized they were missing yet. Perfect. Lowering his mouth to her nipples, he pulled her pants down to her knees, then fiddled with her panty hose until it was down around her knees.

Leslie inhaled loudly and clutched his head to her breasts as he slid a finger between her legs. "I love the way you do me."

Wes smiled inwardly. He always did have away with the babes. He'd banged more than his share before Leslie came along. In a way he was surprised he had stayed with her as long as he had. Usually he became bored with a girl after five or six months and wanted new fluff. But not with Les. She was the best he'd ever had in a long string of conquests. When a guy was good-looking and had money to blow, girls flocked to him like little kids to candy.

His hunger for her rising, he buried his forefinger and felt her quiver and gasp. He stroked, giving her a pleasurable foretaste of the main event, while alternately sucking on her right and left nipples. The aromatic scent of her perfume, which she used lavishly, titillated him. He cupped her right buttock, digging his fingers into her yielding flesh.

"Yessss," Leslie whispered in erotic abandon. "Bring me off, lover."

Wes certainly would try. Kissing the creamy skin below her breasts, he inserted a second finger. Her hips moved of their own accord. Eager to get to the nitty-gritty, he hastily unbuckled his belt and unzipped his fly. He reached in, pulled his pole out, and was lowering the tip toward her when she said the single word he hated most.

"Condom."

Wes paused. He was sure he had brought one along, but for the life of him he couldn't recall where it was.

"Condom?" Leslie repeated, her hooded eyes gazing into his.

"I have one," Wes said thickly, removing his fingers from her and frantically poking his hands into his pockets. What the hell had he done with the damn thing? Next to her panty hose fetish, the most annoying habit she had was always insisting on his wearing a rubber before they could make love. All that business in the news about rampant sexual diseases had gotten to her, and she was absolutely paranoid about coupling unprotected. No condom, no fun and games.

"Condom?" she said a third time.

"Just a second," Wes said, struggling to keep the annoyance out of his voice or she would be pissed. Many a time he had tried to convince her condoms were unnecessary where they were concerned. Pagosa Springs, after all, was hardly New York City or Los Angeles. The incidence of venereal disease was low. But would Leslie listen? No way! Sometimes she was as stubborn as a mule.

"If you don't have one we can't do it."

Wes's left hand sank into his back pocket and found the familiar packet. He yanked it out, ripped it open, and swiftly slipped the condom over his member. "Satisfied?" he said as he reached down to part her legs. Bending at the knees, he aligned himself between her satiny thighs, found her slit and rammed into her.

"Ahhhl" Les cried, stiffening, her fingernails biting into his arms. "Yeah, babe. That's it!"

You're telling me, Wes almost said, but held his peace. He could feel her exquisite sheath enfolding his organ, and he held himself still to keep from spurting prematurely. Another glance at the bend showed him Jay and Stacy were still not coming back to check on them. Lord, but Thorpe was as dense as a brick.

Wes began a rocking motion, arousing her to heights of ecstasy. Her lips and hands were all over him, which was the part of her lovemaking expertise he liked the best. Some girls just lay there like limp sacks of flour. A few had enough sense to grunt now and then to show they were still alive. Some gave as good as they got, tit for tat, so to speak. A rare girl like Leslie became a sexual tigress, devouring her lover with her mouth and her hands. Give him a tigress any day.

His temples pounded, his pulse raced. He panted as he stroked, savoring the unadulterated bliss. To his way of thinking, this was the reason for man's existence. Money was handy to have and drugs made life sweeter, but sex was the only experience that made life worth living

"God, you get to me," Les said in his ear, her breath hot and tingly.

Wes paced himself, wanting her to get off first. He didn't have to wait as long as he normally did. Whether it was the excitement of making love in the Caverna del Diablo or something else, she climaxed intensely, shuddering and squealing and biting his neck. He waited until she began to coast down from her peak, then let himself go, feeling the explosion build and build until finally he exploded.

In the midst of his release, when he was oblivious to everything else around them, he thought he felt something brush against his ankle and assumed it was Leslie's foot.

Then came the slow descent from the peak of pleasure. He sagged against her and she leaned against the cave wall. His loins were drenched, as were her thighs. They kissed lightly until he roused himself and carefully stepped back to tuck his manhood into his pants. "That was great, babe," he said. "You haven't lost your touch."

"Neither have you," Leslie said, pulling herself together. Thanks. I needed that."

"I wonder what happened to those other two?" Wes remarked.

"Maybe they heard us and decided to leave us in peace."

"Maybe," Wes said, securing his belt buckle. "Now where did I drop that flashlight?" He bent and scoured the ground, which was solid rock at that spot. He roved his hands in small circles, first to the right and then to the left, but found no trace of it. "We must have moved a bit," he said, shifting to check farther. In the dark the yellow flashlight should be easy to spot but it wasn't. Annoyed, he squatted and ran his hands this way and that. "Damn it."

"What's the matter?"

"I can't find the stinking flashlight."

"How can that be?" Leslie said nervously.

"Don't lay an egg," Wes said. "I have another one in my backpack."

"You do? Where did you get it?

"It's a spare Scott brought along," Wes lied. He stripped off the pack, found the flashlight, and flicked it on. To his astonishment, when he swept the floor he saw the other flashlight was gone. "What the hell is this action?"

"Where is it?" Leslie wondered, stepping to his side.

Wes scratched his head in confusion. "Makes no sense," he said sourly. Suddenly he remembered that something had brushed his ankle, and a shiver ran down his spine. Had the monster taken it? No, he told himself. The monster would have attacked them on the spot rather than play hide and seek with the flashlight.

Leslie looked around, then laughed and clapped her hands. "Oh, I get it! That Jay is sneaky!"

'What are you babbling about?"

"Don't you get it?" Les said. "Jay heard us going at it so he turned off his light, took yours, and skipped off. What else could have happened?"

"You must be right," Wes said, although in his heart he had misgivings. "Let's find those airheads so I can give them a piece of my mind."

"Don't go off the deep end," Leslie said. "Remember, Jay owes you one for scaring us half to death when you popped out at us."

"Do you think I'm stupid?" Wes said. "I'm not about to say anything that will get King Kong ticked off at me."

"You shouldn't call him that. He doesn't like it."

"Just so he doesn't hear me is all that matters."

Wes grabbed her hand and hurried around the bend. His beam revealed. an empty stretch of passage fifty to sixty feet in length. "They must be around the next curve," he guessed.

The more he thought about the missing flashlight, the more convinced became Leslie was right. If the monster had found them, it would have ripped them to pieces. It had to have been Jay who took the flashlight.

He saw Jay's and Stacy's tracks in a patch of dust. Past the next bend was another long section of empty tunnel. "Where the hell are they?"

"Maybe they're playing a trick on us now.

"Even they wouldn't be that stupid."

"They're our friends. It's not nice for you to insult them."

"Friends? Stacy and you went a few rounds a while ago and you still like her?"

"Of course, silly. Friends fight all the time. You don't stop being someone's friend just because you have a spat."

"Maybe you don't but I'm not the forgiving type. If someone messes with me I hate them for life."

"Sometimes you can be so immature."

"Listen to who's talking. A girl who still plays with dolls."

Leslie wrenched her hand loose and halted. "As you damn well know, I collect dolls. I don't play with them. Collecting is my hobby. It's taken me years to get a doll from almost every country in the world, and one day my collection will be worth a lot of money."

Wes stopped and turned. "Yeah, yeah." He impatiently and motioned for her to move on. "Let's go."

"I want an apology."

"Jesus!"

"I mean it. I'm tired of you insulting everyone all the time. First Jay and Stacy, now me. What's the matter with you?"

"Nothing," Wes said, although in truth he was feeling extremely rritiable. He usually did after coming down off a high, but lately the blahs were lasting longer each time.

"Then apologize."

Wes came close to slugging her. An unreasoning rage flared and he clenched his left fist, ready to swing. At the last moment he realized what he was about to do and turned sharply away. "I'm sorry," he blurted.

"I didn't hear you."

Striving to maintain his cool, Wes said again, "I'm sorry. Are you happy now? Can we keep going?"

"Start walking. I'll be right behind you."

Wes held out his hand for her to take but she shook her head. "Suit yourself," he growled, and stalked off. The bitch! One minute she was humping him silly, the next she was getting all bent out of shape over nothing

Lately they had been fighting more than ever before. Why? Was it his fault? He couldn't see how. Maybe he was bored with her and wouldn't admit the fact. Maybe it was time for him to latch onto a new babe. There was always Lori Donovan. She was a Grade-A fox and had been flirting with him a lot recently. One word from him and she'd leap at the chance to go out on a date. And it shouldn't take more than two or three outings until she gave up the prize.

Jay's and Stacy's tracks led around a curve to the left. There were clefts and cracks in the walls, lending the tunnel an unstable aspect.

Wes gazed at the ceiling, hoping the lousy tunnel wouldn't cave in with him in it. He swiveled and saw Leslie eight feet behind him, her features downcast. What did she have to be sad about? Didn't he always try to treat her right, to show her a fun time every minute of every day? Parties, movies, dances, you name it, he took her. She ate at the best restaurants. And when they occasionally drove to Durango for an all-nighter, didn't he always book a room at the ritziest hotel in the whole town using the phony I.D. he had bought up in Alamosa?

Women never appreciated anything.

"You coming or what?" Wes said.

"Quit being mean."

"You and quit sulking. Yeah, I'm a little ticked off. But who wouldn't be, after all that's happened? Don't take it personally, Les."

"If you say so."

Shaking his head at how inconsiderate she was being, Wes faced forward. His beam swept the ground at his feet, and suddenly he stopped cold in midstride.

Jay's and Stacy's footprints came to an abrupt end.

Superimposed on top of them were the huge three-toed tracks he had come to know so well. From there on, Wes saw only three-toed tracks.

It could only mean one thing.
The monster had Jay and Stacy.

Chapter 19

Not again.

Those were the first words that flashed across Cory Fleming's mind when he revived. Then the pain hit, pain so intense he inadvertently cried out, pain so severe he curled into a ball, his palms pressed to his throbbing temples. The mere act of trying to think heightened the agony. He grit his teeth and let the torment take its course.

After a while he was able to focus his thoughts. He recalled being struck on the forehead, on the exact same spot where he had hit his head when he fell earlier. If the blow had been a shade more powerful, the demon would have caved in his cranium. As it was, his head and neck had never, ever hurt so much.

Where was Ann?

Cory opened his eyes and was surprised to see the lantern, still lit and glowing, on the slope. He was near the bottom of the pit where he must have landed after being hit. Why hadn't the creature finished him off? Grunting, he sat up, searching for Ann.

She was gone.

Panic brought him to his feet but he promptly regretted moving because the pain worsened, driving him to his knees. He spotted the pick a few feet off. And the backpack was still on his back. If his head would only stop pounding, he could begin hunting for clues as to Ann's fate.

The idea of her being dead filled him with stark, almost paralyzing dread. She couldn't be! Not now! Not after they had finally cleared the air and confessed their true feelings. Fate couldn't be so cruel as to deprive him of the girl he loved on the very day she at long last opened her heart to him.

Who was he kidding?

As a budding scientist he knew the one inalienable law that governed human existence---there were no guarantees in life. The rich and the poor, the self-styled aristocrats and the common people, media superstars and the average man and woman on the street, they were all subject to the cosmic constant of random occurrences. Everyone had to take what life had to offer when life offered it.

It was as if everyone on the planet was engaged in a game of roulette where life, health and happiness were theirs if they survived the daily spinning of the great wheel of chance. No one could predict the future, so everyone was a potential victim of the present. A person who had everything one day might lose it all the next. Someone who had never been sick a day in their life might suffer a heart attack and keel over.

Absolutely nothing was certain.

So it was more than likely the demon had already ripped Ann to shreds. It was possible her remains were lying out there somewhere, cold and drained of her vital life's blood. But until he actually saw the pieces, he would persist in believing she was alive. She *must* be alive.

In his soul Cory knew she was the one for him, the woman who would one day be his wife, who might one day bear their children and be his partner in providing a home and the stable love all kids needed. If she was dead, all his dreams were so much shiftless mist, lacking substance and meaning. Somehow, he sensed there would never be another girl he cared for as much as he cared for her.

Without her his life would be empty. Without her, he would bury himself in his test tubes and microscopes and go through life an automaton like ninety percent of humanity already did.

Whoops. Cory caught himself. Here he was. Doing doing it again. Getting carried away. One kiss did not a wife make.

He attempted to stand and succeeded. Shuffling to the lantern, he slowly leaned over and gripped the handle. Straightening caused a spasm to rack his head, and he paused until the pang lessened.

He stepped to the pick, lifted it in his right hand, then climbed the slope until he stood at the same spot where he had been when the demon pounced.

There in the dirt were his footprints, as plain as day, and the demon's tracks, as well. He saw where the creature had moved toward where Ann stood. Saw only the demon's tracks leading up out of the pit. The significance was clear.

The thing had grabbed Ann and made off with her.

Cory hurried to the tunnel, resolved to follow the demon into the bowels of the earth if need be.

He saw no sign of blood, no torn clothing. Ann had still been in one piece.

Soon he came to a fork. The lantern revealed the demon had taken the left branch. Not only that, the thing had set Ann down and pulled her along by the arm.

Cory went as fast as he could. Moving, he found, helped his head to clear and the pain to go away.

Once more he gave thanks his glasses hadn't been busted or he would be up the proverbial creek without a paddle. Had the demon's blow been half an inch lower, he would now be running around bumping into walls and boulders, totally helpless.

Oddly, Cory felt no fear. Only anger. A burning anger that grew the farther he hiked. He wanted to find the demon and kill it, to destroy the monstrosity so no more innocent victims would ever again fall prey to this scourge of humanity.

The scientist in him, however, was more curious than enraged.

If the demon that took Ann was the same one that killed the conquistadors and the Utes, how had it survived all these centuries? Did it enjoy an exceptional life span? Or was it but the most recent descendant in a long line?

Did that mean there a viable breeding population inhabiting the Caverna del Diablo?

Cory wondered if there were similar creatures elsewhere in the world. If so, perhaps they were responsible for spawning legends of an infernal underworld populated by evil fiends.

He could readily imagine a primitive men wandering into a cave in Europe or Asia and encountering some of the creatures, then fleeing. Back on the surface they would have told embellished tales of their adventure, and before long the word would spread among the various tribes that there existed an underground realm inhabited by vile demons.

Cory pondered why it was that no one had reported them in recent years. Given all the spelunkers in the U.S. and the rest of the world, someone should have seen the things. Someone should have reported a sighting.

Or would they? Why would anyone in their right mind report seeing a demon when they were bound to be laughed at?

Ridicule was the typical reaction of those whose preconceived notions of reality were threatened by reputed encounters with the unknown. Just look at the public reaction to reports of flying saucers, Bigfoot and the Loch Ness Monster. Most thought the stories were quaint cases of mistaken identity. Others thought that those who saw anything paranormal were nuts.

Before tonight he had been the same way.

Now he knew better.

The tracks were easy to follow. From the length of the demon's stride, which was twice his own, he guessed the thing had been in a hurry.

Accordingly, when he felt up to it, he began jogging. The lantern swayed with every step. his shadow performing a macabre dance on the walls he passed.

The pick was a heavy burden but he sure as hell wasn't about to discard it. Glancing down, he checked his other weapons. The knife and the two steel bits were still in place.

Cory ran and ran. Every five minutes or so he took brief rests. Sometimes the passages were as straight as arrows, at other times they wound like a slack rope, seemingly taking him nowhere.

The creature's tracks gave evidence of slowing only once, when the demon had evidently scooped Ann into its arms or thrown her over its shoulder. The deduction was obvious because her footprints ended at that point and the demon's stride became shorter, as if it was now burdened with extra weight.

As he crossed another of those rooms where the ceiling eerily glowed, Cory suddenly realized the demon was heading for that vast chamber he considered a world unto itself, the one where he had first spotted it. How he knew, he couldn't say. Intuition, perhaps, or a subliminal hunch. Whichever, he felt certain the tracks would lead him into that boundless dominion the demon must call home.

Getting there would probably take a while.

Getting out might take his life.

"Where are they?" Leslie cried, turning in small circles as she scoured the ground. "They couldn't just up and vanish!"

"Calm down," Wes snapped. "I'm trying to think." He was on his knees, examining the tunnel floor.

"Oh, God," Leslie said, "what if they're dead? What if we're the only ones left? We don't stand a prayer. That thing will hunt us down and kill us just like it has the others."

"Shut up, damn it."

"I want out of here, Wes!" Leslie said. "Do you hear me? You're my boyfriend. Do something! Get us to the surface or we're as good as dead. You're supposed to be the big, tough, quarter---."

Wes uncoiled like a snake and grabbed the front of her blouse. Her bitching had stretched his nerves beyond their breaking point, and he was livid as he glared into her suddenly frightened eyes and said coldly, "Not another word! Not one damn word! I'm trying to figure out what happened to Jay and Stacy, and I can't do that with you running off at the mouth." He gave her a shove, then turned to where the tracks were jumbled and distorted.

How the hell had the thing grabbed Jay without a struggle? Jay wasn't a 90-pound weakling. The guy could pick up the front end of pickup trucks, for crying out loud. Not only that, Jay had beaten all comers in school at arm wrestling.

There should be evidence of a fight but there wasn't.

And why did the creature's tracks mysteriously appear in the middle of the tunnel? As if it had appeared out of thin air?

Wes trained his flashlight on the wall and ran his fingers over the stone surface. There had to be an explanation. A few seconds later he found a clue, a hairline crack extending from the floor to the ceiling. Moving to the right about a yard and a half, he found an identical crack.

The implications made him step back in dismay.

"What is it?" Les said.

"A secret passage."

"A what?"

"Are you hard of hearing?" Wes said. He pointed at the section of wall bounded by the cracks. "There must be another tunnel behind here, covered by this big slab."

Suddenly he remembered the slab he and Scott had stumbled on earlier.

"This whole cavern must be honeycombed with secret passages, just like those castles over in England and Spain and places like that."

"You mean the thing came out of the wall?"

"It moved part of the wall aside, then grabbed Jay and Stacy from behind. They never knew what hit them."

Leslie gasped and touched her hand to her throat. "It might pop out at us any second, too."

Nodding, Wes backed away. Leslie quickly glued herself to his side, her hand clasped around his wrist.

"Please don't let it get me."

"I'll do the best I can," Wes said, although at the moment he didn't care one way or the other if the monster nailed her sorry ass or not. He definitely intended to give her the heave-ho once they were back in Pagosa Springs. If she was to be killed by the monster it would spare him from having to put up with her tears and protests. In a perverse sort of way he wished she would be slain.

They went ten yards. Then Wes turned and ran, going

as fast as he dared and leaving it to Leslie to keep up or fall behind. Amazingly, she kept pace. When they reached a bare chamber he halted in the middle where they could see anything coming.

"Why are we stopping?" Leslie asked.

"So you can catch your breath."

"I'm not winded. You are."

Wes looked at her and discovered she was right. He was breathing heavily. She was as composed as if they were out for a moonlit stroll. It must be all the coke and beer, he told himself.

Leslie was staring at the flashlight. "Do you have another one of those?"

"Nope."

"What happens if it goes out?"

"What do you think will happen?" Wes retorted. He hefted it. "But don't worry. The beam is bright so the battery must have plenty of energy. Well be out of here long before we're left in the dark."

"I wish I had your confidence."

"And I wish you'd stop being so negative. Think positive for once. It would do you a world of good."

"Do you still love me, Wes?"

The blunt query caught him off-guard. He blinked, then looked away, unwilling for her to see the truth in his eyes as he answered, "Of course I do. How can you ask such a dumb question?"

"You're not acting like you do. In fact, you've been treating me like dirt since we argued after making love. You've insulted me and belittled me and you even came close to hitting me. Don't deny it. I could tell."

"I was a little peeved, yeah. So what?"

"So I know you. At times you act like a spoiled six year

old but this goes deeper. I think you don't love me any more and you're not man enough to admit it."

"You're crazy."

"Then why won't you look me in the eyes?"

Leave it to her to start a romantic spat when they were thousands of feet below the earth and being stalked by an inhuman killer! Wes put a lid on his surging emotions and bestowed his most charming smile on her. "There. I'm looking right into your eyes. Satisfied?" he said, and draped a hand on her shoulder. "After all that's happened you're naturally upset. So your imagination is working overtime. Of course I love you and I always will. If I was gruff, I'm sorry. But you can understand why. We're both nervous wrecks and we're jumping at shadows. So is it surprising I'm not my usual self?"

"No, I guess not," Leslie said skeptically.

Wes went to kiss her on the mouth but she turned her face, offering her cheek instead. Provoked, he nearly told her to go take a flying leap off a low cliff. To keep the peace he planted his lips next to her ear, then smiled as if he didn't have a care in the world.

"We should keep moving," Leslie said.

"Whatever you want, honey," Wes said and took her hand before making for a tunnel bounded by jagged rocks.

He was pleased at his cleverness. She'd bought his lies, hook, line and sinker. Which meant she'd be all the more shocked when he sprung his farewell speech on her. Boy, would he enjoy telling her where to go! And he wouldn't feel any guilt whatsoever. She deserved being dumped for being such a putz.

"Do you ever wish you'd lived your life differently?" Leslie asked.

Wes sighed. What the hell was this? Twenty questions?

Did she think he was a shrink? "No, not ever. Why? Have you?"

"Now and then. Sometimes I wish I could be a better person than I am, you know?"

"You're fine the way you are," Wes said, concentrating on the passage, seeking telltale cracks in the walls that might indicate another hidden passage. He didn't want the monster springing out at him when he least expected it.

"I think we can all stand some improvement."

Wes glanced at her and was mildly surprised by her pensive expression. She so rarely thought heavily about anything. "What in the world brought this up, anyway?"

"I flirted with Jay to get Stacy mad."

Wes halted and turned. "When did this happen?"

"Shortly before you showed up. I wanted to get back at Stacy for the fight we had, so I made a play at Jay to try and make her jealous and maybe cause the two of them to go at it."

"What kind of play did you make?"

"It doesn't matter."

"Does to me. How far did you go with him?"

"That's not the issue. The point is I shouldn't have tried to hurt my friend by throwing myself at her hunk," Leslie said sadly. "And now they're both gone and I may never have a chance to apologize.

"So that's what this is about. You feel guilty because they're probably lying in bits and pieces somewhere."

"How could you?" Leslie said, indignant. "Don't you have any feelings at all?

"Don't start."

"Fine. I'll finish it, then."

"Finish what?"

"Us. As of this minute we're no longer going steady,"

Leslie declared. She tugged at his school ring, slipping it off her finger. "You can have your this back. I don't ever want to go out with you again."

"You can't do this."

"Why not?"

"Because. . .," Wes said, and let the sentence trail off. How could he tell her that she couldn't dump him because he was planning to dump her? This wasn't fair.

"A wonderful reason," Leslie said sarcastically. "I'm right, aren't I? You don't love me any longer."

"This is hardly the time or place---," Wes began.

"Answer me."

"What's gotten into you?"

"Answer me, damn it," Leslie demanded, throwing his ring to the ground.

Wes couldn't take it any longer. His self-control snapped. As someone accustomed to always having his own way, he had a short fuse when it came to being given a hard time. He expected others to comply with his every wish since he always knew what was best for everyone.

Unfortunately, Leslie didn't have the brains to realize that. This time she had gone too far. She had driven him over the brink.

His right fist swept up, connecting with her chin and rocking the startled girl on her heels. She staggered, and he slugged her again, grinning as he did, gratified by the feel of his knuckles on her flesh. There was a crunch and her knees buckled.

Leslie sprawled in a crumpled heap, blood dribbling from a corner of her mouth.

Only then did Wes realize what he had done. He swayed as if drunk and dropped to one knee. "Les? I'm sorry, babe. Really. Are you okay?"

Leslie made no reply. Her eyes were closed and she lay completely still.

"Les, honey?" Wesley said, prodding her shoulder. "Come on. Snap out of it. I didn't hit you that hard."

She didn't seem to be breathing.

"Leslie?" Wes said urgently, touching her cheek. She felt cold. What had he done? Was she dead? He picked up her limp wrist and felt for a pulse. He couldn't find one.

Horrified, he stood and took a step back. He hadn't meant to hit her with all his strength. It had just sort of happened. Now she'd gone and kicked the bucket. How could she do it? How could she go and die on him at a time like this? If anyone ever found out, he'd be thrown into prison.

Wes glanced both ways and saw no one. Good. There were no witnesses to worry about. Only he knew, and if he kept his mouth shut, no one would ever suspect the truth.

He could claim the monster killed her. Or maybe he would say she had an accident, fell into a chasm or something like that. He could concoct a cock-and-bull story where he valiantly tried to save her but failed. Everyone would buy it. Practically the whole town knew they were a hot item, presumably deeply in love. The townspeople would believe any yarn he told.

He began to calm down.

There was no way that he, Wesley Aaron Eagen, was ever going to prison. Prisons were for losers. Eagens were winners. It was that simple. If he kept his cool he'd come out on top, just like always. He breathed a sigh of relief and debated whether to leave her there or drag her body into a nook or cranny where no one would ever find her.

Wes mopped his perspiring forehead, then crouched. Better to be safe than sorry. He tucked the flashlight under his right arm, grabbed her wrists, and went to pull.

From back the way he had come rose the rattling of a sidewinder.

The monster was on his heels!

Spinning, Wes took several strides, then paused to stare at Leslie. The thing had perfect timing. It would come on her body and likely tear her apart as it had Scott and Terri. There would be no evidence left when it was through. He would be in the clear.

"Come and get your supper, you rotten bastard," Wes said, smirking.

He raced down the passage. He had covered ten yards when he thought he heard a moan behind him. Stunned, he stopped and looked but Les was right where he'd left her.

The creature uttered its weird cry again.

Wes fled, fear lending wings to his feet, and put Leslie Vanderhorst out of his mind once and for all.

Chapter 20

Jay Thorpe came to with a start and sat bolt upright, his befuddled mind trying to come to terms with the staggering vista that spread before his astonished eyes. He was seated on a high ridge in the midst of a vast wasteland of canyons, ravines, plateaus, assorted monoliths and bizarre formations. For a few seconds he believed he was dreaming, believed he must be imagining himself on an alien world. Then he looked skyward and discovered there was no sky. Rather, where the clouds should be was a ceiling as vast as the landscape itself, a ceiling that gave off a preternatural glow.

Recognition dawned. He was still in the Caverna del Diablo but in a chamber that dwarfed all the others combined, a chamber encompassing more space than the entire town of Pagosa Springs. Glancing around in amazement, he realized the metropolis of Denver would scarcely cover a tenth of the ground he saw.

Someone groaned behind him.

Twisting, Jay saw Stacy and his heart leaped. He moved to her side, kneeling and cradling her head in his lap. She appeared to be unhurt. At least there were no bruises or wounds he could see.

What in the world had happened?

Jay remembered hiking along a tunnel with Wes and Leslie behind them. There had been a scratching noise, a puff of air, and he had started to turn when something struck him on the side of the head and he had crumpled.

It all transpired so incredibly fast that there was no time for him to react or defend himself or Stacy. He stroked her brow and she groaned again. "Honey?" he said softly

Her eyelids fluttered then snapped open, her eyes filled with unbridled fear. She saw his face, exhaled in relief, and mustered a grin. "Hi there, handsome. What the hell happened?"

"Take a look and maybe you can tell me."

Stacy sat up, her features registering dumfounded shock. She gawked at the wasteland, then clutched his wrist. "Tell me I'm having a nightmare, that none of this is real."

"It's real, all right," Jay said, rising and giving her a hand up. "We're somewhere in the stinking cave. How we got here is anyone's guess."

"That thing," Stacy said. "It must have knocked us out and brought us here."

"Why?" Jay said. "It makes no sense. The monster had us dead to rights. It could have ripped us apart like it did the others, yet it didn't."

"Maybe it has other plans for us," Stacy said anxiously.

"Like what?" Jay rotated a full three hundred and sixty degrees, seeking signs of life. In all that near boundless bizarreness nothing stirred.

"Why is it so warm?" Stacy said.

Jay's brow knit. She was right. The tunnels had been cool, some even drafty. This place was uncomfortably warm, so much so he was sweating. The temperature must be eighty degrees or better.

"Is that smoke?" Stacy asked, pointing off to their right.

Turning, Jay spied several brownish tendrils perhaps a quarter of a mile away spiraling toward the ceiling. "I'll be damned. It is."

"We should go have a look. There might be people.

Maybe those are campfires."

Jay made no comment although he felt she was grasping at straws. In the first place, there wasn't a tree, bush or any other combustible material anywhere in sight. Second, it was extremely unlikely anyone else was this far down in the Caverna del Diablo.

"Shall we?" Stacy prompted, gesturing at the smoke.

"I suppose," Jay said He didn't have any better ideas. He headed out, then abruptly halted and reached back over his right shoulder to touch a hand to his spine between his shoulder blades

"What's the matter?"

"Didn't you notice either? The backpack is gone." Jay scanned the nearby ground. "So is the flashlight and the rock hammer."

"The monster must have taken them," Stacy said.

"Damn it," Jay grumbled, putting on a front of being furious so she wouldn't guess the truth. He didn't want to tell her, but deep down inside he was scared. For the very first time in his life he was experiencing genuine fear. Always in the past he had relied on his great size and superbly conditioned physique to see him through any trouble, but this time neither was doing him much good. The monster had them right where it wanted them, and there was nothing he could do about it. He was helpless, a condition he had never known before.

When he was younger he never had to worry about other boys trying to beat him up. They were all too intimidated by his bulk and his muscles to dare pick on him. In high school it was much the same. Everyone knew he was as strong as an ox. No one was stupid enough to get him ticked off. Even on the football field he was top dog because he was so much bigger than his teammates and most opposing players. He'd never been in a situation where he was the underdog. All his life his exceptional strength and size had set him apart and above everyone else.

Now he was being toyed with by a creature capable of ripping him to pieces. By something that must be equally as strong if not stronger. By something larger than he was. His life lay on the line. Worse, so did Stacy's, and much of his fear was for her welfare more than his own. He couldn't bear the thought of something awful happening to her. No matter what, he must protect her and get her to safety.

"Come on," Stacy said, taking his hand. "There's no use crying over spilt milk, as my mom always says."

They walked in silence for a while.

"Do you think the monster got Wes and Leslie, too?" she asked.

"Probably. They were right behind us."

"No, they weren't."

"What?"

"I was just about to say something to you when we were jumped. They never followed us. I looked back several times and couldn't understand what was keeping them."

"We might be the last ones left," Jay said and felt her hand become a vise. To take her mind off their plight he nodded at the smoke and commented, "Then again, Fleming is unaccounted for. It would be just like a brain like him to make some fires to try and signal us."

"God, I hope you're right."

They came to where the ridge sloped down to a barren plain. From their vantage point they discovered the smoke arose on the far side of a gigantic rock formation shaped much like the Denver Coliseum, an enormous dome covering acres. They started down the slope.

Stacy surveyed the sprawling, desolate expanse and shuddered. "This place gives me the creeps."

"We'll be fine. I'll get you out. Wait and see," Jay earnestly assured her.

"Sure."

"You don't believe me?"

"I have complete confidence in you."

Jay was upset by her tone. He noted how she had danced around the question and wished there was something he could do or say to put her mind at ease. But he couldn't bring himself to lie. Besides, she would see right through him. She always did.

"This is a hell of a way to spend Halloween," Stacy said.

"Oh, I don't know," Jay said, adopting a lighthearted attitude in the hope she would cheer up. "Being stalked by a monster is right in keeping with the holiday. Look at all those scary movies that Carpenter guy made." He grinned, but she merely scowled and stared at the smoke.

Their descent took a while. Although the slope wasn't steep, there was a lot of loose earth underfoot. They had to exercise caution.

The whole time, a warm wind stroked their faces, bearing with it a faint, offensive odor.

"What is that smell?" Stacy asked when they stopped briefly at the base of the ridge.

"Beats me, sugar," Jay said. "Reminds me of rotten eggs."

He bore to the right, marveling at the immense, smooth dome they were going around. How had it been formed? He knew next to nothing about geology. Vaguely, he seemed to remember a few science classes dealing with volcanoes and the types of formations formed by volcanic activity. The dome in front of them reminded him of a picture of a geothermal something-or-other he'd seen in the textbook. Of course the notion was ridiculous. There were no volcanoes anywhere in the Rocky Mountains.

It took half an hour to reach a point where they could see the land beyond the dome.

Stacy stopped and cursed.

"We should have known," Jay said, gazing forlornly at three large pools of bubbling yellowish-brown water. Or was it water? He led her closer. The smell of rotten eggs grew stronger, almost making him gag.

"This is far enough," Stacy said, tugging on his arm.

"What's wrong?"

"I have a bad feeling."

Jay would have liked to inspect the pools but he decided not to make an issue of it. Sighing, he stretched to relieve the tension in his body and happened to swivel and gaze at the dome, then past the formation at the section of ridge visible from where they stood.

He thought he would have a heart attack.

Perched at the top of the ridge, silhouetted against the backdrop of the incandescent ceiling, was a huge red figure. It was simply standing there, staring at them.

Stacy glanced at his face, then spun. "Oh, God!" she cried and pivoted, about to flee blindly in the opposite direction. "It's after us."

"Stay calm," Jay said, snatching her wrist. "If we lose our heads now we're done for."

The creature began to descend the ridge, walking slowly and methodically, its arms swinging loosely at its sides.

"Run!" Stacy urged, her eyes pools of abject terror as she tried to tear her arm free. "That thing wi kill us if it catches us!"

Among the many lessons Jay had learned from playing football was that it never paid to lose one's head., Keeping cool when the going got tough was a trademark of great players. If a player let the excitement get the better of him, he might forget which zone he was supposed to cover or which play the quarterback had called. And one blunder could lose a game.

While to the casual fan it often appeared as if most players were reacting to plays on the spur of the moment, in reality the men performed according to strict guidelines, adhering to the strategies set down by the coach. As little as possible was left to chance because the team that could control the ball controlled the game. Planning and strategy always paid off.

Jay would much rather have taken a minute to think things out, to search for something he could use as a weapon or some other means of stopping the monster. But when Stacy went crazy on him, frantically pulling on his hand and jumping up and down in panicked agitation, he gave in and let himself be prompted into full-fledged flight.

They ran out onto the barren plain, a sea of red earth devoid of life, their feet raising swirls of reddish dust.

On the plain the temperature rose higher, causing them to swelter as if they were running under the noonday sun in the middle of July.

Both of them were in excellent condition. Jay figured they had gone half a mile when he slowed and motioned for Stacy to do likewise. Halting to catch his breath, he looked back.

The red figure was far back, just passing the bubbling pools. It still appeared to be walking, not running.

"Maybe it can't move very fast," Stacy said hopefully.

"If it catches up with us it'll be sorry," Jay boasted for her benefit. He studied the lay of the land. Straight ahead lay more flat plain. To the right reared a series of ridges and hills. To their left was the gloomy mouth of a wide canyon. He bore to the right.

"What are you doing?"

"We need somewhere to hide."

"How about that canyon? It's closer."

"Looks to be dark in there. I want to be able to see the thing when it closes in on us."

They jogged energetically until Stacy flagged. Jay could have sprinted for two more miles without tiring, but he slowed down to match her pace.

"Go on," Stacy said, waving her hand. "Don't wait for me. I don't have your endurance.

Jay smiled. "That has got to be the stupidest thing you've ever said to me. What kind of guy would I be if I deserted you now?" He shook his head. "Sorry, babe. You're stuck with me for the duration."

"You have your nerve calling me stupid."

"I love you, too."

Stacy, breathing through her nose, paused between each of her next words. "I'm serious. Only a dummy would have fallen for Leslie's ploy back there."

"What ploy?"

"Don't play innocent with me, lover boy. Your hormones always have been hyperactive, and when Leslie threw herself at you, you just naturally went into heat."

Jay was so flabbergasted that he temporarily forgot all about the creature. "I don't know what you're talking about," he said lamely. "Les and I are friends, nothing more."

"Is that why you were kissing her and kept feeling her up when you thought I wasn't looking?"

A rebuttal died on Jay's lips. He felt like a kid who had been caught with his hand in the cookie jar. If he argued he would only make matters worse. It was better to stay quiet and take his lumps like a man.

"I saw you smooching when I came back from tinkling," Stacy revealed. "You don't know how close you came to getting bashed in the head with a rock, if only I'd been able to find one handy."

Jay stared at the hills and ridges.

"Honestly, sometimes I wonder what you use for brains, honeybuns. Didn't it ever occur to you that Leslie was only using you to get back at me?"

"She was what?" Jay said, his curiosity getting the better of him.

"She was mad because I kicked her ass so she tried to get even by getting you all hot and bothered, figuring I'd notice and the two of us would wind up at each other's throats."

Once again Jay was impressed by his girl's insight. He'd been wondering why Leslie displayed such a sudden interest in him, and now her behavior made sense. "Of all the dirty tricks," he muttered.

"Blame yourself, not her. She set you up for a fall and like a chump you took the bait."

"Why didn't you chew me out on the spot?"

"What? And let the bitch know her little ploy got to me? Get real. You're just lucky I saw through her. Otherwise, I'd have dumped your ass once we made it back to town."

Jay, thunderstruck, broke stride, then had to hurry to jog abreast of her again. "You really would have dumped me?"

"Damn straight. What would you do if you caught me with another guy?"

"Kill the bastard."

"Of course you would. You're a macho lunkhead. But what about us? Would you still want to be my steady?"

"Always."

Stacy looked at him, and smirked. "You're a lunkhead, but an adorable one. And you're mine and nobody else's. Just remember this conversation the next time some bimbo puts the moves on you. Okay?"

"Okay," Jay said, pleased he had briefly gotten her mind off the creature dogging them. He checked to see if they were maintaining their lead and nearly tripped when he saw no trace of it. "What the hell!" he exclaimed, halting. "Where did the thing go?"

After searching about, Stacy said, "Maybe it's hiding."

"There's nowhere *to* hide," Jay said, scouring the empty plain between the dome and them. He was baffled. They hadn't seen any gullies or washes in which the thing could have sought cover, nor were there any mounds, hillocks or boulders to hide behind. The plain was so open, a mouse would stand out like a sore thumb. Yet the monster had mysteriously disappeared.

"Do we keep going?" Stacy asked.

"Might as well," Jay said. "We have nowhere else to go." He didn't add that the creature might be lying in wait back there, perhaps in ditch or a crack they couldn't see from where they were. He continued toward a bald hill, going slowly so as not to force Stacy to overexert herself.

"How far under the surface do you think we are?" she wondered.

"I wouldn't have any idea, babe."

"My guess would be a mile. They say the farther down you go, the hotter it gets, And this place is a hothouse."

Jay gazed at the ceiling, speculating on whether she could be correct. Science wasn't his strong suit. Nor was Math. History. English. Economics. Music Appreciation. You name it. But he doubted they that far down. Half a mile, maybe. In the long run it wasn't important. All that counted was reaching the surface alive.

"There's something I've been meaning to tell you," Stacy said.

"So shoot," Jay said, surprised at how talkative she had become. Probably nerves, he figured. And if talking helped her cope, then he had no objection to her gabbing his ears off.

"My folks want me to go off to college next year."

"You mean go away? Leave Pagosa Springs?" Jay felt a new kind of fear take hold.

"That's the general idea. They're insisting I need a college education, and they even have the college picked out for me. It's somewhere in Kansas, the same school my mom went to."

"Kansas?" Jay repeated, thinking a drive there would take around twelve hours depending on where the college was located.

"I don't want to go."

"Then don't."

"But if my dad puts his foot down I won't be able to say no."

"Hell, you're eighteen. You can do as you want. Tell them you're not going and that's final."

"They've offered to pay for my entire education."

Extremely upset, Jay stopped and faced her. "And what about us? We'll be lucky if we see each other once a month." The thought of not seeing her every single day was more than he could bear. She was his life. He'd do anything for her. In his agitation he pounded his right fist into his left palm.

"Calm down, honeybuns."

"Remember Vic and Sally? They were in love, too. Then

he went off to Berkeley to study anthropology or some such crap and the next time he came to visit he dumped her."

"Yeah, but he also came back wearing an earring. And there was a rumor going around town that he was sharing an apartment out in California with somebody named Maurice."

"That's beside the point," Jay snapped.

"Don't blow a gasket. If I go to Kansas I won't stop loving you."

"You don't know that!" Jay said. "You might meet some hunk who will sweet-talk you right off your feet. Then I'll receive a Dear John letter in the mail. If I do, I promise you I'll come to Kansas, find the son of a bitch, and bust him into so many pieces he'll look like Humpty Dumpty when I'm through."

For the first time in hours Stacy laughed. She placed a hand on his forearm and said, "Whoa there, tiger. Get a grip. We'll discuss this later, if and when we ever get out of the mess we're in."

Jay refused to be appeased. "You'll go to Kansas over my dead body. No wife of mine is going off to another state and leaving me here to cool my heels and worry my ass off."

"Wife?"

"Yeah. I planned to ask you to marry me at the prom," Jay revealed "I've already bought the ring. Have it on layaway at Driscoll's. Cost me every penny I had and then some," he added, breaking off when' Stacy uttered a cry of delight and leaped into his arms. He clasped her to him, awash in a riptide of love, desperately trying to think of the right words to say, the perfect words that would persuade her to say yes, that would keep her by his side forever.

"Oh, you big lug!" Stacy exclaimed, and kissed him on the ear.

"Are you mad at me?"

Stacy drew back and beamed. "Why would I be mad at the guy who is going to be my husband?"

"You mean..."

"Yep!"

Jay cackled and spun in circles, kissing her neck, her cheeks, her rosy lips. He felt deliriously happy, as if he would burst at the seams with pure joy. They were as good as married. Or were they? A sobering stumbling block gave him pause. "What about your folks? How will they take the news?"

"My dad will want to take a baseball bat to your thick skull."

"Then let's elope," Jay said.

"What? And give up my chance at a big, formal wedding with all the trimmings?" Stacy said, grinning. She pecked him on the nose, giggled and hugged him.

Suddenly she stiffened in Jay's grasp and he heard a sharp intake of her breath. She was gazing over his shoulder in the direction of the hill.

Jay whirled.

The monster was on the crest, watching them. The moment he laid eyes on it, the creature bounded toward them.

Chapter 21

One minute Cory Fleming was rounding a comer in a pitch black tunnel, the darkness held back by the flickering glow of his smoking lantern, and the next he emerged from the passage into the stupendous chamber where perpetual twilight reigned. Towering above him was a spire as high as a Denver skyscraper. Nearby was a stone arch under which an elephant could walk with ease.

He shut off the lantern to conserve the fuel, then surveyed the hellish landscape, seeking signs of the demon and Ann. The ground was either solid rock or hard-packed soil lacking the accumulation of dust found in many of the tunnels, so relying on tracks was out of the question.

Tightening his grip on the pick handle, Cory hiked between the spire and the arch.

All was still, the air much wanner than in the passages. He wondered if hidden eyes were observing his every move and fervently hoped that wasn't the case. With the element of surprise in his favor he stood a slim chance of rescuing Ann. Without it, if he was spotted beforehand, the demon could pick him off at its leisure since the creature must know every nook and cranny in the vast subterranean refuge.

Another, equally disturbing, worry bothered him. One he had considered before. What if there were more than one of the things? According to all the tales and legends he had read about or ever heard, demons had at one time been legion. There was supposed to be an army of them at the

Devil's beck and call. Even allowing for gross exaggeration and distortion by people from pervious eras who encountered the creatures, there must have been more than one in order for the population to perpetuate itself.

So there was a distinct possibility there was more than one in the Caverna del Diablo.

The prospect was chilling.

Canyons and ravines crisscrossed the underworld. Mammoth rock formations were everywhere. Way off to his left lay a great plain.

Cory paused and adjusted his glasses. Where in that sprawling region was Ann? Locating her would be like finding the traditional needle in a haystack. He didn't dare shout to draw her attention because the yells would also draw demon. His sole recourse was to keep hunting and pray for the best.

He made for a ravine, running so he would not be in the open any longer than was necessary, his eyes constantly in motion.

Not so much as a mouse stirred, which brought to mind another consideration. What did demons eat? From the marks on the bones he'd seen on the ledge hours ago, he concluded demons were carnivorous and one of their favorite meals consisted of human flesh. If true, there must be other sources of nourishment since humans rarely descended any great depth into the cavern. Rodents, perhaps. Or lizards, since many caves were known to harbor them. Then again, demons might subsist on something else entirely. He had no empirical evidence on which to base his speculation, and a scientist without empirical evidence was like a fish out of water, floundering for facts instead of oxygen.

At the mouth of the ravine he halted to listen. The total

quiet was nerve-racking, more so than in the tunnels. Holding the pick in front of him, he cautiously advanced. Once the lantern cooled off he intended to stick it in the backpack to free both his hands for fighting if need be.

The ravine twisted and turned, its sides as smooth as marble, the stone the color of caramel. Vegetation was nonexistent. He hugged the right wall so his back would be protected and repeatedly checked to his rear to prevent a creature from sneaking up on him.

Minutes of travel brought him to the end, where the ravine opened out onto a level area embracing five acres or more. Domes the size of pickup trucks dotted the tract, behind any one of which a creature might be lurking.

Cory bore to the left to skirt the domes. A quarter of the way around he abruptly inhaled an offensive odor, a smell so rank it brought to mind the disgusting stench of long dead road kills crawling with maggots or rotten garbage so putrid even rats wouldn't touch the stuff. He also heard a gurgling sound and gazing to his left spied a small pool of bubbling yellowish-brown liquid.

Fascinated, he walked over and squatted. He knew better than to touch it. The liquid possessed the same consistency as water, but the stench inclined him to the opinion it was liquid sulfur, which had a boiling point of eight hundred and thirty-two degrees. The slightest touch and he'd be badly burned.

Rising, he moved off, deep in thought. Where there was one pool there were bound to be others, which pointed at some degree of volcanic activity. That would account for the elevated temperature and the muggy air. This great realm, in effect, was a unique microcosm within the vaster body of the earth proper, a habitat perhaps ideally suited to the demons and whatever other life forms flourished.

A rattling arose near the domes.

Instantly Cory spun and raced behind a short spire a dozen yards off. No sooner did he take cover than the noise was repeated, louder and closer. He tried to slow his surging pulse and risked a peek.

A demon was standing beside a dome near the pool, its head cocked, its features lined in intense concentration. The creature stared at the ravine, then at the pool, then walked forward. It stopped, threw back its head, and vented its rattling cry a third time.

Cory was glued to the spire, amazed at how the demon produced the noise. He saw the demon's forked tongue protrude from between its parted lips and vibrate just like a rattlesnake's tail, striking its upper and lower teeth as the forked tip danced wildly. The sight was hideous, but it was nothing compared to the creature's next act. Kneeling by the pool, the demon dipped a hand into the sulfur and scooped the boiling substance into its mouth.

Cory could barely credit the testimony of his own eyes. By all scientific standards the feat should be impossible, yet there the demon was, drinking away, unfazed. He watched as it drank its fill, then wiped the back of its hand across its lips and stood. For a moment he feared the demon would come straight toward him, but it turned and disappeared among the domes.

Cory sagged, feeling weak, the magnitude of the danger hitting home. That thing had been seven feet tall, minimum, and endowed with a physique a weightlifter would die for. What chance did he stand against such an adversary? Who was he trying to kid? All he had to rely on were his wits and his scientific expertise, neither of which seemed adequate for the task.

Should he just give up and leave before he was found out

and slain?

No! He thought of Ann, of the feel of her in his arms and the press of her soft lips. Renewed resolve flooded through him. He was her only hope. No one else knew where they were. No one else could help. If he ran off, if he let cowardice get the better of him, he might as well find a high cliff and jump because he would never be able to live with himself afterward. Some might brand him crazy, but the true test of any love was devotion to your beloved. If he fled, he was not only sealing Ann's fate, he was tacitly demonstrating his affection had been a sham.

Cory looked out. He saw no trace of the demon. Acting on the assumption that it was the one that had taken Ann, he crept toward the domes, setting each foot down softly. Suddenly he realized he was still holding the lantern in his left hand. By now it should be cool. He pressed his right wrist to the metal, confirmed the heat had dissipated, and stopped so he could remove his backpack and place the lantern inside. After zipping the pack shut, he slipped the straps over his arms, gripped the pick in both hands, and ventured among the domes to do battle for the life of the girl he loved.

Provided she was still alive.

"Run!" Jay shouted, and gave Stacy a shove that was supposed to send her fleeing across the plain but instead caused her to stumble and fall to her knees. Before she could stand the monster was there, six feet away, staring at them with its mouth creased in a malevolent grin.

"We're done for!" Stacy cried.

Jay took in the creature's features in a glance. The red skin, the massive muscles, the fiery eyes, the horns and the forked tail. They filled him with dread but he stayed rooted between the monster and Stacy. To get at her it must go through him.

The thing seemed amused by his defiance. It scrutinized him from head to toe, then motioned as if inviting him to attack.

"Don't go near it," Stacy said, on her feet again, her palms flat against his back. "Please, Jay! Let's just back off and hope to hell it leaves us alone."

"We have nowhere to run."

"Look at that thing. You wouldn't last a minute. It wants you to move in close so it can kill you quickly."

The monster glanced at her and hissed.

Jay hesitated. He wasn't completely convinced the creature could beat him so handily. The last time it had taken him unawares. Now he was braced and ready. Sure, it was taller than him, but he knew of basketball players who were even taller. And yes, the monster had more muscles, but muscle alone did not always denote great strength. There were skinny guys on the football team who were stronger than some of the beefier players.

"Please!" Stacy pleaded. "For me."

Reluctantly, Jay slowly retreated, exercising care not to entangle his feet with hers and trip. He tensed, anticipating the monster would rush them. But it didn't move. Only after they had gone fifteen feet did it take a ponderous stride and begin to follow them. "Why isn't it attacking?" he wondered aloud.

"Who cares?" Stacy said. "All that matters is it's letting us leave, so don't do anything to anger it."

Jay knew better but kept quiet. The monster was in no rush because it knew they couldn't escape. It was toying with them like a cat toys with a mouse, allowing them to get their hopes up before closing for the kill. He must be ready when the charge came. There would only be one chance.

The demon continued to trail them, making no attempt to pounce.

"If only we had a gun," Stacy said.

Mentally, Jay echoed those sentiments. He should have thought to bring his dad's pistol or a knife along. But even if he had, the demon would have found the weapon after it had knocked them out and he would be no better off than he was now. He balled his fists and waited.

An agonizing minute went by.

"Leave us alone, damn you!" Stacy shouted stridently. "Go away!"

The monster paid her no mind.

Long minutes went by. And still the crimson fiend stalked them, exhibiting no aggression, grinning wickedly all the while, taking deliberate step after deliberate step, utterly silent.

The ordeal got to Jay. His nerves were rubbed raw. He wanted to end the stalemate, to buy Stacy time to flee while he fought the creature off. But when he slowed, thinking the thing would close on him, the monster also slowed, matching him pace for pace. He went faster. So did the monster. He angled to the right. The thing did the same.

Just when Jay was wondering how much longer this emotionally grueling pursuit would last, Stacy gripped his arm and said, "Maybe we should run."

"Go for it," Jay responded, spinning and sprinting on her heels.

They were near the giant dome, almost back where they had started. He heard Stacy sniff at the same moment he smelled the stench of rotten eggs and saw the bubbling pools giving off their tendrils of spiraling smoke. If the water or whatever was in those pools was bubbling, then it must be boiling, and if it was boiling, it would cause serious hurt to anything that fell in.

A wild idea blossomed. Jay glanced over his shoulder and saw the monster moving at the same speed they were, still playing its demented game. "When I stop at the first pool, you keep going to the far side."

"What? I'm not leaving you."

"This isn't the time to argue, damn it. I have a plan."

"No."

Exasperated, Jay jogged until he was within a few feet of the pool. The rank smell was almost overpowering. Breathing shallowly, he halted and turned.

The monster promptly stopped.

"All right," Jay said to Stacy. "If you want to stay, then you can help me trick this son of a bitch."

"How?"

"Go around the pool to the other side."

"I told you I'm not leaving you alone."

"Damn your stubborn streak!" Jay said. "Listen to me. My plan will work if you cooperate. Trust me. Go to the other side of this pool, and when I say the word, scream your lungs out."

Stacy looked at him, her eyes reflecting her affection and her fear. "Okay. But this had better work. If you get your ass killed, I'm going to be royally ticked off at you."

"I'll keep it in mind."

Stacy pivoted and did as he had instructed. When she was directly across from him she said, "All set."

The monster was gazing from Jay to her and back again, apparently perplexed by their maneuver.

"All right, you ugly fucker," Jay taunted. "Let's see how bright you are." He mimicked the creature's earlier gesture, inviting the thing to come at him.

Oddly, the creature grinned, exposing tapered teeth capable of rending flesh with a single bite

"What are you waiting for?" Jay said. He stepped to the right, starting to move in a circle, his attention riveted on the monsters legs. If the thing didn't do as he expected, he was as good as dead. "What's the matter? Are you too dumb to know when you've been insulted?"

Still grinning, the creature took a short stride.

"That's it, stupid," Jay went on, trying to distract the brute with nonstop talk. If it didn't have a second to think, it wouldn't figure out what he was up to until too late. "Come toward me. Come to papa so he can give you exactly what you deserve for butchering Scott and Terri." As he talked, he continued to move in a circle. "I want to see your face when you buy the farm, bastard. I want to see you in pain."

"Be careful!" Stacy shouted.

The monster stared at her, then shifted to face Jay.

"A little bit further should do it," Jay said, continuing to circle. "Keep looking at me, moron. Don't pay any attention to anything else. Just me. That's it."

Seemingly intrigued, the creature simply listened, moving so as to keep Jay directly in front of it.

"Almost there," Jay said, elated at his success. Another sideways step put him at about the same spot occupied by the monster when he put his scheme into effect. The creature was about where he had been standing. They had reversed positions.

The monster rumbled and began to raise an arm.

"Now!" Jay yelled. "Do it now!"

On cue, Stacy cupped her hands to her mouth and screamed long and loud, a shrill scream that carried out across the infernal wasteland, distorted by the many canyon walls and the steep sides of the many ravines but nonetheless wafting far and wide.

Cory Fleming, warily crossing the dome field, heard the scream and stopped. So, almost, did his heart. Was it Ann? He'd assumed she was somewhere nearby, not as distant as the source of the faint scream must be. Alarmed, he turned this way and that, trying to pinpoint the direction it came from, but in the middle of the domes it seemed to be coming from every direction at once.

He stood still, listening to the scream die out. Either he could go racing off in a desperate search or he could keep scouring the immediate area. Since the demon he had seen couldn't have gone all that far, he opted to confine his quest to the general vicinity and hoped to heaven he wasn't making a fatal mistake.

Fatal for Ann, that is.

In a room elsewhere in the Caverna del Diablo, Wesley Eagen took a sip of beer, then snapped to attention when a barely audible scream reached his ears. He knew it couldn't be Terri or Leslie since they were both dead. So it was either Stacy or Ann. He liked Stacy, if only for her body. Ann, he didn't care for one bit. In any event, there was nothing he could do to help whoever it was so he shrugged and took another sip of brew.

Much closer to the pools where Jay and Stacy were making their stand, Leslie Vanderhorst feebly stirred. Vivid, horrifying memories of being struck by Wes made her cringe and whimper. Had she just screamed? She opened her eyes, feeling nauseous and thoroughly disoriented, then recoiled on seeing the most repulsive face imaginable not inches from her own, the face of a smirking red monster. A hand touched her stomach, another her thigh. Petrified, shocked to her core, she fainted dead away.

At the sound of Stacy's scream the monster turned and stared at her with its forehead knit, as if puzzled by her behavior. It took a step nearer the pool and reached out although she was well beyond its reach.

This was the moment Jay had been waiting for. He galvanized into action, lowering his right shoulder and charging, his powerful legs pumping, transforming every square inch of his two hundred and fifty pounds into a living battering ram. The monster evidently heard him and started to swing around. A heartbeat later he slammed into it at the base of its spine.

The creature flew forward as if shot from a cannon, its arms flung out protectively, and hit the surface of the pool hard. Headfirst, it went under, thrashing and flailing, and sank in a twinkling, its tail the last part of its body to sink from sight.

Jay threw himself backwards as drops of the scalding liquid sprayed in all directions. A few spattered on his arms, a drop on his neck. Those tiny amounts were enough to send waves of agony rippling through him. Landing on his side, he rolled onto his stomach and buried his face in the ground to keep any of the liquid from striking his face. The pool erupted in a foaming, bubbling cauldron, spewing streams of the burning substance, none of which hit him. Abruptly, the agitation subsided.

Worried about Stacy, Jay rose onto his elbows and glanced at the opposite side. She was also on her stomach, staring at the bubbling surface. Then she looked up, caught his eyes, and laughed. "You did it, honeybuns! You did it!"

Jay pushed upright and ran around the pool. She met him halfway, jumping into his arms and giggling in girlish joy.

"We're safe! We're safe!"

"Yes," Jay said, swiveling so he could see the pool. He half-feared the monster would come roaring up out of the depths, but of course the idea was ridiculous. Nothing could survive that.

"I'm so proud of you I could eat you whole," Stacy declared, and bit his chin to emphasize her point.

"Ouch," Jay said, wincing. He lowered her and chuckled. "Any other time or place I'd take you up on your offer. But right now we should haul butt while the hauling is good."

"Why the rush? Why can't we rest?"

"What if it's not the only one?"

Stacy sobered. "Oh, crap. I didn't think of that."

"Come on," Jay said, taking her hand. He headed toward an adjacent canyon. Beyond it appeared to be a high wall which might be the outer boundary. If so, they stood a chance of finding a way out.

"Wait until I tell the gang at school about this," Stacy said proudly. "My hunk took on the monster from the Caverna del Diablo and whipped its sorry butt."

"No one will believe you."

"Why not? All my friends know I don't lie."

"Look around you," Jay said, encompassing the unworldly domain with a sweep of his arm. "Who in their right mind is going to believe this place exists? And do you really expect our friends to believe that monster was real?" He snorted. "They'll laugh you silly."

"I don't. . .," Stacy began, and suddenly fell silent.

Jay knew why. He heard the same sound she did, the

sound of liquid splashing over the edge of the pool behind them.

With a sinking sensation in the pit of his stomach, Jay let go of her hand and spun, knowing what he would see before he saw it although his mind shrieked that it couldn't be, that it was impossible, that no living thing could have survived.

But he was wrong.

The monster was emerging from the pool. Dripping wet, unscathed by its plunge, it looked at them and grinned that wicked grin.

Chapter 22

When Cory Fleming spied a girl lying under a rock overhang that jutted from a canyon wall, he thought he must be seeing things. He blinked in astonishment, moved closer, and nearly whooped with joy.

It was Ann!

Elated, Cory broke into a run and sped to her side. Only then did he think to look around for the demon.

Five minutes ago he had passed through the dome field and entered the canyon. Grotesque formations dotted the floor, with pools of liquid sulfur scattered here and there. The same fetid odor as before, like that of a million rotten eggs, filled the air.

He had found no trace of the demon or Ann until suddenly rounding a curve and there she was, underneath the overhang.

Cory gripped the pick so tightly, his knuckles hurt. What if this was a trap? he asked himself. What if the creature had deliberately left Ann there so he would blunder into the open and be a sitting duck for whatever the demon had in mind? Surely it hadn't gone off and left her there?

He surveyed the canyon in both directions, paying particular attention to the nearest rock formations, yet saw nothing.

Ann moaned softly.

Positioning himself so he faced the canyon floor, Cory knelt, placed the pick by his side, and gently lifted her head onto his leg. There was a nasty bruise on her left temple. Otherwise, she appeared fine. He stroked her cheek, watching the rise and fall of her blouse as she breathed, his relief at finding her alive knowing no bounds. He had to clear his throat a couple of times before he could speak. "Ann? Ann? It's Cory. I'm here."

She moaned once more and her eyelids quivered.

"Ann?"

As if she had been pricked by a pin, Ann abruptly sat up, her eyes snapping wide to reveal unadulterated terror. "Noooo!" she cried, then saw his hand on her shoulder and glanced up. "Cory? It's you! Thank God!"

He wrapped his arms around her, as much to comfort her as to prevent her from noticing the moisture rimming his eyes. "I thought I'd lost you," he said, sounding as if he had a cold.

"Where am I? How did you find me?"

"It wasn't easy," Cory said, trying to control the emotional whirlpool within himself. Brushing a hand across his face, he sat back and gave her a light kiss on the forehead. "You're in that enormous underground world I told you about. I followed the demon's tracks most of the way, but once I got here I had no idea where you were. It was sheer dumb luck that I found you."

“I thought you were dead," Ann said, and kissed him in return, only she planted her lips on his mouth and let the kiss linger before she drew back and grinned. "Umm. That was nice. I plan to do a lot of that from now on."

”I never knew you have such a one-track mind,” Cory joked, and then became deadly serious. "What happened to you? Did the demon give you this bruise?" He pointed at the black-and-blue blotch.

Ann nodded, her grin becoming a scowl. “I saw the

thing hit you. You landed so hard I was sure I heard bones break. It started to go down after you, then changed its mind and grabbed me instead. I screamed and fought but it was no use. The thing pulled me by the arm through tunnel after tunnel until I couldn't take it anymore and tried to get loose. That's when it slugged me."

"And carried you the rest of the way on its shoulder," Cory guessed.

"I don't need to tell you how scared I was," Ann said. "The shock of losing you was more than I could bear." She gently touched his face.

Coughing, Cory rose and helped her to stand. "We've got to get out of here. The demon is bound to return." He snatched up the pick and stepped out from under the overhang. Which way should they go? Back the way he came? He should be able to locate the tunnel that brought them here, so it seemed the wisest choice.

Accordingly, they hurried back down the canyon.

"Why did the thing just leave me there?" Ann wondered.

"Count your blessings. Maybe it was saving you for later."

"How do you mean?"

"Maybe it wasn't hungry."

"Oh."

Cory was a walking bundle of raw nerves. He feared they would encounter the creature on its way to the overhang and knew he would be virtually helpless against its superior size and strength. If only the were a way to kill the thing!

"I came around once for a minute when it was carrying me," Ann mentioned. "The wind revived me, I guess."

"The wind?"

"Have you ever stuck your head out of the window of a

moving car and felt the wind on your face?"

"Who hasn't?"

"Well, that demon or whatever the hell it is, was moving as fast as a car. And it wasn't my imagination. If I had to guess, I'd say it was doing over fifty miles an hour, even with the burden of my weight."

Could it actually go that fast? Cory speculated, wanting to accept her assessment although common sense and his innate scientific skepticism told him no biped could attain such speed. Why, fifty miles an hour was faster than a cheetah could run, and the cheetah was the fastest animal known to man. But what if she were right? If so, then unencumbered the creature must be capable of greater speed, perhaps on the order of sixty or seventy miles an hour. His mind boggled at the concept. It meant the demon could cover a mile in the time it took the average person to walk slightly over a hundred and fifty feet.

"There's something else I think you should know," Ann said.

"What?"

"The thing seemed to be afraid of the lantern."

Cory glanced at her, his curiosity piqued. "What gives you that idea?"

"Because of the way the thing acted when it went into the pit after you. The lantern had fallen from your hand and was between the creature and you. I saw the thing stop and shield its eyes with one hand and back off. The whole time it was hissing like a basketful of snakes. If you want my opinion, the lantern saved your life. I just know that monster was going to finish you off."

A flicker of hope flared in Cory's breast. The demon must have an Achille's heel. If he could discover what it was, they might---just might---make it to the surface alive.

Think! he prodded himself. What could it be? What about the lantern would make such an immensely powerful being act timid? The heat? Obviously not. Any creature able to drink liquid sulfur could endure temperatures that would roast a human alive. What else, then? Light? Was that it? The demon was accustomed to dwelling in near total darkness except for the few rooms and chambers where the walls or ceiling cast weak illumination. He gazed up at the dimly glowing ceiling far, far above.

That had to be it. As with most creatures, the demons were ideally adapted to their environment. Their entire metabolism was geared to subterranean living. Like bats, their hearing must be exceptional. But their sense of smell, since there were so few odors to stimulate their olfactory organ, was probably weak. So, too, their eyes must be in one respect. An eternity of existing in perpetual gloom had rendered them incapable of standing bright light, which undoubtedly explained why they had never tried to establish a foothold on the surface. The sun was more than they could bear. Then again, maybe they had tried and learned from their failure.

All of which meant that for as long as the lantern's fuel held out, he could keep the things at bay.

He frowned, recalling the incident at the pit. The lantern was lit when the demon attacked them. But if he remembered right, the demon had rushed him from the rear. His own body had blocked the light. He mustn't make the same mistake again.

They passed a rock formation in a spiral shape. Before them appeared a boiling pool.

Cory stared at it while mentally reviewing every fact he knew about sulfur. Something nagged at him, something he felt might be important.

Sulfur melted into a yellow liquid at a temperature of two hundred and thirty degrees. At two hundred and fifty degrees, though, it became so thick it couldn't be poured from a beaker. Above two hundred and fifty, oddly enough, sulfur became liquid again, and at eight hundred and thirty-two degrees reached its boiling point. What else? What were the commercial applications of sulfur? The answer hit him like a physical blow. "Elementary," he said, and smiled.

"What is, Sherlock?" Ann said.

"Help me." Cory hurried over near the pool where the ground was coated with fine yellow grains of powder. He quickly stripped off the backpack and removed the pair of dirty socks and the shirt they had found. Neither of the socks had holes. Giving one to Ann, he began filling his with the yellow powder. "Pack yours almost to the top," he instructed her.

Once they both were done, he drew his knife and cut thin strips of fabric from the shirt, then used the strips to tie the open ends of the socks shut.

"What will this stuff do?"

"Maybe make the difference between life and death," Cory said, stuffing the socks into the backpack. Next he spread out the shirt and dumped handfuls of powder on top, forming a mound in the middle. Ann joined in, her expression betraying her puzzled state of mind.

Working swiftly, Cory cut off another strip, then lifted the edges of the shirt above the pile and looped the makeshift tie a few inches from the top to prevent the powder from leaking out. This, too, he put in the backpack.

Cory removed the lantern and gave it to Ann, then adjusted the pack on his back and resumed hiking toward where he hoped to find the tunnel out.

"I have a hunch the demon can't tolerate bright light," he explained. "The stuff we just collected is sulfur. It ignites easily, so we can light it using our matches." He paused. "Sulfur bums very quickly and very brightly."

"I get it," Ann said, clapping him on the back. "My hunk, the genius."

"Please don't call me that."

"Why not? You're the smartest guy in school. Everyone knows it."

"Maybe I am," Cory begrudgingly acknowledged, "but the word makes me think of all the teasing I've had to endure, all the ribbing from kids who looked down their noses at me simply because I was smarter than they were. If I had a dollar for every time someone called me 'Einstein' or 'boy genius', I'd be a millionaire."

"I'm sorry. I didn't know."

"No big deal," Cory said with a shrug, regretting he had brought the subject up. It made him sound like a spiteful dork. He concentrated on escaping. Since leaving the tunnel he had never completely lost sight of the towering spire beside it. Such a prominent landmark was easy to see for miles around, and he now made straight toward it.

"Cory?" Ann said softly.

"Yeah?"

"No matter what happens next, I want you to know I won't ever forget that you came after me. No one else I know except maybe my parents would have risked their lives the way you have."

Cory shrugged, feeling slightly embarrassed. "I did what I had to."

"I just wish we had time..," Ann said, but didn't finish her statement.

"Time for what?"

"Nothing. I'll tell you later."

"Suit yourself."

"There is one thing I can tell you, though."

"Go ahead."

"If anyone ever calls you 'Einstein' or 'boy genius' in front of me, I'll punch their lights out."

"What do we do?" Stacy asked breathlessly as the dripping monster lumbered slowly toward them, its freakish features twisted in a sneer.

"We run," Jay said, and grabbed her arm as he took off. They had outdistanced the creature before. They could do so again.

To his bewilderment, though, the thing suddenly streaked out across the plain, moving so fast its body was a red blur. It swung wide, then curved in a loop until it halted directly in their path, not twenty feet away.

Smirking, the monster stood calmly as if waiting for their next move.

"Oh, Lord," Stacy said, halting.

Jay was stunned. The thing could move like a damn race car! It had been holding back before. Whenever it wanted, it could run rings around them. But why hadn't it done so earlier? "The son of a bitch has been toying with us."

"It's going to kill us," Stacy said. "I can feel it."

"Get behind me," Jay directed, pushing her back. He clenched his fists and assumed a boxing posture.

"Run!" Stacy urged, tugging on his shirt. "We can't fight that thing!"

"There's nothing else we can do," Jay said. "You saw how fast it is."

The creature seemed amused by their conversation. It

strode to within six feet of them, then stopped and beckoned Jay, once again inviting him to attack.

This time Jay did. He heard Stacy wail "No!" but he was already in motion, rushing in close and swinging his fists in furious cadence, pounding his knuckles into the creature's midsection. The monster grunted, then grinned, showing Jay the blows had no effect. Enraged, Jay delivered a hook to the jaw that took the creature by surprise and caused it to stagger back. He closed in but it recovered and lashed out with an open-handed swing that caught Jay flush on the cheek and sent him sprawling onto his back with his ears ringing and his head throbbing.

"I told you we can't fight it!" Stacy cried, reaching his side and grabbing his arm. "Come on! Haul ass!"

The monster was grinning.

"Stay back," Jay said, pushing Stacy aside as he rose and sprang, trying for a tackle this time. His shoulders slammed into the creature's shins with enough force to upend a Brahma bull. It was like slamming into the uprights in the end zone. Every bone from his head to his toes was jarred violently, and he wound up on his stomach, stunned, while above him the monster tossed back its head and uttered it rattling cry. Suddenly he understood. The thing was laughing at him!

"Jay!" Stacy yelled in desperation. "Get up!"

He did, but only because the monster permitted him to rise without interfering. Raining blows, he stepped in close and pummeled the creature's massive body, his fear gone, replaced by an uncontrollable rage at being treated with such contempt. There had to be a way to beat the thing. He had never lost a fight yet. He was in excellent condition, a powerhouse in his own right. Everyone called him King Kong, the toughest guy in Pagosa Springs. Now he intended to be true to his reputation, to show this smirking son of a bitch why he was the most feared football player in all of Colorado.

Jay rammed his fists into the creature's stomach. He struck its chest, its neck, its chin. The monster never so much as flinched. He tried to punch the thing's nose but it jerked its head aside. Then, when he was overextended and off balance, the creature retaliated with a punch to the gut that doubled Jay in half, all the air whooshing out of his lungs as torment racked his body.

He tottered to one side and sank to his knees.

"Jay!" Stacy screeched, darting over and draping her arm across his shoulders. "Oh, God, what are we going to do?"

Jay tried to answer but couldn't. Beyond her the monster moved. In horror he saw it approach. Frantically, he attempted to speak. But all he could do was gurgle and gasp in inarticulate terror.

Stacy stared at him in dismay. He saw the creature grasp her from behind, its hands on her hips, and lift her high into the air. Her face reflected utter shock.

The monster shifted and carried her off. Belatedly, Stacy came to life and commenced kicking and flailing, but the creature ignored her.

What was it doing?

Jay got up, still doubled over and breathing in ragged gasps. He shuffled in pursuit, seeing Stacy twist her head and cast a pleading glance at him. She was helpless in the monster's grasp. Unless he saved her, there was no telling what it might do. But his gut was awash in excruciating pain. He couldn't straighten up, let alone fight.

"Jay, help me!" Stacy cried.

Jay tried. Gritting his teeth against the torment, he managed a tottering run, but despite his best effort he couldn't overtake them. Before he knew it, the monster halted beside one of the boiling pools and turned to face him, its features a mask of supreme evil.

"Jay!" Stacy yelled, staring fearfully at the roiling surface.

Startling insight halted Jay in his tracks. He was five yards from them, too far to help. If he tried a mad dash, the thing might simply release her and Stacy would fall into the pool. Or it might heave her into the middle. He stayed still, hoping against hope the monster wouldn't harm her.

The creature hissed.

"Please," Jay croaked. "Please."

Cocking its head, the monster studied him for a bit, then grinned. In a blinding display of speed and coordination, it changed its grip on Stacy, flipping her so that she was upside down while simultaneously grabbing her left ankle.

"Don't!" Jay pleaded, taking several steps.

The monster's grin broadened, revealing most of its razor teeth. Deliberately, slowly, it extended the arm holding Stacy out over the pool.

"Please, no!" Jay pleaded, his eyes filling with tears.

Stacy had her eyes closed, her hands pressed to her throat. Her lips were moving soundlessly as if she were praying.

"I love her," Jay said, saying the first thing that came into his head to distract the creature while he took another step. He must get close enough to try and grab her. It was a long shot but he couldn't stand there doing nothing. "Don't hurt her and I'll do anything you want! Just don't hurt her!"

Out flicked the creature's snake-like tongue, as if testing the air. It lowered its right arm an inch, dipping Stacy's head that much nearer the surface.

She whimpered.

"You chicken-shit son of a bitch!" Jay roared in impotent

rage. He eased forward. If pleading did no good, maybe getting the thing angry would do the trick. Maybe, if the creature became mad enough, it would charge him and drop her on the ground instead of in the pool. "Why don't you leave her alone and take me on, you bastard?"

The creature lowered its arm another inch. The tips of Stacy's hair touched the liquid and immediately her hair sizzled and smoked.

Stacy began trembling and crying.

"Damn you!" Jay bellowed. He was two yards away. So close and yet so far!

Displaying casual indifference, the monster performed an exaggerated yawn. Its right arm dropped a fraction and more of Stacy's hair crackled and burned.

Beside himself with fury, Jay clenched his fists and tensed to make a reckless bid for her life. He must save her no matter what the cost to himself. She was everything to him.

"Jay. . .," Stacy unexpectedly said, gazing lovingly straight at him.

Without warning the creature suddenly lowered its arm and in the blink of an eye Stacy's head sank beneath the bubbling surface. It happened so swiftly she didn't have time to cry out. Her body promptly went into severe convulsions, her legs jerking spasmodically.

The monster held its arm rigid and grinned at Jay.

"Nooooooo!" Jay screamed, darting to the edge of the cauldron, tears streaming as he watched his beloved's death throes. Blindly, he threw himself at the thing, but it battered him aside with a disdainful sweep of its other arm. He landed hard a few yards from the pool and saw Stacy's blistered right hand jut out of the liquid, her fingers clawing at the muggy air. Then her hand stiffened and went limp. Her legs went slack, her body sagged.

In the same careless manner a human might cast aside a piece of useless trash, the monster cast Stacy's body into the pool and turned, its mocking grin wider than ever.

A burning, berserk wrath erupted within Jay. He vented a bestial growl and came off the ground in a fierce rush, hurtling at the demented monstrosity responsible for the death of his love. His hands outstretched, he leaped at the creature's throat.

As if in slow motion he saw the monster glide aside and knew he had been suckered into doing exactly what the thing wanted him to do. The pool was in front of him. Below him. Enveloping him. Searing heat encased him in a fiery blanket. He inadvertently opened his mouth to scream and felt the heat melt his insides. His world became a red inferno. He weakly tried to move his arms and legs and felt his right hand bump something in the liquid beside him. Somehow, even in his ravaged state, he realized he was touching Stacy's hand. His last conscious act was to close his fingers over what remained of hers, and then the red inferno engulfed him completely.

Chapter 23

“There it is!" Cory exclaimed in relief, pointing at the mouth of the tunnel ahead.

"I can't believe we're going to make it," Ann said.

"We're hardly out of danger," Cory reminded her, scanning the subterranean domain once again. So far their luck was holding. A demon had yet to show up, but he knew and she knew it was only a matter of time.

"Let's light the lantern," he proposed, and halted to dig the matchbox out of his pocket.

"I'll keep watch."

Cory nodded and set to work, anticipating the wick would be as hard to light as before. To his surprise, it caught at the first match. "There you go," he said, sticking the box back into his front pocket. He took the lead, anxious to put the chamber behind them.

At the entrance he paused for one last look.

Far off to the left, near a dry plain, was a red dot.

Cory's breath caught in his throat as he watched the dot move at an incredible speed in the general direction of the canyon where he had found Ann. It reminded him of the Indy 500 where the race cars zipped around the track at speeds in excess of one hundred-fifty miles an hour. On the straightaways the cars were blurred steaks of color.

"Dear Lord!" Ann said. She had seen it, too. “The thing will find out I'm gone.”

"So? We didn't leave any tracks and I don't think it can follow our scent trail. Odds are it won't know which way we went." Cory said, injecting more confidence into his voice than he felt. "Maybe it will figure you revived and wandered off. It should be busy for a while hunting you down."

"Sooner or later it will check out this tunnel."

Cory hastened into the passage. Their footprints in the dust would be all the demon needed to deduce what had happened and come after them with a vengeance. Since they couldn't possibly hope to outrun the thing, they must resort to outthinking it.

Could they? How smart was a demon? Since no one had ever administered a standard intelligence test to one, their intelligence quotient was an unknown factor. He had to assume that they were at least as smart as a human.

Never underrate your adversary.

They hiked until they came to a fork where Cory took the right branch. He had used the other fork when he was chasing after Ann and knew it wouldn't take them anywhere near the surface.

"You hear something?" Ann suddenly asked.

Pausing, Cory listened, fearing the pad-pad-pad of onrushing feet. Other than her breathing the tunnel was perfectly still. "No."

"I thought I did. Sorry."

Cory doubted the demon was after them already but he increased their pace to be on the safe side, her at his left elbow. Twice came to forks. In each instance Cory relied on his gut instinct in picking the branch they took. After the second turn the tunnel slanted upward

"Maybe this is the one that will finally bring us to the surface," Ann said.

"Maybe." Cory reserved judgment. He had traversed other passages where the floor inclined up, only to have them take him lower again. To paraphrase an old adage, he'd believe a tunnel would take him to the surface when he actually arrived *at* the surface.

They hurried on in mutual silence, each racked by trepidation.

The tunnel wound through several rooms and grottos where Cory noticed unique helictite speleothems, formations composed of calcium carbonate. Elsewhere he saw dogtooth spar, crystallized calcite in the shape of small pyramids. Despite their plight he found himself admiring the beauty of the underground world.

After crossing a stretch of tunnel where debris from the ceiling was lying inches deep from wall to wall, they came to a keyhole, a narrowing of the passage where they had to squeeze their way through, with considerable effort.

Cory was forced to remove his backpack in order to accomplish the task.

A limestone passage brought them fifty yards later to a dead end.

Frowning, Cory raised the lantern, examining the walls, then the ceiling. In the process he discovered the dead end was in reality the base of a narrow chimney reaching up into gloomy shadow far overhead.

"Do we go back?" Ann said.

"We'd run the risk of bumping into the demon," Cory said.

"Then what? Make a stand?"

Cory nodded at the chimney. "We scale this and see where it leads."

Ann craned her neck, regarding the shaft dubiously. "What if it leads nowhere?"

"That's the chance we have to take. What do you say?"

She gazed back down the tunnel, clearly displeased. "It's

a case where we're damned if we do and damned if we don't." She sighed. "Hell, I guess we should try the chimney. You go first, though, so you can warn me of trouble spots."

Her request was reasonable but Cory would rather have had her go first so he would be in a position to brace her hould she lose her grip and fall.

Once more he slipped out of the backpack, arranging it over his chest with his arms through the straps. The pick went under his belt above his right hip, an awkward position in which to carry it, but he wasn't about to leave it behind. In his left hand he held the lantern handle.

"All set," he announced, applying his back to the right side of the chimney and the soles of his feet to the other side. By maintaining pressure on his back and his feet, he was albe to inch upward fairly rapidly.

Twenty feet up he broke into a sweat. The chimney was narrow enough so there was no need to extend his legs to their fullest, but the exertion nonetheless taxed his endurance to its utmost. Now and then his legs cramped, compelling him to stop and flex his muscles until the discomfort was gone.

Fifty feet up there was still no sign of an end to the shaft. "How are you holding up?" he called down.

"Just peachy," Ann said. "But I'm telling you here and now that I'll never become one of those spelunkers you were telling us about. This is the first and absolutely the last cave I ever intend to visit."

"Where's your sense of adventure?" Cory quipped.

"Where it should be, back in my bedroom, safe and sound."

Cory chuckled and pressed on. At the seventy-five foot level he began to wonder if he had made a monumental mistake. The higher the shaft went, the harder their descent would be should the chimney turn out to be a dead end.

"Cory?"

"Yes?"

"Why haven't you ever gone out for any sports? I bet you'd be great at track or tennis."

Cory peered between his legs, trying to see her face. Was she serious or what? And of all the times to ask such a question, why did she pick now?

"Did you hear me?" she prompted.

"Yeah," Cory said, pushing himself higher. "Why do you want to know?"

"I'm curious."

"Well, to put it bluntly, I've never had any great interest in running until I drop or swatting a little green ball with an oversized fly swatter. And don't tell anyone, because they all think I'm weird as it is, but I seldom if ever watch a Bronco game."

"Isn't there a law that says every adult Coloradoan must watch at least six Bronco games a year?" Ann joked, and grunted from her exertions.

"You'd think so," Cory said. Next to fishing, Bronco-mania was the preeminent preoccupation of nearly everyone in the state. Once a week during football season they glued themselves to the tube and wouldn't budge for anything short of global disaster. His own dad was a Bronco nut. So, too, were his mother, sister and brother. As the lone holdout in his family, he was tacitly regarded as something of an outcast, a freak of nature who must be missing critical genetic material.

"So why don't you have any interest in sports?" Ann probed.

"Before I answer, let's clarify something. I've gone out for some sports, you know. I'm in the chess club, and I was on the archery squad last year."

"That's right. You won the championship," Ann said. "I remember seeing you shoot a bow in your back yard when we were little." She paused. "But I'm referring to real sports like baseball or basketball, stuff like that."

Real sports? Cory reflected, amused. Archery entailed as much skill, in its own right, as any of the so-called manly sports. And chess could be as grueling mentally as football was physically. But rather than go into a lengthy explanation when the job at hand required most of his attention, he said, "When I was younger I was all skin and bone. I was also smaller than most of the other boys. For a while I tried different sports, until I found out that I couldn't run fast, couldn't throw a football for beans, and struck out every single time at the plate. So instead of making a fool of myself by pretending to be something I wasn't, I stayed at home and read books."

"But you've grown. You're no longer just skin and bones. Why stick with only archery and chess?"

"Because I like them. Any objections?"

"None at all. I just wanted to talk. I don't like being hemmed in like this."

"I understand." Cory felt the same way. Glancing up, he was delight to see the top of the shaft not ten feet above. Just below it was either the rim of a ledge or the floor of another tunnel.

"We're almost there," he informed Ann, and quickly climbed to where he could twist and grip the edge with his free hand. Then all it took was a sharp flip and a roll and he was out of the chimney and could sit up.

Swinging the lantern from side to side revealed he was indeed in a tunnel.

"How about giving a girl a hand?"

He turned to find Ann almost to the rim. Grinning, he put the lantern down and reached out to grip both of her wrists. 'When I say go, shove off with your legs and roll," he directed.

"Just don't let go or you'll never know what a terrific kisser I am."

"Brazen hussy."

"Say go, already."

"Go," Cory said, and heaved, pulling her up beside him. Their faces nearly touched and he couldn't resist the temptation to embrace and weld his lips to hers. She responded ardently, her hands running through his hair. When he broke off, she smirked and clucked in reproof.

"You decided to find out how good a kisser I am right away, huh? It might be best, though, to wait until we're out of the cave."

"Blame my hormones," Cory said. "And if you---."

The rattling cry of a demon wafted up the shaft.

"It's coming," Ann whispered fearfully.

The malevolent reminder of their dilemma had destroyed their light-hearted mood. Cory leaned out and gazed down the shaft but detected no movement---yet.

"We'd better run," Ann suggested, gripping his arm. "Maybe we can find a hiding place."

About to grab the lantern, Cory hesitated, his eyes narrowing as he studied the setup and estimated their chances of success. "No. We'll wait for it here."

"What? Why?"

"This might be our only chance to put an end to the thing," Cory said, and nodded at the smooth walls of the chimney. "It has to climb just like we did so it won't be able to use its hands much. When it get to the top, for a few seconds it will be vulnerable." He pulled the pick from under his belt. "One good blow should do the job."

"But what if you miss?" Ann said. "What if it grabs you as you swing? You know how damn strong the thing is. It can crush you with two fingers."

"Not if I don't let it," Cory said. He extended the pick, gauging the proper radius of his swing, and slid against the left-hand wall. "Take this," he said, removing the backpack.

"What can I do to help?"

"Take the lantern about ten feet off and blow out the flame." Cory tugged on the box of matches and tossed them at her feet. "Take those, too." He tossed them at her feet.

"I don't like this," Ann said.

"When I say to, light the lantern as quick as you can."

"Why don't I just leave it lit so you can see?"

"Because the light might cause it to change its mind and go back down. If I stay still in he dark, it might not notice me until it's too late. And if you light the lantern at just the right moment the thing will be looking toward you when I make my play."

"Your plan is too risky.," Ann objected. "What if it sees you? You'd be dead in seconds."

Cory looked at her. "I'm open to suggestions if you have a better idea."

"I don't have one," Ann reluctantly admitted. "I just wish there was a better way."

"So do I. But this is the best shot we have. Get cracking before the demon gets here."

Pouting, Ann picked up the lantern, the matches and the backpack. Her eyes never left him as she took three steps back, then stopped.

"I said ten feet."

"I know you did. But I'm staying close in case you need

me. Ann crouched and arranged everything beside her, then paused to bestow an affectionate look.

"Do it," Cory said.

A moment later the tunnel plunged into darkness.

He pressed his back against the wall, waiting for his eyes to adjust, feeling his heart thump wildly. Somewhere in the shaft was a vile creature notorious for hating humans with an abiding passion, a creature that wouldn't hesitate to rip him to shreds. If he screwed up he would certainly die.

The air was musty. He kept his breaths shallow, trying to make as little noise as possible. The success of his gambit depended on not being detected. It also depended on whether the demon came up the shaft facing him or facing in the other direction. Either way he would attack, but if the thing was looking toward him when he swung, it might be able to deflect the blow.

The seconds were eternities.

Suddenly, from out of the chimney, there issued a low, sibilant hiss.

Cory's arms began to tremble and he willed them to stop. He must subjugate his fear or he would be a quivering mass of gelatin by the time the demon reached the top. Self-control was the key. As an aspiring scientist he prided himself on his inner discipline and logical frame of mind. Now he must apply both stringently in order to survive the impending confrontation.

How long would the creature take to scale the shaft?

Cory leaned forward a fraction, listening intently for the telltale sounds the demon would make as it climbed. But maybe that was a mistake. Endowed as the thing was with prodigious strength, it wouldn't need to strain. It could easily ascend the chimney without scraping or scratching. He imagined the worst-case scenario in which the creature moved as silently as a ghost, emerging before he realized it was there to clamp its huge hands around his throat and throttle the life out of him. The image made him shudder.

How much longer?

Cory fidgeted, caught himself, and held his body motionless. His eyes bored into the inky shaft. Eventually the demon would show and he must be ready.

He could only pray Ann was on the ball did as he'd asked.

The next instant he was stunned to awaken to the fact that the creature was already there! The inky area marking the shaft shifted perceptibly, thickening like day-old black coffee as the vague outline of a great bulk materialized.

Cory was scared out of his wits. Determining whether the demon was facing him or not was impossible. For all he knew, it had him pegged dead to rights. His palms became sweaty and his nose started to tingle from the dust. Not now! If he sneezed, the creature would nail him for certain.

Panic-stricken, he went to raise the pick when he remembered the creature's eyes, those fiery orbs that seemed to glow with an inner light. Surely, if the demon was facing him, he would see its eyes.

"Now!" Cory shouted.

There was a rasping sound as one of the matches was struck against the side of the match box. A pinpoint of flame flared, caught, and brightened, then was quickly applied to the wick.

The lantern burst to life.

In its golden glow, Cory saw the demon clearly. It was at the very lip of the chimney, its shoulder blades less than a foot away. The monstrosity's three toed feet were braced against the opposite shaft wall, its broad back against the wall nearest to him.

The thing was glaring at Ann and the lantern.

Hissing, the demon started to climb out.

Cory had waited almost too long. Uncoiling, he swept the pick in an arc, driving the point into the rear of the creature's skull. The tip split the tough hide and sank in deep.

Venting a roar like a dragon, the demon stiffened, then reached over its shoulder and grasped the pick handle. One of its unnaturally warm fingers brushed against Cory's hand, and he inadvertently jerked back, releasing the pick as he did so.

The demon gurgled, let go of the handle, and renewed its attempt to clamber from the shaft. A crimson fluid spurted from the hole in its cranium, flowing down its back in rivulets.

"Kill it!" Ann cried.

Cory grabbed at the pick but the handle was slick with the demon's blood and his palms slipped off. With his left hand he yanked a steel bit free and lunged, just as the creature twisted around.

The blazing eyes Cory remembered so well locked on him. He couldn't stop. He sliced the bit into the demon's throat just below the chin.

The monster screeched.

Something slammed into Cory's chest and he was thrown back against the wall, jarring his spine and causing fireworks to explode before his eyes. He slumped, dazed, expecting the thing to be on him in a flash, but the hands that grasped him as his vision cleared were those of the girl who meant more to him than life itself.

"Cory? Are you all right?"

"Fine," he mumbled, glancing at the shaft. The demon

was gone! "Where ...?" he blurted, moving toward the opening.

"It fell," Ann said.

Thrilled at his victory, Cory slid to the edge and gazed over the side. Too late he saw the demon a few feet below, its legs and shoulders supporting its prodigious weight. He tried to scoot back but a red hand shot up and grabbed him by the front of his shirt.

"Cory!" Ann screamed.

Cory clutched the creature's wrist and tugged, but it was like trying to move a steel bar. The demon hissed, its tongue darting out and brushing the tip of his nose. Slowly, inexorably, he felt himself being pulled down. He flung out both hands and pressed against the wall, his body across the opening, his knees gouging into the hard edge.

"No! Fight it!" Ann shouted, seizing hold of his ankles.

Cory strained every muscle in his body in a desperate bid to keep from being torn from his precarious perch. The creature glared, its face, neck and chest now covered with its blood. Radiating raw, palpable hatred, it tightened its grip on his shirt. Cory swore he could see triumph in its satanic eyes. His hands slipped, his body sagged. He was on the verge of being wrenched loose when the unforeseen transpired.

His shirt ripped.

The demon's nails, which were more like talons or claws, shredded the fabric. And since it had been pulling so hard, abruptly losing its hold caused it to jerk downward and lose its purchase on the shaft walls.

The demon fell. But even as it did, it lunged, trying to grab Cory's arm, attempting to drag him down with it. It missed.

The creature plummeted, its tail flapping wildly.

Cory was unable to savor his victory because the very next instant his hands slipped. Aghast, he realized he was about to plunge into the shaft himself.

Chapter 24

Wesley Eagen was one ticked-off guy. He halted in a room where the stalactites were especially long and slender and swept his flashlight beam over the floor. There were no tracks in the dust, which meant no one had been through this part of the cave in ages, not even the monster. Temporarily, at least, he was safe.

He crossed the room and entered a wide tunnel. Safe he might be, but he was still lost and that had him mad as hell. It seemed as if he had been wandering in the lousy cave for years, and he was no closer to the entrance than he had been when Leslie bit the big one. Where could it be? What did he have to do to get out of there?

Frowning in disgust, Wes walked rapidly. The faster he went, the sooner he would reach the surface---or so he reasoned. All he had done so far was tire his legs and reinforce his belief that coming to the Caverna del Diablo was the dumbest thing he had ever done. When the idea was first broached, he'd thought it was brilliant. Now, he wished he had never heard of the cave.

Everything had gone terribly wrong. The only person he knew who could supply him with cocaine was dead. Now he must find another source, another pusher. Fat chance the new one would give him the same deals Scott had and sometimes allow him to buy his coke at a reduced price. He'd have to fork out big bucks each and every time.

And as if having that cloud on his personal horizon wasn't bad enough, now he had to go to all the trouble of breaking in a new babe. Girls, he'd found, were a lot like dogs. They had to be properly trained before they knew how to behave. They had to learn basic manners, such as never talking back to him and always going along with whatever he wanted to do when he wanted to do it. Once a girl learned the fundamentals, they would get along great. Leslie had been great until tonight. Then she had fallen to pieces. Hopefully his next hottie would never lose sight of the fact that he was the boss in their relationship. If she did, he could always dump her and get another.

All these problems could be laid at the feet of one cause. One person. One miserable son of a bitch by the name of Cory Fleming. The geek was to blame for everything that had gone wrong.

If they hadn't decided to bring Fleming out to the cave, Scott and Leslie would still be alive. An evening of innocent fun, of playing pranks, of repaying the nerd for the archery championship loss, had turned into a disaster. His only consolation was that Fleming must be dead, too. If he only knew where to find the body, he would piss on it as his farewell salute.

The thought made Wes chuckle. He negotiated a curve, then stopped in surprise. Before him lay a large chamber, the ceiling aglow, the floor a jumble of formations and stalagmites. It was the brightest chamber he had stumbled on, and he switched off his flashlight to conserve the battery. Wearily, he walked to a rock in the shape of a toadstool and sat down.

What he wouldn't give for a few hours of sleep!

Wes felt burned out and depressed. The effects of the coke hadn't lasted nearly as long as usual. He was on the downward slide that always ended with him feeling like walking puke. Combined with the effects of all the beer he had drunk, he wanted nothing more than to shut out the whole world, to forget all his cares and woes, to put his brain in neutral and give his body an opportunity to recover.

A loud thump came from across the chamber.

Startled, Wes jumped up and spun, flicking on the flashlight in case it was the creature. Nothing moved among the stalagmites. He searched carefully, afraid the monster might be trying to sneak up on him. There was no trace of it. Still not convinced, he moved off toward a passage to his left.

The thing might have nailed Scott and Les, but it wasn't about to nail him without a fight. The Eagen clan had never been quitters, and he wasn't about to roll over and do nothing while some freak of nature tore him to ribbons. If it wanted him, it would have to work for its meal.

At the tunnel he paused for a final check, then wheeled and hurried off.

In the chamber the thump was repeated.

Wes broke stride, debating whether to go back. The thing might be playing with him, just like earlier when it killed Scott and threw Scott's head. Well, he wasn't falling for its stupid trick. He was too smart to be suckered in.

Squaring his shoulders, Wes resumed his quest for a way out of the cavern.

Leslie Vanderhorst fluttered to full consciousness and opened her eyes. She felt weak, confused and strange. There was a buzzing in her ears and her body was warm. Puzzled, she tried to recall where she was and what had happened. She remembered being slugged by the boy she believed had loved her. Now she knew better. She couldn't wait to tell her father. Better yet, she would tell her cousin,

Gary. He would drive over to the Eagen house and beat the crap out of Wes. She and Gary had always been tight, and he wouldn't sit still for anyone using her as a punching bag.

Les seemed to recall another disturbing memory. What had it been? Suddenly a mental image of the repulsive monster she had seen brought her to a sitting position, and she glanced around in stark fear.

Where was she?

Above her was a glowing ceiling as high as the sky. Near at hand were enormous spires and bizarre formations. She was in an oval depression in the ground with only her head higher than the rim. How had she gotten there? Quite distinctly she remembered being in a tunnel when Wes went into his Neanderthal act.

Pain flared in her jaw when she moved her head. Gingerly, she touched the spot and discovered her jaw was badly swollen. Her teeth ached, and her tongue felt thick and sluggish.

Damn Wesley Eagen to hell!

She rose unsteadily and stepped to the side of the depression. Had Wes brought her to this place? If so, why? And what about the image of the monster? Had she really seen it or only dreamed she had? She felt confused and couldn't get her thoughts organized.

Propping her palms on the rocky ground, she pushed up and swung her legs out, then slowly straightened. There was no sign of anyone anywhere. No matter which way she looked, all she saw was desolation.

What should she do? Stay put and wait for Wes to return, or try to find a tunnel to the surface on her own? She certainly didn't want anything more to do with Wesley Eagen. Swinging to the right, she headed toward a high wall.

Her jaw hurt abominably with every step. She wondered if it might be broken and tried opening her mouth. The pain intensified terribly, making her groan. For a second she feared she would pass out but she rallied, suppressing the agony while silently cursing Wes for being the worst son of a bitch on the planet. If her jaw was indeed broken, she'd press assault charges against the bastard. That would teach him to go around battering his girlfriends.

Why hadn't she broken off with him before this? As soon as she had found out what he was truly like, about his violent temper and his drug addiction, she should have dropped him like a hot potato. Instead, she had stupidly continued to date him. And all because he always had money to spend and knew how to show a girl a fun time.

She only had herself to blame.

The constant fun and games appealed to her. Since her twelfth birthday she had lived on the wild side, a regular party animal from the word go. She liked to dance, drink and screw. Not necessarily in that order.

Wesley certainly wasn't the best lover she'd ever had, nor did he have the biggest schlong, but he did always carry the biggest wad of bills she had ever laid eyes on, and to her way of thinking the guys with the bucks were the ones who got the most out of life and had the most to offer their women.

She should know. Since that day when she was twelve and her cousin had humped her in the back seat of his car, she had lived for sex. It had aroused an insatiable need in her, a hunger for every male she saw. Well, not *every* male, just the good-looking ones.

Some of her girlfriends claimed she had sex on the brain. But they were usually the frigid ones who had no intention of putting out until Mr. Right came along. What a drag! Life was too short to let it go to waste. She preferred to take life by the balls, so to speak, and make every minute count.

And look where it had gotten her!

Leslie gazed at the odd terrain, feeling a slight twinge of regret at the lifestyle she had adopted. She promptly dismissed the rare remorse with a shake of her head that increased her pain even more.

Pressing a palm to her jaw, she glanced to the right and spied a pool of water in the shadow of a stone monolith. Eager to quench her thirst, she ran to the pool and knelt. Not until then did she register the smell, a stink reminiscent of rotten eggs. Nearly gagging, she studied the surface and realized the liquid wasn't water at all. Rather, it was a thick yellowish-brown substance that radiated intense heat.

Disappointed, she stood and turned---and nearly fainted again.

Standing twenty feet away, its eyes as red as fire, its mouth creased in a lecherous grin, was the monster of the Caverna del Diablo.

"Cory!" Ann screamed. "Hang on!"

Cory felt her fingers dig into his ankles and frantically tried to brace his hands against the wall but it was hopeless. His body sagged and he dangled over the edge, his knees gouged by the hard rock. If not for her grip on his legs, he would have plummeted down the shaft.

"I can't hold you for long!" she cried.

Cory knew that, knew he must do something quickly or end up as a shattered pile of busted bones and pulped flesh at the bottom, alongside the demon. There was only one tactic he could think of and that was to push off from the wall while simultaneously arching his back, in effect swinging upward until he was level with the rim. On his first try he failed by inches. On his second he lashed out with his right hand and grasped the edge, providing just enough support for him to twist and slide backwards.

Ann helped, digging in her heels for leverage and yanking on his ankles.

He got both hands on the rim and desperately slid back. First his belly touched solid ground, then his chest. He was safe---breathless, but safe!

A hand grabbed his shoulder, and he was flipped over to find Ann straddling him.

"Are you hurt?"

"I'm okay," Cory said.

He reached up, thinking Ann would give him a hand, and was taken aback when she unexpectedly lowered herself on top of him and glued her hot lips to his mouth. Her breasts mashed against his chest. Her hands roamed ceaselessly over his body and through his hair. He tasted her sweet tongue as it entwined with his own. Predictably, his manhood surged.

"You did it!" she whooped when she lifted her head. "You killed the creature!"

"You helped," Cory reminded her.

Ann beamed. "We're safe now. All we have to do is find a way out of the cave."

"Which won't be easy," Cory said. "And as for being safe, there might be more of those things."

"We only saw one," Ann responded, and lavished more kisses on his cheeks, his forehead and his ears.

Cory was growing warm all over. "Yes," he admitted, "but there must be a viable breeding population. Probability factors indicate---."

"Save the scientific mumbo-jumbo," Ann said, grinning. "You just saved both our lives and I want to express my gratitude." She applied her lips to his once more.

Although Cory was convinced they were far from out of danger, he made no protest as she ground her body into his. All her inhibitions had evaporated. She sucked on his tongue and rubbed his thighs, hungry for just one thing.

"What do you think?" Ann asked seductively.

"About what?"

"You know," she said, and licked his throat.

"Here and now?"

"Why not?"

Cory was about to say he could think of a dozen reasons when she locked her mouth on his. He brought up his right hand, intending to push on her shoulder so she would draw back and listen. By sheer accident his hand brushed her breast, and the pliant feel of the mound under her blouse aroused rampant lust within him. Impulsively, he cupped her breast and squeezed. When she moaned and squirmed he thought he would explode in his pants.

He cupped her other breast, relishing the exquisite sensation, his body coming vibrantly alive. No experience he'd ever had compared to this. How different it was from the few times he'd necked with girls before. Then the kisses had been reserved, if not chaste. None of his dates had ever let him go all the way, not that he tried to. He'd been raised to be the perfect gentleman, and his mother had impressed upon him the need to treat all girls with respect. The mere thought of trying to get into a date's pants made him embarrassed. But here he was, contemplating making love as if it were the most natural act in the world. He felt flushed all over and had an urge to kiss every square inch of Ann's voluptuous body.

"Oh, Cory," she breathed.

He lowered his right hand to loosen her blouse so he could get at her breasts. So dominated by passion was he that he didn't realize there was a sound wafting up out of the shaft until Ann suddenly tensed and blurted out, "What's that?"

Involved in nuzzling her neck, Cory replied absently, "What's what?"

"Listen!"

He cocked his head, adrift in a dreamy state where sensual sensations eclipsed all else. Then he heard the noise, too, and his skin crawled.

Ann slid off him, her eyes like saucers.

Cory sat up, listening to the loud rattling from down below. "Another demon," he said.

"Maybe it's the same one."

"After a fall like that? No, the first one is definitely dead."

"Oh God, what do we do?"

Cory rose to his knees, debating whether to stay where they were and use the same ruse they had employed against the first demon. But he no longer had the pick and one of the steel bits was gone, both imbedded in the monster lying at the bottom of the chimney.

He might be able to rig a nasty surprise provided the demon took its sweet time in ascending the shaft. Ann though, would be at great risk. "We run," he announced, and hastened to don the backpack and grab the lantern.

"I'm sorry," Ann said. "I shouldn't have doubted you."

"No harm done."

"Yet," Ann amended.

Cory stuffed the matches into his pocket and started running, not caring where the tunnel led, just so they eluded the monster. If they could gain a substantial lead he would be able to rig the surprise he had in mind.

Fifty yards of swift travel brought them to a room distinguished by fantastic color variations with white stalagmites sprouting among reddish-brown flowstone.

He noticed the display in passing, immersed in thought as he was, then came to a narrow tunnel and barreled into it. The move nearly cost him his life, for less than four feet beyond was one side of a yawning precipice, and he was raising his foot to take a step that would have cast him into the depths below when Ann yanked roughly on his arm, pulling him back from the edge.

"Watch out!"

Cory stared at the chasm, a cool puff of air fanning his hair. There must be an opening up high connecting the ceiling over the chasm to the outer world. How unfortunate they didn't have climbing gear and a rope.

"What were you trying to do? Get yourself killed?" Ann said.

"I wasn't paying attention," Cory conceded. "I've been trying to come up with a means of killing the demon before it can kill us. I have an idea, but I can't guarantee it will work." He hefted the lantern for a better look at their immediate vicinity. To their right the precipice appeared to stretch into the gloomy distance.

"Should we go back?"

"Let's check this out first. There might be a way down," Cory proposed, moving carefully along.

Across the way, at the outer limit of the light, was the other side.

"I hope you're not thinking of jumping," Ann said.

"What, no guts?" Cory retorted, and halted on spying vertical columns of stone in the middle of the chasm. Some were slender, others thick, and all of them were as high as the precipice itself. Evidently the two sides had once been connected by some kind of a bridge which had collapsed due to an unknown cataclysm. Now only the scattered columns remained, isolated islands of stone forming an irregular path to the opposite precipice.

A path?

Cory stared hard, judging the distances between the columns. Some were close together. Others farther apart. While estimating the positions of those near his side was easy, doing so for the columns farther out was difficult because the light from the lantern couldn't penetrate the empty spaces between them.

Then he spied a particularly large column a yard from the edge. "I have an idea."

"How to kill the second demon?"

"No. How to reach the other side."

Ann gazed out over the chasm, did a double-take, and shook her head. "Forget it. I left my wings at home."

"Do you see the columns?" Cory asked, nodding at the large one in front of them.

"Of course."

"Ever play hopscotch when you were little?"

Comprehension caused Ann's eyebrows to arch. She shook her head. "No way, no how. Forget it. Not in a million, trillion years."

"Would you rather have the demon catch us?"

"We'll go back and look for another tunnel."

"And waste valuable time? This way is quicker. And we might throw the thing off our trail. It would never expect us to try such a stunt."

"*I* don't expect us to try such a stunt," Ann exclaimed. "It's suicide. One false step and we're history."

"I'll go first," Cory offered, stepping to the brink.

"No, damn it!" Ann snapped. She grabbed his arm and clung to him. "This is crazy. What if we get over there and can't find another tunnel? We'll be stranded."

"Yet another reason for me to go first. If there's no tunnel, I'll come right back and we'll get out of here before the demon shows up."

"Please. No."

Cory pried her fingers from his arm and raised the lantern overhead. "Trust me. The important thing for us right now is to shake the demon."

"The important thing is for us to stay alive," Ann said. She placed her hands on her hips and regarded him critically. "Everything I'm saying is going in one ear and out the other, isn't it? You're set on doing this no matter what?"

Cory nodded, then leaned over and kissed her cheek. "I love you."

"You fight dirty, you know that?"

Grinning, Cory stared at the gap between the edge and the first column. A single leap would suffice, just so he didn't lose his balance. But would the top of the column hold? It might crumble under him, pitching him to his death. He turned to Ann, pulled the knife from its sheath and forced a casual tone as he said, "Here. Just in case the demon tries to get fresh before you can join me."

"I wish it was a bazooka," she said, gripping the hilt.

"You and me both," Cory said. He extended the lantern. "Take this, too."

"How will you see to get across?"

"I have a brainstorm," Cory replied.

Stripping off the backpack, he felt around inside until he located the pipe they had found, and drew it out. Next he took out one of the socks filled with sulfur, unfastened the tie, and poured sulfur into the pipe. He used his fingers to tamp the yellow powder down, cramming in as much as he could. When the pipe was filled from stem to bowl, he tied the sock shut and replaced it in the pack.

Ann was watching intently. "Will this work?"

"I don't know," Cory said, closing the backpack.

"How long will the sulfur bum?"

"I don't know."

"Is there a chance the pipe will explode?"

"I don't know. Possibly."

Ann took the pipe and examined it. "What if it goes out when you're only halfway across? What if it gets so hot your hand is burned? What if---"

Cory put a finger to her lips. "All we can do is keep our tootsies crossed and pray for the best." He unbuckled his belt and slid the knife sheath off. Once he had the sheath in one hand and the pipe in the other, he inserted the stem of the pipe into the sheath, wedging it tight.

"Oh, I get it," Ann said. "Sort of an improvised torch. Smart man."

"We'll see just how smart in a moment," Cory said, taking the matchbox out. Crouching, he extracted a match, glanced at the chasm, and gulped.

Chapter 25

Leslie Vanderhorst wanted to run but her legs refused to cooperate. Her entire body had gone numb, as if her spine had been severed below her head. She stared, wide-eyed, as the monster walked toward her, its bulging muscles rippling, its awesome form practically crackling with primal power and latent menace. Please let me faint! she prayed. She wanted to be unconscious when the end came, to be spared the physical torment and emotional anguish.

The creature towered above her and inexplicably grinned. Bypassing her, it moved to the pool and knelt.

As if mesmerized, Leslie pivoted to see what the thing was doing. She saw the it lean over the pool and scrutinize the boiling liquid, giving the impression that it was searching for something. But what? It slowly reached down, its arm disappearing into the pool. Not in the least fazed by the blistering heat, it probed around, moving its arm from side to side, before finally smiling and reaching in with its other arm.

When the creature straightened up, it held a huge crimson egg in its hands.

Leslie gawked.

The egg was the size of a basketball, only oval rather than circular. Its leathery shell glistened with the hot liquid. The creature turned the egg over and over, examining it.

Les didn't know what to make of the weird behavior. Did the egg belong to the monster? Or had some other animal laid it and the creature was planning to enjoy an oversized omelette? She watched as the thing exercised great care and placed the egg back in the pool.

Then the monster stood and faced her.

Les quaked, feeling its flaming eyes bore into hers. Her mind shrieked that she should flee but she was glued to the spot.

Suddenly the creature was next to her and sweeping her into its arms. In a flash they were speeding across the wretched landscape so fast it made her head swim. She glimpsed gigantic spires, tremendous arches, formations of every shape and size. Then her captor entered a canyon, and she was borne to a large dark opening in the canyon wall, a cave within a cave as it were, and deposited in front of the entrance.

Without a backward glance the monster walked into the cave, vanishing within its depths.

Now what? Leslie wondered, marveling that she could still think calmly and rationally when she should be overcome with fear.

She twisted, gazing up the canyon, her intuition telling her to get the hell out of there before the creature came back. Hope sparked in her breast when her body finally obeyed her mental commands. She shuffled a few steps, then broke into a run, disregarding the pain in her jaw.

Go, girl, go!

Leslie flew. She had always been an excellent runner and jogged regularly. That, and aerobics, helped to keep her shapely figure in its prime.

The mouth of the canyon was far off, but if she could get out of there and find a place to hide, she stood a chance of eluding the monster.

Nothing else moved. She was the only life in all that vast

expanse, the only living being other than the creature. Or were there more of the things? She might not be as bright as Cory Fleming but she was smart enough to put two and two together and conclude that the egg indicated there must be a female of the species somewhere.

Or had the male laid the egg himself?

So many questions and so few answers.

She started to breathe unevenly and paced herself. If she pushed too hard she would tire and collapse well shy of the canyon mouth.

Again and again she told herself, I can do it! I can do it!

Leslie looked back and saw no sign of her captor. So far, so good. In a way it was funny. She never had thought of herself as very tough, yet here she was resisting a walking nightmare, determined to fight for her life with her dying breath. If only she'd had such courage a month ago, she could have told Wesley Eagen to go screw himself and she wouldn't be in the predicament she was in now. Yes, sir, life was funny sometimes.

Minutes ticked by.

Any moment Les dreaded discovering the monster on her tail but she reached the end of the canyon unchallenged and bore to the left, remembering a maze of formations that would serve to conceal her until she figured out her next step.

Once past the first one she relaxed a bit. Farther and farther she went until she was in the middle of the maze, and there, beside an enormous boulder shaped remarkably like a squat frog, she stopped to rest.

Leslie leaned against the boulder and inhaled deeply, her heart pounding, her every sense alert. The ground was too hard to bear prints so the monster couldn't follow her that way. Her main fear was the thing had a nose like her dog's and would scent her out like her Boston terrier did with bones she sometimes hid around the house. Thinking of little Blackie made her smile. What she wouldn't give to be cuddled with him in bed right that minute! He always slept with her at night,'his cold nose pressed against her side. Blackie was the perfect companion when she wanted to be by herself and temporarily forget all about the pressures of the outside world.

Her mind strayed, and she began to doze. With difficulty she snapped her head up. There would be plenty of time for sleep after she escaped from the Cavern del Diablo. Until then she must do her best to stay awake.

She thought about Wes, her anger returning. How she'd love to see that bastard behind bars for what he had done to her! Why, she'd even go so far as to formally press charges. The chauvinistic son of bitch believed he had the right to lord it over every girl he met. It was about time he was made aware of the realities of life.

Leslie stretched and for a moment closed her eyes. When she opened them again there was the horrid monster, not fifteen feet away, staring at her. Flooded with terror, she leaped up and whirled to flee, but she only took three steps before shock brought her up short.

A second monster blocked her path.

"I still wish you wouldn't do this," Ann said anxiously as Cory stepped to the edge of the chasm and held a lit match close to the sulfur-filled pipe.

"Just keep your eyes peeled for the demon. I don't want anything to happen to you now that we've found each other."

"You're worried about me? I'll be fine. Just concentrate on getting across alive."

Cory nodded and gripped the knife sheath firmly. He must move quickly once the sulfur was lit as he had no idea how long he would have to reach the other side before the sulfur went out. If he recalled his studies correctly, sulfur burned bright but fast. Allowing for the amount crammed into the pipe, he estimated he would have thirty seconds, at best, to traverse the chasm.

He didn't fear the pipe exploding---not too much, anyway. Since there were openings at both ends, the internal pressure should be equalized by gas escaping from both the bowl and the stem. If not ... well, he could still be a scientist with one hand.

"Are you sure you don't want me to take the backpack?" Ann asked.

"Positive," Cory said, glancing down at the straps looped tightly around his shoulders. The pack was on as snug as could be. With any luck it wouldn't throw him off stride. He looked at her, admiring the play of golden light from the lantern on her lovely features, and smiled. "Here goes nothing.

"Whatever you do, don't fall."

"I'll try to keep that in mind."

Cory took a deep breath, stepped backwards to give himself room, and touched the match to the sulfur. Instantly the pipe flared with flame and smoke, and at the very moment the sulfur ignited, he launched himself into motion, running full tilt at the brink, and jumping.

The first column was only a yard away. He alighted smack in the middle and shoved off on the same leg, angling toward a second column slightly to the right of the first. Relying on pure instinct, moving by reflex alone, he leaped from column to column. Most were close together. A few gave him hairy moments when he feared he would miss and plunge into the chasm.

In his right hand the sheath grew hot as the sulfur sparked and crackled.

Seven columns brought him to within six feet of the opposite side. There were two columns to go. The first he reached easily, coiling his leg for the next jump even as he landed. Like an ungainly kangaroo he sailed upward, slanting toward that last stone perch. His foot was inches from making contact when the torch hissed out.

He couldn't see!

Cory felt his foot smack onto the column. He didn't dare try to stop or his own momentum would pitch him over the side. So as he landed he tensed his leg muscles and flung himself wildly toward where he hoped the edge of the precipice would be. For a second he hung in the air, hearing Ann shout his name, aware that if he came down short of his goal he would never see her lovely face again.

In a tumble he crashed down onto solid ground and frantically threw himself forward. Or tried to. He felt the rim under his left heel, felt his foot slip and his own weight start to drag him backwards. He was going over the side! The realization was enough to lend desperate strength to his limbs, and with a superhuman effort he reversed direction and dived, hitting hard on his elbows and knees, bruised but safe on firm earth.

"Cory? Did you make it? Oh, God! Cory!"

Cory wanted to answer but his throat seemed parched. His body throbbed to the beat of his speeding heart. Adrenaline coursed through him. He felt vibrantly alive, and grateful to be so.

"Cory? Answer me, damn it! Are you there?"

"I'm here," he croaked, rising to his knees.

"Are you hurt?"

"A little worse for wear but nothing major."

"Hang on. I'm on my way."

Cory rose, about to tell her to wait so he could provide detailed information on the alignment of the columns. He also wanted to hunt for a tunnel before she committed herself to joining him but she sprang before he could get a word out of his mouth, the lantern held high.

Dreading a misstep, he saw her leap to the second column, then the third. He could barely stand to look. If she perished he would blame himself forever since it had been his idea to try and cross.

The swaying lantern lent her a ghostly aspect as she jumped with the grace of a gazelle. He recalled that she had taken ballet lessons for years. All that rigorous training now came in handy, enabling her to land with pinpoint precision and perfect balance on top of each of the columns. She made it appear easy.

And then she was coming down on the last column and leaping yet again, her face swinging up to seek a landing spot on the precipice.

Suddenly he saw that she was heading straight at him and she had no way of stopping. He tried to back up, to get out of her way, but a second later she alighted and was unable to check her impetus. Her arms flailing, she rammed into him and they both went down in a tangle of arms and legs. He thudded onto his back, bearing the brunt of the collision, with her on top of him. Pain racked his left shoulder.

Ann lay still for a few seconds. Then she shifted and raised her head to stare into his eyes. "What were you trying to prove?"

"Who, me?"

"Were you trying to catch me, or were you just standing

there like a dummy?"

"Me, a dummy? The boy genius? Need you ask?"

Ann grunted and sat up, holding the lantern where she could inspect it for damage. "Had I known you were such a klutz, I never would have thrown myself at you."

Cory burst into laughter: She gazed at him in confusion until she realized what she had said. Then she chimed in, their mirth relieving their tension.

"Are you okay?" she inquired at length.

"Get off me so I can find out," Cory replied, then slowly rose when she moved to one side. The pain in his shoulder was minor. "I'll live," he announced.

"We're lucky the lantern wasn't broken," Ann said.

"They built things to last back in those days," Cory said, examining his torch. The pipe was badly scorched and part of the leather sheath had been singed by the intense heat. His hand, thank goodness, was fine.

"So what now, fearless leader?"

Cory handed her the pipe and sheath. "Stick these in the backpack and we'll be on our way." Swiveling, he scanned the top of the precipice for as far as the light permitted but saw no indication of a tunnel. "I thought you were supposed to wait until I found a way out," he mentioned.

"Sorry. I was so worried about you, I completely forgot."

"And you call me a dummy?"

Ann had the pack open and was stuffing the pipe inside. "If there's no way off this cliff, maybe we should stay here a while and rest. We'd be safe here. The demon can't get at us without us hearing or seeing it."

"You hope," Cory responded. "No, we'll keep moving. I don't want to stop until we're back on the surface." He glanced across the chasm and listened for sounds of the creature. How much of a lead did they have? If it should show up now and spot them, the risks they had taken in crossing the abyss would have been for nothing.

"All done," Ann said.

Cory took the lantern and moved out, scouring the wall flanking them. He hiked over forty yards and saw no trace of an opening.

"Maybe we goofed."

They were almost to the end of the precipice when Cory spotted a hole at the base of the wall. "Look at this," he said, hurrying over and squatting.

The opening was the size of a manhole cover.

"That looks like a tight fit," Ann said.

Cory thrust the lantern into the cavity, seeking to ascertain its dimensions. The hole ran back into the wall. He couldn't tell if it ended in a room, a chamber, a tunnel, or went nowhere. There was only one way to find out. Ducking his head in, he eased onto his knees and warily advanced, disliking the feeling of being closed in.

"Must we?" Ann said.

"Unless you'd rather stay there until I see where this leads."

"Yeah. Right," Ann said and entered.

The hole proceeded in a straight line for about sixty feet, then turned to the right.

The farther Cory traveled, the more claustrophobic he became. He began to understand why some people were uncomfortable in elevators and other confined areas. Before, he had wrongly imagined the problem was all in their heads. It was amazing how firsthand experience could broaden a person's perspective.

Abruptly, the hole widened, then came to an end. He halted and poked the lantern out, dreading another chasm. Revealed in the flickering light was a spacious room adorned with the usual stalactites and stalagmites. Overjoyed, he slid to the floor and waited to assist Ann.

From behind him came a faint noise.

Cory spun, expecting to see the demon charge out of the darkness. The dancing shadows gave the illusion of creatures swarming from everywhere. He grabbed for the knife, then remembered he had given it to Ann. Instead he clutched the other steel bit and held it ready to stab or slash.

"What's the matter?"

Cory looked at her, kneeling in the opening, and put a finger to his lips. The noise he had heard was repeated but it wasn't a scratching sound. Nor was it the rattling or hissing he associated with the demons. Rather, it was an odd sort of plop such as a dripping faucet might make.

Cory moved in the direction of the sound. The plops formed a regular tempo, one after the other at spaced intervals. Soon he spied the reason. Near the center of the room was a sump, a crater into which water dripped from an overhanging stalactite.

Fingers touched his elbow, and Ann whispered in his ear. "Is that what I think it is?"

"Water," he confirmed.

"Can we drink it?"

Cory moved to the sump. He wedged the steel bit under his belt, then dipped a finger into the pool and gingerly touched his fingertip to his tongue. In many instances, water found in caves was invariably too acidic or contained too high a mineral content to be drinkable. This water, however, tasted as fresh and pure as that from any mountain stream. "It's safe," he informed her.

Ann plunged a hand in, took a sip and smiled. "You have no idea how thirsty I am," she said. Bending, she drank in greedy gulps.

Cory imitated her example, drinking until he couldn't drink any more. Stepping back, he wiped his slick mouth with the back of his hand and sat down to speculatively eye the pool. This was the first and only water they had found since entering the cavern. While water was sometimes found at great depths, more often than not it was close to the surface. Were they, then, near the entrance?

"A penny for your thoughts," Ann said. She was leaning on the sump rim, glistening drops falling from her chin.

Cory told her.

"Then what are we waiting for? Let's keep going if we're that close."

"We might not be. Don't get your hopes up yet."

"I want to get the hell out of here," Ann emphatically stated. She lifted the lantern and made a circuit of the pool, scouring the perimeter of the room. "How can you just sit there like a bump on a log when we could be safe soon?" Almost back by his side, she pointed to their left. "There! Do yo see it?"

Twisting, Cory spotted the outline of a passage. He sighed and stood. "All right. Hold your horses." Once again he took off the backpack, this time removing the flask of whiskey.

"Shouldn't we hold off celebrating until we're safe and sound?"

"Funny lady," Cory joked. Opening the bottle, he upended it. The contents splattered at his feet. Once the flask was empty, he dunked it in the pool and watched air bubbles form. "The human body needs water more than it does food to survive. So in case we don't find a way out soon, we'll take some along."

She frowned, tapping her foot.

"Just a bit longer," Cory said. He didn't blame her for being impatient. After all they had been through, he was just as eager to reach the surface. But they might be making a fatal mistake if they let their enthusiasm blind them to the dangers still facing them. When the bubbles stopped he raised the flask out of the pool, replaced the cap, and stuck the bottle in the backpack. His fingers brushed another of the steel bits, which he pulled out.

"Do you want the knife back?" Ann asked.

"You hold onto it," Cory said, aligning the second bit under his belt close to the other one. It took but a moment to put on the backpack. He motioned for her to take the lead, but she gave him the lantern and moved aside.

"You first, Crocodile."

"Crocodile?"

"You know. *Crocodile Dundee*, the movie about the guy who goes around saving his fair maiden from giant crocodiles and stuff like that."

Grinning, Cory walked to the tunnel. No one had ever rated him as the rugged hero type before. And the last time he had been compared to a movie star was when his brother took to calling him Ernest P. Worrell, which was not exactly the most flattering of comparisons to someone who prided himself on his intelligence.

The lantern illuminated a twisting tunnel that led up.

Ann grasped Cory's arm. "Look! We're on the right track. I can feel it in my bones."

"I hope so," Cory said. Her excitement was contagious, and he found himself hurrying forward, anxious to find out where the passage would take them.

"You know, it's our obligation to tell the sheriff and everyone else about what happened here," Ann said. "We can't make up stories just because we don't think anyone will believe us. People have to know the truth."

"You're talking as if we're already out."

"We almost are. Lighten up, dear heart," Ann said. "You have nothing to worry about."

Cory went around a comer and halted at a junction. He was about to remind her that they did, indeed, have cause for worry when the light disclosed a more effective reminder at their very feet.

It was the track of a demon.

Chapter 26

Leslie Vanderhorst swooned. The shock of being trapped by the two hideous monstrosities, of having nowhere she could flee, of being in immediate mortal jeopardy, was more than her system could take and she sank to the ground in a slow faint. She felt her left side contact the hard earth and all went black.

When next she opened her eyes, she curled into a fetal position and covered her face with her hands, fearing the creatures were right beside her, waiting to pounce. How long had she been out? Why hadn't the things harmed her while she was unconscious? She lay still, listening, paralyzed with fright. After a while she mustered enough courage to peek between her fingers. Neither of the monsters were in front of her.

Her fear worsened. The things must be behind her! What were they doing? She braced for the worst and waited for them to do something. Minutes passed.

Perplexed, she remained motionless until the strain and the prompting of her own curiosity became too much to bear. Mustering her courage, she, twisted and glanced over her shoulder.

The monsters were nowhere to be seen.

What the hell was going on? Leslie wondered, sitting up. Why had they gone off and left her ? Confused, she stood and ran a hand through her hair. Was it possible the creatures had never been there at all? Had she imagined the whole thing? No. She couldn't bring herself to believe that. They *had* found her. There must be a reason they hadn't killed her, although at the moment she couldn't think of one.

Leslie scoured the sea of formations but saw no sign of the creatures. She broke into a run. She wasn't about to stay put when the fiends might come back at any second. They should have finished her off when they had the chance because she wouldn't give them another.

She realized she must be even more careful than before, avoiding open spaces where at all possible. With luck she could elude them and find a tunnel to the surface.

Her jaw still hurt something terrible. She would have given anything for an ice pack or a painkiller. Her torment was compounded by sharp pangs which made her want to scream. She knew she had to be strong now, stronger than ever.

Mentally she vowed not to faint if she should encounter one of the monsters again. They wouldn't take her easily. She would fight them tooth and nail.

Les covered about a hundred yards. Ahead was a formation with three spires branching of from a common trunk, sort of a rock tree, and beyond it a slab of stone the size of a house. Between the two was a shadowy area, and as she neared the tree something moved in that murky space, something huge, something with a reddish tint.

Leslie cut to the left, threading among monoliths while trying to quell the terror nipping at her soul. Had the creature seen her? Maybe not. Maybe it had been looking the other way.

Forty feet away another monster stepped into view, its malicious gaze fixed right on her, its mouth curled in what could only be a smirk.

She stopped so abruptly she nearly tripped over her own

feet, then spun to the left and raced for all she was worth. Deep into the formations she went. When she finally halted under a monumental arch, she was so out of breath, she gasped for air.

Nothing was on her heels.

Bending at the waist to relieve an ache in her side, Les attempted to make sense of their bewildering actions---or, more precisely, lack of them. She knew the one had spotted her. It could have caught her easily but it didn't give chase. Why? Was it so confident she couldn't escape that it was letting her roam free?

Leslie straightened, grimacing, and moved off. Staying in one spot too long might prove fatal. She picked a different direction, hoping to throw the creature off her trail if it was following her, but she only went about twenty feet when the same or another abomination stepped into sight up ahead.

Wheeling, she fled, casting an apprehensive glance back. The monster just stood there, not even bothering to pursue her.

She slowed to save her strength, aware she was wearing herself down to the point where she would be unable to lift a finger against her tormentors.

Were their tactics deliberate? An awful idea occurred to her, one with bloodcurdling implications.

What if they were playing with her? Was that how the monsters got their rocks off? Capturing people and subjecting them to a perverted game of hide and seek? Were they having fun at her expense, waiting to close in when she couldn't take another step?

Leslie halted, refusing to play by their rules. She would bide her time, get her wind back, and wait for their next move. It wasn't long in coming.

A creature appeared near a spire off to the right.

She turned to the left.

Another red giant popped up directly in front of her.

Les again changed course, sprinting flat out, thinking she now knew how a mouse trapped between two cats must feel. Were they closing the net on her? Or were they herding her as cowboys herded cattle, working her toward a special destination?

She ran for a couple of minutes, then had to halt because of the persistent ache. The instant she did, a monster showed itself fifty feet to the right.

Damn you! Leslie mentally screamed.

The thing stood still, its features coldly impassive.

Anger replacing her fear, Leslie ran anew. She had no idea where she was. If she had to guess, she would say somewhere near the middle of a maze.

Rounding a boulder, she found herself in a circular space ringed by solid rock over eight feet high. There was no way out! She stopped and started to pivot when steely hands clamped on her shoulders and she was pushed to her knees.

This was it!

They were through toying with her.

She tried to stand but it was like attempting to rise with the weight of a brick wall on her back. Craning her neck, she looked up into the blazing eyes of one of the creatures.

Gone were the grins and smiles. It was getting down to business now.

The thing hissed, its forked tongue swaying before her like one of those Indian cobras before the flute of a snake charmer. Its left hand lowered until its fingers closed on her breast.

Recoiling, Leslie tried to pull the warm, leathery hand

off, but it might as well have been glued to her body. Loathing made her shudder as the creature squeezed and massaged her, tweaking her nipple every so often for added measure.

Les swung her fist and was brutally flung to the ground. Before she could stand the creature seized her by the arms, flipped her over, and started tearing her clothes off.

"No!" Leslie fumed, swatting ineffectually, her rage at being so grossly violated making her heedless of the danger of arousing the monster's wrath. She reached up and slapped its face, only to receive a slap in kind that rattled her teeth, lanced her jaw with worse anguish, and rendered her dazed.

Unhurried, the creature removed every last stitch of her clothing, pausing only once to hold her underwear up to its nose and sniff. Then it straddled her, knelt over her abdomen, and placed its hands on both her breasts, resuming where it had left off, its tongue flicking sinuously in and out of its mouth.

Leslie struggled to full consciousness and wished she hadn't. The feel of the creature's palms and fingers rubbing on her bare skin repulsed her like nothing else ever had. It was worse than the few times boys had manhandled her on dates. This was unbearably vile, unspeakably obscene. This was the ultimate transgression of her as a person.

The creature shifted to run its hands down over her stomach. A finger probed lower.

Leslie bucked in a futile attempt to unseat the thing. She even tried to bite it.

The creature froze, then exploded, striking her again and again.

Her vision blurred. A fog enshrouded her brain. She was vaguely aware of the thing seizing her arm and felt a peculiar sensation in her shoulder.

When, a minute later, the fog lifted slightly, Les saw the monster holding what appeared to be the arm of a mannequin. She saw it rip off the middle finger and pop the digit into its mouth as if the finger was a piece of popcorn.

The sight was so comical that she laughed inanely.

Weakness pervaded her. She experienced dizziness. Her chest felt wet, her back clammy. As she observed the thing eat a second finger, she struggled to pull herself out from between its thighs. Her right hand touched the ground but she couldn't feel anything under her left hand. A second later she realized she had no feeling whatsoever in her left arm.

"Oh, God!" Leslie moaned as the monster took a healthy bite out of the wrist.

Flesh dangling from its lips, blood dribbling over its chin, it looked at her and grinned.

A devastating numbness coursed through her. She opened her mouth to scream, but the best she could do was vent a pitiable whimper.

The monster of the Caverna del Diablo took its sweet time consuming her arm, bones and all. She heard it chew, heard it smack its lips, heard every crunch and crackle. She felt gore spatter her chest.

When the thing grasped her other arm, Les prayed for the end to come swiftly. It tore the arm from her with a quick, savage wrench.

Gratefully, almost eagerly, she slipped into limbo.

"Do you think it's the same one?" Ann Weatherby asked.

"I don't know," Cory said, swinging the lantern in an arc to reveal a dozen or more tracks. "It could be. Maybe it knew of another way past the chasm, a shortcut that got it here ahead of us."

He stared down the three passages bisecting the tunnel they had been following. The tracks came out of the passage on the far left and went to the right-hand fork, bypassing the middle passage.

He took Ann's hand and led her into it.

"Maybe there's more than one after us."

"Maybe," Cory acknowledged, inwardly afraid she was right. They might be able to give a single demon the slip. Eluding two would be difficult. Three or more rendered their prospects nil. He walked rapidly, wishing he still had the pick.

"There's something that's been bothering me," Ann commented after they had put the junction far behind them. "Why now?"

"Beg pardon?"

"Why have these things appeared now? Why is this happening to us? I mean, lots of folks have visited th Caverna del Diablo over the years and never reported seeing the things. Why are we the unlucky ones?"

"Perhaps the creatures hibernate for long spells, like ground squirrels and marmots and hamsters. Or maybe they're more like cicadas. They can stay underground for up to seventeen years. Or it could just be a case of us being in the wrong place at the wrong time."

"Hamsters hibernate? I didn't know that. My sister has one and it's active all winter long."

"Because your house is warm and cozy. Hamsters outdoors, though, always sleep through until Spring."

"Like bears, huh?"

"Bears aren't true hibernators. They sleep heavily during cold months but their body temperatures don't fall much below normal like the temperatures of true hibernators do. And they wake up every now and then to go out and forage for food."

"So this whole nightmare can be blamed on bad luck?"

"Who can say?" Cory replied. "Besides, I could be wrong about the hibernation business. Maybe these demons are more like reptiles than mammals or insects."

"Meaning what?"

"Reptiles are cold-blooded. Turtles, frogs and toads become dormant in cold weather and stay that way until Spring hits. They can't get up and move around like bears do. If my supposition is correct and these demons are reptilian, they should be moving around at all until April or so."

"But it's not cold down here," Ann said. "In that big chamber it's like a sauna. The demons might not be affected by the change in seasons."

"The truth is, we just don't know."

"Maybe we're making more out of it than there is," Ann said. Maybe it's just the fact that today is Halloween."

Cory glanced at her.

"You heard me," Ann said. "Halloween is when all the ghosts, spirits, fairies, elves and witches are supposed to come out and roam the earth. What if the same is true for demons?"

"You don't really believe that nonsense?"

"Unless you can come up with a better explanation, yeah, I do," Ann said.

Cory shook his head in amusement. He didn't say anything more because he didn't want to offend her but the notion was absurd. His scientific nature scoffed at any and all superstitions, and the idea of goblins and spooks roving the earth on All Hallows Eve, as the ancients called the holiday, stemmed from primitive beliefs prevalent during Druid times. The old ways died hard, he figured. There would always be those who believed in the existence of things like werewolves, vampires and ghouls, no matter how much scientific evidence to the contrary was presented.

Cory went around a corner and nearly stopped in surprise, although not due to a threat. A profoundly disturbing thought, shattering in its significance, shocked him to his core.

Not six hours ago he would have laughed like crazy if anyone had the gall to insist demons were real. Now he knew they were. Did that mean there might be a kernel of truth to other legends about spectral entities and sundry monsters? Did werewolves and vampires, in fact, exist? Were there things such as goblins and ghosts that roamed the earth at appointed times?

The idea was mind-blowing! It set every scientific precept in which he believed on its ear. It meant there was an entire goblin universe out there, a universe where evil creatures of the outer edge dwelled. It meant there might actually be such a being as Lucifer or Satan or whatever he was called. And if the living embodiment of Ultimate Evil was real, what did that infer about the living source of Absolute Goodness?

Cory put a stop to his train of thought and focused on the passage stretching before them. It bothered him to think of such things. Such reflections were better left for later, if and when they escaped from the Caverna del Diablo.

"Have you ever seen a ghost, Cory?" Ann asked.

"Of course not," he answered somewhat testily. Why was she bringing the subject up now, of all times? Especially when he had just been questioning the reality of ghosts and other supernatural beings.

"My great-grandmother did. She insisted to her dying day that she saw the ghost of her husband come into their house one stormy night and stand by the foot of her bed, just watching her. She tried to speak to him but all he did was stare. And when she got out of bed and went to touch him, he vanished."

"What does that have to do with our current situation?"

"Not much, I suppose, but I've always viewed it as proof that there's more to our existence than meets the eye. Our situation confirms it."

Thankfully, they came to a chamber and Cory turned his attention from the nature of reality to finding out if the demons had been through the chamber recently. He checked the cave floor without coming across a single track. "Are you hungry or thirsty?" he asked when he was done. "We can afford to rest."

"I'd rather keep going," Ann said.

The floor continued to slope upward. They were several hundred yards from the chamber when the lantern flickered, the flame dwindling for a bit and then burning bright again.

Ann gripped Cory's arm. "Are we running out of fuel?"

"I'll check."

Stopping, Cory put the lantern down. By dipping a finger in the tank he determined it was a third full. "We should be okay for another hour or two. The mixture is uneven so don't be surprised if the wick sputters now and then."

"I don't want to be in the dark," Ann said.

"We can always use the pipe and sulfur," Cory proposed, hiding his own concern. Having the lantern had made all the difference in the world, allowing them to go faster and giving them a means of keeping the demon at bay.

"Let's hurry," Ann prompted.

Cory moved swiftly. Four curves brought them to another chamber. He was well inside before he discovered there was no other way out. Checkmated, he scowled and made for the passage.

"Do you hear something?" Ann asked.

Cory stopped. At first he heard nothing out of the ordinary. Then he detected a faint whisper, vaguely reminiscent of a sound he felt he should know but couldn't identify. It was coming from off to the left. Moving toward it, he passed scores of stalagmites.

Beyond, something moved.

Something that was flowing over the cave floor.

Drawing closer, he was astounded to smell water. He rushed over and beheld an underground stream. It had to be five feet wide.

None had ever been reported in the Caverna del Diablo although other caves were known to contain them.

"A stream?" Ann said. "Does this mean we're close to the surface at last?"

"It could."

"That water has to come down from the surface somewhere, right?"

"Not necessarily."

"We can't follow it back to its source?"

"No," Cory said, nodding at the wall to their left. From out of a gaping hole at the bottom poured the racing water. Crossing the chamber, it disappeared under another wall on the opposite side.

"Damn," Ann said. "Sometimes you're too smart for our own good."

"Would you rather we wasted time on a wild goose chase?" Cory said.

Crouching, he dunked his left hand into the stream. The water was icy cold, the current strong enough to sweep a grown man away.

Ann knelt and scooped a handful to her lips, splashing water at her feet. "Brrrrr," she said after tasting it. "This must be runoff."

"Possibly," Cory conceded. The cold temperature was a telltale clue the stream might be fed by the packed snow that crowned the highest peaks most months of the year.

"Do you ever answer a question with a yes or a no?"

"Not if I can help it," Cory teased.

Laughing, Ann clapped him on the back. "It's going to take me a while to get used to your quirks. I just hope I can get you to lighten up, to cut yourself some slack now and then."

"Figures," Cory said, grinning. "We're not even going steady yet and already you're trying to change me. My dad says that women aren't satisfied unless they can remake their men the way they like. He says that when a bride stands at the altar with the groom, she doesn't see him as he is but as she wants him to be."

"Now I know where you get your brains," Ann said, all smiles.

Cory was delighted to see her relaxed and happy for the first time since they entered the cave. She had temporarily forgotten about their ordeal, and he was reluctant to say or do anything to remind her. "I'd like you to come over and have supper with me and my folks once we're out of here."

"You'd better be careful. They're liable to think we're serious about each other."

"I thought we were."

Ann leaned over and put her forearm on his shoulder. "We are, bright boy. Make sure you never forget it." Chuckling, she kissed him on the cheek.

"I won't," Cory vowed, returning her kiss, feeling as if he was unequivocally the most fortunate guy alive. They *must* make it out! For the first time in his life he had something marvelous to look forward to.

"We'd best boogie, handsome," Ann said.

Adverse to ruining their tender moment, Cory gave her another kiss, then stood and turned to check the chamber.

Out of the comer of his eye he saw Ann begin to rise, saw her left foot slip on the slick stone floor edge of the stream.

Spinning, Cory grabbed for her just as she threw her hands out toward him. Their fingers brushed. And then she fell, sinking into the stream, completely out of sight in the blink of an eye.

Shocked, Cory saw her hand thrash the surface. Without any hesitation, he threw himself into the water after her.

Chapter 27

Wesley Eagen wanted to lie down and rest. It seemed as if he had been wandering in the Caverna del Diablo forever and he was no closer to finding the entrance than he had been hours ago.

There had been no thumping sounds behind him for quite some time. He flattered himself that he had cleverly lost the monster somewhere in the confusing labyrinth of passageways. His main worry now was his flashlight. The beam had grown noticeably weaker although it was still bright enough to pierce the darkness forty feet ahead.

He was also hungry. The last of the beer had been downed a long time ago, the food well before that. His stomach rumbled intermittently, aggravating him no end. Why hadn't he thought to bring some candy bars along or at least some chewing gum? Sighing, he entered a narrow room where the floor was covered with waist-high stalagmites.

"Where the hell am I?" Wes grumbled, further annoyed because he had started talking aloud to himself, a sure sign he was in bad shape. His voice echoed hollowly off the walls.

"I hope to hell I run into Cory Fleming," he said as he threaded among the stalagmites. "I need to pound someone and it might as well be that bastard. He's to blame for everything going sour. He's a lousy jinx."

A puff of warm air struck his face.

it distracted Wes and he accidentally banged his left foot

against the base of a stalagmite, stubbing his toe.

"Damn it!" he fumed. "I hate this stinking cave. Hate it! Hate it! Hate it! For two cents I'd find a case of dynamite and blow it to kingdom come."

Wes paused to transfer the flashlight from his right hand to his left. "They should post signs warning people about this place. Maybe I'll sue whoever is responsible when I get out." He chortled. "Yeah, that's the ticket. Make myself a couple of million so I don't have to leech off my old man anymore."

The next tunnel was wider than any he had seen. He played the beam over the walls and plotted how he could make his fortune. "Doctors and surgeons and bozos like that get sued all the time, don't they? Geeks are always claiming they were put through emotional trauma, I think they call it. Well, I can claim the same thing. I lost poor Scott. Les went and bit the big one. I'm as traumatized as they come."

Snickering, he took a turn.

"And I can act as good as the next jerk. Why, put me on the witness stand and I'll bet I qualify for an Academy Award. I'd have the judge and jury eating out of my hand."

The more Wes thought about it, the more liked the notion of suing someone. Wasn't that that American way? Make a mint off a lawsuit and live in the lap of luxury for the rest of your days?

Wes wearily rubbed his eyes, then yawned. All that coke and beer were catching up with him. If he'd known he was going to wind up lost, he never would have indulged. All he needed was ten or so hours in the sack and he would be in tiptop shape, but fat chance he'd get to sleep any time soon.

More warm air caressed his cheeks.

Wes's brow furrowed. Warm air? Where was it coming from? Up until now he had felt occasional breezes, all either cool or chilly. So how come this air was warm? Mystified, he forged on, traveling hundreds of yards before he came to another chamber. Making a desultory sweep with his light, he spied an exit but decided to take a brief break.

He sat on an essentially flat formation the size of his bed. Putting the flashlight beside him, he removed his backpack and stretched out. He could feel the tension draining from his body.

Drowsy, he closed his eyes, planning to rest a minute or two. That was all.

What was that? Wesley sat up with a start, certain he had heard a noise, and was shocked to see the flashlight lying on the floor a yard away instead of beside him where it should be. He must have bumped it while he was sleeping and knocked it off, and the beam was now pointed at the far wall. Thank God it still worked!

Rising, feeling groggy, he arched his back, stepped over to the flashlight, and leaned down to retrieve it. As his fingers wrapped around the handle a low hiss from close by caused his breath to catch in his throat.

Terrified, he swept the light up and around and noticed in passing that his backpack was missing. A second later he learned why.

Thirty feet off stood the same red monster he had tangled with earlier, an ugly red brute sporting breasts the size of full-grown cantaloupes. She held his backpack in her left hand while shielding her eyes with her right, and she wore a mocking smile that revealed teeth a piranha would love.

Wes whirled and ran, fear dominating his being wanting only to get out of there before the creature attacked. He let her keep the backpack, certain if he tried to take it she would do to him as had benn done to Scott and Terri.

At the tunnel he glanced over his shoulder and saw her in the same spot, making no move to catch him. But he wasn't fooled. She was toying with him. She wanted him to get away so she could come after him and hunt him down again. Why else hadn't she slain him when she'd had the perfect chance?

Wes ran doggedly, partially rejuvenated by his short sleep, heedless of where the tunnel was taking him just so it got him in the clear. He crossed two more rooms and jogged along a passage with a lower ceiling than usual, the stalactites a hand's width above his head.

Suddenly the ground underfoot buckled and he tumbled end over end.

Wes screamed. He didn't know if he was falling into a fissure, a chasm, or what, and he anticipated being dashed to bits when he struck bottom.

The impact came the very next instant. His right shoulder smashed into an immovable object, jarring the flashlight from his hand and spearing tremendous pain up and down his arm. His breath exploded from his lungs and total darkness enfolded him.

Stunned, he lay on his side, his cheek pricked by a sharp stone or pebble.

Gradually other sensations made themselves known. Foremost among them was a terrible pain in his right wrist. His ribs hurt. And unless he was mistaken there was a gash on his chin from which blood trickled onto his neck.

Wes licked his dry lips. With difficulty, he lifted his head. The flashlight must be nearby but he couldn't see it. He had to find the damn thing before the creature came after him or he would be helpless. Fighting waves of fright, using his left hand only, he groped in all directions. His fingers touched what seemed to be a broken, blunted stalagmite and clumps of earth.

Then something touched him.

Wes jumped when a hand fell on his back. He tried to jerk aside but another hand seized his left shoulder, pinning him to the ground. The first hand roamed upward, felt in his hair, then traced a path over his face, the fingers lingering at his eyes and nostrils. He smelled the musty scent of old leather.

The monster hissed.

Too scared to move or speak, Wes winced when the creature roughly picked him up as one might lift a small child. His cheek grazed a large rubbery ball that he realized wasn't a ball at all. He felt a nipple poke him in the ear.

In a burst of speed the monster executed several prodigious leaps, bearing him out of whatever he had fallen into, and raced like wildfire along an inky passageway.

Wes could see absolutely nothing. His face and hair were fanned by wind as the creature sped through the cave faster than a human could ever hope to run. The sensation reminded him of driving in a convertible with the top down. He made no attempt to break loose. Should he succeed, he'd hit the floor so hard he'd bust bones for sure. And since she could kill him whenever she wanted, rather than make her mad he preferred to stay quiet.

How could the damn thing see?

Gradually his eyes adjusted. Even so, he could only distinguish the walls and the ribbon of tunnel before them. He figured the monster must have eyes like a cat, the result of a life spent entirely under the surface, which was another reason not to put up a fight. She could see his every move. He'd be lucky to land a single punch.

The tunnel looped and twisted like all the rest, the creature navigating it with consummate ease, at home in her natural environment. Her footfalls and heavy breathing were the sole sounds punctuating the inherent stillness of the Caverna del Diablo.

Just when Wes was beginning to think she would keep running all night, they emerged from the passage into a vast twilight realm that brought to mind the pictures he had seen of the surface of the planet Mars. The terrain had that same dry, alien aspect.

Changing direction, the monster headed out across the forlorn landscape, going faster than ever.

To Wes everything was a blur. He gave up trying to note landmarks. His right arm was pinned uncomfortably between his body and hers so he tried to shift position to ease the discomfort, but she was holding him so tightly he could hardly move his fingers let alone the arm. Resigned to the inevitable, he put his mind to work on a way to escape.

The bitch must have a weakness other than bright light. Her body gave him the impression of being solid muscle but maybe she was soft in the gut. Better yet, he might try to jab her in the eyes. If he could get her down on the ground and find a large rock to bash her brains in with, it would be all over but his shouts of joy.

He was surprised the legendary monster had turned out to be female. The painting at the cave entrance was of a male, and he had just naturally assumed the monster must be the same. In a way, though, it figured the creature was a bimbo. Women were nothing but trouble. His mom, for instance, was always giving his dad grief, always nagging him about doing this or that or criticizing him about his parenting. She didn't like the way his dad had raised him, didn't think lavishing money and gifts was the right way to instill character. A lot she knew! Here he was, almost out of high school, and he was far from being a serial killer or some other kind of psycho. He was no worse than most of the kids in his class.

The creature slowed down.

Wes saw a cluster of formations ahead and then they were among them, winding right and left at a dizzying rate. Closing his eyes, he composed himself so he would be ready to spring into action when she stopped.

Not ten seconds later she did.

Wes opened his eyes to discover they were surrounded on all sides by more rock formations.

She let go of him and he dumped onto his backside at her feet. Pain shot up his arm and he inadvertently cried out.

Grinning, the creature stepped to one side, cocked her head, and uttered a rattling sound that was ungodly loud.

What was that all about? Wes asked himself. Comprehension dawned when an answering rattle came from a distance.

There were two of them!

Once the other one arrived he wouldn't stand a prayer. Frantically, he started crawling, but the female slammed her foot down on his shin to prevent him from going anywhere. He tried to push her leg off his but it was like trying to push a tree.

"No!"

Wes rained blows on her knee. If he could break it she might leave him be long enough for him to slip off. Too late he glimpsed a crimson fist the size of a sledgehammer sweep at his head. A hand grenade went off in his skull, blowing his consciousness to smithereens.

He was still alive?

Aching all over, Wes blinked and gazed up at the ceiling. Why did he feel as if he was lying on the shore of a lake on a hot summer day? He swore he could feel a warm breeze on his chest and legs. He rose on his left elbow, looked down at himself, and had to bite his lower lip to keep from screaming.

He was stark naked.

Wes looked around. The female was gone. There were walls of solid rock encircling him except for a gap near his feet. His clothes were nowhere to be seen.

At the base of the wall ten feet away lay a short pale rod or pole, and near the gap, in deep shadow, was a bundle or pile of something or other.

Wes stood, his right arm tucked to his waist to minimize the pain. Securing a weapon was his first priority so he dashed to the pole, bent over, and scooped it up. It took several seconds for his mind to register the grisly reality. Strips of jagged flesh were hanging from white bone. Grooves in the bone had been made by teeth gnawing to get at the marrow. At the end of the bone were short stubs that had once been fingers.

"God, no!"

Wes cast the arm down and backed away, his stomach coming up to his throat. He gagged, leaned on the wall, and shook uncontrollably.

Get a grip, Eagen! He would share the same fate if he didn't haul ass. Turning, he moved toward the gap, his gaze on the odd bundle in the shadows. Was it another body part, maybe from someone he knew? His curiosity got the better of him. Stepping over, set eyes on a large clump of hair matted with blood.

Timidly, he nudged it with his toe and it flopped over. His senses swam. Bile spewed into his mouth. Nauseated, he stumbled back.

Attached to the hair by a strip of scalp was half of Leslie Vanderhorst's face. A single eyeball, locked open, seemed to glare accusingly at him. The part of her nose still left had been flattened like a pancake, and her lips were badly mangled.

"Les, no!" he blurted, bumping into the wall. Or so he believed.

Hands gripped him around the waist from behind.

Wesley tried to wrench loose but he was held as if his efforts were nothing. He looked over his shoulder.

The female was smiling, the forked tip of her tongue sticking between her parted lips.

"Let me go!" Wes shouted, swatting at her fingers.

She hissed and flung him to the ground. When he tried to rise, she slapped him.

Blood filled Wes's mouth. He coughed, spit it out, and used his good arm to propel himself in a mad scramble away from her. She followed leisurely, her powerful arms swinging at her sides.

If only he could get past her! He glanced at the gap in the wall, so near and yet so far. His arm hit something on the ground. It was the bone. He thought it was called the radius, which hardly mattered. What did matter was that the thick end of the bone, the end once attached to Leslie's elbow, was jagged enough and sharp enough to slice skin. In a flash of inspiration he grabbed it, twisted, and stabbed the female's right foot, cutting into her flesh close to her middle toe.

Venting an enraged rattle, the monster tore her foot out from under the bone, the force of her causing her to stumble into the wall.

Like a greyhound out of the starting gate, the bone clutched in his left hand, Wes bounded to the gap, making his bid for freedom. A hasty glance showed him the creature was raising her foot to examine it. What a dunce! By the time she got around to hunting him, he would be well-hidden.

Wes cut to the right, darting behind a huge stone mound. Using formation after formation to screen his line of travel, he covered a mile in better than four minutes. When he reached the last of the rock shapes he halted to get his wind back and see if he was being pursued.

The female had yet to appear.

Snickering, and without thinking, Wes leaned his right arm on the hard stone surface. An intense pang shot from his wrist to his shoulder. The arm might be fractured or broken. He would be lucky if it didn't become infected before he found help.

A ravine thirty yards away drew his attention. Shadowy along the bottom, it promised an ideal sanctuary, one the monster wouldn't expect him to use. The thing would count on him trying to find a tunnel. He could rest and recuperate.

Wes spring into the open, running as if he heading for the end zone and his team needed every point to win, his legs driving like pistons. Once in the ravine he crouched behind a boulder and peered back. Evidently his plan had worked because none of the monsters were on his trail.

Hot damn! Wes sank into a corner bounded by the boulder and the ravine wall. The cool shade refreshed him. His aches and pains subsided a little except for his arm. He would rest until he felt up to searching for a tunnel, then he would make another attempt to find the surface.

That had been too close for comfort, Wes reflected. But the Eagen luck had run true to form and he'd saved his hide. Another minutes, and he would have wound up in pieces like Leslie.

Poor Les! He remembered her partially consumed face and that single eye staring at him as if he were to blame for her death, which was sheer bull. She had brought it on herself but in typical female fashion she seemed to be blaming him even from beyond the grave.

How in the world had her remains gotten where they were? The creature must have carted her down to this inner world, then eaten her.

Was he the last one still alive? Or had the creatures brought one or two of the others, too? He debated whether to search for his companions but dismissed the idea as stupid. The others were on their own. He had to look out for *numero uno*.

Wes was upset about his missing clothes. Sitting bare-assed on hard rock was a royal pain in the butt. Suddenly he realized the pun he had made, and he had to press a hand over his mouth to stifle budding laughter.

He still had it, even with his life on the line!

He was tired but didn't dare sleep. The last time that he dozed off, the monster had capitalized and closed in. It was too bad he didn't have any blow. That would keep him awake for hours.

A hissing sound filled the ravine.

Wes stiffened. Holding his breath, he eased to the edge of the boulder and glanced out.

There were two of them, the female and a male that was even taller and more massive than she was. They stood close to the mouth of the ravine, hissing at one another. To his amazement they were clearly communicating, carrying on a conversation in that damnable hissing. Every so often one or the other would make a gesture as if stressing a point.

Would they check in the ravine?

Finally they separated, the female moving to the left, the male to the right, both as quick as alligator lizards in their movements.

Wes crept back into his corner and slumped against the wall. For the time being he was safe. If they came back he would need a weapon so he scoured the nearby ground and spotted a rock about the size of both his fists combined. He would have liked one bigger but it would have to do. Flattening, he crawled out to get it, constantly glancing at the open space fronting the ravine.

He picked the rock up in his left hand and shifted to start back when the shadows enveloping him darkened as if a cloud had passed in front of the sun. Only there was no sun. His spine tingling, he looked up into the leering, vicious face of the female monster.

"No!"

The creature seized him by the leg and the arm and lifted him over her head. Pivoting on her heel, she hurled him from the ravine, throwing him a good ten yards.

Wes crashed down with a thud. Panic coursed through his veins, overriding the torment in every cell of his body. His left arm was numb but he pushed to his knees anyway, then stopped, petrified.

Above him loomed the male monster.

He felt its stony fingers dig deep into his biceps as it raised him off the ground, then casually flung him aside. His head struck first. Pinwheels of light burst before his eyes. Vaguely, he was aware of his wrists being grasped in bands of granite and of his arms being held flush with the ground.

When his vision gradually cleared, he almost wished it hadn't.

The male held his arms immobile. Standing by his feet was the female, who now knelt and savagely pushed his legs so far apart, it was a wonder she didn't split him down the middle.

Wes screamed, his groin on fire, certain his manhood had been ruptured. He saw her bend forward. What was she up to? Eyes wide, he saw her hands descend and felt her fingers on his organ.

"No!" he whined. "Please no!"

She smiled her enigmatic smile and lowered her face.

In abject horror Wes felt her teeth scrape his most private of parts, and shuddered. Tears overflowed his eyes, pouring down his cheeks. He wanted to scream but couldn't, not until a moment later when the creature opened her mouth as far as she could and revealed her razor-sharp teeth glistening with red saliva. She looked him right in the eyes, then bit down with all the force in her powerful jaws.

Chapter 28

A frigid cocoon enveloped Cory Fleming as he plunged beneath the surface of the rushing underground stream. Freezing cold water got into his nose and ears and soaked him to his pores. He had taken a breath right before submerging, and it was well he had because the raging current tumbled him like a cork in a whirlpool, flipping him every which way. He became completely disoriented. Encased in a pitch-black watery womb, he hurtled along through the Caverna del Diablo at breakneck speed.

He had no idea where the surface was. Struggling against the sweeping current, he tried to angle in the direction he hoped was up. The water buffeted him harder, carrying him swiftly along, as helpless as a rag doll in the grip of a washing machine.

Where was Ann? He was more worried about her than he was about himself. She had fallen so quickly that she might not have had time to fill her lungs with air. She might readily drown.

The stream swept around a curve.

Cory smacked against a rock wall, then flashed down a straight stretch. To cushion future blows he curled into a ball and clutched his ankles, his head tucked tight to his chest. His glasses, miraculously, were still on his nose, and he gripped the left temple piece to prevent them from being swept off.

The stream executed several turns, a dull roar testifying to the ferocity of the rapids.

Cory prayed there were no underwater obstacles such as gigantic boulders. Ann and him would be smashed to pulp in a microsecond. He also hoped the stream wouldn't pitch them over a high waterfall or throw them into a bottomless sinkhole. The risks were endless.

Once more the current carried him around a curve. Suddenly it slackened dramatically. Uncoiling, he detected a glimmer of light and shot toward it in strong, even strokes.

His head cleared the surface in a spray of water and he gratefully sucked in cool air. Drops on his lenses blurred the world around him but he could see sufficiently to determine he was in a great horizontal shaft, a dimly glowing ceiling less than a foot above his head. He faced forward, seeking Ann, but saw only a bluish-black torrent speeding into a dark maw.

From out of that hole came a dull rumble.

A waterfall! Cory was certain of it. He threw himself backwards, swimming for his life, but the current swept him along. The rumble became a roar. He stroked and stroked, in vain. Looking at the maw, he saw foaming bubbles. In desperation he tried to brace his hands against the wall but the smooth sides were like greased glass.

The next instant Cory was propelled through the hole as if shot from a cannon and found himself falling, his arms flailing, toward a large pool twenty feet below. Twisting frantically, he got his head pointed down and held one hand over his glasses. When he hit it was like taking a jump off a high diving board and not being properly set for the impact. His shoulders bore the brunt and then he sank like a rock, dazed.

The cold water snapped him alert. He could see light and struck out for it, having to kick extra hard because of the added weight of his clothes and the backpack. His lungs were close to bursting when at last he reached the surface a dozen yards from the cascading waterfall.

Gasping and sputtering, he dog-paddled and took stock.

Situated in a sprawling chamber, the pool was thirty yards in diameter. To the right and left were typical calcium and aragonite speleothems. High, high above, the ceiling formed an arch.

The walls and the ceiling, as in other chambers in the cavern, cast a pale radiance.

Cory swam toward the side opposite the waterfall. The pool, he discovered, was the consequence of an immense rimstone dam, the water flowing over the rim at several points. Beyond, the stream resumed its swift course. He gripped the rimstone, about to climb out, when he heard a sound that electrified him into action.

Someone coughed.

Swinging around, he spied Ann sprawled on a dry patch of ground. She was coughing and sputtering, her arms flung out.

Pulling himself out, in three bounds Cory was at her side. Kneeling, he clasped her to him. "Ann! Ann! Are you all right?"

Ann groggily looked up at him in blatant shock, water seeping from her nose and mouth. "Cory?" she gurgled.

Smiling in relief, he helped her to sit up and patiently waited for her coughing fit to subside. At last she began breathing normally and wiped the back of her hand across her face.

"Are any bones broken?" he asked. "Do you have any internal injuries?"

"No," Ann said weakly, shaking her head. "I don't think so. All I did was swallow half the stream."

Cory hugged her, then kissed her cheek. "I thought I'd lost you."

"It was a close call," Ann said. She squeezed him with all her strength. "I can't believe we were both dumb enough to fall in.

"I didn't fall."

Ann pushed back, studied his face, and blinked rapidly a few times. "Oh, my God," she said. Throwing herself at him, she buried her face in his shoulder and began crying in great racking heaves.

"What's the matter?" Cory said, confused, afraid she was injured after all. "Is there anything I can do?"

She didn't respond. She cried and cried, her hands grasping his shoulders as if she was clinging to him for dear life.

"What is it?" he persisted.

"You," Ann said, the word muffled, almost inaudible.

"Me? What did I do?"

"You jumped in after me, didn't you?"

"Yeah. So?"

Ann raised her head and kissed him, mashing her lips against his, molding her body so the two of them were as one. Minutes later she said, "I didn't realize just how much you cared for me until now."

"I love you."

"Believe me, I know. And it's scary."

"Being loved?"

She nodded.

Although Cory didn't quite understand, he shelved the topic for later discussion. Paramount was scouting the new chamber to see if there was a way out. Standing, he pulled her upright, and the two of them slowly surveyed their surroundings.

"There," Ann said, pointing.

Cory saw it, too, a tunnel hundred of feet away. He took her hand. "Do you want to rest or can we keep going?"

"Don't hold back on my account," Ann said, grinning sheepishly. "Just keep me away from the stream."

They headed for the opening in the far wall. Suddenly there was a tremendous splash at the rimstone dam, and they both turned.

Looming above the rim was Evil Incarnate. A red demon, its skin dripping wet, glared down at them and uttered a rasping hiss. Prominent on its neck under the chin and visible on its head were fresh wounds.

"It's the same one!" Ann exclaimed, "The one you stabbed! It followed us somehow!"

Cory could scarcely believe his eyes. How had the creature found them? Had it been watching and seen them plunge into the stream? More importantly, how could the one he stabbed still be alive? But there was no denying the hole under the monster's chin, nor the hatred etching its features as it clambered off the rimstone and started toward them. "Run!" he yelled. "I'll hold it off."

"No. We're in this together."

"Don't argue," Cory said, pushing her, his eyes on the demon. She stubbornly stayed by his side.

"Where's the lantern?"

Cory stared at his empty hands. In all the excitement he had forgotten about it. The last he remembered, he had been holding the handle when he dived into the water. The current must have torn it from his grasp. He grabbed at the steel bits under his belt and only found one. The other had gone the way of the lantern.

"Hey, what's wrong with that thing?" Ann said.

Cory glanced up and was bewildered to see the demon

stumbling as if drunk. The creature's legs gave out and it fell onto its hands and knees, then vigorously shook its head. Inexplicably, it toppled onto its side and lay there feebly moving its limbs in a futile effort to stand.

"What the hell?" Ann said.

"Stay here," Cory directed, and ran toward it, the bit in his right hand. Maybe the creature was weak from loss of blood. Maybe the wounds he inlicted had finally taken their toll. Or maybe ,there was another reason for its weakness.

Think! he goaded himself If he could deduce the reason he might be able to use the knowledge to his advantage should they tangle with another one.

His mind raced faster than his feet. The demons were reptilian, weren't they? At least they appeared more like reptiles than any other species. And true reptiles were unable to endure cold temperatures, which was why turtles, snakes, frogs, toads and lizards all hibernated in the winter. The cold made them weak and sluggish. Prolonged exposure resulted in death.

If the demons were biologically similar, cold temperatures should have the same effect on them. Was the one on the slope suffering from having jumped in the stream? Had its thirst for revenge made it reckless?

Cory was almost there. Footfalls behind him alerted him to the fact that Ann had not followed his advice. Frowning, he jumped over a rivulet, and there was the demon on its back now, the flames in its eyes undiminished by its weakness. He lunged and stabbed, the steel bit sinking into the creature's side. If he thought the monster was helpless, though, he was mistaken.

The demon lashed out, its movements leaden compared to its former swiftness but it was still fast enough to clip

Cory on the shoulder. He tottered back, pulling the bit loose as he did, and collided with Ann. She cried out. He heard her slip and fall, but he couldn't afford to turn his back on the demon to see if she was unharmed.

The thing was trying to rise, and already on one knee.

Cory sprang, lancing the bit into the demon's arm. Predictably, the creature jerked its arm back, exposing its chest, and he struck again, the bit cutting deep into the monster's torso. A hand cuffed his face. Bending at the knees, he thrust the steel tip into the demon's stomach. The thing retaliated with a fist to the head that knocked him down the slope.

Seeing stars, Cory refused to give up. He got to his feet and charged, resolved to end the conflict then and there. The demon had other ideas. Weakened but far from out of commission, the creature looked up at the rimstone dam, coiled and leaped. Demonstrating fluid grace, it grasped the top, arced higher, and dived into the pool.

Confused, Cory stopped. If cold water adversely affected the demon's metabolism, why had it done that? To get away from him? Because it knew he would kill it and the only way out was to get beyond his reach?

"Cory?" Ann was four yards off, holding her right wrist with her left hand.

"I'm fine," he said, hurrying over. "What about you?"

"I think I sprained my wrist when I fell."

"We'll check it later. Right now let's make tracks."

She needed no convincing. Together they hastened to the passageway, both of them glancing repeatedly at the dam.

"Where is it?" Ann asked as they halted.

"Laying low would be my guess," Cory said. "I hurt it, hurt it bad. If we're lucky it will crawl into a hole somewhere and die." He faced the dark opening and shrugged out of the backpack. They would need light.

"What are you doing?"

He placed the pack down and clasped the zipper. "The lantern is gone but we still have the sulfur.

"Which is soaking wet and won't do us any good."

"Not so, true heart," Cory said. "This type of backpack is waterproof. I've seen them on sale at the mall in Durango so I know. If the waterproofing did its job, the contents should be slightly damp, no more." He opened the pack and reached inside, frowning as his hand closed on a damp sock. Drawing it out, he saw the sock had been saturated and was now streaked with yellow.

"So much for water-proofing," Ann said. "It must have sprung a leak."

The second sock was as wet as the first. Cory next removed the big bundle, which was also drenched, and unfastened the tie.

"Now what, handsome? The sulfur is bound to be useless."

"Maybe not," Cory said, unfolding the shirt. As he'd expected, the outer layer of sulfur was indeed moist. But he hadn't been underwater long enough for all the powder to become soaked. Several handfuls in the center were dry. "See?" he said, taking the pipe and sheath out.

Ann smiled. "My genius."

Cory looked at her. "I used to resent being called that. Coming from anyone else, I still would be ticked off, but in your case I'll make an exception."

"I'm honored."

Working rapidly, Cory crammed sulfur into the pipe and replaced the socks and the big bundle. Rising, he pulled the matchbox out of his soaked pocket.

"Are the matches waterproof too?"

"No, silly. Some in the middle might be dry, though." Cory proved his prediction by finding five untouched by the water. "Hold these, please," he said, giving her the improvised torch and the five matches so he could don the backpack.

She turned toward the pool and gasped.

Cory spun, his breath catching at the sight of the demon standing between them and the dam. "Let's go."

"What does it take to kill that thing?"

"A shotgun at point-blank range might do the trick. Unfortunately, we don't have one."

Cory went a few feet into the tunnel, paused until she joined him, then moved as fast as they were able.

For the time being they moved in the dark. The sulfur was their last resort, to be saved for the right moment.

"That thing must want us real bad to have trailed us so far," Ann said.

"I think it wants me the most," Cory said to alleviate her worry. "I was the one who buried a pick in its head and caused it to fall down the shaft."

"You did good, man of mine."

Cory's face grew warm. His admiration of her was growing by the minute. The dip in the stream had left her bedraggled and waterlogged but she hadn't become hysterical as some would have done. And she still retained her sense of humor despite all that had happened. Here was a girl--- no, a woman---who had a fine head on her shoulders.

He stopped again and again to scan the tunnel and listen for sounds of pursuit. If the demon was back there it wasn't advertising the fact. The next attack, when it came, would be swift and devastating, and he must be ready to light the pipe at a moment's notice

"Cory, I forgot to tell you. I lost the knife in the stream."

"No problem. I lost the lantern so we're even."

"Could I have one of those rods you're carrying?"

"A steel bit, you mean," Cory corrected her. "Sure. Hold out your hand." Her fingers touched his waist so he knew exactly where to place the tool.

"Thanks. You have more, don't you?"

"Yes," Cory said, not bothering to mention they were in the backpack. Since stopping with the demon in pursuit would be foolhardy, he kept going. He could always grab a steel bit later.

"I lost my watch, too," Ann said. "Do you have yours?"

Cory could feel the strap on his left wrist. "Sure do," he answered. When last he had checked, shortly after finding the lantern, he'd been astounded to learn they had been in the Caverna del Diablo for over five hours. Another five, if not more, must have elapsed since. Provided his calculations were correct, dawn would soon herald a glorious new day in the Rocky Mountains.

The passage contained fewer twists and turns than most they had traversed. Twice they passed through benighted rooms.

An hour or so after entering the tunnel they spied a pinpoint of diffuse light ahead. The light enlarged as they approached, and ten minutes later they stepped out into a chamber to be immediately hit by a blast of chill air from above.

Cory peered upward, expecting yet another of those glowing ceilings. To his amazement he saw sparkling stars in a lightening sky tinged by pink and orange to his left, where the eastern horizon must lie.

"The sky!" Ann exclaimed. "It's a way out!"

Not quite, Cory realized. The high walls were smooth, lacking a single purchase hand or foot. Unless they could sprout wings and fly, the opening did them no good, and he told her so.

"There has to be a way, damn it," Ann insisted, moving around the perimeter. "We can't be so close and still be trapped."

Her frustration goaded Cory into searching for a chimney they might be able to climb. Concentrating on the walls, he failed to watch where he was stepping and his left foot bumped something that gave off a hollow thump. Glancing down, he was surprised to behold, of all things, a vase. Crouching for a better look, he saw the clay vessel was marred by a random spider's web of thin cracks. The clay was dry to the touch, the outer surface flaking off on his fingers.

"What do you have there?”

"An old Indian vase like the kind the Anasazis made at Mesa Verde," Cory said, referring to the cliff dwellings at Mesa Verde National Park which he had visited with his parents on two occasions. The spectacular ruins of the pueblos drew thousands of tourists every year

"What's it doing here?"

"Beats me," Cory said. Mesa Verde had to be sixty or seventy miles from the Caverna del Diablo. There were other, lesser-known pueblos scattered throughout the southwest part of Colorado, many so remote that only a few hikers and hunters ever visited them. As far as he knew, none had ever been found in the vicinity of the cavern. Yet the vase hinted there must have been Anasazis in the area at one time.

Ann was gazing wistfully at the opening "I give up. I can't find a way up there." She sighed, her shoulders slumping in resignation. "I guess we have to keep on looking."

"Hang in there. It's only a matter of time before we're out of here," Cory offered as encouragement, although his own doubts filled him with trepidation. He moved toward another passage, pausing to stare at the steadily brightening sky before venturing into it.

"I don't know how much more of this I can take," Ann said.

Cory shared her dejection.

The tantalizing sight of the surface world had raised his fading hopes to new heights, only to have them dashed on the bitter rocks of reality. They were still lost, still at the whimsical mercy of Fate, still prey for the crimson devil on their trail.

The dark tunnel ahead only accented their plight.

Ann stayed close by his side. "I never thought my life would end like this."

"Don't talk like that," Cory said gruffly, more irritated because his own thoughts were becoming morbid than because hers were. "We're breathing, aren't we? We have food and enough sulfur to last a while. We have water in the whiskey flask." He wagged the pipe. "We're a lot better off than we were before we found that prospector's remains, so don't count us out yet."

"Sorry," Ann said softly. "I didn't mean to upset you.

The tunnel entrance forked, one branch angling sharply to the left, the other to the right. Neither passage offered a clue as to which would be best to take.

"Have a coin?" Ann asked half-heartedly.

Thinking deeply, Cory surveyed first one, then the other. That tinge in the eastern sky had allowed him to get his bearings. They must have been moving south when they stumbled on the chamber, which was a break for them, since the cavern entrance was at the south end of the cave system. But neither of these forks would take them in that direction. Either they retraced their steps, or they took a chance on---

"Cory!" Ann screamed.

He heard the thud of heavy steps as he whirled and knew he was too late.

The demon was on them, its red eyes ablaze with fury.

Chapter 29

Cory gave Ann a shove and shouted, "Run!" He tried to back up to give himself room to maneuver, when out of the darkness lashed the creature's forearm, clubbing him. His feet left the floor and he slammed into the tunnel wall, then fell, his mind in a fog, his back in torment. There was a commotion, the sounds of a struggle, and Ann screeched.

"It's got me! Help!"

He could see their shadowy figures, the demon holding Ann by the front of her blouse, Ann kicking and punching but having no effect.

"Hang on!" Cory shouted, wincing as he rose. By some fluke he had managed to hold onto the matches and the pipe. He tucked the torch under his left arm and fumbled with the matchbox, trying to light one of the dry matches.

Ann began sputtering and wheezing as if she were being choked to death.

"Hang on!" Cory repeated, his leaden fingers finally responding to his will. He struck the head of the match on the friction strip, and as the flame flared he touched it to the pipe bowl.

Brilliant light lit up the tableau, revealing Ann's flushed face and parted mouth, revealing the demon's hand clamped on her throat. The thing hissed and swung toward Cory, squinting against the bright glare.

Cory leaped straight at the demon's face, his crude torch spewing fire and smoke. He jabbed the torch at its eyes and had to duck under a savage swing that might have crushed his skull. Thrusting before the demon could protect itself, he rammed the scorching pipe into its right eye.

A piercing, wavering cry erupted from the demon's lips. Releasing Ann, it staggered back, its hands covering its eyes.

Ann sank to her knees, rubbing her throat and gulping air.

Knowing he only had a few seconds of light left, Cory snatched her wrist in the same hand he held the matchbox and hauled her upright. He spun and fled with her in tow. She recognized the urgency and did her best to keep up.

Behind them the tunnel shook with an elemental howl of boundless rage.

Cory flew around a bend. The demon might give chase at any second. They must cover as much distance as they could and hope they found somewhere to make a stand. He glanced back at Ann, who forced a wan smile, just as the torch burned out. Should he refill it with sulfur or keep going? If they stopped now the creature would easily overtake them. He pressed on.

Minutes later he was elated to see a patch of pale light ahead. He ran faster, his hopes soaring anew when they emerged in a chamber with a high ceiling. Near the top was an opening, a cleft through which the pale light filtered. He stopped short, agog. There could be no mistake. It was another opening to the outside, only this one could be reached with some effort.

Ages ago, the left side of the chamber had collapsed, leaving a tremendous pile of earth, rocks and boulders. Talus, it was called, forming a ramp that slanted from the cave floor to within a few feet of the cleft. The ramp was broad at the base of the wall and narrower near the top.

"Cory, look! We can get out!" Ann cried, pulling loose

and dashing to the pile. She laughed and started scrambling up it.

"Slow down!" Cory advised, hurrying to catch up. There were loose stones and rifts where a person might slip if not careful. In her excitement she could hurt herself, not that he blamed her. He felt equally as thrilled but he refused to let his emotions get the better of his logic.

Ann was ten feet above the floor and climbing with remarkable alacrity.

"Be careful, for crying out loud," Cory warned, glancing at the tunnel before beginning his own ascent.

The demon had yet to appear. Perhaps he had injured it worse than he thought. He stuffed the matchbox and the four loose matches into his left pocket, the pipe into his right, and started climbing. In spots the dirt was so loose it cascaded out from under him. He was amazed Ann hadn't taken a tumble.

Thirty feet up was the first rift, a gap over a foot wide where the underlying earth had buckled. He stepped over it, checked on Ann's progress, and chuckled. At the rate she was climbing, she'd be halfway to Pagosa Springs before he even stepped out of the cave.

As if she were a mind reader, she called down. "Come on, slowpoke! Do you have a death wish or something?"

Cory shook his head, convinced he was playing it smart by taking it slow. The higher they went, the steeper the slope became. Up near the cleft they would have to be especially wary.

As he climbed, he wondered what had happened to the others. Had Jay, Stacy and Les found a way out? He didn't care one iota about Miklin and Eagen but the rest had never done him any harm, and he prayed they were okay. If Jay had managed to find the entrance before midnight, by now a rescue party might be on its way from Pagosa Springs.

A second rift gave him pause. Five feet wide and nine feet deep, it would be difficult to jump. He couldn't get the momentum needed to make a decent leap. He looked right and left, puzzled as to how Ann had gotten across, and saw a point where the rift narrowed to only two feet. Stepping over to it, he tensed, then vaulted into the air and came down on all fours, digging his hands into the earth for added traction.

The next forty feet were increasingly treacherous. The top layer of earth was like sand, shifting and sliding at the slightest pressure. He set each foot down slowly, not moving the right until he was sure the left was firmly in place, and vice versa. Total concentration was required to keep from falling.

Because he wasn't watching Ann, he had no idea she was in trouble until he heard her cry out. He glanced up to see her hurtling toward him, out of control. She bounced twice, then rolled, gathering speed with every toss of her body.

Cory rose directly in her path. All he had to do was step aside and she would sweep on by, falling until she hit the bottom or fell into one of the rifts. Either way, she might be seriously injured. To prevent that, he dug in his heels, crouched, and braced for the collision.

Extending both hands palms out, he saw her frenzied attempts to stop, saw dust flying out from under her, then saw her glance his way a second before she barreled into him with the force of a runaway train.

He went down. Even with his legs braced, the kinetic energy she had built up was irresistible and she went over him like a steamroller over asphalt. Flipped onto his back, he grabbed her legs and held on tight, determined to stop her no matter what. She dragged him over ten feet before his extra weight brought them to a lurching halt.

Dust swirled around his face, making him cough. He craned his neck and saw her grinning at him. "You think that was funny? You could have gotten us both killed."

"I wasn't worried. I just knew you'd save me, Sir Galahad."

"Be serious."

"I am."

Cory disengaged himself from under her and stood up, brushing dirt from his clothes. "You do know, don't you, that Galahad never had time for the fairer sex? He was always too busy, either on quests for the Holy Grail or slaying enemies of King Arthur."

Ann made a face as she rose. "Okay, then, Mr. Know-It-All. Sir Galahad you're not. How about if I call you Pee Wee Herman instead?"

"You do, and the next time you fall I'll just wave as you go by."

She laughed.

Cory was about to join in her mirth when his gaze strayed over her shoulder. Just coming out of the passage was their infernal nemesis.

The demon spotted them instantly and bounded toward the pile, venting a roar that goaded Cory into gripping Ann's hand and rotating. "Come on!" he shouted, his legs pumping.

The demon hardly slowed when it reached the slope. In great leaps it raced up after them, covering six feet in a stride and vaulting the rifts as if they didn't exist.

Clawing at the dirt with his right hand, climbing in an adrenaline-induced frenzy, Cory chided himself for being the biggest fool who ever lived. He should have filled the pipe when he had the chance. The oversight might cost both of them their lives, and here they were on the verge of escaping. He looked at the demon, which had reduced the gap by half, then scoured the nearby ground for a large rock. There were plenty to choose from, and he scooped up one that weighed close to fifteen pounds.

The creature uttered its rattling cry as it closed in.

Cory caught Ann's eyes. She glanced at the rock, then nodded. Their legs churning, they fled higher, dirt and small stones tumbling down the pile below them. He kept one eye on the earth underfoot and the other on the demon. His timing must be perfect. If the thing suspected what he was up to, it would simply dart out of the way.

Ann was watching the demon, too.

The creature wore a wickedly triumphant grin as it drew within eight feet of them. From its newest wounds trickled thick blood. Its right eye was swollen shut, yellow pus seeping out of the comers.

The demon focused on Ann and reached out to grab her, its claws poised to rip and rend.

Cory wasn't about to let the fiend lay a finger on her. He waited until the very last instant, until the creature's hands were inches from her body, and then he unwound, spinning and throwing the rock with all the strength in his lean frame.

Unable to stop or turn aside, the demon was hit in the face. Had it been on level ground the tactic would have done little good but on the steep slope the unexpected blow rocked the creature on its heels. Tottering, it slipped backwards.

Releasing Ann, Cory grabbed another rock and hurled it at the demon's chest. It struck with a resounding thud.

The creature went down in a whirl of limbs, gravity carrying it lower and lower until, in a spray of fine dust, the thing came to rest on the chamber floor.

Cory kept going. He came to a yard-wide rift and took it on the fly, then stopped and turned as Ann alighted beside him.

The demon was slowly rising, its legs wobbly, its movements sluggish, just like back at the pool.

"What's wrong with it?" Ann asked breathlessly.

"Blood loss, maybe," Cory said, moving higher. Quickly, he removed the backpack and worked the zipper. "Climb to the cleft," he directed. "I'll catch up when I can."

"Like hell I will. I'm not leaving you."

"Please," Cory said, taking out the last pair of steel bits.

"No."

"For me."

"We're in this together, buster."

There was no time to argue. Cory gave her the bits, then pulled out one of the sulfur-filled socks. He tugged the matchbox from his pocket and swiveled.

The demon had recovered sufficiently to scale the pile and was charging upward, gaining speed with each step. Whatever was wrong with it seemed to come and go, and at the moment it was as ferocious as ever.

Crouching, Cory reached into his soggy pocket and found one of the four dry matches. It *had* been dry, anyway, until he put it in his pocket. Now it was damp, and he wondered whether it would ignite.

"Here comes ugly," Ann said.

Cory looked, saw the creature twenty feet below them, and hurriedly closed the pack. Grasping the sock by the tied end in one hand, he held the match in the other and lowered it next to the matchbox. The sock was also damp, compounding the chances of success. Should his plan fail, both of them would die.

"Look," Ann said.

The demon had stopped and was regarding them suspiciously, wary of another trick. It angled to the right, cocking its head from side to side, its fingers clenching and unclenching.

Cory scowled. Once the creature saw the sock and the match it might deduce his purpose. "Come on bastard!" he baited the brute, hoping to provoke it into attacking. "Or are you scared of a human?"

The rush, when it came, was so swift that if not for the rift, the demon would have been on them before Cory could get the match lit. As it was, he saw the creature spring forward, and he struck the match against the box. Nothing happened. Again he tried, producing a spark but no flame.

The demon was only ten feet lower, raw power in motion, intent on the kill.

A third time Cory tried the match. Flame sparkled to life. He hastily touched the match to the sock, which sputtered and smoked but refused to catch.

"Cory!"

She didn't need to tell him. He knew the monster was almost upon them and glanced up to see it about to leap over the rift. The thing paused for the span of a heartbeat, and in that moment the sock crackled and blazed as the sulfur within caught on fire.

Twisting, Cory tossed the crude incendiary flare at the demon's face---and missed.

The thing saw the sock coming and darted to the right to evade it. But the sulfur suddenly incinerated in a great, white-hot tongue of searing fire, so bright that for half a minute a miniature sun bathed the chamber in bright light.

Screeching, the demon threw its hands over its good eye and stumbled. It blundered to the edge of the rift, then over the edge, plummeting seven or eight feet before its massive body became wedged in the crack.

Cory didn't waste another second. He snatched up the backpack, motioned at Ann, and sped toward the cleft. With any luck they would be out of the cave before the demon extricated itself.

The slope became steeper. The stones looser. They were forced to exercise supreme care, testing each step before they put a foot down.

Above them, the cleft beckoned "I didn't realize it was quite so high," Ann said.

Cory scoured the slope to their rear for the tenth time. The demon, he reasoned, must be out of commission or it would have appeared already.

The cleft was about the size of a refrigerator door. It wasn't more than three feet above the top of the slope.

All they had to do was reach it.

"I'll go first," Cory volunteered, easing onto all fours for the final stage of their ascent. "This way, if I fall you'll have time to move out of my way so we both don't wind up at the bottom."

"Oh, sure. That's going to happen. You didn't move out of the way when I fell."

Cory crawled. At the very pinnacle of the pile he stopped, rose onto his knees, and extended his right arm as high as it would go. His hand draped over the edge of the cleft. Securing a purchase, he raised his other hand and tossed the backpack through the opening, then gripped the edge with both hands and pulled, his shoulders protesting the strain of lifting his one hundred and fifty pounds. But he made it. He got his chest onto the rim, then his stomach, finally his thighs. Squatting, he looked at Ann, who smiled, and beckoned for her to scale the final few feet.

The next few minutes were some of the scariest of his entire time in the cave, scary because at any moment the demon might appear and attack the girl he loved. Before he could reach her side it would all be over.

His skin itching, he watched her make agonizingly slow progress, slow from his point of view although she was moving as fast as he had. When she reached the top he flattened and lowered his right hand for her to grip. Once she did, it was a simple matter to haul her up beside him with her bracing her feet against the wall to make the job easier.

They sat on top of the cleft, facing one another, both of them winded, both of them grinning like idiots.

"We did it!" Ann exclaimed.

Had they? Cory turned. In his concern for her safety he had failed to see what awaited them. He did so now and was flabbergasted to behold a series of walls and doorways, as if he were at one end of a room and gazing through a half-dozen others. A hundred feet above was an enormous rock overhang, and in between was a patch of steadily brightening sky.

"What the ... ?" Ann blurted.

Cory stood, the backpack in his left hand, and entered a room bounded by walls made of stone and adobe. Lined up against one side were various vases, bowls and gourds, each decorated with fantastic black and white abstract designs consisting of swirls and triangles and assorted other shapes.

Dust covered everything.

"Where are we?" Ann asked in awe.

"Unless I'm mistaken," Cory marveled, "we're in an

ancient pueblo like the one at Mesa Verde."

"A cliff dwelling?"

Cory nodded and moved to the doorway. "These rooms were individual apartments. Some pueblos had thousands of inhabitants."

"Then there might be people here," Ann said hopefully.

"Probably not. Most of the pueblos were abandoned ages ago. For years there have been rumors of undiscovered cliff dwellings far up in the mountains." He touched the adobe, which was as sturdy as the day the place had been built. "This could be one of them."

"I don't really care," Ann said. "I just want to see the sun again and breathe fresh air."

Cory took the hint, leading her through room after room, eight in all, before they came out onto a terrace. Spread out before them was a spectacular sight.

A winding, verdant valley meandered into the distance, rimmed by rugged mountains crowned with glistening snow. To the east the crown of the sun had risen, a golden arch hinting at the beauty to come. On both sides and below them were scores of cliff dwellings. The valley floor itself was two hundred feet below.

"How will we ever get down there?" Ann said.

Cory set the backpack down and moved along the terrace rim, seeking a means to do just that. He knew the Anasazis had relied on wooden ladders and occasionally stone steps to get them from level to level, and there were a few ladders in sight, but all on lower levels. In any event, the ladders were bound to be so rickety that they would be unable to bear a person's weight.

He went to the next terrace, which bordered a high cliff. If his memory served, sometimes the Indians chiseled handholds to take them up and down. A casual scrutiny confirmed this. A succession of handholds ran from the bottom of the cliff to the top. While the idea of trying to climb down two hundred feet was unnerving, the top of the cliff was only thirty feet or so above their heads. Like most cliff cities, this one had been constructed on the side of a plateau from the top of which the Anasazis could keep a lookout for their enemies.

"Are you thinking what I think you're thinking?" Ann asked, standing at his side.

"We'll go up and scout around. There might be an easy way down somewhere else."

Cory stepped to within arm's reach of the grooves in the rock surface. "Maybe I should go first to see if it's safe."

"Be my guest," Ann said. "But what about the backpack?"

Cory turned and saw the pack lying where he had dropped it. "Blast. I forgot."

"Allow me, dumb one," Ann said, smirking. She pecked him on the cheek before running gracefully across the terrace to fetch their meager supplies.

Cory gazed out over the sprawling valley, and stretched. Waves of fatigue washed over him. Every muscle ached. His eyelids felt as if they each weighed a ton, Until that moment he hadn't realized how tired the grueling events of the long night of terror had made him. He thought of his comfortable bed and yearned to curt up under his blankets and crash hours. Heck, the way he felt, he wouldn't be surprised if he slept the clock around.

For as long as he lived he would never forget this ordeal. And how strange that such unthinkable horror should spawn a romance between him and the girl he had adored for years. How strange that out of a nightmare a dream should come true.

Cory chuckled, thinking of how his parents would react

when he broke the news to them. Young Thomas Edison, as his dad sometimes called him, actually had a girlfriend. Would wonders never cease! After their initial shock they would probably be delighted, especially his mother, who was always asking him when he was going to find a girl to carry on the Fleming line.

Speaking of which, where was she?

Cory turned, a grin curling his lips, a grin that froze as did his blood at the sight on the next terrace.

The demon stood close to the edge, holding Ann in its brawny arms, a hand pressed tight over her mouth. No sooner did he lay eyes on them than the creature dangled her over the side and exposed its pointed teeth in a grin that mocked his own.

Chapter 30

Cory's first impulse was to rush to Ann's aid. He took several swift steps before it occurred to him that doing so would get both of them killed. Once he came within reach, the monster had only to let go of her so she'd plummet to her death, then pounce on him. And maybe that was exactly what the creature wanted.

Ann was holding herself still, her frightened gaze alternating between Cory and the drop-off below her feet.

The demon had a hand under each of her arms, supporting her as easily as one might hold a toy doll.

"Don't hurt her, damn you," Cory said, knowing he was wasting his breath but unable to think of anything, else to do or say.

The demon glared.

Cory had the feeling it was waiting for a particular move on his part.

Abruptly, the creature withdrew its left hand, and Ann started to fall. She involuntarily screamed. At the same instant the thing seized her left wrist and held fast. Her fall arrested, she blanched and swayed back and forth.

Rage pulsed through Cory. The creature had deliberately done that to torment him, smirking in its depraved fashion the whole while. He longed to kill the thing, to put an end to the horror. But how? The sulfur had been his edge and now he couldn't get at it.

The demon motioned with its free hand, beckoning him to come closer.

Cory stayed where he was, thinking furiously, trying to come up with an idea to turn the tables. Maybe his best bet was to stall. The sun would be up soon, and he doubted very much that the creature could endure bright sunlight.

Clearly annoyed, the demon gestured again, then pointed at Ann. To emphasize its point, it bobbed her up and down several times.

The message was plain. Either Cory did as the creature wanted or Ann would die. He moved slowly forward, his rage mounting. There really wasn't any choice. The demon had them over a barrel and knew it. At the junction of the two terraces he halted, stalling, hoping for a brainstorm.

The demon motioned emphatically.

Cory advanced cautiously, taking short steps. One of the steel bits he had given Ann now lay near the creature's feet, and he still had one wedged under his belt. A quick stab into a vital organ might do the trick, but he had no idea where the creature's vital organs were located. Did it have a heart and lungs like humans? Or, as was more likely, did the thing possess a totally alien physiology?

"Don't let it get you, Cory," Ann suddenly spoke up. "Save yourself."

"Not on your life," he responded.

Hissing in anger, the demon drew Ann onto the terrace and cuffed her across the face, not once but three times. After the third blow it released her and she slumped, unconscious, onto the terrace rim, her body half an inch from eternity. The thing put a foot on her shoulder, then grinned at Cory.

"You son of a bitch," Cory growled, dreading the result should the demon give her the slightest shove.

Unperturbed, the creature motioned for him to keep coming.

Cory took measured strides, resisting feelings of despair, his right elbow crooked, his right hand partially screening the bit from the demon's view. Where should he strike first? The neck? No, he had tried that before and the thing was still alive. The same with the chest and the head. What about the eyes? He studied the monstrosity from head to toe and inspiration struck.

The demon exuded confidence. Its right eye was still swollen closed. Its left was a mirror of living hellfire.

Cory stopped and pointed at the thing's foot resting on Ann. To his surprise, the demon took a step to the side and faced him, its broad shoulders squared, its claws poised to rend. So he was right. It wanted him more than it did her. It wanted revenge. He smiled and saw its brow crease. Another stride brought him within a yard.

Saliva dripped from the demon's parted lips.

"Here I am, scumbag," Cory said to distract it from noticing his hand as he gripped the steel bit. "Let's get this over with once and for all."

The creature acted as if it was puzzled, tilting its head and intently staring at him.

For the first time Cory noticed how heavily the demon was breathing, each breath laboriously drawn out, reminding him of someone who had just participated in a ten-mile marathon. Was it in worse shape than it appeared to be? Was that why it wanted him in close, so it wouldn't have to exert itself hard to kill him? Or did the air outside the cavern have an adverse effect on its respiratory system? He saw the demon's good eye narrow and flick toward the eastern horizon. Perhaps the true reason it had lured him so close was that it feared the sun and needed to end their clash quickly.

Ann groaned.

The demon glanced at her, and in that instant Cory struck, lancing the steel bit at the the creature's abdomen. Inhuman reflexes enabled the thing to shift to the left to evade the stab even as its hand closed on Cory's wrist and squeezed. Absolute agony shot up to Cory's shoulder. He tried to wrench loose but the demon shoved, sending him to his knees beside Ann and close to the bit lying on the terrace. His left hand wrapped around it as the demon savagely twisted his right arm to make him drop the other one. Gritting his teeth against the anguish, Cory lanced the bit in his left hand up and in, the point cutting deep into the demon's genitals.

As if jolted by a stun gun, the monstrosity stiffened, then backhanded Cory across the head and tottered back.

Knocked flat, Cory saw the demon double over, clutch its groin, and shuffle toward the nearest doorway. He rose into a crouch. By all rights that last blow should have cracked his cranium or at the least stunned him. Yet it had been no worse than a punch from any of the guys at school---which meant the demon *was* weaker.

There would never be a better opportunity.

Cory took a moment to pull Ann away from the edge, then dashed after the crimson fiend. The thing had crossed the first apartment and was entering the second, still bent over, blood dribbling from its fingers. It was paying no attention to him.

From five feet off he launched himself into the air and came down on the demon's back to thrust and hack in a fury. The creature hissed and tried to yank him off his perch but couldn't quite reach his leg. Rattling, it ran at a nearby wall and spun around at the last second, ramming him into the adobe.

Cory thought his back would burst. Stunned, he

slumped, and was tossed to the apartment floor. He smacked down hard on his left side. His head pounding, he looked back to see the demon coming toward him. It had yet to straighten up, one hand cradling its organ while the other, caked with blood, reached out to end his life.

Cory rolled away, felt its nails snatch at his arm. Rising, he held the steel bit at waist level, ready to attack again. The demon, however, had stopped, its lips curled to expose its fangs.

Cory sensed the thing was on its last legs. He sprang, lashing out at the demon's head, and discovered he was wrong. With a lightning swing of its right arm the demon smashed him to the floor. Landing on his back, his chest a welter of pain, he barely glimpsed the huge foot sweeping at his face in time to throw himself to the right and avoid it.

He shoved upright, his legs shaky, expecting the creature to charge. Instead, it was heading deeper into the pueblo, weaving erratically and careening off of door jambs as it passed through doorways. For some reason it was trying to reach the cavern and considered getting there more important than finishing him off.

Cory gave chase, the hunted becoming the hunter. He must slay the monstrosity or risk never having another good night's sleep for as long as he lived. He needed to know the demon was dead, that it would never endanger him or anyone he knew ever again. If he had to chase it into the Caverna del Diablo, he would.

The creature tripped, recovered, and barreled onward. Seven of the eight apartments were traversed when it tripped a second time, tried to straighten, and sprawled onto its stomach.

By then Cory was fifteen feet behind it. His legs were

close to giving out, his body close to complete exhaustion. From a reservoir of stamina he didn't know he had came additional energy, enough to propel him in a final mad rush. He reached the demon just as it stood and turned, crashing into it, the impact driving the teetering monster backwards through the last doorway. Unable to stop, he felt the demon grip his throat as they toppled to the apartment floor.

Fetid breath fanned Cory's nostrils. He was eye to eye with a living embodiment of all that was evil and vile, nose to nose with the living personification of humankind's most primitive fears, with hatred made flesh. The demon's fingers were constricting iron bands, cutting off his air, and he desperately tried to batter the creature's arm aside. Its tongue flicked out, licking first his left cheek, then his right. Repulsed, he delivered a punch to the jaw, and in response the demon opened its mouth wide and bit down on his left shoulder.

A burning sensation rippled through his body. He felt those razor teeth biting through flesh and sinew, felt them scrape against his bone as blood flowed down his front and back. The demon yanked backwards, and he saw a chunk of his flesh in its mouth. Sickened, he tried to push it away, but the thing held him in place.

The demon grinned and began chewing slowly, noisily, blood dribbling over its lower lip.

Cory sagged. It was going to eat him alive! Bite by bite it would consume him until all that remained were his white bones. Then it might go back for Ann, sun or no sun. When he thought of her lying helpless on the terrace his fury returned, dispelling the weakness in his limbs, giving him the strength to sweep the steel bit on high and plunge it into the demon's good eye.

For a heartbeat nothing happened.

Giving voice to a tremendous screech, the demon came up off the floor and hurled Cory to one side. Its hands clawed at the imbedded bit. Staggering back, it tottered toward the cleft. Then it was at the edge. At the last second it seemed to realize where it was and tried to lurch back but its left foot went over, throwing it off balance, and with a rattle of defiance it plummeted from sight.

Cory had to try twice before he could stand. The weakness was back, reducing his limbs to putty. He shuffled to the cleft and halted shy of the opening to peer down and scan the jumbled pile of earth and rocks.

The fall surely must have killed it. In its weakened state it couldn't possibly survive.

Then where was it?

He scoured the pile from top to bottom but didn't see so much as a trace of red skin. "No, no, no," he said. He was about to rise when he spied a red foot jutting from a rift. The foot was motionless. By tilting his head he made out the legs and part of an arm. Balancing precariously, he saw the head, the eyes open but no longer firey red. They were solid black, and lifeless.

Corey rose and shambled out. He needed to check on Ann, then get to a hospital before he bled to death. If only his damn legs would cooperate. They were growing numb, as were his arms. He wondered if demon bites were toxic to humans, and that was the last thought he had before the ground leaped up to meet his face.

When Cory opened his eyes and saw a brilliant sun directly overhead, he blinked in confusion and tried to rise. Dizziness convinced him otherwise.

"Oh, no, you don't, Galahad. Just lie still until I say so."

He saw Ann materialize above him and knew how people who claimed to see angels must feel. "You're all right?"

"I have a headache but I'll live," she responded, kneeling by his side. "You're far worse off than I am. I tried to stop the bleeding but couldn't entirely."

"How long have I been out?"

"About five hours. It's close to noon."

"Did you drag me out here?"

Ann nodded and stroked his chin. "It wasn't easy. Thank God you're not as heavy as Jay. What happened to Beelzebub?"

"Who?"

"That thing that looked like a devil. I remember reading about Beelzebub in English class when we studied that blind buy who wrote *Paradise* something- or-other."

"Oh," Cory said, understanding. "His name was John Milton and he wrote *Paradise Lost* and *Paradise Regained*."

"Yeah, he's the one," Ann said, pressing her palm to his forehead. "So what happened? Did you kill it?"

"Dead as dead can be."

"Thank God." Ann placed a hand to his brow. "Did you know you have a fever? Not much, but you have one."

"I do feel warm," Cory admitted.

Ann stared down into the valley. "I've been watching like a hawk but I haven't seen a sign of anyone. We must be way out in the middle of nowhere."

"And it's time we were on our way." Cory held up his right arm. "Give me a hand."

"I will not. You lie there and rest. Eventually someone will come by. You'll see."

"We're not waiting. Help me."

Cory grunted as she grasped his wrist and gave him a

boost up. "Grab the backpack," he directed, moving toward the cliff face. His shoulder was stiff and sore, the blood flow reduced to a trickle.

"You're not thinking of climbing up there in your condition, are you?" Ann asked as she complied.

"Unless you can carry me on your shoulders I am."

"You'll fall."

"You'll catch me."

"I'm serious, damn it."

Cory jabbed a finger at the cliff. "Do you think I like the idea? Of course not. But we have to leave now and get as far from this pueblo as we can before nightfall. There are more of those things down in that cavern, and I wouldn't put it past one of them to come after us."

Ann offered no further objections as Cory walked to the end of the terrace and peered up at the top of the plateau. The same thirty feet that had seemed so inconsequential earlier now seemed like an insurmountable distance. He reached out and tested one of the grooves. The edges flaked off under his grip but the rest of the handhold was solid.

"Let me go ahead of you," Ann suggested.

"Some other time," Cory quipped, taking hold of another groove. He slid his right foot into a low niche, then did likewise with his left. He felt dangerously light-headed and hoped he wouldn't suffer more dizziness while he climbed.

"Please be careful."

"I'm not about to kick the bucket. We haven't had our first date yet." Craning his neck, Cory focused on the rim above and began to climb, a torturous labor that set his torn shoulder to throbbing and caked his body with sweat. Each handhold had to be cautiously tested before he dared apply his entire weight. If he were to lose his grip but once, he knew he lacked the strength to pull himself upright again and would plunge to his death.

How long the climb took he couldn't say. At length, when it hurt terribly just to lift his left arm, he poked his head above the cliff and saw a tree-dotted slope unfold before him. So he had been wrong. The pueblo wasn't situated on the side of a plateau It was on the sheer side of a mountain.

Cory crawled onto solid earth, then crouched and waited to assist Ann. Once she was safe, he took her hand and hiked toward the bottom. Neither of them spoke. They were both exhausted, both in a daze from the harrowing night of sheer hell. Not until they were almost down did Ann break the silence.

"I've been doing some thinking."

"Uh-oh."

"Cute," she said, then asked earnestly, "Do you think we should tell the truth about what happened? I know we talked about it before, but..."

"I doubt whether anyone would believe us if we did," Cory said. Forgetting himself, he shrugged, and promptly aggravated his sore shoulder. "I honestly don't know, gorgeous. We'll have to make up our minds when the time comes."

"I don't like to lie."

"Me neither. But I don't want to be committed to a sanitarium because I go around claiming there are such things as demons and they feed on human flesh."

Ann snickered. "You're exaggerating. No one would have you committed."

"You never know." Cory spied a meadow through the trees. "People are more open than they were back in my dad's youth. A person can talk about UFO's and Bigfoot and not be laughed to death. But if you bring up the subject of the Devil or demons or angels, people are likely to think you're a religious nut. And believe it or not, there are psychiatrists who consider any and all religious beliefs as indicative of mental psychosis."

"They think you're crazy for believing in God?"

Cory nodded.

“They're the ones who are crazy.” Ann chewed on her lower lip. "So you're saying that if we tell the truth, we're in for major grief?"

"Bingo," Cory said. He was about to elaborate when there arose a loud rustling in the underbrush to their right and he spotted a large shape moving rapidly toward them. The demon! It had to be! He stepped in front of Ann, prepared to go down swinging, when the brush parted and out rode a tall man on horseback.

"Whoa, there!" the rider said, reining up. He was in his fifties, a square-jawed man wearing jeans, a flannel shirt and a wide-brimmed black hat. His surprise was evident. "Well, I'll be! I *did* hear voices. What the dickens are you kids doing way up here?"

Cory simply stared. His mind couldn't seem to accept the fact that here was another human being, that they were truly safe at last.

The man smiled. "Cat got your tongues? I'm Rex Tyler. My ranch is over yonder." He jerked his thumb over his shoulder. "I don't get up this way much but a few head wandered off and I've been searching for them all day."

"We're glad to see you," Cory said, fighting back tears of profound relief as the reality hit home. "I'm Cory. This is Ann. We've spent the night lost in a cave. Please, will you help us?"

"Why sure, partner. I can have you back at my ranch

inside of two hours, and by tonight I'll have you in town."

The rancher's brow knit. "If you don't mind my saying so, the two of you are sorry sights." He bent and peered at Cory's shoulder. "You look like you need a doc, son. What took that bite out of you?"

Cory glanced at Ann, who had tears streaming down her cheeks. She swallowed, smiled, and nodded.

"A mountain lion," Cory said, facing their benefactor. "A mountain lion jumped us."

"Those big cats can be nasty when they want to be," Rex Tyler said. "You're lucky to be alive."

"Don't we know it," Cory said.

PAGOSA SPRINGS (AP News)-This small town in southwest Colorado is still in mourning for the loss of six high school students now presumed dead in the Caverna del Diablo, one of the largest caves on the North American continent.

Two weeks of extensive searches by experienced spelunkers have failed to turn up a trace of the six, who reportedly went to the cave on Halloween "to have some fun," as one of two other students who found their way out told police.

Relatives of the lost six have demanded that the cave be sealed so future tragedies can be avoided.

Authorities, however, say they are reluctant to close off forever a cave of such natural beauty and wonder as the Caverna del Diablo.

FINI

Be on the lookout for more great reads by David Robbins!

A GIRL, THE END OF THE WORLD AND EVERYTHING

Courtney Hewitt lived a perfectly ordinary life. Then several countries let fly with nuclear missiles and chemical and biological weapons and her life was no longer ordinary. Now Courtney has chemical clouds and radiation to deal with. To say nothing of the not-so-dead who eat the living.

ANGEL U
LET THERE BE LIGHT

Armageddon is a generation away. The forces of light and darkness will clash in the ultimate battle. To prepare humankind, the angels establish a university of literal higher learning here on Earth. Enroll now---before the demons get you.

ANGEL U
DEMIGOD

Gilgamesh the Destroyer. Demon-slayer. Son of the Moon. Two parts god, one part human. He wants nothing to do with the war between Heaven and Hell. Then Gilgamesh learns that he is not who he thought he was. He is not *what* he thought he was. To learn the truth, Gilgamesh will venture where few have dared.

ENDWORLD #28
DARK DAYS

The science fiction series that sweeps its readers into a terrifying Apocalyptic future continues. The Warriors of Alpha Triad face their greatest threat yet. Their survivalist compound, the Home, has been invaded. Not by an enemy army. Not by the horrifying mutates. This time a shapeshifter is loose among the Family. Able to change into anyone at will, it is killing like there is no tomorrow.

ENDWORLD #29
THE LORDS OF KISMET

From out of the horror of World War III, a new menace is spawned, Claiming to be the gods of old, their goal is global conquest. Three Warriors are sent to bring the Lords down---but there is more to the creatures than anyone imagined.

ENDWORLD #30
SYNTHEZOIDS

The survivors of the Apocalypse have endured a lot. Mutations. Chemical toxins. Madmen. Now a new threat arises---living horrors, thanks to science gone amok.

BLOOD FEUD #2
HOUNDS OF HATE

Chace and Cassie Shannon are back. The feud between the Harkeys and the Shannons takes the twins from the hills of Arkansas to New Orleans, where Chace has a grand scheme to set them up in style. But if the Harkeys have anything to say about it, they'll be ripped to pieces.

THE WERELING

The original Horror classic. Ocean City has a lot going for it. Nice beaches. The boardwalk. Tourists. But something new is prowling Ocean City. Something that feasts on those tourists. Something that howls at the moon, and bullets can't stop. The Jersey Shore werewolf is loose.

HIT RADIO

Franco Scarvetti has a problem. His psycho son has whacked a made man. Now a rival Family is out to do the same to his son. So Big Frank comes up with a plan. He sends his lethal pride and joy to run a radio station in a small town while he tries to smooth things over. But Big Frank never read Shakespeare and he forgets that a psycho by any other name is still....a psycho.

WILDERNESS #67
THE GIFT

Evelyn King is sixteen and in love. She tricks her father and sneaks away with the warrior she loves---straight into a pack of killers.

WILDERNESS #68
SAVAGE HEARTS

Nate and Winona King thought they were doing the right thing when they rode deep into the Rockies to return a little girl to her people. But some good deeds are fraught with perils.

WILDERNESS #69
THE AVENGER

From out of the past comes a threat the King family never expects. A killer who wants an eye for an eye.

WILDERNESS #70
LOVE AND COLD STEEL

The heart wants what the heart wants. But what if your heart leads you and the one you love into danger?

Made in the USA
Coppell, TX
15 July 2023